TASTE OF GRACE

TASTE OF GRACE

An Earthly Pilgrimage
by
Pauline Landes Browne

Copyright:

©2003 USA by Pauline Landes Browne

All rights reserved. No part of this publication may be reproduced, stored in a retrieval system, or transmitted in any form or by any means — electronic, mechanical, photocopy, copy, recording, or any other — except for brief quotations in printed reviews, without the prior written permission of the publisher.

Published May 2004 by:

KiwE Publishing, Ltd.
P.O. Box 28007
Spokane, WA 99228-8007
USA
E-mail: kiwe@kiwepublishing.com
Web Site: · http://www.kiwepublishing.com

ISBN: 1-931195-48-X
Library of Congress Control Number: 2003117147

Cover photo of Rio de Janeiro courtesy of www.bigfoto.com

Printed in the U.S.A.

To my fair sons and daughters:

George and Mary
Greta and Guy
Paul and Carol
Natalie and Al
Elizabeth and Maurício

CONTENTS

Introduction ix
Prologue 1
Chapter 1 - At the Foot of T'ai Shan 5
2 - Living Three Cultures 14
3 - Learning the Word 23
4 - In the Center of South America 28
5 - A Child's Vision 37
6 - Starting New Churches 47
7 - College Years 56
8 - Princeton Idyll 65
9 - First Thing in the Morning 74
10 - Twins 82
11 - Berkeley Interlude 93
12 - Outside East Gate 102
13 - China Years' End 112
14 - Assigned to Brazil 123
15 - Brazil's Wild West 135
16 - The Wild South 145
17 - Farm School in Eden 157
18 - Double Duty: Sâo Paulo 169
19 - Cruzada ABC 177
20 - Goiânia: Empty Nest 188
21 - Choosing Mozambique 199
22 - Independence for Mozambique 209
23 - On the Shore of the Indian Ocean 219
24 - Down by the Geba River 230
25 - Dad Browne 238
26 - Promised Land 247

Introduction

Things which fill our days suddenly disappear or shrink away. We find ourselves standing alone and wondering. Is there anything that we can count on, anything that endures? I have chosen the word *grace* as the expression of that which cannot be destroyed, uprooted, or taken away from us. We pass away, but the grace of God continues and multiplies. The experience of this grace is the meaning of this narrative.

My family through many generations has been bound up in the church of Jesus Christ so that our lives belong to all people of good will who have reached out in mission to the world. This book is a report to the many persons and cooperating bodies that have made our saga possible. Since we have been affiliated with the Presbyterian Church throughout all our years we mention this one entity, though there are very many others as you will see as you read.

Many persons have helped me write this book. I would mention my children and grandchildren, especially Sibby Browne. I have had the continued support of Chalmers' brother and sisters, Frenchy, Joan, and Bea. Two editors have very helpfully reviewed my work, Bob Hostetler and Nancy Young. My brothers and sisters, George and Mary Lou and Phil and Mary Louise have taken care of a myriad tasks, small and large, to put the manuscript in shape and get it to a publisher. To these and many others I extend my heartfelt thanks.

More recently Marthy Johnson and KiwE Publishing have undertaken the task of preparing the manuscript and publishing it. I am truly grateful to each of them.

P. L. B.

Prologue

We met quite formally at a reception in the Library of Princeton Theological Seminary. Still, it was astonishing that Chalmers Browne, born on the hilly northeastern shores of China and I, Polly Landes, born in the low river valley of central South America should find our way to each other.

Was it in the stars? God created the great luminaries to rule over the days and nights. What further sway they may have over earthlings is not clear. The ultimate power comes from the King of kings, who also is mindful of the fall of a little sparrow. Given this faith, chance and coincidence are no longer random or reasonless. They are related to eternal wisdom and grace. We perceive our lives as ordinary happenings like getting up to the sunshine or rain of each morning, but at times happenings are filled with wonder.

Chalmers had stars in his eyes. He was quick and intense. He had the gift of finding pleasure in many things. He liked to study Hebrew, to paddle a canoe, to go for a walk in the sleet of a November gloaming.

I liked the way Chalmers planted his feet, and the swift way in which they carried him through his week of study, work, and choir trips. I soon discovered his devotion to duty. I wrote him a Valentine as if I were the furnace at the Friar Club where he worked in the kitchen and on janitorial duty. The furnace consumed a great deal of his precious time. He had to wake her in the morning, stoke her several times a day and bank her at night.

The center of Chalmers' life was prayer. His sense of calling to the ministry was profound and unswerving. After our marriage, as Chalmers took up his duties in our first parish, there was no doubt in our minds that we were jointly called to this service.

That first parish consisted of two churches in Ohio, Salineville and Oak Ridge. About ten miles separated the white, spired Presbyterian church in Salineville from the little brick Oak Ridge Presbyterian church standing on a hillock surrounded by fields and farms. Chalmers had bought a Plymouth roadster and the drive between churches through wooded areas and meadows was a time of togetherness for the two of us.

Becoming householders in the old manse on the hill above the church in Salineville was an adventure, including my experiences in answering the manse door. The doorbell rang and I opened it to the dry cleaner who had come to collect Chalmers' suit. He asked me for my name. "Pauline Landes," I said. "Oh, no, no, no! Pauline Browne!" He gave me a look of astonishment, wrote my name (the Browne without the *e*), and departed as quickly as possible. The next time I answered the bell, a stranger stood at the door, a man who was looking for the new minister whom he had not yet met. "Is your father at home?" he asked.

There were times when I opened the door and found Aunt Sadie standing there. She was a woman who, though past a reasonable age to live alone, persisted in staying out on a farm by herself with her cats. We invited her in and served her lunch or tea. She told us with great gusto the colorful stories of her life. After about two hours Chalmers would say, "Aunt Sadie, I'm going to the post office to mail some letters. Would you like to ride along?" Aunt Sadie graciously accepted and, collecting the nosegays she was taking to friends in town, rode off in state beside the young minister.

And there was the June day when Chalmers came home to announce that a young couple was coming to be married in the manse. I picked pink rambler roses that grew wild along the fence and decorated the living room. No young couple could have been married more lovingly. Chalmers was gifted with warm understanding of people at these important times in their lives. After the ceremony we shared lemonade and cookies.

Chalmers not only loved people, he liked them. He entered into the lives of the pottery workers who commuted from Salineville down to the river town factories along the Ohio. He appreciated the dour

Scots, whose ancestors had burnt the brick and built the church out on Oak Ridge, and the more recent immigrants from eastern Europe. As he visited in field and barn, Chalmers had equal appreciation for the elderly farmer who, as he mowed, left standing a clump of purple thistle frequented by butterflies, and the child who showed him his pet calf. And I heard about all these special people when he returned home for supper.

The young people of the parish were at once a great joy and a despair. They were full of idealism, enthusiasm, and shifting loyalties. In both churches the young people flocked to the young minister, including the gang which had climbed through a window and was roaming about inside the Salineville church in the middle of the night. Chalmers stayed to have a heart-to-heart talk with them, returning to his worried wife at two o'clock in the morning.

When we first came to the parish, one boy went home to tell his mother that the church had a new "manager." A year later, when our first son was born, a little girl went home from church indignant because "the preacher had taken the Sunday School offering and bought himself a baby." Her parents had told her it would be too expensive to get a baby brother or sister for her. It was only after long years that we came to know how great an influence a minister has on young people. Back for homecoming, we saw our "young people" stream into the Salineville Presbyterian Church with their spouses and children.

I liked Chalmers' evening sermons best. At the close of a long Sunday he found pleasure in making a Bible story come to life and drawing nourishment from it for our lives.

Chalmers loved the minor key in music. There was also a minor strain in his personality. During his first year in the ministry he came into a time of depression when it was hard for him to perform his many tasks. Sometimes it was early Sunday morning before he knew what he was going to preach about that day. After several months God cleared away the clouds of depression and drew him once more into His marvelous sunlight. Throughout our lives there was a sense of Presence as we walked with the Master amongst the churches in many lands. The Spirit led us subtly and simply through

- 1 -

At the Foot of T'ai Shan

In the province of Shantung in northeast China, T'ai Shan, a mountain sacred to Confucius, rises from the plain. Pilgrims climb the many steps to the monastery at the top. High up, the mountain air is clear and sweet. Weary sojourners find refuge and quiet in the old temple hostel.

George and Irene Browne, a young missionary couple, came to these lodgings in the late summer of 1915. They were seeking rest and healing after a year of strenuous work. In October they descended the mountain and turned in at the mission clinic in the small town of T'ai An. George Chalmers, their first son, was born there on the 15th of October. His parents chose his name in the tradition of the Browne family: *George* for his paternal grandfather and *Chalmers* for his mother's father.

George Browne and Irene Cowen had met at the Outgoing Missionary Conference in New York City in 1913. There they were both assigned to China. They sailed on the Chiyo Maru, a small Japanese passenger ship going to Shanghai.

The two new recruits studied Chinese in Chefoo, Shantung Province. A romance bloomed, and they announced their engagement. A senior missionary, Dr. Corbett, cut through the red tape that would have obliged them to go to separate mission stations. They were married on May 14, 1914. Irene wore a beautiful wedding gown of white Chinese silk and George donned a frock coat. They provided an exciting and romantic occasion for the missionary community.

After their honeymoon, the Brownes went to their station at Ichowfu. They both taught—Irene in the girls' school and George in the boys'. Irene also taught in the women's Bible School. George itinerated, preaching the Word as he had hoped to do. Establishing a Christian home was part of their missionary task. They lived in the "old Johnson house, next to the church, overlooking the city wall and the moat where we skated on occasion." (*Burning Hearts and Itching Feet,* by George Francis Browne). It was to this home that they brought their newborn son, Chalmers, as soon as they were able to travel.

A second child, Mary Elizabeth, joined the family when Chalmers was sixteen months old. This little sister died of dysentery six months later. Those were the days before antibiotics. In the hot summers many children died of this disease because of unsanitary conditions, lack of sewer systems, and hordes of flies. Only the grace of God gave them courage to continue at their post in the face of their loss. Chalmers was too young to understand, but he felt his parents' anguish. They found consolation in their love for this remaining child. Soon after Mary Elizabeth's death, George and Irene suffered another shattering blow. News came of the death of George's father. George felt it all the more because he knew what a sacrifice his father had made in letting him go so far from home.

A year later, in 1918, the family returned home to America on furlough. Chalmers' parents took him to visit Grandmother Browne, who had settled in Wooster, Ohio, with her unmarried daughter, Natalie. Next they visited Irene's parents on the farm near Rural Valley. While they were with the Cowen grandparents, Beatrice Irene was born on August 5, 1918, at the hospital in New Brighton, Pennsylvania. Chalmers was old enough now to understand and welcome a sister.

As he moved about in strange surroundings Chalmers was learning many new and surprising things. One morning his mother was arranging his bath in the galvanized iron washtub that he had seen used to boil clothes. He cried and struggled, afraid that he was going to be boiled alive. Fortunately his mother realized the reason for his distress. Smiling, she let him touch his hand to the water and see that it wasn't hot. Those were happy days of reunion, of much talking and explaining, and of rejoicing in the work God had entrusted to Irene and George. Chalmers became acquainted with grandparents, aunts and uncles who, back in the mission field, had been known only through letters. After a year of speaking in churches and visiting with their families and friends, Irene and George with their two small children returned to China.

The mission station at Ichowfu was a busy place. George and Irene taught in the schools, preached, and attended to the many who now came to their door with all sorts of needs and requests. There were fun times too—parties, canoeing on the river, skating when the river froze over. In the winter, blocks of ice were cut and stored in rice husks for cooling iceboxes in the summer months.

A second son, Francis William Browne was born in Ichowfu on November 16, 1920. He turned out to be a jolly little fellow and not as stubborn as his older brother.

As a small boy Chalmers acquired the reputation of being able to sleep through anything. Once, when the family was traveling by train, Chalmers' father prepared to waken him well before their destination. "Let him sleep a little longer," said a fellow passenger. "It is a long way still to your station."

"You don't know how heavily my son sleeps," was the answer. Mr. Browne took Chalmers up by his feet, touched his head several times against the floor, then returned him to the bench where he had been lying. Chalmers went right on sleeping.

His mother told of a time when Chalmers decided he was going to stay up all night. His parents said that would be all right. He sat on the sofa after dinner. His mother was writing letters and his father was doing accounts. The clock kept up its rhythmic ticking. After a bit Chalmers said, "I'm going to lie down here on the couch for a bit, but I'm not going to sleep." When his parents were ready to retire, his father carried him upstairs and tucked him in.

As the three siblings grew older, it was Chalmers who would say at bed time, "Come, it's time to go to bed."

Chalmers, Beatrice, and Francis remember with awe an occurrence they heard their father recount many times: the story of his encounter with the bandits. Mr. Browne was returning home from a mission meeting. He had been asked to escort a young Chinese woman doctor who was to join Dr. Emma Flemming at the mission hospital in Ichowfu. Mr. Browne and the doctor traveled by train to the end of the line. They then hired a boat and boatmen to convey them along the Grand Canal to Ichowfu. It had been raining and the banks were muddy. They loaded supplies, including medicines for the hospital and household goods for the mission families, and set out.

They rounded a bend in the Canal and heard shouts: "Stop!" A boat with armed bandits pulled up. Usually, bandits let "Jesus Church" people, as missionaries were called by the locals, go by. But now several armed men jumped into their boat.. They held a gun on George while all the other men in the boat fled, including a newlywed husband who was taking his bride home. The woman doctor and the abandoned bride huddled together while the bandits took George's money, his watch, and the wedding band from his finger. The bandits proceeded to appropriate all the supplies and medicines.

Suddenly gunfire erupted from a fort on the hill above them and from soldiers stationed on the far bank of the canal. The bandits fled. The remaining passengers lay flat in the boat until the barrage ceased and one boatman returned. They retrieved their cargo from the bank and decided to go back to the nearest village. On their way they met yet another gang of bandits. Mr. Browne warned them, "Soldiers are on the march along the canal!" These bandits also fled. Finally Mr. Browne and his small company were able to reach the city from which they had started. The doctor decided to stay there for a time.

The next day when George went down to the riverbank, the boat, which he had left in the care of the boatmen, was completely looted. He decided to return to Ichowfu by land. The mail carrier offered to let him ride one of his two mules. But the mule, used to carrying only mailbags, refused to carry a rider. It sidled off the road, planted its feet firmly, and would not budge. George continued his journey walking beside the mailman over the hills and along the muddy valleys for two days. Days later he stumbled exhausted into his home. The incident affected his nervous system for months.

Partly because the bandits were still threatening Mr. Browne, the Mission transferred in 1923 to Chefoo where they were to serve for the remainder of their time in China.

Temple Hill in Chefoo, the missionary complex of schools, hospital, and missionary residences, became home to Chalmers and his family. For a year they lived in a Chinese house built around a courtyard. A flat roof over the kitchen made a wonderful play area for the three children. One time they built an airplane with chairs, blankets, a lampshade frame and other assorted findings. They were concerned that their parents might not like the requisitioning of household property for this enterprise, but when he found out, Dad joined the fun and added a fan that made a whirring noise like the engine of a plane.

As Chalmers grew he developed new interests. The upstairs windows looked out over the harbor, which was used as a naval station during the summer. Chalmers liked to watch the ships steaming in and out of the bay. He was very proud that his father could read the names of the British and American ships standing a mile or more out on the water.

The British and American communities in Chefoo afforded a rich variety of social experiences. Mr. Browne was often invited to preach at Sunday services at the Navy YMCA. The family met sailors and other personnel at different functions. Many times Mr. Browne was asked to sing at gatherings. There was also entertaining back and forth among the British and American families. In the American homes the British liked to drink coffee. Conversely, the Americans enjoyed the tea served by the British.

Chalmers learned to read and write with his mother. In Chefoo he went to the C.I.M. (China Inland Mission), a British school with rigorous rules and discipline. The boys and girls were strictly segregated after fourth grade. For example, on Sunday afternoons the children who lived in the dorms went for walks. If the boys and girls happened to meet, the boys lined up on one side facing away from the road and stood thus until the girls had passed.

When Chalmers started going to the C.I.M. School, he and two Booth girls, missionary daughters, rode donkeys the two miles across town. Later he and Beatrice went by rickshaw. When he was older he walked through town. These trips to school brought him in contact with life in the center of Chefoo. In an interview for his Oral History project at Columbia University, Chalmers reported:

"I walked sometimes. Needless to say this was part of getting into a feeling of Chinese life. I remember watching the making of *yang chau dze*, or noodles. They would come out through the mill, hand ground. It seemed to me that they were twenty or thirty feet long and they were hung way up to dry. There were men who made little toys out of bamboo or cornstalks, and the glass noisemakers that you sucked in and out on, that were on display.

"There were the more terrifying glimpses: not only pigs being slaughtered, but a man being led along who had been, probably, under some kind of torture because every half inch across his back and his chest had been cut and was slightly bleeding.

"Another time in a procession, a man, the guilty one, walked with his crimes on placards in front and behind him. Someone walked in front banging a bell. We knew that he was on his way to the west parade grounds, where he would be executed."

At school, Chalmers learned to be respectful and to respond with a "Yes, sir," or a "Yes, ma'am." He learned to eat everything on his plate at lunchtime. He cherished a bible that he received from the school. Standing by the window looking out on the bay, he leafed through the pages of satiny, fine paper redolent of printer's ink. Inscribed on the flyleaf were the words, "Remember Jesus Christ," the motto of the school. In later life Chalmers often chose this verse from II Timothy 2:8 as the text for a sermon.

During these growing-up years, Chalmers was surrounded with love. Both George and Irene had come from homes where love abounded and they passed on this unmeasured love in their own home. Two facets of this love stand out in the stories Chalmers told of his young days: fun and discipline, not mutually exclusive.

Chalmers' father was fun-loving. He relished a good joke and delighted in puns and practical jokes. Mr. Browne could play Santa Claus to perfection for the station. At one Christmas celebration he dropped one boot down the chimney. Below they could hear him grunting and saying, "I can't get down this chimney. I'll have to go around by the door." In a few minutes he appeared without one of his boots, but with his bag of presents.

In the life of a missionary child, discipline was of special importance. It was necessary to know and abide by the high standards of the group so as to feel accepted and cherished. Thus, teaching discipline was an act of love. One day a week there was a prayer meeting at the station. As a schoolboy Chalmers attended and knelt to pray with his seniors and fellows. On one occasion he dropped off to sleep on his knees, and snored, a lapse for which he was teased later.

There were four servants who kept the household running while the Brownes carried out their missionary tasks. As in many third world countries still today, chickens, instead of coming all plucked and wrapped in cellophane, were delivered with the squawk still in them. The stove burnt coal briquettes which had to be fashioned and dried. Clothes were washed by hand. Padded garments and other clothes were sewn at home. The children were taught to respect these Chinese helpers. They were not allowed to order them around. Hu-Shir-Fu, Wang-deh-Sao, Wang-deh-geh and Li-kwei were not only respected, they were loved because they were kind and gladly cared for the family.

The caliber of these household helpers was evidenced when the table boy left. Mr. and Mrs. Browne called the remaining servants together and suggested that three persons could do all the work needed. Instead of hiring a fourth helper the Brownes would divide the table boy's salary amongst the three remaining servants. At first the servants were pleased. But soon one of them came to the Brownes and said: "We would like to do the work and receive the extra pay. But we couldn't in good conscience take a job away from someone who needs it." So a new table boy was hired.

Chalmers' relation to his father was one of admiration and respect but his temperament was less precise, more Scottish than that of his father. He was committed to obedience and struggled all his life to please his father, never quite sure that he was good enough.

Chalmers' mother was a quiet-spoken, orderly person, someone to be counted on always. She was fun, too. Her fun came from a deep enjoyment of life. Her ripply laughter bubbled up as she told of a funny incident or participated in family play. Chalmers reminded his mother of her brothers. She found great pride in her stalwart sons and pretty brunette daughter. Chalmers knew his mother was always there for him and he dedicated a winsome, wholehearted devotion to her.

When Chalmers was about eight years old, his mother underwent gall bladder surgery. She did not come out of the operation as hoped. For days she was critically ill. The members of the station prayed for her day and night. Finally she rallied. The family felt God's healing presence in their midst.

The next year found Irene back in the hospital after a miscarriage. One Sunday Francis stayed with his mother at the hospital while Chalmers and Beatrice went with their father to the worship service at North Hill on the other side of town. While Chalmers and his father and sister were away, Irene noticed that something strange was going on just outside the hospital. Shots rang out. From the window Irene and Francis could see men in yellow crouching behind the compound wall. Answering fire came from amongst the grave mounds in the cemetery beside the hospital. Green-clad soldiers of one warlord were battling the yellow-clad followers of another.

Because of this conflict, when the service on North Hill was over, the Americans who lived across town were taken to the American embassy. There they were served a meal and detained until the emergency was over. In the late afternoon with the "all clear" signal, they returned home. Of course, the Brownes hurried to the hospital, and the family was very glad to be reunited without mishap.

Life returned to normal and the children went back to school. One day Chalmers was walking home through the narrow streets observing the busy life about him—the vendors, carts, rickshaws, dogs, pigs, oxen, and even camels. The houses and shops crowded on either side. At an open place he came upon a new well being dug. He peered down into the darkness, but couldn't see the bottom. Wondering how deep it was, he dropped a stone down the well. He heard only a low thud. The next morning his father called him into the study.

"Did you throw a stone down a well?" asked Dad Browne.

Chalmers said, "Yes I did."

"There were men working down in the well. The stone might have hurt one of them," his father explained.

Then they talked over the need for much care because they, as Americans and Christians, were guests in China. Their behavior would influence the way people understood and judged all Americans and Christians.

- 2 -

Living Three Cultures

Seven busy years rolled by and in the summer of 1926 it was time again for the Browne family to spend a year in the United States. Chalmers was now eleven years old. The family went to Shanghai, where they embarked on a steamer for the west coast of America. Unless one were prone to seasickness, an oceanliner trip was very enjoyable. Chalmers found a companion his own age on board. They played shuffleboard and swam in the ship's pool. At teatime each afternoon, they would find a table out on deck set for four. Between them they consumed all the sandwiches and cookies with gusto.

In the United States the China family settled in Wooster, Ohio, with Grandmother Browne and Aunt Natalie. The Browne home was a tall frame house on the corner of Beall Avenue and Pearl Street. In some ways it was a difficult year of intergenerational adjustments. Noise bothered Grandmother, and three lively children could not help making a noise. Being reprimanded by Grandmother sometimes hurt feelings.

Beall Ave. School was only a block down the street from Grandmother's house. How different this school in America was from the C.I.M. School in Chefoo! The three children enjoyed the new school experiences, adjusting quickly to the new ways of doing things. The Wooster culture differed from both the overseas expatriate community and the Chinese culture, but they soon made friends. Playing at recess and after school with their friends filled their days with excitement.

Playing a special game of tag with his friends one day, Chalmers had a humiliating experience. Part of the game was to get across the street without being tagged. He ran into the street without looking carefully enough and was struck by a car. He glanced off the car onto the side of the street. Stunned, he got home with the help of a playmate. What hurt much more than the bruises and abrasions was to be held up as a horrible example at school.

Matters in China were unsettled. The fighting between warlords continued to spell danger. Missionaries from the interior stations came into the port cities. The mission compounds were crowded. Missionaries on furlough during this crisis were asked to remain in the United States.

So the Brownes moved to Wheeling, West Virginia. There, Mr. Browne served as the associate pastor of the First Presbyterian Church. Among his duties, he was in charge of the Eighteenth Street Mission. On Sundays the Browne family went to Sunday School and morning service at the downtown church. They ate their noon meal in a hotel dining room, a treat and a time of togetherness for the family. After dinner, they proceeded to Sunday School at the Eighteenth Street Mission. Thus the Brownes became acquainted with many families and young people. Chalmers and Bea made their profession of faith during this time.

After the year in Wheeling it was back to the Wooster area, to the town of Fredericksburg. Mr. Browne became pastor of the Presbyterian/ Methodist Church. Chalmers started high school in Fredericksburg. He began to take on responsibilities such as mowing, not only their own lawn, but those of neighbors. He was hired to do other chores. One afternoon the family decided to go to Wooster to visit Grandmother Browne. Chalmers wanted very much to go along, but he had promised to do some work for a neighbor. He stayed behind to keep his word.

But Thanksgiving and Christmas brought opportunities to visit with Grandmother and Aunt Nat and other aunts, uncles, and cousins. Once, when they were visiting in Wooster, Chalmers' father wanted to listen on the radio to the football game. But the noise was annoying to Grandmother. Dad took himself and the radio under a blanket on the floor and Chalmers crawled under the blanket to listen, too. Chalmers sometimes went for walks with his grandmother. One evening, when the new moon shimmered in the sky, Grandmother said, "You know, I see seven moons." Chalmers, who could see only one, was intrigued.

In Fredericksburg the young people of the church had a very lively organization and enjoyed many good times together. After church on Sunday evenings, they gathered in someone's kitchen to churn ice cream. One time they put sour cream, which had been set aside to make butter, into the ice cream by mistake. They wondered why the ice cream had such a funny flavor until someone discovered their mistake. The boys often ended a day by going skinnydipping in the creek.

In his brash younger days Chalmers had said that there were two things he was not going to be. "I'm not going to be an aviator because by the time I'm grown up, aviators will be as common as taxi drivers. And I'm not going to be a minister." His father was a fourth generation preacher. He didn't want to become a minister to follow a family tradition. But by his high school days Chalmers, in a meeting where vocation was being discussed, said he was considering the ministry. Perhaps he was heeding his dad's expressed maxim that "every young man should consider the ministry as a calling. But no young man should go into the ministry if he could be happy in another vocation."

The Brownes lived in Fredericksburg for two years. In 1930 they went back to Chefoo. They were finally housed in permanent quarters. They lived for the remainder of their overseas service in what was called Dr. Hill's house. Dr. Hill had built a very large cottage and installed all sorts of wonderful systems such as one for pumping water into the house and one for heating in winter.

Mr. and Mrs. Browne took on their regular tasks. Mr. Browne was asked to add to his work that of station treasurer, which entailed care of mission property as well as bookkeeping. Mrs. Browne became principal of Ai Dao Bible School for Women. The Brownes helped construct a new building for the Bible School. It was a long structure facing south, slightly curved so as to catch the sun's warmth. The women were very grateful for this solar warmth in their bedrooms and classrooms in the cold winters.

At the Ai Dao Bible School the intricate and delicate Chinese art of cutouts had been adopted and adapted. It became a flourishing industry. The women created greeting cards, albums, and wall decorations. Besides helping to finance the schooling of the women, these cutouts, with their scenes from the Bible as well as from Chinese life, carried the message of good news.

Chalmers and Beatrice did not stay on in Chefoo for their schooling. They and their parents decided that they would go to Korea, to the P'yongyang Foreign School, Chalmers as a high school sophomore and Bea as an eighth-grader. Most of the young people of similar age from Temple Hill were going to P'yongyang for secondary school. The young people had to make a trip of two days to reach this American school judged to have high standards and a wholesome atmosphere. The school came into being to meet the need of missionary families. It also accepted children of business and diplomatic families.

Getting ready to go to boarding school was exciting. In Fredericksburg Chalmers had worn long trousers for the first time; before he had worn knickers. Now he packed some of each. Enough clothing for a school term, including jackets and blankets for the cold North Korea winter, were packed into suitcases and *coris*. (A *cori* is a woven basket with a second fitting snugly over it as a top, thus making the *cori* expandable.)

Chalmers and Bea started out with five other Chefoo "mish kids" on a coastal steamer. They went out to the ship by sampan. Climbing the straight-up swinging ladder onto the ship's deck was breathtaking. The ship had cabins for sleeping and a common room where they ate supper, then breakfast the next morning. They had learned to avoid cold cuts and raw vegetables because of the danger of dysentery and cholera. They stuck to cooked food that was still hot. Sometimes this rule meant going hungry.

The ship made the crossing to Chemulpo, Korea, in a day and a night. Korea at this time was under Japanese occupation. The travelers had to go through immigration and customs, a nerve-wracking business. The Japanese officials were sometimes very slow and uncooperative. One time when a customs official insisted on shaking out each item in Bea's *cori*, the young people were frantic. They were sure they had missed their train to P'yongyang. Suddenly a man dressed in a business suit appeared as they were stuffing everything back into suitcases and *coris*. "There is a station up the line where you can catch the train if you hurry," he said. He piled all their baggage on a handcart and, getting between the bars, pulling the cart himself, ran ahead of them to the station. They made the train just in time, but never found out who that mysterious man was or what prompted him to help them.

It was a relief to be aboard the train and know that oneday of travel northward would bring them to their destination. Chalmers as the big brother was in charge of his and Bea's passports and ticket money. He was soon navigating the intricacies of travel as they made the trip again and again. The train carried them through a new kind of countryside, greener than the part of China they knew. Chinese architecture consisted of compound walls and tile roofs. Here the houses stood out amongst the fields with their thatched roofs and clean-swept yards. Rice fields added gold to the landscape at the end of summer or vivid green in the springtime. The people dressed in white and the children wore colorful garments, instead of the dark clothing used by the people in China. Korea seemed at once gentler and brighter.

At last they made it to the train station in P'yongyang. Chalmers and Bea followed their older schoolmates into taxis and up a main road to the school. They turned onto a winding smaller road and came to the dorms. The boys were housed in the old dorm and the girls in the new. Across from the dorms were the tennis courts and below them the schoolhouse. Residences for the principal and teachers were nearby. The playing fields lay across the road. This was the hub of Chalmers' daily life for the next three years. The gymnasium, which doubled as an auditorium, was built during the time Chalmers was at P'yongyang (PY). The students helped raise the money to construct this building by soliciting buyers for the bricks.

Life at PY was fun. One of the primary reasons was the people, the teachers and fellow students. One person who had a tremendous influence on Chalmers' life was his scoutmaster at PY, the Reverend Bill Shaw, known as Uncle Bill. Uncle Bill charmed Chalmers in part because he was so different from Dad Browne. Dad had an intransigent side, demanding obedience, sometimes without the possibility of discussion. Uncle Bill was laid-back. He added a new dimension to Chalmers' understanding of a Christian man.

Studying, of course, was paramount at PY. The arts and sciences were a wide-open world, always beckoning on to new facts and ideas. Chalmers was by nature a gatherer. One of his favorite expressions was, "I like to see the whole picture." He wanted to read widely and put off organizing; but when he did finally bring things together, he could be brilliant. Scouting and athletics, with their close organization and set rules, were a rest and support to a nature that craved order but had difficulty finding it. Chalmers played soccer and tennis. He ran track for the school, taking part in meets with teams from Korean boys' schools.

Chalmers had a strong tenor voice, with overtones like those of the trombone which he played with the school orchestra. Sometimes the orchestra played for Sunday school. The community held Sunday services in the worship hall of the Theological Seminary across the main road. Near the Seminary stood homes for missionaries involved in evangelistic work or teaching in the seminary and other schools for Korean students. There was also a university campus to the south, and residences not far away for missionaries of the Methodist Church. A real colony of expatriates had formed here, but always a part of the community of faith, Koreans and Americans together.

The Women's Bible School shared the area of the PY Foreign School (FS). This Bible School had an enormous effect on the growth of the Presbyterian Church in Korea. Bible women, as the lay evangelists were called, received their training during the year. In the spring women came from their villages, and camped out at the Bible School for a week of study. They gathered in the courtyard for their daily classes, bringing the life of the country people close to the foreign students. When these women returned to their homes, they carried fresh and life-changing ideas to their communities.

PYFS outings were special! Each year a surprise holiday was announced at breakfast. Classes were canceled and the whole school prepared for a hike and an all-day picnic. The girls rushed to make sandwiches and the boys assembled the necessary gear, including drinking water.

A romantic outing was to Keija's Grove in the moonlight, when the cherry trees were in bloom. The glimmer of the gray tile of the high gate and memorial arch enhanced the dreamy quality of the night. The young people wandered about the paths along the river and sat under the trees to talk and laugh while moonlight filtered down on them through the cherry blossoms.

With Uncle Bill Shaw, the scouts went to the caves. The trip started out by rail. When they left the train they walked for ten miles up a valley and among the hills. At the end of the valley the group clambered up to the opening of the largest cave and made camp in its mouth. The next day they explored the caves. Through a passage at the back of the first cave, they entered a second. They groped their way to find the entrance of a third cave. Each scout carried a flashlight, for the darkness was thick. The tiny beacons of light in their hands barely cut through the blackness. They all sat down on the floor of the cave and turned off their flashlights. The darkness was like nothing they had ever experienced. They were glad to turn the flashlights on again. There was still another cave with a gaping crevasse before it. There was no way to tell how deep this cleft was. By tying a rope to a boulder, the boys could swing on the rope, one at a time, across the chasm. They were then in a large cave with a stone table surrounded by stone benches. When the first explorers from PYFS had come to the cave, the story went, they had found skeletons sitting on the benches. Sometime between visits, the skeletons had disappeared.

Besides exploring the caves the scouts hiked the wooded hillsides. One morning Chalmers and a schoolmate were detailed to make breakfast while the others went hiking. Chalmers made a fire with the wood they had gathered. His companion got out the pans and the oatmeal and went to the spring for water. The water was full of leaves and twigs after a rain. What to do? Chalmers found a clean T-shirt. They strained the water through the shirt and had the oatmeal steaming when the hikers returned.

Time flew and the Christmas season came. More exciting than the trip to PY was the trip home for the holidays. They traveled by train to Mukden in Manchuria and from there by steamer to Chefoo. They arrived for this first Christmas back home as night still hung over the harbor. Dad was standing in the prow of the sampan as it edged towards the steamer. He held a flashlight high, eager for a first glimpse of his children. Not only were Dad, Mother, and Francis welcoming, but the servants also welcomed them with their favorite dishes.

On a later trip through Manchuria they missed their boat and had to spend the night in a Russian hotel. They had asked the treasurer at the school for a little more travel money. "You have plenty," he had advised them. Now they were unable to rent two rooms. So all five of the travelers, two boys and three girls, engaged one room. The three girls shared a double bed, Chalmers slept on a cot and the other lad slept on the couch. The girls dressed the next morning, while the boys kept their faces discreetly turned to the wall. When the boys were ready, they were served breakfast. The eggs were a little past their prime, but they did catch their steamer that morning.

After Chalmers and Bea had graduated, Francis, on one occasion, was traveling home alone. He had bought his passage and gone aboard the steamer. The captain appeared at his cabin and asked. "Do you want me to sail?"

"What do you mean?" asked Francis.

"There is a storm coming. You are my only first class passenger. You have a right to order the ship."

"But you're the captain. What do you think we should do?"

"I would not go out in the tempest that is brewing," said the captain.

So Frenchy gave the order to stay in port. They were in a harbor, but the storm that night tossed the small ship so fiercely that Francis was wretchedly seasick for the first time in his life.

At home, seeing friends and going to parties intermingled with participation in their parents' work. Mr. Browne was in charge of the museum. Dr Corbett had started this program in downtown Chefoo. It was at the museum that Chalmers and his brother and sister could give a hand. The Chinese house had a large front hall, an inner courtyard and other rooms off the courtyard. Through the many years, interesting specimens, curios and examples of Chinese art were collected and displayed. The first part of the tour was a lantern slide presentation of the life of Christ, explained by the director. After this talk the visitors could wander through the building. On Sundays Mr. Browne held a service at the museum. Bea played the organ and Chalmers his trombone. Vacation days flew by.

Holidays over, Chalmers and Bea returned to P'yongyang, but now with a surer knowledge of what to expect and keen anticipation of school activities with friends. Frenchy soon joined them.

Nevertheless home was still the center of affections. In the hot summers the "Chefoo Riviera," with its beautiful beaches, was a source of great pleasure. But the process of leaving home was a real one. For Chalmers it included a search for an outlook on life that was his own. He did not discard the values of his upbringing, but they were weighed and imbued with new meaning.

During this phase of school life he had an experience of call. A team of young people from America on a preaching mission arrived at PY for a series of meetings. At one of these services Chalmers felt God's touch and summons to the ministry. The focus for his life was set.

Scouting, orchestra, running, and playing soccer did not prevent Chalmers from taking part in several dramatic events. One was a production of Gilbert and Sullivan's HMS *Pinafore*. In his senior year he was the editor of the *Kum and Go*, the school's news sheet.

Still there was time in the midst of all the activity for a prank. One morning all the boys dressed, then rolled up their pant legs, donned their bathrobes and tousled their hair. Looking as if they had just tumbled out of bed they went to the dining room for breakfast. Miss Logan, the dorm mother in charge of the dining room, bit her tongue to keep back an immediate reprimand. At the end of the meal the boys threw off their robes, rolled down their trousers and stood in their go-to-school a-tire. When Miss Logan confessed that she had been about to take them to task, one young man, who had been studying Proverbs in Miss Logan's Bible class quoted: "Even a fool when he holds his tongue is considered wise." Miss Logan was able to laugh with them.

Chalmers' class chose him as valedictorian. The school invited his father to be the speaker at the graduation. His family was present for this special occasion. Chalmers was now ready to step out into the next phase of his life.

- 3 -

Learning the Word

Chalmers was packing to go to the College of Wooster. His parents, reasoning that travel was part of a good education, arranged for him to travel via Europe, a journey halfway around the world. Eleanor and Billie Booth, missionary daughters, were also leaving for the United States. The trio traveled together. They started in Italy.

Chalmers enjoyed Italy—the exuberance and color, the charm of olive orchards and vineyards on hillsides looking down to the blue Adriatic, and the grace of the Greek and Roman art. He liked the food, steaming soup with cheese melting on top. Chalmers was slightly color-blind, so that dark red and dark green looked the same to him. Bright red, orange, and gold were his favorite colors, but the blue of lakes and the sun green of valleys and mountains in Switzerland also provided a spellbinding experience. The history, William Tell and John Calvin, stirred his imagination. His visits to France and England were like coming home to his cultural heritage.

The three travelers arrived on American soil in September 1933. Chalmers chose Wooster as his college and lived at first with his grandmother and Aunt Natalie. He shared the household tasks—mowing the lawn, stoking the furnace, and shoveling snow. In 1934 Grandmother died. It was a solemn experience for Chalmers, but he was a great support to Aunt Natalie.

Across Pearl Street from the Browne house stood the large red brick residence of the Millers. The Reverend Clarence Miller was twice widowed and lived with his daughter, Grace. One day he walked across the street and asked Aunt Natalie to marry him. She accepted, and they were married in the summer of 1935. The brick house became her home and a haven for nieces and nephews in the years that followed.

Chalmers moved up to the Livingstone Lodge, on the edge of the campus. There were two "Inkies" (incubators), Westminster for girls and Livingstone for boys. These were established especially for missionary children studying at the college or at the high school in town. Chalmers roomed with three other "mish kids," Dave Cunningham, Bob McClanahan and Jim Love. They arranged their rooms so that they had sleeping quarters and a living room for study and socializing.

Chalmers majored in English and speech. Dr. Lean, a longtime friend of the Browne family, was head of the speech department. Chalmers delighted in the excursions to other colleges for debates. In preparation, Dr. Lean would have each student debate one side and then the other of an issue. Chalmers found it stimulating to study a subject from both points of view and marshal the arguments for either side. Professor Lowry, who later became president of the College of Wooster, was then teaching Shakespearean Tragedy, which added a depth of understanding not only of literature but also of philosophy and theology.

Among his other courses Chalmers liked history and geology. All through his life he "saw" rocks and brought stones and fragments home. One year the Latin class organized a Roman feast. Chalmers was detailed to learn to carve a roast pig. He did the research and carved for the banquet.

Chalmers sang in the choir and played his trombone in the Wooster College marching band. On the track team he ran the mile. At one meet Wooster's best runner was incapacitated. The opposing team was jubilant, sure they would win. Chalmers outdid himself and won in his teammate's place. He also helped organize a soccer team and played on it.

There were several Christian organizations on campus, collectively called the Big Four. Chalmers belonged to the YMCA and to Student Volunteers and was much involved in their campus activities. At least one year he went to a national rally of the Student Volunteers. One spring, as a committee of one, he made signs and put them up all around campus: Keep off the Grass!—a single-handed campaign for the beauty of the lawns.

Chalmers did not go to dances because dancing was taboo in his family but parties and other doings he entered enthusiastically. At homecoming time, each dorm built on its lawn some representation of Wooster's prowess on the football field with dire predictions of what was about to happen to the competing team. Imagination and skills in executing ran wild. Livingstone Lodge on several occasions won first prize for its lawn fantasy.

During the summers Chalmers worked. Dr. Mellott, who lived in Wooster, handled the student summer sales program for Thompson's New Chain Reference Bible. Chalmers took the training and set forth each summer to sell this study bible. He was a conscientious salesman and returned to campus each fall with several hundred dollars earned.

Three years is a long time to be away from home. At the beginning of Chalmers' senior year Bea came to college. Chalmers settled her in the girls' Inky, Westminster Hall. That Christmas of 1936 Chalmers and Bea went to Rural Valley to celebrate with Aunt Mary and others of the Cowen side of the family. When they arrived, Aunt Mary had a final day of teaching, the day when the pupils exchanged small gifts. Chalmers decided that Aunt Mary needed a Christmas tree for her classroom. He and Bea walked to the tree farm. They cut their own tree and carried it all the way out to the schoolhouse. It was a welcome surprise. The tree moved to Aunt Mary's apartment to add to the family festivities.

Chalmers' senior year passed swiftly. Mother and Dad Browne were in China. Aunt Mary, Aunt Nat and other relatives helped him celebrate at his graduation. He received honors and won a Phi Beta Kappa key. College days were over, but Wooster still remained the place most like home for him. That summer Chalmers persuaded Bea to join him in bible selling. One summer was enough for Bea, though she did well. At the end of the summer Chalmers went to Princeton Seminary under the auspices of the Presbytery of Wooster.

One interesting feature of the campuses of both the seminary and the university at Princeton are the iron rail fences around the grounds.

Stuart Hall, a massive, turreted building where lectures and classes are held, stands just inside the fence on Alexander Street. Chalmers roomed in Alexander Hall with Bob Allen, a Wooster classmate. At the very heart of the campus stands the white, New England-style chapel with its columned portico. It looks out across the lawns shaded by venerable trees seeming small and aloof amidst the large old buildings. However, its presence hallows the whole life of the Seminary family.

During his first year at Princeton, Bea visited Chalmers. She was struggling with hard questions and brought them to her brother. "Why, since God's pardon was already so plenteously available, did his Son have to come in human form and die on the cross?" Bea posed her questions and Chalmers listened. He then took her into the quiet chapel and prayed with her. Her questions were not all answered, but she was again put in touch with the Source and her life was back on track.

In Chalmers' time the students of Princeton Seminary belonged to eating clubs. There were four of them: Benham, Warfield, Calvin, and Friar. Warfield and Calvin were very sedate clubs. Benham and Friar were less inhibited. The Friars gave the impression of outright rambunctiousness. The Friar Club was just off campus on a side street that led to the university. There was a rooming house of university students next door to the Friar Club. A Princetonian asked a Friar Club member how much they drank. The answer was: "Lots of water, tea, and coffee."

"You can't fool me," answered the interrogator. "I hear you singing those rowdy drinking songs every night." Chalmers found employment with the Friar Club as a busboy. He stoked the furnace, washed pots and pans, and became a close friend of Pete, the Friar cook. Pete was a gourmet cook, much sought after by high-quality restaurants until his drinking habits started interfering with his work. He came to the Friar Club because there was no liquor to tempt him. The benefit was indeed mutual.

While at Wooster Chalmers had dated a young woman named Beryl. During his first year at seminary, he invited Beryl for a visit. They were very good friends and they had much to talk about. At the end of the visit Beryl told Chalmers that she felt their friendship should remain just that. "Ministers move about," she said. "I want a little white cottage by the side of the road with clambering roses." Years later I was to meet Beryl. My admiration for her was great. She was a woman of depth and wisdom and cheer. I was awed that the man who had chosen Beryl as a special friend had chosen me to be his wife.

Chalmers worked very hard at Princeton Seminary. He continued his Greek and added Hebrew. Hymnody became a favorite subject. Further voice training as a member of the choir and in speech provided satisfaction. Delving into church history and other learning specific to a theology course honed a mind and spirit that were reaching out for truth and meaning.

The Princeton Seminary Choir spent most of its weekends barnstorming. They sang in two or three churches each Sunday. At each service one of the members spoke briefly about his vocation and the meaning of the gospel in his life. With his colleagues listening, the speaker had to be honest about himself and about Princeton Seminary. The disciplined music under the direction of "Jonesy" (David Hugh Jones), and the testimonies of the seminary students became a strong message of hope and encouragement.

Midway through his first year at Princeton, Chalmers welcomed his parents back to the United States. They settled in Wooster where Bea was studying and where "Frenchy" started his undergraduate studies. Christmas holidays were joyfully spent together.

The next summer the whole family went on a trip. They enjoyed Washington, D.C., visiting the monuments and museums. The family sought tourist homes for accommodations each night. Chalmers always checked out the restaurants at mealtimes to be sure they did not serve liquor. From Washington they traveled south and spent some time at Montreat, North Carolina. They wandered over the wonderful hillside conference grounds. Many friends from former days greeted them with warm southern hospitality. They heard eminent speakers in the large auditorium and were caught up in the sense of an extended Montreat family.

Chalmers was devoted to his home and to his family. At the same time he felt a responsibility to create his own life with God. He wanted to be as independent as possible financially because that was part of the measure of his own growth and individuality. His sense of God and the mission of the church were strong. He was holding in abeyance any decision about his future work, knowing that the contingencies of life are in God's hands.

- 4 -

In the Center of South America

The Cuiabá River meanders through the Pantanal, the vast swamplands in the center of South America. Traveling on a riverboat through the maze of these wetlands, Philip Landes and his bride, Margaret Hall Landes, reached the city of Cuiabá in July, 1915. They had come as the first Protestant missionaries to the interior of the state of Mato Grosso. My mother, Margaret Bookwalter Hall and her twin sister, Julia, were born on January 7, 1884, in Santa Barbara, Brazil, the sixth and seventh daughters of Mary Elizabeth Miller Hall and Charles Moses Hall.

Charles Hall had traveled to Brazil with his father, Robert Hall. In the aftermath of the Civil War, many Southern families, finding their farms and businesses in shambles, moved to other parts of the United States or abroad. The emperor of Brazil, Dom Pedro II, was seeking good, honest settlers for his vast, underpopulated country. He offered attractive incentives to American immigrants: hospitality in a large mansion on arrival in Rio de Janeiro, advantageous terms for the purchase of land, and help in getting established. The Halls settled with a group of other Americans on a fertile tract of farmland in Santa Barbara in the state of São Paulo.

Also joining the colony was the family of James William Miller and Sarah Boyd McGill Miller. It was in this setting that Charles Hall met Mary Elizabeth Miller. Though he was more than ten years older than she, he courted and married the sixteen-year-old girl. Charles' father, Robert, was killed by a mentally unstable man who fancied he had a grudge against his victim. Charles then took over the farm and he and Lizzy established a gracious, Southern-style home in this new land.

My cousin Carolyn Smith Ward writes: "The quiet, resourceful mother and the energetic, vibrant father provided the family with the steady, happy influence that made for a strong, loving and stable family life."

Charles and Mary Elizabeth Hall had twelve children, ten girls and two boys. Two daughters died before reaching adulthood. The children had their early schooling at home. Margaret and her sisters went to high school at the Methodist Boarding School for Girls in Piracicaba, São Paulo, not too far from their home.

Charles Hall had been reared an Episcopalian. Mary Elizabeth Miller was a Presbyterian. Their family was brought up to observe simple, Christian piety. On Sunday, the children memorized Bible passages. Charles built a nonsectarian chapel on his property where services were held whenever a preacher visited.

The Hall home extended hospitality to all who came. Bachelor missionaries were among those who visited. Five of the Hall daughters married missionaries. Margaret saw most of her sisters married, including her twin sister, Julia. Margaret stayed on at the farm as her father's right-hand manager. Philip Landes eventually came along and asked her to marry him. She prepared for her wedding while Philip made an exploratory trip as far as Cuiabá.

My father, Philip Sheeder Landes, was born in Botucatu, in the state of São Paulo, on June 22, 1883, the second of ten children, three boys and seven girls. Before long the family moved to the state of Paraná. Grandfather George Anderson Landes grew up in the farmland of Lancaster County, Pennsylvania. His father died when George was quite young and he had to go to work. With the help of friends and the constant moral support of his mother, he graduated from Princeton Theological Seminary.

Grandmother Margaret Sheeder Landes was born in Gettysburg, Pennsylvania. Her father was a Lutheran minister newly arrived from Germany. In 1880 Margaret and George were married, and set out for Brazil as Presbyterian missionaries. The Landes family settled in Curitiba, the capital of Paraná.

There the children studied at the Escola Americana. During the holidays Philip sometimes accompanied his father on itineration trips. He slept in huts, ate out of the common pot, cooked over the smoky fire in the middle of a one-room cabin, and learned to drink "chimarrâo," the bitter tea brewed from mate leaves. On returning from one of these trips, George Landes found Margaret and the children sitting on their household effects in front of their rented house. The owner had been persuaded that it was his Christian duty as a Roman Catholic to oust these Protestant interlopers. The eviction was illegal since Brazilian law guaranteed religious freedom, but Roman Catholics in those days were sometimes carried away by their fervor. Soon, with the help of Brazilian friends, George and his family were comfortably housed once more.

Philip finished high school at Mackenzie College in São Paulo. He taught English to help himself along. He then went to the College of Wooster where he graduated in 1907. In the fall he entered Princeton Theological Seminary.

The news of the death of his sister Pauline, only two years younger than he, shocked him profoundly. She was nearing the end of her medical course when she died of pernicious anemia in 1908. She was Philip's inspiration and he decided on graduating from Princeton in 1910 to study medicine at Cornell University. But he came to realize that he would not be able to practice medicine adequately in Brazil's interior and be a minister at the same time. He therefore left Cornell at the end of his second year and applied to the Board of Foreign Missions of the Presbyterian Church to serve as a missionary in Brazil.

To begin his missionary work Philip and a friend, Franklin Graham, made an extensive survey trip by mule. Franklin chose his field of service in the state of Goiás and Philip picked Cuiabá as the center of his endeavors. Philip then hurried back to Vila Americana to marry Margaret.

After the wedding, they visited Philip's family in Curitiba. They took their "honeymoon" trip to Cuiabá. It was a wearying journey, first by train and then up the river by paddle wheeler. They arrived at the port of Cuiabá on a pitchblack night. On the riverbank, holding lanterns high, the Dias family waited to receive them. They were the only Protestant family in the city.

Things were strange and different as they settled into their new home. The mud-and-brick stove had no chimney, so the smoke burned their eyes and rose lazily to the soot-blackened walls and rafters. Milk was delivered to the door from canisters on the back of a mule and measured by cup or liter into a vessel provided by the purchaser. Fishermen brought their catch to sell from door to door. There were no vegetables. Margaret asked Philip to bring home some salt on his next trip to the store and was shocked to see that it came in rock form and was mixed with dirt. To make the salt usable, Margaret melted and strained it, then let it dry.

The Dias family, my parents' primary helpers and friends, had come to Cuiabá from the northeastern state of Ceará. There they had embraced the Protestant faith. The enterprising Sr. Dias was working on a hydroelectric power plant on the Cuiabá River, and on a telephone system for the city.

Nine months after their arrival in Cuiabá, on March 26, 1916, Margaret and Philip welcomed me into their home. The house where I was born faced a small square in which stood a marker inscribed "the center of South America."

Close to the central square of Cuiabá, about a mile from our house, Father and Sr. Dias had rented a barn-like room where my father began to hold services on Sunday evenings. He had benches made by a carpenter, one by one, as he had money to pay for them. In those days the exchange rate from dollars to Brazilian coin was poor. My parents found it hard to stretch their salary to meet family needs and those of church work. They walked everywhere over the cobblestone streets. Soon Margaret had worn out her shoes and brought up her need for new ones. Philip said, "The money we have must go to pay for the benches we ordered." This was the couple's first clash. Margaret did get her shoes, ordered from the cobbler, and the benches were eventually paid for.

On the first of January, 1919, my brother George Newell Landes was born. He was a small, delicate baby, and a most cherished son.

My earliest memory is of a dream. In my dream I was in the cavernous dining room of the house where we lived. Its deep corners were filled with shadows and mystery. It was evening. My mother was sitting near the dining room table holding my baby brother in her arms. Around them, in the light of the kerosene lamp, flitted black and red imps, scrawny, like giant mosquitoes. I frantically swatted at them to keep them from snatching away my brother. I remember this dream as a token of sisterly love which did not always persist when my brother grew old and inquisitive—enough to break my toys.

Not very long afterwards, Aunt Maud, Father's third sister, came to start a primary school in a front room of our house. The next year my Landes grandparents retired and came to Cuiabá for an extended visit. My grandmother, being a true Yankee, did not regard Southern women highly and my mother felt the stress of her disapproval. My grandparents lived with us for a while, then rented a house closer to the center of town. Philip appreciated his father's help and counsel in the church work. Grandfather was a quiet, kindly man of God. After six or seven months my grandparents left to settle in Rio de Janeiro where their son Ray worked.

My mother played our little pump organ for services, taught Sunday School, went visiting and often cared for sick people. She had learned practical nursing from her mother. My parents planted a vegetable garden and raised chickens. When people started coming to ask for vegetables and chickens, Mother shared with them, but also encouraged people to plant their own gardens and raise their own chickens.

"Here are some eggs," my mother would say. "Set them under your hen and you will have some chickens of your own."

After my brother George was born a young black woman named Isaura helped my mother take care of us. We had an enormous backyard. Isaura would take us out under the fruit trees. She knew how to make toy animals out of green mangoes, berries, sticks, and leaves. She taught us to blow iridescent bubbles through grass rings using the milky sap from the stalks of a hedge plant.

Father didn't limit himself to preaching in Cuiabá. He began to make trips to neighboring towns. He had gone to a village named Guia to hold services for a week. Guia is about twenty miles from Cuiabá, an easy day's journey on horseback. When the week was up, he did not return and Mother became uneasy. She consulted Sr. Dias, who exclaimed,"Dona Margarida! Do you mean to say that Sr. Felipe has gone to Guia by himself? Don't you know that it is election time and political parties are fighting each other? It is dangerous!"

My poor mother, who tended to be a worrier, was fully alarmed. To her great relief Father came home the next day and told us what had happened.

Father had preached several evenings in a house which Sr. Laurindo, a new believer, had made available. Father slept in a hammock with the windows of his room open to the street. One night a man came to the window, wakened him, and said, "You had better leave town right away or we will shoot you. We don't like Protestants preaching in our town. We are good Roman Catholics, 'graças a Deus.'"

"I am perfectly within my rights," my father answered. "The constitution of Brazil guarantees freedom of religion and freedom of speech. I shall continue to preach about God whom you yourself just mentioned." Father went back to his hammock.

The next evening the room was filled with attentive listeners. As Father arose to speak he noticed some well-dressed men on the front bench. He did not recollect having seen them before, so he preached with renewed ardor. After the service he shook hands with everyone, greeting especially the newcomers. After they had left he was told that those men were of the opposing political party to that of the man who had threatened to shoot him. They had heard of the threat and had come to protect the preacher. The next day my father saddled his horse and rode around to all the farms and ranches of his protectors and thanked them for their support.

When I was almost five, my sister, Mary Elizabeth, was born on January 17, 1921. She was a cute, cuddly baby, a joy to all of us. My parents named her for Grandmother Hall, who had died two years earlier, only a year after Grandfather Hall's death. Little Mary Elizabeth was blessed with her grandmother's name and with her kindly good sense.

Both Mother and Father told stories. Father told marvelous ones out of his imagination. Mother told us Uncle Remus stories about Bre'r Rabbit. My mother sang us nursery rhymes and songs of the South. One evening Father was putting me to bed. He told me a story and heard my prayers. I complained about a scratch on my leg so minor that he could hardly see it. But he put some alcohol on it. I wanted his sympathy, so I cried. Father said to me very gently, "We all get scratches. You must learn not to cry over the small ones." We learn kindness and wisdom by living, passed on by those who are wise and loving.

It was with grateful hearts that our family welcomed Adam and Nettie Martin with their children, Betty, James, and Paul, as missionary co-workers. It was especially wonderful for me because I now had Betty for my best friend. My parents had extended their term of service well beyond the expected seven years. The church in Cuiabá was growing. Construction of a proper church building was started on a plot on the main street not far from the Roman Catholic cathedral on the square. As soon as the Martins were settled and able to take over the work, we left for the States.

We traveled by ocean liner for thirteen or fourteen days from the port of Santos to New York City. Crossing the equator was an event. Mother remembered winning the costume contest on her previous trip to the States when she represented the Statue of Liberty, so she made costumes for us now. She made a blue and white crepe paper Dutch dress and cap for chubby little Bibette (our nickname for Mary Elizabeth), a clown suit for George, and a fairy crown and wand for me.

My mother's youngest sister, Ella, had married a doctor, John Calvin Turner, and settled in Miami, Florida. We spent six weeks with the Turners while Father went north to arrange for housing and for his course of study. My cousin Johnny Turner and I went to kindergarten together. Kindergarten enchanted me with the bright construction paper, crayons, and the marvels our teacher taught us.

Father came for us and took us to Princeton where we had an apartment in Payne Hall, across Alexander Street from Stewart Hall. Father was studying for a master's degree at Princeton University as well as taking courses at the Theological Seminary. Father sang us fun songs that he picked up at the university, such as "MacNamara's Band."

Aunt Maud came to stay with us. She taught me to read and write from a Robert Louis Stevenson primer. I liked the poems. The first in the book was:

> *When I was down beside the sea,*
>
> *A little spade they gave to me*
>
> *To dig the sandy shore.*

When Aunt Maud left us I went to Miss Fine's School, where I was placed in second grade. French was my favorite subject because we had a big dollhouse in this classroom, with windows and doors that opened and shut, furniture, and doll residents. We learned to say, "Pierre et Marie" and "Ouvrez la porte, fermez la fenêtre".

Mother found living in the States strange and at times difficult. Windows that were shut against the wintry winds instead of wide open to the soft breezes gave her claustrophobia. More formality in social customs left her ill at ease. Wearing hats and heavy coats and galoshes caused exasperation. Moving around with three small children into strange surroundings taxed her strength and resources.

Father began working as an assistant pastor at the Tioga Presbyterian Church in Philadelphia. He was taking a few extra months in the United States in hopes that my brother George, who was a fragile child, would grow stronger before we returned to the heat of the Cuiabá River valley. We moved to Philadelphia. Father had rented an apartment for us. I attended third grade at the local public school. Coming in at midyear I found that the children had already formed their own circles so that at recess I hung back and watched the others. Carl, a small boy who seemed also to be on the outside, and I became playmates and fast friends.

Summer came and we went with Aunt Maud and Mother to a cottage on the ridge above Northfield, Massachusetts. Here we could open the screened windows wide and enjoy the shade and sunshine amidst the sweet-scented pines and firs.

When Father came to spend a couple of weeks with us on the ridge, he took me into the hills above our cottage, where we found all sorts of treasures—tangy wild strawberries, blueberries, bluebells nodding in the light breeze, and wintergreen, which had dark, shiny leaves that were sweet to chew.

I made friends all along the ridge. One gentleman who lived in a cottage on a back road loved to play games. With Mother's permission I would go to his house to play. Some of the games were rather active, and during a game of snatching things, I knocked his glasses off and they shattered. I was devastated. For the first time in my seven years of life I felt responsibility for my own actions. I did not want to pass on the responsibility to my mother, and yet I did not know what to do. So I did nothing except feel terrible guilt. My friend never told my mother.

It was a wonderful summer, but that fall we moved back to Payne Hall in Princeton. Christmas that year was very special. We received gifts from our aunts and other relatives and from the people of the Tioga Presbyterian Church. I had more dolls than I ever dreamed possible. We opened packages of games, books, and toys galore. The fly in the ointment came later, when we were packing to go back to Brazil. We were unable to take all our new riches with us and I mourned my left-behind dolls.

One Sunday afternoon some of the children from our apartment building were going for a walk. I asked for and was given permission to go along. We reached the far side of campus and my friends were merrily going "just to Stony Brook," they said. So I tagged along. Yet I knew that I was going beyond the bounds set for a walk without an adult. At the brook we skipped stones across the water, and no thought of time entered my mind. We returned home by the old railway tracks now overgrown with weeds. We enjoyed balancing our way along the rails. By the time we reached home it was dusk. Strains of "Träumerei" were coming from someone's gramophone. For a long time thereafter that music evoked a sickening feeling of guilt in me. My mother had been frantic. Much relieved to have me home, she punished me by grounding me and giving me a hymn to memorize.

One Sunday my Sunday School teacher at the First Presbyterian Church of Princeton said at the end of the lesson, "So we should love Jesus very much." My mind took in the message and I thought: "If we should love Jesus, I will love him with all my heart."

- 5 -

A Child's Vision

On our return to Brazil, we spent a few days with Mother's twin, our Aunt Junie, in São Paulo. Our trip from São Paulo to Cuiabá always took two weeks or more. The train carried us halfway across South America. Its wood-burning engine chugged along, sending bright sparks flying through our coach windows to turn into gritty black cinders.

The train stopped each evening at some town. All the passengers alighted to spend the night at a hotel. We children would trudge along behind Mother and Father, carrying whatever bags we were assigned. It seemed an interminable walk to the hotel. But ah! Here came a taxi and Father hailed it. The redolent fumes of the hot motor and the warm smell of well-worn leather upholstering were the sweetest perfume. Even now when an old car passes me on a hot day, a whiff of burnt motor oil brings a nostalgic sense of comfort. We breakfasted early, having coffee with milk and lots of sugar and sometimes freshly baked bread with butter. Then we set out for the train. How different the town looked by daylight—low houses, some white, some blue or pink or green, and many dirt-brown or peeling. Dust swirled from the passing horses and oxcarts carrying the commerce of the day.

It was a relief to get back on the train. The moving air, though hot, fanned our cheeks. We were traveling directly west, and when we reached the banks of the Paraná River, all the passengers descended from the train with their baggage and took the ferry across the wide river. On the other side we found another train waiting to take us as far as Pôrto Esperança on the Paraguay River. We waited there for a river steamer plying between Pôrto Esperança and the bustling border town of Corumbá, one of the hottest and most humid spots on the globe. My wax crayons melted while we waited for the boat to Cuiabá.

Two paddle wheel steamers carried passengers and freight up and down the river. These boats had two decks. Passengers occupied the upper deck with its large central covered area, open to the breezes, and cabins fore and aft. Meals were served on long tables in the central area.

The time it took a steamer to make the trip depended on the season. In the rainy season, the river ran full and the trip took about a week. In the dry season it could take twice as long because the boat would ground itself on many a sandbar. Out came the winches and cables and the crew affixed the cables to a sturdy tree on the bank. When the river men had hauled the vessel back into midstream we forged ahead until we came to another curve and sandbank.

The ever changing scenery on the riverbanks was like a nature movie or a safari. There were always alligators sunning their grey-green backs, and a great variety of birds. Pink spoonbills and snowy egrets, poised on the tree branches, took off in startled flight at our coming. All sorts of smaller waterfowl strutted or flew about. The most impressive birds were the "professors," as we called them. These long-legged black creatures with white vests stalked about the sand holding their wings precisely as if they had tucked their hands behind their backs under their coattails.

The cabins were so hot and stuffy that Mother let me sleep on deck in a hammock. Mother was ever watchful because at times the boat passed under overhanging branches that might rain spiders or fiery caterpillars on us.

I was sleeping on deck one night as we were moving through an area of low hills slowly unfolding against the dusky sky. In the misty, luminous predawn Jesus came aboard. I found myself in his lap as he sat on one of the benches. We talked. I do not remember what he said. But the wonder and happiness of his presence were very real and lasting. The next morning I told my mother that Jesus had taken me on his lap and talked to me. "You must have had a dream," my mother said gently. Whether a dream or not, the experience remains a reality of my life.

The steamer made it up the river and we were back home. Changes were taking place in the Mato Grosso mission field. Besides Reverend and Mrs. Adam Martin, who were stationed in Cuiabá, an agriculturalist, Mr. Homer Moser, and his wife, Edith Moser, arrived to start a farm school at Buriti. Prior to our furlough in the States, Father and Mr. Martin had discovered Buriti and negotiated its purchase on behalf of the mission. Buriti was a wild and beautiful 4-square-mile tract of land on the high plateau above the Cuiabá River valley. The physical difficulties the Mosers faced were immense. All provisions had to be transported from Cuiabá. Two old adobe houses with tamped dirt floors served as living quarters and school.

In Cuiabá the church structure had grown to an impressive brick building, high-ceilinged with large windows. The interior was whitewashed, making it light and airy. The completion of the new building was celebrated with jubilation.

With Mr. Martin in Cuiabá, Father was now able to travel to more distant farms and towns. The interest of several families in Rosário Oeste encouraged him. We went with him on one of his trips to Rosário. Father and Mother had acquired a buckboard, or trolley with no top. Two mules pulled it. We had three pack mules to take our gear, and one horse, Traveller, to keep the pack of five mules together. Mules will follow a horse.

Our first day on our way to Rosário took us as far as Guia. The next morning our cavalcade continued through rolling country. Our road was a cleared dirt strip through the wooded river bottoms and over the prairies of coarse grass and sparse, dwarfed trees. We all wore straw hats against the hot sun. That afternoon we were going up a small rise. The wheels of the buggy slipped into a gully and the buckboard rolled onto its side, dumping us into a growth of spiny pineapple plants. We were scratched but not badly hurt. The trolley was soon righted and we were on our way again.

Night fell before we reached the farm where Father had planned to stop for the night. It was very dark and quiet and mysterious in the woods. The mules plodded on. The road descended from the ridge and we found the farmhouse near the river. There were no lights. Everyone had gone to bed. At our call the old farmer came out squinting in the light of a smoking kerosene lamp. "What brings you to my door at this time of night?" he greeted us. The farmer's family now piled out of the house, gathering around the trolley. They were greatly amazed, never before having seen such a vehicle. "Is this where the pilot sits?" asked the farmer, whose major means of transportation was his canoe. The family gave us a room in their house for the night. Mother didn't sleep very well due to the yipping of a litter of new puppies under the bed. The next morning one of the young men of the family went with us for a few miles to show us a shortcut.

As we moved along into the afternoon, the day grew hotter. My little sister, Bibette, began to cry. My mother took her on her lap and felt her forehead. She was burning with fever. "Oh, my little head," Bibette wailed. "Oh, my little head." We were nearing the town of Brotas. Father turned in at the crossing. He usually passed Brotas by because he had found no welcome from its people. We entered the central square. The Roman Catholic Church dominated the dirt plaza. Clumps of grasses and bushes grew in the sparse soil, and low houses rimmed the square. Crowds of children gathered about us, shy and curious. Father asked if there was an empty house in town. An excited chatter followed. One man stepped forward and said he thought Sr. Honório's house was unoccupied.

By good luck Sr. Honório was in town and came over to us. Yes, he would rent his house to us for a week. His family was out on their farm. As soon as they struck a bargain, Father and the "camarada," who traveled with us and saw to the mules, went to the river for buckets of water to wash and disinfect the house. In the meantime Mother had made a pallet for Bibette in the shade. She gave her aspirin and bathed her hot body. The next morning Bibette's fever was down and she ate some cornmeal mush for breakfast. Father saddled the horse and went on to Rosário becaus he had promised to hold a service that evening.

While Father was gone we cooked our meals outdoors, boiled our drinking water, and swam and played in the river. In the afternoons Mother played the folding organ. The children, hearing the music, gathered in our front room. We sang hymns and, tentatively, some of the children started chiming in. On the second day more children and some adults came to sing. When Father arrived back on the third day he found the house full of people learning to sing hymns. That night he held a service. We stayed in Brotas a week with singing in the afternoons and services in the evenings.

Then we were off to Rosário. When we reached the east bank of the river we had to wait for the "balsa" or ferry. Everybody standing about joined forces to get the trolley—and the mules—aboard the raft. The ride across the river with the cool breezes blowing off the swirling water delighted us. The mules pulled the trolley up the steep bank on the west side of the river.

Father and Mother conducted the promised series of services and also medicated some of the people who came to them. There was neither doctor nor pharmacy in Rosário. I was given the task of watching a man to whom Father had given thymol against internal parasites, to make sure that he ate nothing during the next four hours. Thymol was a dangerous medicine when mixed with oil.

At Rosário, some huntersgave me a *paca*. They had taken the baby from the mother's womb alive. A *paca* is a large rodent that grows to the size of a pig. This baby fit in my cupped hands. I fed Paca with milk sopped in cotton. She sucked greedily. She soon graduated to a baby bottle.

When we returned to Cuiabá Paca adapted well to the house and large yard where many fruit trees grew. Paca loved fruit and would wait for hours under her favorite mango tree in expectation that a mango would fall. We all loved Paca, and Paca was devoted to us. She would trot around behind Mother until Mother sat down. Then she would jump into her lap. But when Paca was about five months old, she bit the lady who came to help mother with her sewing. Mother bandaged the seamstress' leg and Paca was banished to a back room. Several weeks later Paca became aggressive with another guest. It was obvious that we couldn't keep Paca. We had a family council and sadly agreed to send Paca away.

Soon after, we moved to a house across the street. This new house had a long cement stairway from the dining room down into the yard. A huge mango tree shaded the yard with branches that reached up to the dining room windows.

Once settled in our new house, Father and Mother planned a trip to Pocon, and we set off enthusiastically. In Pocon, we stayed at the home of some friends. The householder and his wife were an older couple who had several grown sons living with them. We were surprised to notice that they had very little to eat. They squatted on the floor and ate with their hands from a single plate. Their diet was meager, a mixture of manioc meal and green bananas fried with a little oil. Mother had brought canned goods and large loaves of sandwich bread which we shared. We liked it when Mother spread slices of bread with condensed milk for us.

This family had the most loquacious parrot I have ever known. It seemed that he knew what he was saying. The first time he heard the organ he became very excited. He stood on one foot, then on the other, and walked back and forth cackling, "Wy! Morena. Wy, Morena! Wy!" In the morning he would start asking for his coffee. "Qué café, Morena qué café." ("Morena wants coffee"). He could sing a little ditty:

Papagaio verde do bico dourado,

Leva esta carta p'ro meu namorado.

(Green parrot with golden beak

Take this letter to my sweet.)

Each evening Father preached, Mother played the organ, and we sang lustily so people could learn the tunes and the words. Few people knew how to read. "What a Friend We Have in Jesus" and "Master, the Tempest Is Raging" were favorites.

When it was time to return to Cuiabá, a young woman who had been attending the meetings implored my parents to let her travel with us. Father and Mother were reluctant as space in the trolley was limited. However, they finally relented and we started out. When we had traveled for about two hours and Pocon was far behind, the girl said, "Oh, my! I have lost my wallet." Father stopped the trolley. Bento, the camarada, rode up. A conference took place. "You dropped it from the trolley?" asked my father. "How far back?"

"I don't know," answered the girl. "It had all my money in it." Father told Bento to ride back for a kilometer or two and see if he could find the wallet. I was already mounted on our horse, Traveler, and Father told me to drive the pack animals. Everything would have been fine if we had not come to a ford. One mule, after drinking, decided to follow the stream instead of the road. Before I knew it, the other mules were following the first. I pressed Traveler into a gallop and dashed downstream to cut them off. We urged the mules onto the farther bank and finally got them turned back to the road. Traveler knew his business. But low branches had pulled off my hat and my face was scratched. Bento came back without finding the wallet. Mother gave the girl a little money. We never knew if she had really lost a wallet.

Soon after we were back in Cuiabá, Maria came seeking work. Mother needed a helper. Maria was a big-boned woman with dark chocolate skin. At first Mother despaired of her. She was taciturn, almost sullen. All her movements were slow. Before long we found out how much Maria had been mistreated. She was an orphan. Relatives had made her work for them and had taken from her any money she had earned. She ran away and was again exploited in the city.

Maria soon began to show remarkable ability. She listened to Mother's explanations and understood about germs and the need to keep flies away from food. Still deliberate and somewhat solemn, Maria became a dependable part of the family. Maria went to church with us and was soon an enthusiastic member. Her understanding of the faith was grave and full She drank in all the knowledge of which she had been deprived for so long. She learned to read and write.

At our church we had a talents competition. Each person was given a small amount of money to use along with his or her talents. Maria bought some corn with her money. We had a hand grinder. Maria made corn meal and sold it door to door, making more with her talents than anyone else.

Some new friends came into our lives. A young missionary couple, Reverend Roy Harper and Evelyn Harper arrived to live with us and learn Portuguese. Father gave them lessons and we all talked Portuguese with them. After a time the Harpers rented a house a block away from us. Aunt Evelyn taught me my first piano lessons. Uncle Roy had a harder time than Aunt Evelyn with Portuguese. One day he embarrassed the girl who worked for them by asking her if her father was a sinner. He meant to ask if her father was a fisherman. The word for fisherman is *pescador*, the word for sinner *pecador*.

One hot afternoon I was in the backyard. I looked at the flight of steps up to the house and felt I couldn't possibly climb them. By resting every other step I made it. Mother took one look at me and put me to bed. I had the measles. George and Bibette came down with the measles too.

The next day the Mosers arrived from Buriti with a very sick baby. Their son, Paul, had double pneumonia. The Harpers took them in since we had measles at our house. Aunt Edith asked Mother to help nurse Paul. The Mosers had lost their infant son Bobby Lar two years earlier and were frightened. Mother called on our good friend, Dona Amelia, a stout Portuguese woman with a heart of gold, who believed that the best remedy for measles was to sweat them out. Despite the heat she piled blankets on us. We weathered the discomfort and the measles, and to everyone's joy Paul got well, too.

Then something marvelous happened in our household. Our brother Phil was born on April 23, 1926. He was named Philip Harper Landes. Fortunately Phil was a beautiful, hardy baby and Mother was able to trust Maria to wash his clothes and sterilize his bottles. George and I both had the flu and bronchitis while Mother was still unable to care for us.

Phil entered a busy family life centered about the church work. Evening services were held in the church on Sunday and Wednesday. After church Father and one of the elders, Sr. Nonato, would walk towards home together. Clovis, Sr. Nonato's son, and I would walk sedately behind our fathers, holding hands. Clovis was sixteen and I ten. I still have a small gold bracelet that Clovis gave me.

Because carnival time offers so much that is injurious, especially to young people, who are initiated into evil ways in the name of fun, the Protestant Church in Brazil sought alternatives to carnival festivities. The Cuiabá Church believers took off for a daylong picnic out to the Coxipó River. We played in the clear waters and on the sandy bank and delightedly buried Maria's big feet under a mound of sand. I was personally glad to get away from the revelry in the city because the young men and boys wore horrible masks and tormented children. I must have been frightened at a very early age because I felt a real terror of these bogeymen which entered my nightmares.

When Phil was almost a year old Mother decided we should go on a vacation to Guia to be away from the dust and heat of the city. Father took us to Guia and returned to his work in Cuiabá. For us Guia was a splendid place. Sr. Laurindo's house was roomy and pleasant. In front of the house stood two large shade trees which we called bat trees because the bats liked to gnaw the fruit. We took benches out under the trees and played to our hearts' content. After lunch and a rest, Mother would take us to the river, to the women's beach where the river spread wide and shallow. We splashed and swam with other children in the cool, sparkling water.

On the most memorable day at the river, Mother saw a dark object floating along the current. She thought someone upstream must have lost a quilt. She motioned to us to bring whatever it was to shore. With a great deal of cavorting we pulled the big, black cloth to Mother. To her horror it turned out to be a priest's cassock. Mother knew that the Catholic Church that stood on the square was being given a thorough cleaning by the faithful women of the town. She also knew that there had been several outbreaks of smallpox through the years. At times of crisis, people took the stored banners and vestments from their nooks and chests and carried them in procession. Priests waited on the sick and dying. The smallpox germs or spores could remain dormant in their clothing for years. We were urged out of the water and bathed with lots of soap. Mother sent a telegram to Father asking him to bring smallpox vaccine. We were vaccinated. We didn't hear of anyone getting smallpox.

By this time, people knew that I loved to tell stories from the *Arabian Nights* or Portuguese versions of fairytales. We gathered under the bat trees. As I told the stories the warm evenings would be peopled with exotic characters from many lands.

April brought with it Phil's first birthday. Father came for the occasion. Some of the church people from Cuiabá came with him to enliven the week of services my parents held during the next week, before we returned to the city.

In these growing-up years for me, romantic-tragic daydreams mingled with the real-world activities of studying math with Father and learning to make cornbread with my mother. In my daydreams I would cry in private at the thought of how terrible it would be if my parents should die. I also cried about my sins. I had a real concept of the imperfection of my human state. So I went one day to my Father's study with a certain amount of trepidation and told him about my sorrow for my sin and asked if I could make my profession of faith. Father listened gravely and asked me questions. I joined the church with the next communicant group. I was growing up.

-6-

Starting New Churches

The old-style Brazilian houses were flush with the sidewalk. After the heat of the day people brought wicker chairs or benches out in front of their doors. Neighbors would wander up the walk or saunter across the street to visit with friends. The children played games. I walked up and down the block with my arms linked with my friends Virgilina and Ada.

As we were strolling one evening Father returned from a trip, dusty and tired, but eager to show us what he had cradled before him on the saddle. It was a tiny field deer. "The mother deer ran away in a panic when I came close," Father told us. I was afraid she might not come back to take care of her baby, so I brought her to you." I resorted to cotton soaked in milk as I had with Paca. Bela, as we named her, grew into a graceful spotted creature that stepped daintily or cavorted about the yard chasing her short, white tail.

The Mosers took an extended health leave and we were going to Buriti to take care of the farm and school until they could return. Buriti occupied an area of wild, scenic beauty hugging the edge of the high plateau above the Cuiabá River valley. The land fell away from the plateau in deep ravines and craggy escarpments.

We had hoped to make the trip up the sierra from Cuiabá to Buriti in one day, but the last rays of the sun were slanting through the treetops and lighting up the red face of the cliffs ahead and we still had miles to go. Clouds rolling over the mountains presaged a storm as we stopped for some supper. Thunder rumbled and lightning arched across the dark, scudding clouds. We took shelter under a shed which road workers had put up (only a thatched roof, but a cover). Wind brought driving rain and Mother pinned up some blankets on the windward side so that we were just damp rather than thoroughly soaked.

The next morning dawned fresh and pink against the stony face of the mountain. On our way again, the road climbed steeply, turning back on itself around outcroppings of the hills. Sometimes the road ran between the cliff and fearful chasms. Portâo do Inferno (Gate of Hell) was such a place, deep in the forest of overhanging tropical trees. We skirted the precipice on a narrow ledge along the sheer stone mountainside watching for jaguars that lived in these jungles. We eventually emerged into more open country and sunlight.

Continuing across the plateau we reached the edge of Buriti property. The road curved through sandy terrain, where tall grasses and bright flowers blew in the wind, until we came to the small valley with its stream and buriti palms and the low houses of Buriti School.

Buriti was a magical place for us. We delighted in the sandy paths for exploring, in the brook for swimming, and especially in the joy of horseback riding. We would gallop with the wind or go slowly, searching with sharp eyes under each clump of trees as we looked for tart, sweet wild pineapples. We picked other wild fruit, which abounded in the woods and fields.

This untamed corner on the edge of civilization was a jumping-off place for explorers. It attracted all sorts of naturalists since it was at the meeting point of three ecosystems: the river swamp valley, the forests reaching north to the Amazon, and the plateau of grasslands and forest stretching as far east as what is now the Federal District and Brasília. An Englishman named Colonet spent some time studying butterflies at Buriti. He taught us how to become butterfly collectors. There were so many beautiful butterflies that ranged from the big, luminous blue ones that floated in the shadowy depths of the forest to the bright red, white, and black ones with an *88* stenciled on their wings.

We had brought Bela with us to Buriti. Soon she began wandering in the woods. We would find footprints of many deer at the edge of the clearing. Bela had evidently found those of her own kind. But she would return often to us and almost knock us down in her demonstrations of affection. Bela didn't go back with us when we returned to Cuiabá—we left her free with her own kin.

We lived with the girls in one of the two small houses that were the original buildings at Buriti. A long back porch served as dining room with kitchen attached. A new building was being erected, which was to be the girls' dormitory. We could run along the stone foundation and talk to the workers. The chief builder was Hans, a gifted constructor from Germany.

Time came for Mission Meeting. Once a year all missionaries of the South Brazil Mission gathered, usually in São Paulo, to determine the assignments and work budget for the next year. Father and Mother and the Sallys, who were visiting our field, decided to rent a truck and go to São Paulo by the new motor road.

We started out one fine morning, each finding a seat amongst the baggage and boxes of gasoline tins. There would be no filling stations along the route until we were well into the state of São Paulo. The unpaved road kept Rigoletto, our driver, busy finding the part of the road with the fewest bumps. As we were going along a level part of the road, he chose the right side because of a gully on the left. Hidden under grass was an anthill, the hard-as-rock kind that termites build in the fields in Brazil. As the wheel went over it the truck tipped crazily and turned on its side, spilling passengers, baggage, and boxes. Mother was the only passenger badly hurt. She had been in the truck cabin with Phil on her lap. Something struck her temple. A great lump appeared on the side of her head and, as was later discovered, she also broke several ribs. But the immediate worry was over George and Bibette. They were nowhere to be seen. The men began to move the bags and bundles cautiously. Suddenly, the two of them appeared prancing over the hill. Happy to be out of the truck, they had run up the near hill and back. Everyone gave a deep sigh of relief.

The truck was righted and reloaded. Rigoletto refilled the gas tank. We had to push the truck up the first steep hill. On the downgrade the motor caught and we sailed along again. As we started up the next hill the motor coughed, sputtered, and died. We all tumbled out and pushed the truck up a long hill. Fortunately, there were seventeen passengers on the truck, mostly men. I was quite strong for a twelve-year-old girl, and thought it a lark to help push. On the downgrade the motor started again and ran smoothly until the next hill. So we traveled, pushing uphill and riding on the downgrades.

Exhausted, we came to a valley with a crystal-clear stream out in the midst of virgin, unspoiled nowhere. We stopped to rest and eat our meal. Rigoletto, though he was uncomfortable with a head cold, did not rest. He was under the truck checking all systems. Even the wheels and brakes were studied. He was still at it as the sun dropped close to the horizon. Another truck drove up kicking up dust as it halted by our truck. Rigoletto and the driver greeted each other with an *abraço* (hug). The newly arrived driver started looking over our truck, walking thoughtfully around it. He hunkered down near the gas tank and ran his finger over the damp top. "Hey, you've got kerosene in this tank! No wonder the truck can't climb a hill," he called. Somehow a box with kerosene had been loaded with the gasoline and Rigoletto's head cold had prevented him from detecting the kerosene.

We slept that night at a farmhouse and the next morning we reached the São Lourenço River finding it in spate, rolling along tumultuously between its jungle banks. The ferry was tied securely to the bank. "Only the old Indian would dare to take the raft across these treacherous waters and he isn't here," the men at the crossing told us. However, the Indian turned up before long and agreed to take the truck across. "People," he said, "will have to cross in canoes." We embarked in the frail dugouts for a scary passage across the tossing water.

Late in the afternoon we came to a stream that had no bridge. We left the truck and helped each other across on stepping stones. The ford was downstream from the road so that the truck must manage a sharp curve through the stream. At the top of the far bank the truck began to make wrenching noises. Rigoletto removed the offending gearbox, but had no spare parts for the repair. He asked a truck bound for Cuiabá to have gear parts sent to us.

That night it rained. We huddled with other passengers under the tarp thrown over the truck. Father and the other men slept under the truck. I think that was the most uncomfortable night I have ever spent. Mother was in pain. By morning she had a fever and a cough. It was excruciating to cough with broken ribs. The gear parts arrived by the next afternoon and we made it to Rondonópolis that night. There the Thompsons, a missionary family of another denomination, took us in. Mother had a bed to sleep in. Father would have liked to go on to São Paulo when the truck started on the next day, but Mother was feeling too ill.

The Thompsons included us in their busy lives and made us feel at home. They had a library in which I found some marvelous books. One, a romantic account of Bruce of Scotland, fired my imagination. I read the biography of Hudson Taylor in two volumes.

We had to wait until Mother could travel and until a truck came along. In the meantime we got acquainted with some Bororo Indians. The Bororo tribe is one of the least aggressive of Mato Grosso Indians. The women would sit at the edge of the village while the men walked boldly down the streets. Mother asked one of the Indian women her name. The woman's face clouded and she answered sullenly, "Buzzard." She wouldn't tell Mother her true name because the Indians believe that the person who knows one's name has power over one.

Mother's health improved and we returned to Buriti. One day on her way to one of the planted fields of the farm Mother met a boa constrictor hissing angrily in the middle of the path. Mother sent a boy who was with her running to fetch a farm worker who came with his machete and killed the snake. It was a young boa constrictor about six feet long, big enough to be a threat to chickens. Rattlesnakes were common at Buriti and we watched for them when we went to pick pineapples.

We baked our own bread at Buriti. I learned to be the family baker. I gathered dry corncobs, bark, and kindling to coax the fire in the woodstove to a red blaze.

George and Bibette decided to help by chopping wood at the chopping block. Each of them had a hatchet. George said, "Not that way, Bibette," as he leaned over to fix the piece of wood against the block. Bibette had already raised her small axe and brought it down on George's head. At George's terrible roar Mother rushed out and gathered him up as blood poured from the gash. She sat him on the bed and slapped a handful of boric acid powder on his head. She held it like a compress on the wound and the powder stanched the bleeding. We kept George awake and gave him aspirin. His young head healed quickly, leaving only a scar on his scalp.

The Mosers returned in good health and we moved back to Cuiabá. We did not stay there long. The Reverend Rodolpho Anders accepted the call as the first Brazilian pastor to the Presbyterian Church in Cuiabá. We received him, his wife, Dona Elvira, and their one-year-old son, Euricles, into our home with affectionate care. We knew that they would find the transition from their home in Rio de Janeiro to Cuiabá a difficult one. Dona Elvira had become ill on the train trip, so we took care of Euricles for her.

With the Anders established in Cuiabá we moved to Rosário. Our household goods went by truck and Father rented a Buick sedan with driver to take the family. We could reach Rosário in one day, but we didn't make it. The river had overflowed and the road was a swamp. The heavy Buick sank in the mud. As the day waned it became stiflingly hot, but the mosquitos were whining outside so we kept the windows rolled up. Water, water everywhere, but we didn't dare drink the swamp water. We told stories and sang songs and drifted off into intermittent sleep. Finally morning dawned and soon a truck came along and pulled us out of the morass.

We moved into the large, traditional house the Mission had bought for the work in Rosário. The largest room was the dining room, which became the meeting room for Sunday School and services.

We had a large unpaved work patio behind our house and a large backyard with fruit trees. We soon had a vegetable garden, chickens, and three cows. Mother milked the cows herself. All the water for the household, the animals, and for watering the garden was drawn by hand with a bucket and pulley from our well.

Father had a shed built at the end of the patio. It had one zinc wall and three made of wire netting. Thus we had a fly-free dining room. Early each morning it was my job to churn the butter. The cream hung in the well all night to keep cool. I took the cream into the shed dining room and beat it with a spoon until the globules of butter formed.

Maria was in charge in the kitchen. Sr. José came to cut wood. He and Maria took to each other and were talking about getting married.

We were concerned because Sr. José was the adventurer type and we weren't sure he would make a good husband. He did, however, tell marvelous stories. In season he was an ipecac gatherer. Most of the men in Rosário went into the forests when it was time to harvest rubber and ipecac, a medicinal root. His best story was about the time he and a companion were in the woods and their food ran low. Sr. José decided to go hunting in open country. At noon he was thirsty and found a stream and knelt beside a fallen palm tree to drink. He cupped his hands and brought the dripping water to his mouth. The second time he dipped his hands in the stream an anaconda grabbed them with its teeth. The anaconda pulled and Sr. José braced himself against the palm trunk and pulled. Sr. José realized that he would not be able to hold out indefinitely against the huge snake. His rifle was slung on his shoulder and his knife was in his belt. But he had no hands with which to use them. He gave a hard yank, bringing the snake's head within reach of his mouth and gave the snake's snout a hard bite. The snake let go. He went back to his friends shaken but with a story to tell when he returned to Rosário. As things turned out Maria never married José.

The congregation that gathered for Sunday School and worship wasn't large, but it was growing. Dona Maria Paula was an exceptional new believer. She had struggled over her devotion to the little statues of saints which she kept in niches in her parlor. She prayed to them daily and placed flowers and lighted candles before them. One day she brought a parcel to my father. "Here, Dr. Felipe," she said. "I can't destroy them; they have been my friends. But I must give them up. Do whatever you decide with them." Father took the package respectfully. Later, on his next furlough, these little images illustrated his talks about the spiritual needs of people in such places as Rosário. Dona Maria Paula learned to read from her great-granddaughter who was going to school. Her great desire was to read the Bible.

From Rosário our family went with Father on a trip to Diamantino. The road we traveled ran sometimes between thickets of bamboo whose fronds overarched our way, and sometimes through deep forests of mighty trees. Rare fern and creepers grew in the gloom. We rounded a bend to come upon a gnarled tree holding clusters of large, exquisite lavender orchids, whose heady perfume had reached us before we saw the bright blossoms. But the town of Diamantino was a dreary place. The surface mines of gold and diamonds had long since been exhausted. The people were victims of diseases that stunted them physically and mentally: Chagas disease, which attacks the heart; goiter; and intestinal parasites. In the midst of the more normal citizens there was an inordinate number of idiots. Despite their strange, lethargic existence, the townspeople were cheerful and welcoming. We came away sobered.

Rosário also had its share of poor people. Mothers, some of them wives of tenant farmers living on the outskirts of town, brought their children to our house in the afternoons. I helped my mother with her baby clinic. We talked with the mothers and enjoyed cuddling the babies. Mother taught the women to bathe their babies and use simple remedies for skin abrasions, and cornstarch for diaper rash. Most of the babies were undernourished. Often the mothers had not themselves the nourishment to be able to nurse their babies adequately. Twin girls, six months old, looked like wizened little monkeys. Mother would have sterile nursing bottles and boiled milk and water ready. She mixed a formula for each pint-sized child. The mothers then sat happily giving the good milk to their babies. One extra bottle of milk went home with each baby. In most cases the children fattened up and developed remarkably in a few months. They babbled and laughed instead of whimpering. I resolved that when I grew up I was going to start a home where mothers could learn to take care of their children.

During the two years we spent in Rosário I was supposed to be studying my geography and spelling with Mother and my math with Father. Mother rarely had a minute to devote to books. Father, it is true, assigned me work in my arithmetic book. He would then depart on one of his journeys. I grappled with the fractions and weights and measures and turn to Mother for help. But she would say, "Don't ask me about math. I don't understand it myself." I had to do the best I could until Father returned.

A bachelor minister, Mr. Good, arrived to take over the Rosário field, since we were due to go on furlough. Father took him on a trip to the farms and towns where he was to work. The parting from Maria was hard. Mother and Father offered to take her with us to the United States. She had heard, however, about prejudice against black people in America and declined. Instead, she accepted the invitation of the Tylees, missionaries returning to their work with the Niambiquara Indians. The Tylees had a little daughter two years old and were expecting a second child. The family needed Maria. With the Tylees was a nurse named Pauline, who was a new recruit in this mission to the fierce Niambiquara tribe. Before accompanying them into the wilderness Maria saw us off on the riverboat.

- 7 -

College Years

When life changes, hope is a good companion. With delight we settled in Northfield, Massachusetts for a furlough year. I enrolled at Northfield Seminary, a girl's middle school founded by D.L. Moody. I studied in the preparatory to high school, but also took some courses in first-year high school. That experience was one of the most exciting of my life. I had not been to school in a classroom with other students and teachers since my short sojourn in third grade in Philadelphia and Princeton. I responded to history, grammar, literature, and algebra with great enthusiasm. I made the Dean's list without having known of its existence.

The great auditorium at Northfield Seminary was a place of wonderful happenings for us. We attended a professional production of Shakespeare's *Macbeth*. Phil was only four. Mother tried in vain to find a baby-sitter for him. We took him to the play and he was as excited about it as the rest of us. He went about for days chanting, "When shall we three meet again, in thunder, lightning, or rain?"

I came home from school one day to find Mother in the living room with a letter from Brazil in her hand. From her face I could tell it was not good news. The Niambiquara Indians had fallen upon the mission station and killed everyone. Mrs. Tylee had been bludgeoned and left for dead. After the Indians left, she was able to crawl to a telegraph station and so get help. Later, her child was born safely. Investigators found Maria's body with thirteen arrows in it. I sat beside Mother and cried. "Don't cry, Polly," Mother's voice was pleading. For her sake, I dried my tears. Maria and the Tylees could not gain from our sorrow. We could only thank God for their lives and sacrifice and resolve to honor their courage in our hearts and our lives.

In the winter we learned to ski down the slope behind our house and in the summer we learned to ride our bikes. We went for walks up on the ridge where we had been for a summer when I was seven years old. Now at fourteen I found that everything on the ridge had shrunk to about half size.

While we were in Northfield Father studied at Hartford. He didn't finish his thesis in the doctoral program because he didn't want a degree that would put him above his Brazilian colleagues. So he never became "Dr. Landes," though he was often given the title.

As we prepared to return to Brazil, Father decided to take us by way of Pasadena, California, to visit Grandmother and Grandfather Landes. We traveled across the United States by train learning the names of the states and their capitals as we went and marveling at the vastness and diversity of our country. The good visit with grandparents was brief. In San Diego we embarked on a Norwegian freighter carrying Oregon apples to South America.

We sailed the Pacific Ocean to the entrance of the Panama Canal. We watched as the ship slowly entered a lock, the gate closed, and the lock filled with water, which raised the ship effortlessly to the next lock. So lock by lock we went from Pacific sea level up into the hills of Panama. There we followed a channel hewn out of the rock to make a passage deep enough for seagoing ships. Looking up at the rock walls we thought of all the American and Panamanian men who labored here to create the waterway between the two oceans. When we reached the other end, the locks lowered the ship to the Atlantic, our ship sinking each time a lock was emptied. It was a fascinating journey with Father explaining the sights to us.

In Brazil once more, we didn't return to Mato Grosso. Father was assigned the job of evangelist-at-large, going on preaching missions from field to field where his colleagues worked. Mother settled with us in São Paulo, near Mackenzie College, a university founded by Presbyterian missionaries. Bibette, George, Phil, and I studied at the Escola Americana, the grammar school attached to Mackenzie. At first it was strange to be studying in Portuguese, but soon we were quite at home.

I went on to the preparatory school of the university. I studied math, Latin, and sciences. I studied English and more Latin with Miss Moore at the American Grade School.

I was studying piano with my cousin Joyce, Aunt Junie's daughter. Our house was always full of young people, among them a very talented pianist, José Del Nero. He and I went through a friendship to a sweetheart stage. I was most in love with his music. I had dreams of living in some romantic place with a husband who played the piano divinely. But there came the clash between customs. Zinho, as we called José, wanted me to go walking with him clandestinely. I lived in two worlds, between the Anglo-American community of my extended family and my Brazilian world. There was no way I could feel comfortable betraying my parents' trust. So our courtship came to an end.

Father was soon off again to north Brazil. The revolution of 1933 caught him far from home. The state of São Paulo, the richest in the union, attempted to secede on the grounds that it was being docked disproportionately for the running of the federal government. There were fiery speeches and much knitting of socks and kneepads for the soldiers. Father had a hard time getting permission to reenter the state to be with us. The revolution was mostly sound and fury. Few shots were fired and an agreement was reached after a few months of hot patriotism on both sides. This revolution was typical of the Brazilian temperament.

The time came to think ahead. Father helped me choose a college. My requirement was that there be a swimming pool. We selected Wilson College, a Presbyterian women's college in Chambersburg, Pennsylvania. I applied for a Curran scholarship, established by Dr. Curran of Philadelphia for young women who desired to enter some type of Christian service. The scholarship would pay my board and tuition. To compete I had to pass four College Board exams: the aptitude test, English, math, and Latin. There was no College Boards center in Brazil and Father was off traveling again. So I went to Dr. Waddell, president of Mackenzie College, and asked him to officialize a center for the examinations at Mackenzie. He did, and I took the first three tests. The Latin test did not arrive on time. When it did come I had succumbed to a severe attack of asthma and couldn't take it. I assumed I had lost my chance to enter college in the fall of 1934. I was distressed and aimless.

In late August we received a letter from Dr. Warfield, president of Wilson College, offering me a place at Wilson and a Curran Scholarship! My parents asked me, "Do you want to go?" There was only one answer; I wanted to go very much. The whole family got into motion and I was ready in time. I even had a beautiful blue evening dress bought ready made, a great luxury in Brazil in those days. I boarded a Munsen Line steamship and waved good-bye to my family gathered on the dock to see me off.

There were very few passengers to enjoy the wide decks and the other amenities of this floating hotel. I would wake early to watch the sun rise amidst the configurations in the clouds along the horizon, as the new day tinted them in rainbow colors. I found a friend in an American girl who was on her way from her home in Argentina to study at Agnes Scott College in Atlanta. The purser and the telegrapher would join us for strolls on deck in the lovely starlit evenings.

Mother had suggested that I get in touch with the stewardess, who could help me with any problem. As it turned out, I was the one who helped the stewardess. There was on board a young American woman who had been working in Rio de Janeiro for an American firm. She became ill and was being sent home to her family. She was afraid to leave her cabin. She was sure that the noises she heard, the clangings and grindings on the ship, were from torture machines being prepared for her. How was the stewardess to carry out her regular duties and keep an eye on this disturbed woman? The stewardess asked me if I would sit with the ill woman. I welcomed the chance. The stewardess suggested that if she should become overwrought, I read to her from the prayer book which she kept by her bedside. The book contained psalms and other beautiful prayers. There was something oddly different, however. Then I realized that there was no mention of Christ, no prayers in his name. I concluded that she was Jewish. The day before we reached New York it took all our persuasion and a bit of our muscle to get her to the beauty parlor, which she conceived as a torture chamber. I didn't see her leave the ship and I have wondered many times since how things turned out for her.

My Aunt Evangeline, Father's sister, met me and took me under her wing. She put me on the train to Chambersburg, where I disembarked with other Wilson-bound students. The Cumberland Valley is a wide and bosomy land of apple orchards and grazing cattle on Amish farms, with the mountains just beyond. It was a good place to grow into America.

I was very homesick for my mother and home and Brazil, but "the gang" kept me going. A number of us, mostly recipients of Curran scholarships, many from missionary families, banded together. I roomed with a missionary daughter from China, Ethel Dickson, my first year. In our sophomore year the gang moved to the second floor of Main Hall. Anita Poole and I roomed together. Anita reached out to me in my loneliness. She introduced me to the classical music she loved.

My main passion was English, in which I majored. I minored in French. Never before had a term paper impinged on my helter-skelter education. Miss Hoffman, my freshman English teacher, endeared herself to me by handing back my first term paper with this inscription, "If you correct your spelling, I will grade your paper." I had used the word *different* many times, always spelling it *diferent*, like *diferente* in Portuguese. This was only one of a great number of misspellings. Anita helped me correct them. Thus I received a B rather than the F which the paper deserved. It was a while before I was able to shed the influence of Portuguese.

Christmas holidays came. I spent ten days with Aunt Evangeline in New York. She worked as a nurse at the Presbyterian hospital. I caught cold while with her. She arranged me on the sofabed with all I needed for the day and turned on the radio. I had never had a radio available to me before and was fascinated.

I enjoyed visiting Anita's family before returning to Wilson. Anita was the youngest of four siblings. Her family had weathered the Depression years and was still struggling to keep afloat, but they were most hospitable and always had a place for me in their home.

Summertime came with no possibility of going home. I got a job at a camp for girls in Vermont as the waterfront guard and swimming instructor. The job was easy because swimming was in one of those beautiful, clear New England brooks that babble happily over stones. In no place was it deeper than to the girls' waists. I was also in charge of crafts for the younger girls.

In some ways camp was a strange experience for me. I cannot now remember any counselor or camper as an individual. Most of them came from the towns thereabouts and I felt very foreign. It was as if I spoke a different language. I wrote letters to my family, read, and daydreamed. In my daydreams I saw a young man riding a bicycle. Later, when I met Chalmers, I discovered that during that summer he had been riding a bicycle as he sold New Chain Reference Bibles. At the end of the summer, Aunt Maud and her friend Betty took me up the Mohawk Trail. The trees were at their most colorful.

After another year at Wilson I spent a summer with Aunt Maud at Kearn Hatten Home for girls at Bellows Falls, Vermont, where she was the director. Towards the end of the summer Mother came home with my brothers and sister. Aunt Maud and I met them at the dock in New York. As they came down the gangway, I was shocked. They looked very worn, sallow, and in need of comfort and good nourishment. Father and Mother had been reassigned after I left for college and I could see why Mother and Father had decided she should bring the family home early, before furlough time. I had not realized how hard Campo Grande, where they had moved, had been on these adolescent siblings of mine.

Mother, Bibette, and Phil settled in Ventnor, New Jersey, at the Doane Apartments for missionaries. George soon went off to Stony Brook School on Long Island for his senior year in high school, while Phil and Bibette went to high school in Atlantic City, riding the tram each day. I went back to Wilson for my junior year.

Our family spent the summer of 1937, between my junior and senior years, on a farm near Meadville, Pennsylvania. The Gasteigers, friends of ours from Harrisburg, had invited us to summer at their old farmhouse. Their older children had jobs, and two of the boys, Dean and Edgar, spent the summer with us. It was a relaxing time, picking blueberries and currants, reading, or going into town to the movies. Dean and I had a crush on each other—Dean got over his at the end of the summer, but it took me longer.

Bibette joined me at Wilson. She, too, received a Curran scholarship, and for one year we were in college together. We didn't see a great deal of each other. But it was good to share letters from home and friends and know we could see each other whenever we wanted.

Margaret Disert, dean of students, was a remarkable person and a role model for Wilson women. At the beginning of my senior year she went over my three-year record with me. My grades hovered in the B's with an occasional C or A. "What you have accomplished so far," she said, "reflects in large measure the preparation you had before you came to college. Your senior year will show what you can really do." My grades improved perceptibly. In my senior year I valued more consciously Wilson's gracious ways. Father had returned from Brazil and came to my graduation. It was wonderful to have him there for all the events. My mother and brothers did not come, a great disappointment to me. They were in Davidson, North Carolina, where George was studying at Davidson College.

When the family was reunited at Davidson we prepared for a trip to California. Father bought a secondhand Ford from a dealer in Davidson and all but Mother and Phil took driving lessons. Mother didn't want to drive and Phil was only thirteen. When we applied for licenses we expected a road test, but the officer instead presented us with an open Bible and asked us to swear upon it that we would obey the laws of the land and of the road, whereupon we were issued licenses.

To be all together in our first car and on our way to adventure, that was happiness. We traveled the southern route, going first to Georgia to see Mother's aunt and cousins. As we drove on across the country there had been rain in the desert and as we pressed on, the sands as far as eye could see were abloom with every kind of small bright flower—gold, orange, violet, and bright red.

From the start our Ford was a disaster. A tire blew out, and the bushings in the wheels had to be changed. Each time a problem cropped up we were delayed for several hours and paid roundly for the repairs. The dealer who had said the car was in very good shape became a joke.

We were glad to reach Grandfather and Grandmother's home in Pasadena, California. Aunt Evangeline and Aunt Jessie were living with their parents. My grandparents had slowed down and we enjoyed the gentle days sitting with them in their garden. We also had fun with the aunts on excursions to see the beaches and the Palomar telescope.

We returned east via Salt Lake City and we visited the Mormon Temple. As we walked along the portico, Father took one of the available forms for requesting a visit from a missionary. He filled in the name and address of the Davidson Ford dealer as a form of revenge.

We collected our possessions in Davidson and moved to Princeton where again we had an apartment in Payne Hall. Bibette went back to Wilson for her sophomore year. Father and Mother set off to take George back to Davidson.

On their return trip, as they were arriving in Princeton, a car hit the Ford. The passenger door flew open and Mother was thrown out on the side of the road. Once again she broke ribs and had a bad bump on her temple. She was taken to the Princeton hospital. Father phoned from there and I went over to see Mother in the middle of the night. When we got back to the apartment, I treated Father's cuts and bruises. He was more bruised in spirit than in body. He felt terrible about causing an accident that hurt Mother, so he sold the Ford for what he could get and never owned another car.

I had been getting ready to go to Cleveland to enter nursing school. Father asked me to put off going for a semester so that I could stay with Mother as she recuperated. I gladly agreed. I loved Princeton and nothing could be better than staying at home for a while. By this simple choice God moved me into paths of his own choosing.

- 8 -

Princeton Idyll

Mother was coming home from the hospital the next day so I was giving the apartment a thorough cleaning. I was in some old clothes and there were runs in my stockings. It was about 10 o'clock in the evening. The doorbell rang. I felt embarrassed opening the door in my work clothes, especially when I saw a dapper gentleman with a moustache on the threshold. He told me he was George Browne, a schoolmate of my father's at Wooster and at Princeton. He was in town for a short visit to his son and had hoped to see Philip. I invited him to come in and told him that Father was at the hospital visiting Mother. We talked and I found out that he was a missionary to China and that his son Chalmers was a middler at the Seminary. "I hope you can meet him," said Mr Browne as he rose to leave.

Mother came home a bit unsteady, but in good spirits. We were happy to be together. Phil was a mature and tractable twelve-year-old and my favorite little brother. As mother mended I had time to go to classes with my father. He was enthusiastic about Dr. Emil Brunner's lectures and I decided to audit the course.

In late September the president of the Seminary, Dr. John Mackay, held a reception for faculty and students. As we circulated in the main hall of the library, I met a friend, Dr. Mackay's daughter Helena. I asked her if she knew a student named Chalmers Browne. "Yes," she responded. She led me over to a small group standing in an alcove and introduced me to Chalmers. As he took my hand and I raised my eyes to his, my impression was of a slender figure, wavy dark brown hair and pleasantness.

Not long after on a sunny afternoon Chalmers presented himself at our kitchen door with a bowl of spaghetti from the Friar Club, where he worked. It was a custom of the Friar Club, one of the Seminary students' eating clubs, to share with the missionary families at Payne Hall a platter of beef stroganoff or a stew left over from a Friar meal. It was a special treat when it was our turn to receive some of the chef's good cooking.

As I took the bowl from Chalmers' hands with my thanks, I commented on the gorgeous weather. "Wonderful for a walk," I said.

"Would you like to go for a walk?" asked Chalmers. "I can be back in a few minutes." We walked down by the new theater. Chalmers had ushered there for the premiere of *Our Town* when the author, Thornton Wilder, played the role of the commentator. I found out that he didn't like eggplant, that he did like to sing, and that we both liked to play tennis and were both left-handed.

The years of young adulthood are an extraordinary, bittersweet time. Living with my parents gave me an opportunity to think and pray, and I made up my mind that I was going to return to Mato Grosso and work with women and children. I applied to the Board of Foreign Missions of the Presbyterian Church for service overseas. I knew I wanted more training and continued with plans to get a nurse's diploma. But in the meantime it was good to share my family's home and meet people. We were attending the First Presbyterian Church. Dr. Niles, the pastor, and his wife became good friends. I started teaching kindergarten children in the Sunday School.

Betsy Hopkins, a classmate of mine at Wilson, and of Chalmers' at PY, was in Princeton at the Westminster Choir School. Jim Crothers, who had also studied at PY was a senior at Princeton Theological Seminary and was courting Betsy without the desired response. On a lovely fall day the Princeton University football team was playing a home game and Betsy went to the game escorted by an out-of-town beau.

I was quietly minding my own business at our apartment when Jim came over. He reminded me that we were both on a student volunteer committee and suggested we look over some pertinent material he had in his room. I went with him, and when we had thoroughly studied the material, Jim invited me to go for a bike ride. The afternoon was sunlit and the golden and scarlet leaves rejoiced from every tree against the warm blue sky. No one could refuse to go biking through such splendor. We returned after an hour, having had a glorious time. I told Betsy and that did it. In no time she and Jim were engaged.

I made many friends amongst the missionary families in our building. One missionary mother, having served a term in Japan, asked me what I felt about being a missionary child. She was fearful for the development of her small children away from their own culture. I told her that, whereas there were genuine drawbacks to being reared abroad, there were many compensations that far outweighed the negative factors. It is no small thing to be bilingual and bicultural.

Another couple, Jean and Alan Clark, had grown up in Korea, studied at PY and returned there as missionaries. Across the way from them lived Bod and Carol Booker, missionaries to Persia. With them was living Yayah Armajani, a Persian. He was a student at the Seminary.

Yayah, whom we called Army, and I became friends. He introduced me to the struggles of a person emerging from an ancient culture with a religion and a prophet of their own, Zoroaster. He found it strange that in this Seminary where he was studying for the Christian ministry not much thought was given to the great teachings of Zoroaster, who had deep insights to share concerning the things of the spirit. Yet to some of our western world, Zoroastrians were considered pagans. I could listen and learn, but had very little to offer to this discussion.

Another young man, Bruce, became a good friend. We went to concerts together. His invitations were always issued well in advance of the occasion. Chalmers came puffing up at the last minute with stars in his eyes and I was obliged to say that I already had a date. On most Sundays Chalmers was away with the Seminary Choir. Many times Bruce walked with me to the Presbyterian Church for the evening service. Evidently there was a sort of unwritten rule of which I was unaware that two young people sitting Sunday after Sunday together in church were declaring a special relationship. Mrs. Niles came to speak to me in favor of Chalmers. I was amused and perplexed because I had no romantic liaison with either friend.

Chalmers took me canoeing and biking. Much later, when we were engaged, Chalmers confessed that he had wanted to kiss me when we stopped during our bike ride, in the stillness of a country road to admire the view. Any time Chalmers spent with me was snatched from his very busy schedule.

We welcomed the Thanksgiving break and invited Chalmers for Thanksgiving dinner. In the late afternoon he and I went for a long walk. The wind was piercing and icy snowflakes pelted us. As we turned homeward in the gathering dusk, Chalmers took my arm and we clung to each other for warmth as we hurried to the hearth of my parent's home. We felt very close.

There were a number of small children in the apartments we lived in. I proposed to the mothers that I run a nursery in a basement room for a couple of hours five mornings each week. The mothers were glad to have their children under supervision in the same building and we settled on a weekly stipend that would keep me in pocket money. It was fun to get to know the smaller members of the missionary crew.

We had minimal equipment and where we got that I don't remember. The eight or ten youngsters and I did fun things together. I had two Bobbies, Bobby Clark and a rather less aggressive Bobby. These two were always vying for attention or for toys or just vying. One bright day a new boy of about the same age—four or five—joined us, Albert Pittman, son of missionaries to Brazil. Albert decided to make his place in the group. Since Bobby Clark was the most active of the old guard, he picked him out and socked him. Bobby was looking up in surprise when the other Bobby came over, feathers ruffled. "You can't hit my Bobby," he cried. Bobby Clark's eyes widened. "Bobby loves me!" he exclaimed in an awed voice.

On a Saturday, when there was no nursery school, Bobby Clark had come up to our third-floor apartment. At lunchtime his mother came out into the ground floor hall and called up to Bobby to come home. Bobby was steadfastly determined to stay at our house. I was with him at the top of the stairs looking down at his mother when Chalmers appeared at the apartment house door. More than ever I wanted Bobby to go home. I took a handkerchief from my pocket and unfurled it. I took it by one end and said "See, Bobby. Can you catch it?" and I let the handkerchief flutter down the stairwell. Bobby followed it with his eyes for a second, then was off down the stairs to catch the handkerchief. Of course, his mother caught him. Chalmers' brown eyes looked up at me amused. He was learning about my devious ways.

I had all these wonderful opportunities to meet many people and do a variety of things, yet life was becoming hard for me to manage. I had to be candid with myself—I had fallen in love with Chalmers. But there was no sign that he was more than a very good friend.

Christmas holidays were approaching and the Seminary students had planned a Christmas party before the end of classes. Bruce, well in advance, invited me to the Christmas party. I had to refuse. I could not in good conscience appear at a Seminary function in his company. Later that week Chalmers invited me to the party. I wanted to accept. What was I to do? I had refused one invitation and felt I must refuse this one. So, I stayed at home and heard the merriment coming from Stuart Hall across the street.

Several days later Chalmers came over in the evening and invited me to go for a walk. The moon was full. There was a drift of fallen snow over the ground. We walked through university quadrangles enjoying the soft moonlight against the grey stone, the fretwork of the leafless trees, the mellow campus lights and the deep shadows. We reached the University Chapel and stood listening as someone played Bach on the great organ. The world was filled with wonder and music. Chalmers asked me, "May I kiss you?" I was startled since I had wanted him to kiss me, but had never thought that I would be asked. So I didn't say anything and we kissed. We walked home as on moonlight.

After delivering me home, Chalmers went to his dorm and climbed through a window into George Winn's room. George looked at him and said, "You're engaged!" So there was some rowdy rejoicing among his friends. The next day I found out I was engaged and I worked up a storm. How could Chalmers, I asked him, go and tell his friends that he was engaged without letting me know first?

He was mock penitent and got down on his knees and formally asked me to marry him. After that we went in to Father's room where he was studying and Chalmers asked him for my hand. That made it all very official since Father graciously gave his consent. My mother appreciated Bruce's more sober qualities and his gentlemanly ways, but she knew I was the one who had to make the choice for myself. She knew I was in love and she welcomed Chalmers.

Chalmers invited me to go home with him for Christmas. His mother and father were living in Wooster during their furlough, which was about to end. They were going to return to China in January. Chalmers wanted me to meet them. I told Mother of this invitation. "You can't just appear at the Brownes' house without an invitation from them," she remonstrated. I relayed this message to Chalmers.

Long distance phoning was rare in those days. We walked down to the telegraph office on Nassau Street and Chalmers sent his parents a night letter. In addition to his request to bring a guest for Christmas he added, "Have bought a hat." "They'll understand," he said, seeing my perplexity. The invitation from Mr. and Mrs. Browne was forthcoming. Then Chalmers and I were off for our first trip together. We rode the coach all night and were in Wooster the next morning.

Dad Browne and Bea met us at the station. Their welcome was warm and so was Mother Browne's when we reached the steps of their home. Aunt Mary was there, too, to add her quiet, sedate welcome. No one gave a hint of the fact that they had quite naturally expected that Chalmers' friend who was being invited for Christmas was one of his dormmates. A young woman was a surprise. The "hat" message had gone undeciphered. They rallied quickly and Dad asked me if I would consider going to China as a missionary. My response was that I was open to God's leading and was ready to serve anywhere God chose to send me.

The next morning was Christmas Eve. As I was leaving my room Chalmers met me in the hall. He asked for my clear plastic raincoat. He wrapped me in it like a package and took me to the breakfast table. "Here is your Christmas present," he said. delivering me to my new family. They have been a gracious and thoughtful family who have treated me with courtesy and loving-kindness. I have ever desired to be a good daughter to them. Bea and Frenchy were awed by their big brother who had suddenly fetched himself a bride.

Dad helped Chalmers buy an engagement ring for me, the most beautiful diamond in the whole world. After it had been placed on my finger at the family table, Chalmers and I were about to set out for a party at the home of friends. "Now don't crow, Chalmers," admonished Dad.

Chalmers and I stopped at the Episcopal Church first. We felt the need to worship together. The service was simple, but the Eucharist was celebrated. We had our first communion together, not asking or being asked if we were welcome at the table of the Lord in this church, just knowing that the Lord welcomed us.

The Christmas interlude was soon over and I was on my way back to Princeton to spend New Year's Day with my family while Chalmers stayed on with his. The Brownes arranged a berth on a sleeping car for me, and my dreams were sweet.

In Princeton I had to come down from the rosy clouds and face a difficult moment. Bruce came to invite me to go to New York, to the theater, with him and his parents. When he was announced, I shrank from appearing in the living room. But there was no alternative, so I went out and showed him my ring and told him I was engaged to Chalmers. I had not seen him since before the Christmas party, but I felt he was vexed with me for not having given him a hint about what I had not had a hint of myself. The awkward moment passed and we have been friends since.

When Chalmers returned from Christmas break, something very interesting happened in the kitchen of our apartment. Jim and Betsy had come over and the four of us were chatting and drinking coffee. Jim pulled a small package out of his pocket. Betsy took from the box a ring with a diamond and Jim placed it on her finger. Jim and Betsy were formally engaged.

I started attending some classes with Chalmers. I had taken one year of Hebrew at Wilson to satisfy a Curran Scholarship requirement. Now it was interesting to read the Psalms in Hebrew. I attended Dr. Gamon's class, with his permission.

One day Dr. Gamon asked if he could call on me. I responded affirmatively and recited. Dr. Gamon was awed that a woman could read Hebrew. Years later we were awed in turn when Dr. Gamon learned Portuguese so that he could deliver some lectures in that language at the Presbyterian Seminary in Campinas, Brazil, where my father was a professor.

Bea and Frenchy came for a visit at spring break. We had a gathering of friends, and Frenchy was helping me in the kitchen. I asked him to open a couple of cans of tuna fish. I was making two salads, one with tuna and the other with fruit. "Shall I put it here?" asked Frenchy.

"Yes," said I, meaning in the bowl with chopped vegetables. I turned just in time to see Frenchy emptying the cans into the fruit salad. I scooped the fish out quickly and everything was set right, but for a moment something was fishy in the fruit salad.

Phil's birthday in April posed a problem for me. How was I to organize the kind of party that would appeal to a bunch of thirteen- and fourteen-year -olds? I turned to Chalmers. Would he play some games out on the campus with Phil's guests? He did. From our small balcony I looked out and saw him join the boys. He wore a bulky navy blue sweater with his Wooster "W" on it. When the group came in I had cake and ice cream for them.

Chalmers had a demanding job at the Friar Club. Sometimes I would go over to the club when he was waxing floors, and read to him. Chalmers brought along a book on marriage which we read together.

Towards the end of the academic year the Friar Club had a special event at which they recognized those who had made the Club run: the prior, the steward, and the cook. Betsy and I and the gals of other Friar men were invited to the special dinner. The food was delicious and there were speeches and toasts and much hilarity. As the tables were being cleared there came a great crash from the kitchen as though all the cups and plates in the establishment had suddenly hurtled to the floor. Bob, the steward, who was especially jumpy because his girlfriend, Esther, had not yet made up her mind to marry him, leaped to his feet and rushed out to the kitchen. The two Friar men on duty as busboys that evening were dashing out the back door, leaving a large pile of shattered crockery in the middle of the kitchen floor. Bob followed in pursuit. They came running in the front door, creating pandemonium. After the uproar, the perpetrators confessed that they, including Chalmers, had been saving up all the broken dishes for months for this occasion to add a bang to the party.

Of the four eating clubs, two were very sedate, Calvin Club—which had been my Father's club—and Warfield Club. The two unruly clubs were Bennam and Friar. The Friars outdid themselves in singing drinking songs and other nonclassical ditties. The Bennamites excelled in impersonations and hoaxes. One day the Friar Club received a phone call from the movie theater in town. The film about the life of Peter Marshall, pastor of a Presbyterian Church in Washington, DC, and chaplain of the Senate was showing. The movie theater offered each seminary student a free ticket. The word spread. Friar Club members went to the movies to find that the phone call was not from the theater. They knew well whence the phony message had come.

Father was going back to Brazil and George was transferring from Davidson to Wooster. Mother was moving to Wooster to provide a home for him, for he had been suffering repeated attacks of asthma. Mother and Father hoped that a change of climate and a chance to be at home would improve his health. Phil was in high school, Bibette had one more year at Wilson, and Chalmers had one more at Princeton. And I? What should I do? Father counseled me to forget about going to nursing school. I think he realized that it was not really my vocation. "One year at nursing school will be all drudgery without much profit," he opined. So it was that I decided to accept Chalmers' suggestion that I sell the New Chain Reference Bible that summer.

- 9 -

First Thing in the Morning

We did our salesmanship training in Wooster. Then, armed with two bicycles, we went by train to Tidiute, Pennsylvania, where I stayed with the Merkles. Paul Merkle had been at Princeton with Chalmers. His family was supportive as I tried for the first time in my life to sell. One day when I was discouraged Mrs. Merkle reminded me that sometimes people really don't have money to buy a bible. My letters to Chalmers, who was selling in another town, were expressive of my depression and loneliness. He was surprised, but stuck with me. Biking up and down the hills and dales of northwestern Pennsylvania was good for body and soul and I got the knack of the job.

We worked through churches. Usually the pastors welcomed us cordially and helped us to find customers. We didn't go to the movies because some of the denominations with which we worked disapproved. We did go to weekday meetings in churches as well as to Sunday services. The great variety of people and beliefs were, as Chalmers expressed it, "more interesting than the movies." I went to a Wesleyan Methodist prayer meeting one evening. The praying reached agonizing proportions, as if God had to be taken by storm. Their ardent faith was impressive. By contrast, the next day I sat on the front porch with a woman who belonged to the Christian Science Church. As she rocked gently she explained to me how God is ever eager to give. He knows our needs before we are conscious of them and in kindness gives us what is good.

Chalmers would work in one town and I in a neighboring one. We would meet on weekends whenever possible. One Saturday I took a train up into the hills to Spring Grove. The countryside was shimmering with feathery grasses in the slanting golden sunlight. The trees and meadows were full of gladness and I was on my way to see Chalmers. The folks where he was lodged made room for me and they fed us at their board. We had rhubarb custard pie for Sunday dessert. In the evening Chalmers and I went walking under the stars. Monday morning we went back to our work. The last week on the job we spent in Warren. Chalmers worked in one part of the city and I in another. We roomed in separate homes. Chalmers' landlady was upset with me because I went up to Chalmers' room. She told us we could meet in her living room.

As we wound up our summer's work we decided to bike at least partway home. On our first day we traveled about forty miles to Titusville, where the Bickerstaffs were living. They were retired missionaries from Brazil who had been close friends of my grandparents. They took us in, fed us supper, and gave us comfortable beds. Mr. Bickerstaff made a practice of getting up at 4 a.m. to put the oatmeal on to cook. We had steaming bowls of cereal for breakfast, then set out for the home of Chalmers' Uncle Rob on the Allegheny River north of Kittanning.

The day was beautiful. We were seasoned bike riders. But as the day wore on and the hills grew steeper, we began to droop. We descended to the swift rivers and pushed our bikes to the top of the high ridges. As darkness descended we had miles yet to go. Chalmers pushed his bike with one hand and with the other against my back gave me support as we struggled up yet another steep hill. At ten o'clock we reached the railway bridge across the Allegheny, where we stopped to consider. We could follow the river downstream for ten miles or more to the bridge at Kittanning or we could risk crossing the railroad bridge hoping that no train would catch us on the crossing. We opted for the railway bridge at hand and made it. At their home just beyond the bridge, Uncle Rob, Aunt Alberta, and their daughter, Ruth, took us in with every kindness. We fell gratefully into bed. The next day I could hardly move after the fourteen-hour bike trip. After a couple of days of visiting we shipped our bikes and went by train to Wooster.

Chalmers and I joined Mother, George, Bibette, and Phil, who had settled in an apartment for missionaries near the College of Wooster. We had a few brief, carefree days going on picnics and other family outings. We saw Bibette off to Wilson. Then it was time for Chalmers to return to Princeton. A year of separation loomed like some giant cloud over us after the year of sharing our days and work. After Chalmers left I went out in the evening dusk to the pine grove near the Henderson Apartments. The pines were young, but yet they crowded round and I poured out my despair beneath them. The pines have grown in these last fifty years and now stand high and dark and wise.

I tried selling bibles, but Wooster was already saturated. I tried halfheartedly to sell women's clothing. I shrank from the job of pushing merchandise, so I bought a sewing machine and took a Singer sewing course and worked on my trousseau. As always, Mother and I shared the housekeeping.

In the meantime. Chalmers was facing a tough year. He started field work in a Trenton church as director of youth activities. The minister was not satisfied with Chalmers' style and dismissed him. It was a jolt to Chalmers' ego. Our separation was harder on him than on me. He developed physical stress symptoms and in his confusion heard voices negating our relationship. Nevertheless, Chalmers came to Wooster for Thanksgiving. The celebration time pales in the remembrance of the day Chalmers was to leave. I woke early and went down to the living room where Chalmers was sleeping on the couch. I wanted to tell him of my sense of dislocation. Mother would have liked to return to Brazil where Father was carrying on alone, but didn't want to leave me. I suggested that I move to Princeton and find a job so as to free Mother and be near Chalmers. We spent a sad day as Chalmers tried to come to some sense of poise. Between us was this question—should we continue our engagement? Finally, I said, "Since you aren't sure right now what we should do, I will continue to wear your engagement ring until you do know. In that way Aunt Natalie and other people who love you will not be burdened with this matter until we are sure."

And so it was. Even though Chalmers came for the Christmas holidays, we lived through a year of uncertainty. We wrote to each other weekly, but as friends. One bright spot in my days was Professor

Howard Lowry's Shakespeare Tragedies course, which I audited. Hamlet and King Lear were good medicine. Then spring came, and with the resurrecting earth, Chalmers' peace returned. He wrote to me that he was ready to get married. We planned our wedding for May 21.

I wrote to Dr. Webb, pastor of the Olivet Presbyterian Church in Harrisburg and a longtime friend of our family, inviting him to participate in the ceremony. His answer was that we really should wait a year until Chalmers had a job and established himself, but we had set our course. Chalmers was to graduate on May 10 and I went to graduation in Miller Chapel on the beautiful Princeton Seminary campus. Aunt Maud also attended and drove us back to Wooster.

On the way home we were scheduled to have supper with the Webbs in Harrisburg. But Chalmers had a hard time getting packed up to leave. We were very late and along the way we tried to phone the Webbs, but didn't succeed. We arrived at their home after eight o'clock. They had organized a surprise party for us and we did not show up. We felt awful that we had disappointed the Webbs.

It was good to be home in Wooster. Chalmers stayed with Aunt Nat and Uncle Clarence. The only time we could find for our wedding, if we were to be married on May 21st in the college Chapel with its busy schedule, was 7:30 a.m. Dr. Webb and family were coming from Harrisburg on Monday, the 20th, planning to go on after the wedding to visit friends in Illinois. So we settled for that rather unorthodox hour.

Bibette and Bea put flowers in the chapel. I had made my dress of white organdy. Mother had helped me buy a fingertip veil. The night before, Chalmers picked lilies of the valley in Aunt Nat's garden to pin in my veil. Bea and Bibette were my bridesmaids, dressed in blue organdy, and Muggy Webb, who was five, wore pink and was our flower girl. Chalmers wore his dark blue suit and looked very distinguished. Frenchy was best man. George and Phil were ushers.

The service was simplicity itself as we met before the communion table. Doug, the minister of Westminster, and Dr. Webb officiated. Dr. Webb had come to take part in our wedding despite reservations as to the timing, whereas Doug, who had been our pastor, wholeheartedly encouraged us.

I find the Lohengrin wedding march sad and fateful, maybe because the bride in the story was getting married against her will. We consulted Jonesy at Princeton and took his suggestion for an alternative. My companions and I moved down the aisle to the strains of "Liebster Jesu" as arranged by Bach. Art played it trippingly. Chalmers and I exchanged vows and rings in a sort of high fog, which, though we did not perceive it at the time, turned out to be the cloud of the presence of God. Chalmers gently threw back my veil and we exchanged the traditional kiss.

We turned in the midst of all the well-wishers surrounding us and joyously started our life journey together to the more stirring Mendelssohn march. In the foyer of the Chapel we greeted our remarkable friends who had turned out in the early morning to be with us.

Chalmers and I are the oldest in our families. We knew we were in for a very noisy ragging from our brothers and sisters and their friends. So we made some counter plans. Aunt Maud had offered us the use of her car for the honeymoon and we told our brothers and sisters this fact. We thanked Aunt Maud and explained privately that we wanted to go honeymooning on our bikes. The night before the wedding Mother prepared a supper for all our guests. She made a coconut cake, which was traditional in our family for weddings. At this meal we quietly told all our adult guests of our plans for the next morning and thanked them and said our good-byes.

After the wedding service we all went out to the Melrose apple orchard. The trees were in full and riotous bloom. Frenchy had borrowed a movie camera. We processed and reenacted some of the wedding for posterity. Mrs. Bryan drove us back into Wooster. Frenchy, who was with us, had a class and asked to be dropped off at the college.

Mrs. Bryan then drove us out to a farm of friends where she had, the day before, taken our bikes and clothes for the road. The family on the farm had a delicious breakfast awaiting us with strawberries and ham and eggs. We changed, and after thanking the dear people, were on our way.

We biked slowly, stopping to rest and be glad. No conventions separated us; we were husband and wife, responsible to each other, a truly amazing estate. This day was to be savored and prolonged. We had lodging at a beautiful inn in Leroy (now Westfield). We checked into our room and then went back out into the lovely spring day. We had a meal at a teahouse down the road from the inn. We walked in the meadows and picked violets. We sat for a while under a tree as the moon came up, full and gracious, smoothing out all the countryside. How to explain fifty years later in a jaded time the fire and altogetherness of the gift of virginity which we brought to each other? We were twenty-four years old. All the maturing years came together for us in each other. The next day we slept until two o'clock and we were still tired. Dinner at the inn revived us. Two days spent reading and talking and walking were good for body and spirit.

Frenchy made a surprise visit. He wanted to consult Chalmers about his own vocation. "Do you think Dad would mind if I don't become a minister?" he asked. Chalmers assured him that Dad, of all persons, would not want him to become a minister out of a sense of duty. Frenchy also had marriage on his mind. He and Joan had what they called a platonic friendship, but this state of affairs was obviously changing. Frenchy was checking out with us what marriage meant.

We packed up our small belongings on the third day and started out eastward on Route 224. Railways were still carrying a major portion of the nation's freight and the highways were not crowded with huge trailer trucks. Summer was exploding into lavish green. The time of the singing of birds had come. We rode along the shore of a lake and stopped at night in a tourist home. By Saturday we had reached Deerfield, where Chalmers had friends from bible-selling days. We were warmly welcomed into the home of the family where Chalmers had lodged earlier. Three or four years earlier this region had still not recovered from the Depression and the people were hurting. Chalmers had been able to share in their distress and trials. Now he was pleased to see the confidence that had returned. On Sunday we went to the Presbyterian Church with the family. Many friends greeted Chalmers. This was Memorial Sunday and Chalmers, when called upon to help with a new hymn, taught the congregation "For All the Saints."

On Monday we had our first disagreement. Chalmers proposed that we make our next stop in Canton at Aunt Bess and Uncle Will's. Our clothes, not elegant to begin with, were by this time travel worn and dirty. I did not want us to appear as hobos at the Miller's lovely city home, but Chalmers figured he knew his aunt and uncle well enough and we knocked at their door. We were received as graciously as if we had stepped from a bandbox. I was grateful to Aunt Bess for her womanly understanding.

We returned to Wooster on Tuesday, a week after our wedding. We found "the union"—our brothers and sisters and their friends—highly incensed and offended at us for escaping their plans for a send-off.

They had bought much rice and tied all sorts of signs and cans to Aunt Maud's car. In revenge they had dumped rice in the suitcase we had planted in the car as a foil. That rice kept coming out of the corners and folds of the suitcase for years.

My mother had a harder time than I in adjusting to the changes in our lives. I was all wrapped up in Chalmers and Chalmers was not only concentrating on his new role as husband, but was also busy with his new responsibilities as a minister. Mother, who had given so much to us, was now feeling bereft of her daughter and far from Father in Brazil. Newlyweds need space and understanding, for their behavior can appear callous towards their dearest ones.

We had planned our wedding without knowing if Chalmers would receive a call to a church. A few days before the wedding Chalmers received a call from a yoked parish of two churches, Salineville and Oak Ridge, in eastern Ohio. A couple of weeks after we returned from our bike trip, Chalmers was ordained by Wooster Presbytery in the Presbyterian Church at Ashland. The key to Chalmers' feelings at this momentous time in his life can best be expressed by the hymn he chose to be sung at his ordination:

> Be Thou my vision, O Lord of my heart;
> Nought be all else to me save that Thou art.
> Thou my best thought by day or by night,
> Waking or sleeping, Thy presence my light.
> Be Thou my wisdom, and Thou my true Word;
> I ever with Thee and Thou with me, Lord.
> Thou my great Father and I Thy true son,
> Thou in me dwelling and I with Thee one.

- 10 -

Twins

In June we started commuting from Wooster to our churches. Dad and Mother Browne made it possible for Chalmers to buy a car. Our neighbors, Don and Ruth Zimmermann, were leaving to go as missionaries to Japan. Chalmers bought their car, a blue Plymouth roadster with a rumble seat. The manse in Salineville was still being repaired and painted. Several minister friends advised us to be patient and not move into the house until all the work was completed.

While we were still driving back and forth to Wooster, Chalmers officiated at a funeral. Judge Smith, one of the two elders at Oak Ridge, died before we got to meet him. We missed having his wise counsel. Mrs. Smith's strength of spirit continued to give guidance and balance to the congregation. A wedding also took place that first June. The couple had been engaged for seven years. Chalmers, who was to officiate at the wedding, forgot his order of worship book and had to borrow one from a minister in Wellsville.

We did eventually move into the manse. Our bedroom furniture came from Aunt Natalie and Uncle Clarence's house. But we had no stove and were wondering how we could acquire one, since we had no money. The Presbyterian minister in Wellsville had just bought a new stove and sold his old stove to us for five dollars. We had an icebox out on the kitchen porch, and I did our wash on a washboard. A missionary friend, Mrs. Campbell, had a washing machine she wanted to sell for ten dollars. We didn't have the ten dollars. Bibette and Bea came to our rescue and bought it for us. When paychecks began to come in, Chalmers and I bought some Sears unfinished furniture. I sanded and Chalmers varnished. Our dining room set was finished in oak and Chalmers' desk in a dark stain.

Mother was packing to return to Brazil and I drove back and forth to Wooster to help her. She gave us a clutter of things collected over her two years in the States. One of our rooms upstairs in Salineville received this amorphous mass of things too good to throw away and yet not of high enough priority to sort through immediately.

We started out each Sunday with Sunday School and a worship service in Salineville. After a quick bite of lunch we made the thirteen-mile trip to Oak Ridge, where Chalmers preached his sermon a second time. Sunday school followed. It was almost time for young people's meeting when we returned to Salineville. An evening service with preaching ended the day. Between Sundays the parishes continued like twins, calling for two of everything.

Chalmers was involved in counseling a young couple who were considering divorce. His Princeton orientation had been to keep such confidential matters secret even from his wife. So I could only stand by and see him struggle with crushing realities with which he was still ill prepared to cope. Later, as he gained experience and we grew closer, he no longer felt he had to go it alone.

Phil came to visit us for a couple of weeks before he and Mother rejoined Father, now a teacher at the Presbyterian Seminary in Campinas, Brazil. Phil was a strapping young man of fifteen and very eager to drive a car. When he went calling with Chalmers out in the country, Chalmers let him take the wheel on back roads. One summer afternoon they came to the hairpin turn into the Frischkorn's driveway. Phil didn't quite make it and ended up with the new preacher in the potato patch. Chalmers got the car back on the driveway. Herb and Ruth were laughing. Herbert said,"The Wright brothers drunk again." When the preacher and his young brother pulled up, the Frischcorns had straightened their faces to receive them. "Don't worry," said Herb, "the vines will bounce back by tomorrow and the potatoes will never know."

After Mother and Phil left for Brazil, I missed my mother very much. It was especially traumatic since we now had no parents near by. Chalmers' parents were under house arrest in Japanese-occupied China. We had no direct communication with them since no mail was getting through.

In the Oak Ridge congregation the state of the session was a worrisome problem. Mr. McGarvey, the remaining elder, was old and frail. The previous winter he had had a bout with pneumonia. Yet no one in the congregation felt worthy to become an elder. The fact that the late Judge Smith had occupied the position with dignity and saintliness for many years served to underscore this view. At a congregational meeting in the fall, Chalmers pointed out that, if our remaining elder should die, the congregation would be without a session, and would not be able to do any business. The church would have to call upon the Presbytery to take any necessary measures.

The Presbyterian Church has a government much like that of the United States. A congregation elects officers who make up a session. The next highest court is the Presbytery, made up of the ministers of a region and delegates from the church sessions. The highest court is the General Assembly, made up of delegates from the Presbyteries.

Without a session, a church has no power. One of the members suggested that the meeting go into a committee of the whole. Thus Chalmers, the moderator, could step out and they could deal with the matter as a family. The committee presented two names as the congregation's choices for elders, Mr. McBane and Mr. Ed Serafy.

In the days that followed Chalmers spent long sessions with these men before they consented to take on the eldership. Mr. McBane had never prayed in public, a fact he felt disqualified him for leadership. Finally he asked, "Would it be all right if I wrote out a prayer?" When Chalmers called on him to pray at the next service and he read his prayer, he was satisfied. Ed Serafy's concern was quite different. He was a bachelor living with his father and mother, who had immigrated to this country from Germany. The family was of Baptist background and questioned confessionalism and infant baptism. Chalmers talked about the things that unite us as a Christian family and the choice each person has in the Presbyterian Church according to conscience. Chalmers was able to put their hearts at rest. The congregation ordained its two new elders and Mr. McGarvey continued to serve on session for two more years.

In the Salineville Church the matter of sacred music reared its head. The congregation was preparing to buy new hymnals. One of the women of the church, who today would have been an elder, was determined that a hymnbook of her choice be bought. Chalmers and most of the session wanted *The Hymnbook*, a Presbyterian publication. The situation was delicate. It was finally resolved by acquiring two hymnals, *The Hymnbook* and a book of gospel songs.

Not many months went by before I noticed that Chalmers was having a rough time. His malaise showed itself principally in his being unable to tackle his studies and other duties. He read most of the day. As Sunday approached he couldn't bring himself to prepare a sermon. Matters became accute when he got up one Sunday morning and still had no sermon. He rallied at the eleventh hour and got through the day, but it was scary. I wrote a letter, for advice, to Dr. Bonnell, pastor of the Fifth Avenue Presbyterian Church in New York and teacher of pastoral counseling at Princeton Seminary.

In the meantime Christmas came and carried us along on familiar and well-loved songs and scripture. We had an influx in our home of our brothers and sisters and friends from Wooster. I was beside myself as hostess because that room full of "amorphous stuff" was not in shape for my guests. I took Martha Wylie, a friend, into my confidence. She and I stayed at home while the others went to an event at Oak Ridge, and we cleaned the room and readied it for company. While we worked I told Martha about our problems and Chalmers' stress. We discussed whether or not inviting a child into our home might help. We decided it might since Chalmers and I wanted children.

After Christmas Chalmers received a letter from Andy Blackwood, a Princeton classmate. Andy's wife was from Wooster, and Andy asked if Chalmers would exchange pulpits with him so that he and Mary Ann could visit her folks. Andy's church was in New Jersey, not far from New York. We jumped at this fortuitous opportunity to go to the New York area.

It was lovely to drive east together. We went first to New York and saw Bea who was at Biblical Seminary. Dr. Bonnell took time to see Chalmers. He gave him several hours of that Saturday afternoon. It was a great blessing. Chalmers now found a freedom in his personal life that made it possible to do his work and enjoy the God-given gifts of reading and sex without a sense of guilt. We enjoyed meeting another congregation and Chalmers found it stimulating to preach in Andy's pulpit. We returned to Salineville through a frosty January day with new heart.

We invited the young people of the Salineville Church to our house for spaghetti. I had the unique spaghetti sauce recipe that Pete of the Friar Club had given me. The sauce I cooked up was indeed marvelous, but I soon realized that there wasn't enough spaghetti. I had to duck out and run down the hill to buy more spaghetti to match the enthusiastic appetites of the young people.

Chalmers and I were ecstatic: I was pregnant. We were also somewhat giddy at the realization that we were actually going to be parents. The news made a stir in the congregations, and it was pleasant to find our people involved with us in our new prospects. Some were concerned because I was so young, only nineteen, and relieved when I told them I was actually twenty-five. Others were surprised, since they had assumed that because we wanted to be missionaries, we weren't planning to have children. I was told to stop running, which was my favorite way of going places. We were interested in all the proffered advice.

Spring-cleaning time came. It was a most important activity in Salineville. This town in the valley was built over coal mines. All heating was done with very soft coal. Inside, wallpaper had to be cleaned and outside porches had to be scrubbed down. The labor took days.
In April Joan and Frenchy were married in Wooster in a double wedding ceremony with Art Kaltenborn and Helen Phillips. It was a gala occasion and we drove over from Salineville for the event.

That summer was fun. We planted a vegetable garden with lots of instruction and help from our neighbors and farm friends. We got good results and canned beans and tomatoes in the fall.

I went to Bibette's graduation in June. It was very special to be back among the dear old buildings and trees at Wilson. The weather was beautiful. As I sat on the grass for the pageant that happens each year, another alumna and I talked. I told her I was there for my sister's graduation. "And are you coming to Wilson too, dearie?" she asked. I guess the folks in Salineville and Oak Ridge could be pardoned for thinking of me as very young. George Butterick preached at the baccalaureate service. I was proud of my sister and rejoiced that I could be there to represent the family.

Chalmers took two weeks of vacation and we went to Chautauqua, New York. We lived in one of the two Presbyterian houses. We went to concerts and lectures in the open-air pavilion and, at one concert, Chalmers took me to sit behind the orchestra and taught me to recognize the different instruments. We went for walks and sat in the evenings for vespers by the lakeside to sing "Day is Dying in the West," a hymn written at Chautauqua.

Back in Salineville Chalmers and our two congregations were planning fall programs. But at the manse the more absorbing preparations were for the coming of our baby, due in November. We decided to buy a crib with wire netting sides and top. This crib would protect the baby from insects in whatever country we might go to as missionaries. A friend, Margaret, had her baby first, a little girl. I went to visit her full of enthusiasm. She had had a difficult labor and regaled me with all the details, scaring me half out of my wits. Chalmers helped me see things in better perspective.

It was in the wee hours of November 18 that I woke Chalmers and he phoned Dr. McColough. We were soon off to the hospital in East Liverpool, eighteen miles away. Chalmers stayed with me that livelong day until George Philip was born that evening at about 6:30. Weighing in at six pounds and four ounces, he came wide awake and really eager to take on the world.

Somehow, the next day, not only Chalmers appeared at the hospital but Bibette and Joan and Frenchy as well. When I saw them all I burst into tears. Full of solicitude they asked me what I wanted and I answered, "Grape juice." It materialized immediately and tasted very good.

A ten-day stay in the hospital was mandatory in those days, but finally I was home again with little George and Chalmers. Bibette was still with us, helping us get used to the new regime. She soon had to get back to her work in New York as Portuguese translator for The Reader's Digest.

The 7th of December—Pearl Harbor, declaration of war! My brother George came over to Salineville to tell us he was enlisting. He felt he wasn't really concentrating on his studies. He wanted to choose his service, which would be possible if he enlisted. We were reluctant to see him drop his college studies, but we honored his decision.

Our little George, whom we took to calling Buster, thrived. Dr. McColough was a great old-fashioned country doctor in the best tradition of service. He helped me with feeding and any sniffles or other small matters of care.

There were five Protestant churches and a Roman Catholic church in Salineville. Chalmers took our communicants class to each church so that the youngsters could learn about the many parts of the body of Christ. The Catholic priest received the class. One boy asked, "What do you think about Protestants?"

The priest answered, "You are not members of the visible church, but you are members of the spiritual church."

The five pastors of the five Protestant Churches and their families shared a potluck supper each month. Usually the wives made the casseroles and cakes, and the men washed the dishes. In April we had a good get-together. For some reason that day the ministers were busy talking and I found myself at the sink washing the dishes for five families. I wasn't feeling very well, but I finished the job. I was sicker than I thought. Dr. McColough ordered me to bed. "Keep her there," he told Chalmers. I had a miscarriage and it was a while before I was fully well again.

Bea came for a visit, bringing Sam, to whom she was newly engaged. Both Bea and Sam were studying at Biblical Seminary in New York, Sam aspiring to the ministry. Sam went calling with Chalmers and, as a born and bred New Yorker, found crunching through the snow to farmhouses an exotic experience which put him in awe of pastors of rural congregations. Sam confessed to Bea that he had not been able to drink Salineville water. I'll admit that the water, full of minerals, was hard to get used to. The next day we went for some spring water up the far hill. We liked Sam and he survived us.

After a long winter, brighter, warmer weather arrived. That summer Buster and I enjoyed going to Oak Ridge with Chalmers for Daily Vacation Bible School and for the women's meetings. Chalmers visited in the parish while we quilted and studied. He was always welcome for the potluck meal that the women provided, delicious, hearty Ohio farm fare.

We received the good news that Dad and Mother Browne were on their way home! They were on the Gripsholm, a ship which had picked them up at Lorenzo Marques in Mozambique. They had traveled on an Italian ship that far, and were exchanged there for Japanese prisoners. Bea and Sam set their wedding day for the 31st of August, putting it off to the last possible date, in the hope that Mother and Dad would arrive in time to attend. The Gripsholm docked in New York just a week before the wedding, and Bea met her parents with Sam beside her to greet them. Chalmers, Buster and I waited on the platform in Alliance for their train from New York to pass through. We had a short family reunion as Mother and Dad descended from the train and took their first grandson in their arms.

On August 31 we started out from Salineville. We were late because Chalmers had attended to business until the last minute. Buster didn't like sitting on my lap through a wedding, so I took him outside. I was dis-appointed to miss the beautiful wedding. Then Bea and Sam were off for a honeymoon aboard a ship on the Great Lakes. We had a chance at last to visit with Mother and Dad and really show off our son.

Summer over, we were even busier with the life of the two churches. We were enjoying rural Ohio life and we loved the people. I had been surprised, not at how intelligent and well-bred the men and women were, but at how well informed. The radio, the services such as the agricultural extension, the constant study in church groups, and their mobility made the farmers and their wives much better equipped than the people in rural Brazil. We were perfectly happy to continue in our parishes. Nevertheless, we wrote a letter to the Board of Foreign Missions offering ourselves as missionaries overseas.

We had talked the matter over many times. Because we were brought up as missionary children, we felt we had an understanding of cross-cultural living. We felt a desire to serve in China or Brazil. We knew the dearth of opportunities in many other countries, the extreme lack of resources in small communities. "What can we do?" was our question. "We can tell people about the good news that God cares and seeks them. And we can live with them and share what God gives us," was Chalmers' answer.

We felt no care for ourselves and our children. Besides our faith that God would be present with us, the Presbyterian Church provided its missionaries with salaries, medical care, and furloughs for educational opportunities, vacations, and visits to churches in the United States.

The churches needed to know us and what we were doing, and we needed to know the people who were standing behind us and their dreams and prayers for the people abroad we were living with. We sent in our papers to the Board and then rather forgot about the matter.

Chalmers and I were both glad when Dr. McColough said my health was good again and we could think of having a second child. How especially delicious the love that comes when one is hoping for a child! The hope became reality.

With this pregnancy my allergy returned. The roses along hedgerows must have been my undoing. For almost nine years I had been free from asthma. Now it returned with a vengeance. Dr. McColough would come after his office hours and give me a shot of adrenalin. The effect would last for a few hours. I tried to be quiet during the night so that Chalmers could get his sleep. One morning, awakened by my sobbing, he dressed quickly. "I'll see the young people off to camp and I'll be right back," he promised. Our neighbor, Cliff Randolf, also an asthmatic, had recommended an inhaler named Breatheasy. When Chalmers returned we bundled Buster into the car and set off for the Breatheasy Agency in a nearby town. We put out the money for a Breatheasy inhaler with trepidation. But after that I never spent a sleepless night as long as I had Breatheasy.

A surprise call came from the Board of Missions in New York. A representative was coming to visit us. We met his train in Lisbon. The visit was delightful. Our guest was a charming gentleman. I had prepared a luncheon. Our "pride and joy" behaved himself in his sunny little-boy fashion. All would have been well except that we did not get our new friend to his train on time. We stood outside the train station. "What about a bus?" asked Chalmers.

"We can get a bus?" asked Dr. Smith.

It wasn't far to the bus station. And there was a bus leaving for New York in less than half an hour.

"That was fortunate," I said as the bus pulled away and we waved.

After this fiasco our hopes were none too high for an overseas appointment. But in due time we were informed that we were accepted and were expected to attend the outgoing missionary conference in early fall. Going on a trip with a small child was a new challenge.

Bea and Sam were living in New York City and agreed to keep Buster for the two days of the conference.

The conference was a blur. I had thought that I would be willing to go to any country except a very cold one like Alaska. Of course my secret hope was Brazil and Chalmers' desirewas China. We were assigned to China. I had to find a place where I could cry without anybody, including Chalmers, knowing.

We were duly commissioned and, while our contract was being processed, we returned to our work with the Salineville and Oak Ridge churches.

Our two churches were able to minister to the wider community through their pastor. One afternoon a distraught young woman appeared at our door. She had a small baby in her arms. Just before leaving for duty with the army, her husband had rebuffed her. Now she had his baby. She wanted to know if she was truly married. Chalmers was able to find the registry of their marriage, and he was able to help her understand how bewildered her husband must have felt at the dual responsibilities that had fallen upon him all at once. Chalmers helped her write to her husband. She and I made cookies together. We packaged them and sent them to our soldiers, to her husband and to George. Her husband was eventually discharged and they were reconciled.

I went to the hospital very early Sunday morning, November 21. Chalmers stayed with me until he had to go to his Sunday service in Salineville. I spent an uneventful day in the hospital. Chalmers checked in after his services at Oak Ridge. Since things were quiet he and Dr. McColough went home. It was 1943 and the Second World War had drained personnel from the hospitals. There was only one nurse on the obstetrics floor that Sunday evening and there were two of us in labor. Dr. McColough and Chalmers were summoned from Salineville. I asked the nurse as she checked me, "Can you deliver a baby?"

"I could, but would rather not," she answered.

The nurse gave me a sedative and I held out until Chalmers and my doctor arrived. Margaret Irene was born at daybreak on November 22, 1943. She was indeed a different personality from her brother. Curled up in a little ball, eyes closed, her serene highness was very sure of her right to be cared for.

Mother Browne came to stay with Chalmers and Buster while I was in the hospital. After nine days we were allowed to take Margie home and it was good to have my sweet, gentle mother-in-law to welcome us home. She couldn't stay long because Irene Elizabeth had been born on November 24 to Bea and Sam and Mother hastened to welcome home her second granddaughter.

The summons to missionary service came in December. Chalmers resigned from the parish. We were leaving the people who had taught us our job with singular kindness, good humor, and a strong faith. Dad came to get Buster and took him to Cincinnati. Our friend, Margaret Russell, who had lost her own little daughter shortly after birth, took care of Margie during the last hectic days as we closed down our household and sold our possessions. We took a train from Salineville and were on our way, via Cincinnati, to Berkeley, California, where we would study Chinese.

- 11 -

Berkeley Interlude

We took up residence on "the Court" on Regent Street in Berkeley, a block away from Oakland. Six cottages on the court housed missionary families, all of us preparing to go to China.

Betsy and Jim Crothers lived right across the court from us. The Rhodes of PY days were next door. We made new friends, and we all functioned as an extended family.

The Chinese Language School from Peking was for the duration of the war on the campus of the University of California. There Chalmers and I started our studies. We had excellent native Chinese teachers. One of them was Mrs. White who had been a lady-in-waiting to the Empress Dowager. She had fallen in love with an American diplomat and gained the consent of the Empress to marry him. She was a Chinese lady with much to tell us about the last days of the empire and of Chinese culture. Though Chalmers could speak Chinese, he was illiterate in the language. His ability to speak, however, enabled him to take advanced courses in Chinese literature at the University proper.

Sam Wylie was by this time a chaplain in the Navy in the Pacific theatre. Bea and Rene Beth came to stay with us while he was assigned to troop ships taking Marines across the Pacific. Our apartment had only one bedroom, so Chalmers and I slept in the dining room on a bed that folded into the closet during the day. Bea and her baby daughter squeezed into the bedroom with Margie and George. Our two went to bed early. Though Rene Beth was only three months old and petite, she had a strong mind of her own and stayed up with the grown-ups. It was a great advantage to have Bea with us because she was willing to look after the children in the mornings while I went to classes.

California had a beautiful continuing education program for adults. One day Chalmers met a man on the streetcar reading Chinese. He was a gardener at the University and was studying Chinese. I enrolled in a course in preschool education. It consisted of a weekly evening seminar and a laboratory session one morning a week. Parents enrolled in the course could place their children in the lab nursery. George started his school experience in this nursery school and thrived. In the nursery we were assistants to the director and learned by observing and participating.

These were war years and we didn't have a car, but the University was within walking distance. Sometimes we took the children over to the campus on warm, sunny days. There were many paths to explore, nooks shrouded in shrubbery and flowers, two great Chinese stone lions, and a sundial.

Our own court, with its sidewalks and circular drive away from street traffic, was a busy playground for the children. White slatted gates into tiny gardens, and trellises with clambering red roses invited our children to climb. Parents would run out shouting "No!" and "Get down!" Then we put our heads together and decided that whatever parent saw a child climbing a trellis would show the child how to come down safely. The children soon had their fill of climbing and turned to other play. Even if a child should climb, we no longer feared disaster.

How to share toys on the court became an issue. We parents decided that toys would belong to everybody. A tricycle belonged for the time being to the child riding it. This worked very well, but there was a catch. We noticed that the rule was extending to the parents and that no one was feeling responsible for these community toys, to put them away at night or mend them. So, having made the point with the small fry, we went back to family ownership with parents teaching their children to take care of their toys.

George played with several children his own age, but George was small for his age. In his frustration at being pushed around he began to bite. The other mothers were incensed. I reasoned with George, but it did no good. So the next time that George used his teeth, I bit him, and the biting stopped.

Sam's ship was coming into port at San Diego to stay for a while. We were sorry to see Bea go to be with Sam. We now arranged for a nurse for Margie in the mornings while I continued Chinese conversation and writing of characters at the University.

One evening Chalmers and I were doing our homework. About nine o'clock Chalmers said, "I think I'll go buy a paper." The newsstand was not far and though the evening was cool Chalmers left in his shirtsleeves. After a half hour I began to wonder where he was. In another hour I became concerned. I went out to see if he had taken his bicycle. No, it was in its accustomed place. The Coles had the only phone on the court and I went to talk to them. They advised me not to worry. "He'll be back soon," they assured me.

Another hour went by and no Chalmers. I decided I must go out to the avenue as far as the newsstand. As I turned the corner from the court the lights were on brightly in the house just to our right. The curtains were not drawn and I saw through the window Chalmers seated in the living room talking with the family. I breathed a sigh of great relief and went home and crawled into bed. About two o'clock Chalmers came home. He had been passing the house when someone called him. The family was having a crisis and wanted a minister. They knew we were all church people on the court. He had felt so drawn into their need that he was unable to break away.

One evening Margie was riding home on Chalmers' shoulders and he pointed out the stars to her. He sang "Twinkle, Twinkle, Little Star" to the children. From then on a favorite, they would ask their daddy to sing it. George had fears. He became especially apprehensive when the fire engines passed on Regent Street with sirens shrieking. Chalmers took him to see the engines at the fire station and explained about the work the men he met there did. What calmed his night fears, however, was the reading of comforting passages from the scriptures, especially Isaiah chapter 65:25, "The wolf and the lamb shall feed together, and the lions shall eat straw like the bullock: and dust shall be the serpent's meat. They shall not hurt nor destroy in all my holy mountain, saith the Lord."

We were expecting a child again, somewhat sooner than we had envisioned. I began studying harder to make up time because I knew that when a third baby arrived I would have precious little time for Chinese.

Chalmers and I both got mumps at the same time. Dr. Oaks, our family physician, told his church people about our predicament, and many members came to our rescue, doing our laundry and bringing us food. Other friends helped us take care of the children.

We recovered and our son, Paul Chalmers, was born on October 10 at the Alta Bates Hospital in Oakland, a block from the court. Paul was wonderful. He had a little turned-up nose and slits for eyes that gave him a puckish look. We took him home on Chalmers' birthday, October 15, a great big beautiful birthday present wrapped in a baby blanket. Mrs. March, a retired missionary, came to help take care of Paul.

Our clothesline extended on pulleys over a narrow space between the court and a neighbor's wall. From our porch I would hang diapers, then send them flapping over the geraniums below. How many diapers had we washed and hung in our lives? I wondered. I savored the balsamy fragrance of geranium on the cool breeze, which on foggy mornings brought the dissonant voice of the foghorn from the bay.

We visited the Chinese Presbyterian Church in San Francisco where services and Bible study were in Chinese. Many of the young people were restless and wanted to move to English. They asked Chalmersto teach a Bible class for the young people in English. He was glad of the opportunity to be among Chinese people. We were introduced to some of the best Chinese restaurants in the world as we mingled with these new friends.

We celebrated George's birthday with a cake with four candles and we sang "Happy Birthday." Margie could not understand why all the attention was for George. With each gift George unwrapped she pleaded "It's me! It's me!" Four days later it was her birthday. We repeated the festivities, this time for Margie. She basked in the attention and opened each present with great satisfaction. After enjoying the cake with two candles, as we sat in the midst of the wrappings and toys, Margie leaned back and said, "Do it again!"

We watched and marveled as the nations gathered in San Francisco to create the United Nations, and we continued our studies until D-Day arrived at last! Now we would be able to go to our task. Chalmers had fretted as to whether he should join the armed forces as a chaplain. Sam, a chaplain in the Navy, and Frenchy, an infantry captain ferrying trucks over the difficult passes on the Burma Road somewhere between

India and China, urged him to stick to our plan. "When we return," they said, "There will be a terrible need for you."

Now our turn had come with word that Chalmers would be able to leave for China in early April 1946, but there would be no passage yet for families. Another disappointment was that the house we had expected to rent in Wooster had been ceded, by some lack of communication, to another couple.

Sam and Frenchy were back and reunited with their families. We stopped by in Wooster just long enough to say hello since this was a time of adjustment for them after being so long separated.

Bibette was living in an apartment in Philadelphia and her place became the gathering point for the family. She was able to rent a second apartment in the same building. Mother was there, and my brother George, who had just returned from military duty. Our family now swelled her quarters to the bursting point.

My brother George was planning to marry Mary Lou Beebe, a College of Wooster friend. Her parents had been missionaries in Thailand and Mary Lou's father was now pastor of the Presbyterian Church in a small town named Pennsylvania Furnace. Chalmers stayed with our children while I went with Mother, Bibette, and George to Pennsylvania Furnace for the wedding. It was a wonderful time of rejoicing in this quaint old community.

Bibette was involved in her own romance. Our cousin, Francis Hodgkiss, son of Aunt Junie and Uncle Frank of São Paulo, had come on company business to the United States. Bibette and he fell instantly in love. As Francis had to go on to Canada, Bibette made a visit to him there. So the state of affairs became apparent. Both Bibette and Francis were agonizing over the fact that they were first cousins. They did a lot of research, including a consultation with Uncle John Turner in Miami. They decided it would be all right to get married.

In the meantime Chalmers had looked at For Rent ads. He found a basement apartment in Ocean City, New Jersey, where in the off-season the rent was affordable. Mother moved with us to this three-bedroom flat, a block away from the boardwalk.

Chalmers had just enough time to get his cholera, typhoid, and other inoculations and collect clothing. The cold sea breeze whipped at our clothes on the morning of April 2, 1946, as I pushed Paul's buggy along the boardwalk. Chalmers held Margie and George by the hand. We were on our way to the little train station in Ocean City to see Chalmers off to China.

Chalmers sent us a letter and a photograph from the west coast. He was to sail on the USS *Breckenridge* that very week. He was missing us, but thought ahead to the time when we would be joining him. We stayed in Ocean City during April and May. The children and I enjoyed walking on the sand and on the boardwalk each day when the weather permitted.

In June, with the coming of the summer season, the rent on the apartment went far above our housing allowance. Fortunately Father was now coming to join Mother for their furlough year and they had requested a cottage for the summer at Montreat, North Carolina. We packed up and moved again.

Montreat, conference grounds of the Presbyterian Church, occupies a valley and the lower slopes of beautifully wooded mountains. There are year-round residences, but the large, comfortable cottage that we lived in was meant for summertime only.

Paul was eight months old. He was enjoying life with his grandparents. Father took him for walks in his stroller. Paul could repeat words already. Mother would say to him, "Paul, say *spoon*." He repeated "Spoon". After a series of easier words she would say, "Say, *ladies and gentlemen*." Paul just looked at her with innocent brown eyes.

Margie and George were having one cold after another. I took them into Ashville to Dr. Bell, who had been a missionary in China. He was upset that I was planning to go to China with my three small children. "Things are very uncertain and potentially dangerous," he argued.

"Dr. Bell," I countered, "In China I have a husband and a house to live in."

Dr. Bell decided that if we were going to be where medical services might be dubious, the children should have their tonsils out now, so we scheduled the tonsillectomies. My stories at bedtime became tales of going to the hospital and having tonsils out. I told the children that their throats would hurt, but they would soon be all well again. They embraced the idea of going to the hospital as a lark and looked forward to chipped ice.

We went to Ashville on the bus and walked over to the hospital. When they were ready for the operating room we all went to the staging area together. George was taken into the operating room first. Margie was incensed that he got the first turn. The next morning I found the children alert, and still in an adventurous spirit. I thought I would take them back to Montreat by taxi, but they begged to go on the bus. We made the trip home as they wished. They were tired when we reached home and went to bed gladly, but were soon as bouncy as ever.

I watched the mailbox at the post office hungrily for letters from Chalmers. They were too few, for he was very busy. Chalmers was the first missionary to arrive back at the Chenhsien mission station in Hunan province. He had an adventurous trip up the Yangtze River to Changsha, capital of Hunan, and then by rail to Chenhsien. All transportation was crowded with displaced persons trying to get back to their homes. At one point Chalmers heard one of the passengers singing softly. He recognized a hymn tune. He went to the man and asked if he were a Christian. Yes, he was. They introduced themselves and spent some happy hours singing hymns together.

Chalmers took up residence in what was known as the Blackstone house, named for the missionaries who built it. The problem of famine was acute. Chalmers wrote of the overwhelming feeling of helplessness when a little girl died, lying in the road, while he went for help. He met Mr. Hoffman, the UNRRA (United Nations Relief and Rehabilitation Administration), representative in that district. There were not enough supplies coming into the area to meet the desperate need. Two contingents of American soldiers had been stationed for a time in Chenhsien and had left behind surplus supplies under seal. Mr. Hoffman, on his own authority, broke the seals and with Chalmers' help started distributing the food. Later, Mr. Hoffman had a terrible time justifying his action to the military authorities.

It was a lonely, uphill battle and I was very glad to hear that Muriel Boone and Dr. Edie Millican had arrived. They were both old China hands and pitched right in to assist in the social service and medical work as well as the church work. The Church had gone under ground during the Japanese occupation. Many had fled and were now coming back. The church building had been used as a stable. Though the pastors had carried on as best they could, it seemed that everything was to be done over at once.

I was beginning to be very concerned. The United States was still in a postbellum mode. It was almost impossible to rent a house, and train passages had to be reserved well in advance. It was August; we were to sail in September and I had heard nothing from the Board of Foreign Missions. I wrote asking that arrangements be made. A week later I found a letter from the Board in the mailbox and tore it open hastily. It began: "We are now able to inform you that you will be sailing on November 18." There was no expression of concern anywhere in the letter about the delay.

I walked out into the beautiful sunlit day and leaned against a rough tree trunk. The summer cottages would be closed after Labor Day. How was I to manage two more months without a home for my children? Loneliness for Chalmers swept over me and I ached to the very roots of my being.

When Bea and Sam heard of our plight, they invited us to share their apartment until we found a place. We packed up and traveled to New York City. Rene Beth was now two, the same age as Margie.

The new member of their family was Mary Gertrude, a very busy ten-month old. One morning as Bea and I lingered over a second cup of coffee, Mary crawled over, grabbed the tablecloth to pull herself up to her mother and brought the pot of hot water all over herself. Bea wrapped her quickly in a blanket and rushed her to the hospital. Mary was extensively burned, but the burns were not deep. With care she recovered quickly. In the midst of their own concerns Sam and Bea put up not only with the four of us but with the baggage I had accumulated to take to China and repacked on their living room floor.

Mother and Father were able to get a small apartment, again in offseason Ocean City. The children and I moved down there. Phil was serving his stint in the army at a base not too distant and came to spend his time off with us.

Mother and Dad Browne were living in Cincinnati with Dad's cousin Bertha. They wanted us to visit them for a week before we went on west. Once again we packed up and set forth. Mother and Dad

Browne loved the children and we were enjoying our visit, but once more a discouraging letter arrived. Our sailing was postponed to mid-December. Why couldn't we have known in time to stay in the apartment in Ocean City where we were settled? Our visit with Mother and Dad Browne extended to a month rather than a week.

When we were ready to go to San Francisco, my mother came to make the cross-country train trip with us and to see us aboard the ship for China. How good it was to have her sweet company on this bittersweet trip of parting! In Berkeley we stayed with Dr. and Mrs. Oaks and their adopted daughter. Dr. Oaks' sister, a beautician, dropped in to visit. After we became acquainted she said to me: "It's all very well to be a missionary, but you don't have to look like one." She gave me a permanent which made me look much like a curly poodle.

Mother had to relinquish Paul to me at the dock gates. She was not allowed to go aboard. It was just as well since she would have been horrified at our quarters. The ship had not been refurbished and was still a troopship. We moved into a hold with two hundred canvas hammock beds arranged in tiers.

- 12 -

Outside East Gate

As we weighed anchor the slanting rays of the sun warmed the buildings and coast line turning everything to a rosy pink. The city was beautiful in the tender light, like all the warm, dear things we were leaving. We sailed slowly under the Golden Gate Bridge still bathed in the reflected glow of the setting sun.

Descending to the hold we found the area assigned to our family, two tiers of bunks with the aisle space between. It was a regal amount of room compared to what each soldier had been given. That night I placed Paul on the lowest bunk, where he would not have much distance to the steel deck, and I took the bunk just above him. Like little monkeys George and Margie climbed up to their beds above me. We had the bunks across the aisle on which to spread our clothes, books, and toys.

As we moved out to sea, the ship began to heave and roll. We were hitting the edge of a storm and my children were soon seasick. I did not usually get seasick, but I couldn't keep from joining them. There were passengers all around us in far greater distress than we. As soon as we moved into sunlight and fresh breezes the four of us were again fit.

At five each morning, I woke to keep an eye on Paul. On the third morning I dozed off, waking with a start. Paul was missing. Rushing to the nearest stairway I found and grabbed Paul who was already halfway up the steps. My heart beat wildly. The deck above had open railings with nothing between a small child and the sea. I had seen a playpen on an upper deck and had asked a steward for it to no avail. On our way to breakfast that frightening morning, I met Joe Esther, a neighbor of Berkeley days. I asked him to bring the pen to our hold, and he did. Paul slept in the pen after that.

The mess hall was two decks up. Two couples offered their help in getting the children to meals. The Hilschers took Margie, who found it hard to go with strangers, and the Melroses took George. Paul went with me and enjoyed sailor food. The fare was good and plentiful.

The ship's crew provided a play area for the children on the top deck, with protective canvas threaded through the railing uprights. I took my threesome up there whenever the weather permitted. On the first day I held each child up to look out over the sea. Margie's surprised comment was, "It would be the ocean if there were some sand!"

We were at sea for Christmas. The ship's officers did everything to make the day special for the children. A large Christmas tree with lights and trimmings stood in the mess hall. Santa presented each child with a gift. We had our own family celebration. We read the Christmas story, sang carols, and had our own presents. Christmas was especially poignant so far from any home and from Chalmers.

We reached Shanghai on the last day of 1946. We spent New Year's Day in the harbor waiting for the ship to be unloaded. Most of the boats in the calm harbor were sampans. People lived on these boats and fished for their livelihood. They had the help of cormorants, large, floppy birds with collars around their necks to prevent them from swallowing their catch. They were rewarded with pieces of fish small enough to slip down their restricted gullets. I was awed, but then I saw a woman brushing her teeth at the side of a sampan. She fished with cormorants, but, like me, she brushed her teeth.

By the evening of January 2 we were on our way with favorable winds, and we reached Hong Kong in the wee hours of the 4th.

It was exciting to awaken. The children and I were soon dressed to meet Daddy, and our bags were all packed. While waiting for all the red tape, which seemed interminable, I had time to admire the wide sweep of the harbor with the hills rising around it. The sunshine gleaming on the city burnished the bright colors of buildings, the tropical verdure, the red flame of poinsettias and the deep blue of the bay—one of the loveliest harbors in the world.

At last, Chalmers came aboard to help us ashore. We all hugged him deliriously. Then Chalmers stood back and looked at me. I was dressed in a three piece wool suit and a pale blue blouse. I had tried to slick down my frizzy hair. He asked, "Don't you have any more suitable clothes?" He was dressed in khaki and boots. I think he was really shocked by the contrast between my clothes and the drab, faded blue padded pants and jackets of the women in Chenhsien where I was going to live. I assured him that indeed I had brought along slacks and jackets.

Chalmers took us to the hotel where we were put up in dormitories, one for the men and one for the women. George went with his daddy to the men's dormitory. We met in the dining hall for breakfast. Chalmers and I arranged for the care of our children and began the wearisome job of locating our freight. All the freight off the ship had been piled helter-skelter in the huge godown sheds along the docks. It took us three days to locate our baggage amongst the innumerable crates, trunks, and boxes.

One morning I noticed that George had some bites on his arms. I asked Chalmers to check his bed. Chalmers found nothing. We traveled the next day to Canton where we were warmly received and housed by the personnel of the Presbyterian hospital. It was suppertime when we arrived and we were invited into the hospital dining room. One of our missionary nurses took Paul on her lap and started feeding him with a spoon, but quickly put it down and took up a pair of chopsticks like those with which she fed children in the wards. Paul was quite willing to eat this new way.

In Canton all of us newcomers became ill with some virus or germ new to our bodies. We had to stay in Canton until we were well enough to travel. It was good that we were in a mission hospital.

The train trip from Canton to Chenhsien was to be a twenty-four-hour trip. We packed enough food for one day. There were no sleepers, so the children slept in our laps and on the hard benches. When morning broke we expected to be nearing home, but we were told that the train was three hours late. We had nothing left for breakfast except some orange juice and I divided it amongst the three children. Paul started to drink his and began to cry. We looked at him and saw that his neck was swollen. He had the mumps, and George's bites turned out to be chicken pox, which broke out more thoroughly on Paul and Margie a few days later. We amused the children by looking out the window and commenting on the passing scene. I saw with relief that many of the grasses and weeds along the banks were the same as those along train cuts in the United States or Brazil. Finally we trundled across the shaky bridge over our own river, slowed as we traversed the town, and stopped at the Chenhsien station.

What a flurry! All the new people to meet! Yang Shir Fu and Tang De, two of our new Chinese family, helped Chalmers with the baggage. Soon we were hustled off to the compound and our new home at "Dung Men Wai" (Outside the East Gate), the name of our end of town taken from the long-gone wall of the city and one of its gates.

There were two houses close to the compound gate. Muriel and Edie occupied a two story house on the right. Our house to the left of the gate was bigger. The large living room and the dining room had fireplaces, upstairs one iron stove somewhat warmed one of the three bedrooms. It was very cold—the thermometer hovered around 30 degrees. When we climbed into bed that first night, I thought I had never touched such cold sheets.

That very first evening after supper, Chalmers and I had found ourselves in a crucial disagreement. Chalmers wanted to be at work. The young people of the Church ran an educational and recreational program at a downtown hall. Chalmers expected to go right back to the job of participating in this activity. I desperately wanted him home for that first evening. I felt so strange and lonely in this big, new house and new land. We found through the days as we explored our feelings and our needs that we had both been feeding on the wonderful thoughts of when we would be together again, but with different scripts. Chalmers had spent desperate moments all by himself, needing the comfort of being loved and cared for. I had battled the difficulties of being a pilgrim with three small children. I wanted to rest in the love and care of a trusted companion. We had to adjust to the needs of each other in conscious ways.

I soon found that I had very wonderful people around me. Yang Shir Fu bought our fresh food daily, since we had no refrigeration or electricity, and prepared all our meals. Chalmers talked over any plans and weekly did the household accounts with him. I had no household obligations. Tang Sao, a homely older woman with a big voice, washed our clothes and swept and dusted. Tang De Geh was her son. He made the coal and dung cakes that burned in our fireplaces and stoves and did the yard work. He ran errands and carried messages since there were no telephones. A sweet young woman served as *amah*, taking care of the children while I studied Chinese, and accompanied Muriel or Edie in their tasks.

I spent the mornings with the children and taught them. George was following the Calvert School by correspondence kindergarten curriculum. I adapted the activities for Margie and Paul. It was fun to crayon, mould clay, read stories, and sing with them. George did Calvert first grade the next year.

The street running by our gate separated our compound from the mission school and the hospital compounds. The principal of the primary and secondary school was a scholarly Chinese gentleman. There was no missionary personnel teaching at the school. The mission hospital stood in its own compound on a hill in the midst of shade trees. One day I went with Dr. Edith Millican on her rounds. As we entered the hospital, a man was being carried in. Edie saw to him at once and after examining and medicating him she shook her head. He had a very pernicious form of malaria and had come to the hospital in the extremity of his illness. By the time we left the hospital that day, he was dead. Malaria, tuberculosis, intestinal parasites, eye infections, and especially malnutrition were the most common maladies. Edie treated them all, sometimes on a round-the-clock schedule.

Muriel Boone was our other American missionary colleague. She did a little of everything. She preached, she taught, she oversaw the orphanage and the kindergarten down town. She visited and held women's meetings and she had a well-baby clinic where I helped. We bathed the babies, medicated their minor abrasions and fed them powdered milk formula. The mothers watched and helped and learned to use the milk powder and soap, both of which were new to them.

We were soon to have another missionary family join us, Bill and Ruth Meyers and their two small sons, Bobby and Billy. Chalmers rounded up a crew and went over to the other missionary residence on the far side of the hospital. The building needed cleaning and repair. As Chalmers was helping, he went to the well to draw water. But the wooden bucket made of staves wouldn't turn over on the surface of the water. Chalmers drew the bucket out and was about to dash it into the well when one of his coworkers said, "Not that way, Bang Mu Shir (Pastor Browne). Here, let me show you." He gave the bucket a special little flip. The bucket descended, submerged, and came up dripping full. "You see, the staves are set but not fastened in these bands and would fall out if you clapped it hard against the water," explained the worker.

The house was readied when the Meyers arrived. Bill had worked in China for a number of years prior to becoming a Presbyterian minister and marrying Ruth. She had no experience overseas but courageously undertook to bring up their boys in what were to her very severe conditions.

When the chill rains had given way to sunshine, Chalmers decided to make some outdoor play equipment for the children. George and Margie had found friends among the children who lived on our compound and were beginning to talk happily in Chinese. With the help of our carpenter he put up a jungle gym, a swing, and a seesaw under the trees beside our back porch. Before long there were flocks of other children who came to play, too.

Shortly thereafter Margie came in from play with her face swollen and red, her eyes almost shut. I bathed my tearful daughter and took her to Edie. Edie said she thought it was scabies and prescribed applications of sulphur water. "We will know for sure when the swelling goes down." Sure enough, the next day we could see little lines across her skin where the minute mites had tunneled. The boys picked up the itch too and were swabbed with the smelly sulphur water. Edie was having serious problems, too. She would come home from eighteen exhausting hours at the hospital, grab a bite and crawl in bed. No sooner did she fall asleep but someone would climb the stairs in their house and walk into her room seeking her medical attention. We had tried to keep our compound open to all comers, but now decided to place a gateman again at the entrance to screen visitors.

All through that year distribution of UNRRA food continued. Chalmers was supervising three distribution centers. A group of volunteers—students, teachers and nurses—canvassed the villages and farms. They listed the families and issued tickets according to the number of persons in each household. The tickets were exchanged for rice, oil, and any other available foods at the centers. The recipients brought their baskets on poles to carry their allotted supplies home.

Chalmers was working at the distribution center located at the school compound when I received a message for him. I took Paul and went to deliver it. The street was crowded with people who had not understood the system and had come to beg for food. They caught hold of my belt and held on to me thinking that I might give them food. For a time I despaired of breaking away. I eventually wrenched myself loose, and clutching Paul to me, shoved my way across the street. On our return Chalmers sent a man with us to escort us across the street.

People didn't know how powerless I was. We were strictly forbidden to give food to anyone who entered our compound. One day a woman with a small child at her waist came to our door with a bowl in her hand. I had to tell her I couldn't give her a bowl of rice. The look in her eyes haunts me to this day, even though I knew the rules were necessary to prevent utter chaos and graft.

The Japanese had ravaged the fields and killed the water buffalos for meat, so there had been no crops the year before. Now the farmers were malnourished and developed ulcers on their legs as they tried to ready their fields without the water buffalos. Nothing but rest and a good diet would restore flesh and muscle. At the hospital they were given a place in a huge army tent pitched on the grounds.

The hospital issued them a protein-rich powder, provac, to eat with their rice. They planted seed in the communal garden so they could have vegetables. Sometimes it took weeks to gain back their strength, but in time Chalmers would see one of them waving to him from his work in the fields as he drove between centers. There would be a harvest this year.

Chalmers had pastoral duties also. Pastor Tsao and Pastor Chen were the two Chinese pastors in the area with whom Chalmers shared the ministry of the Church. The field was large and required a lot of travel. The thriving Chenhsien church stood on our street, at the end of our compound. Chalmers enjoyed preaching in Chinese, but Muriel and the other pastors persuaded him to take a few months off without preaching to concentrate on his Chinese, an incentive for his studies which could so easily be put aside for more pressing matters.

I had my request of him too. I wished for an occasional family outing. Edie and Muriel backed me up in this. So on a delightful sunny day, Chalmers and I started out with the children for a picnic lunch. We turned downhill from our compound to cross the clear, small river that curved around the northern edge of Chenshien. We crossed a narrow, arching masonry bridge and walked beside the terraced paddies now green with the new growing rice.

There we came to the foot of the mountain we could see from our house. Tang De Geh had come along with his carrying baskets. He placed Paul in one basket and Margie in the other and hoisted the pole to his shoulder. He started up the path with a steady running gait. The ascent was steep and the path a series of stepping stones, wide and flat. Chalmers and I helped George, who valiantly climbed up and up with us. The wind soughed softly in the ancient pines that arched their branches over our heads. We stopped for a rest and looked out over the river and fields to the distant mountains. Azaleas and rhododendron were still blooming in the shade, delicate pink and orange and red.

At the very top of our mountain stood an ancient temple, a vague two thousand years old. Up here in the clouds that ringed the mountain it was ageless.

Legend had it that a very pious boy went on a long journey to find help for his sick mother. On his way he met a white stag that carried his mother to a great herb doctor, and she was cured. This lad also played chess with the gods on the top of this mountain. There is a flat stone near the temple marked off into a crude chessboard where they played. One day the gods took the boy off with them to their dwelling place, and on another stone one can see the mark of the boy's foot as he pushed off into the sky.

Two ferocious stone lions guarded the entrance to the temple. Having mounted the steps we entered the hall, so dark that it was very difficult to see more than a glint of the many images of Buddha in the cases lining the walls. The monks here were Buddhists in a very eclectic sort of way, mingling Buddhism with the folk religion of the region. The hall was high ceilinged and awe inspiring.

Along the stony pathways around the temple the birds sang in the branches of the trees. We wandered a bit in this quiet, airy top of the world. Then after our picnic, we returned down the long, winding path with its wide stone steps.

In the hottest part of the summer Chalmers and I took off a couple of days to roam by ourselves in the beautiful countryside. We left the children with the *amah* and Aunt Muriel for the day and returned to be with them at night. We explored paths, finding little ponds with ducks swimming about. We sat under the high pines to hear the music of the wind running delicate fingers through their branches. We listened to the birds and were especially intrigued by the wild doves who with their mournful cooing drummed out a syncopated rhythm. We came home each night weary but singularly refreshed.

When harvest time came, the desperate famine was over. The relief centers closed down and the leaders in the movement were invited to a feast. The food was delicious. At the end of the meal they served the foreigners coffee. Never having used coffee themselves, they mixed a whole jar of Nescafe in a quart of water. We sipped at it politely.

Muriel, Edie, Chalmers, and Bill and Ruth Meyers had gone to a meeting in Hengyang. When I arose the morning after they left, Tang De Geh brought me a bundle he had found on our front doorstep. It was a wee baby girl. For two days we fed her and bathed her and cuddled her. We wanted to keep her. But when the rest of the team came back, they were adamant that it was impossible to keep her; we would be flooded with baby girls. So, to my distress, the baby was borne off to the orphanage. I visited her there, but, sadly, an epidemic of boils broke out and many of the children died, among them the baby from our doorstep.

During this year I had a bad spell of asthma. The Breatheasy we had ordered from the United States had not arrived and my supply gave out. I spent two weeks in bed feeling desperate and lonely. Chalmers was immersed in his work. The children went outdoors with their *amah* to play. I took too much antihistamine in an effort to ease my labored breathing and only succeeded in making myself more miserable with the side effects.

When I was well again, we enrolled Margie in the downtown kindergarten. Muriel wanted me to help the teacher, a slender young Chinese woman who seemed ill at ease with me around. I couldn't talk to her because I had no Chinese vocabulary in the field of child development and preschool teaching. I should have been willing to learn by just being in the kindergarten several times a week. Instead, I beat a hasty retreat.

I was having a hard time with Chinese anyway. I could speak enough Chinese to communicate with help and to invite people politely into my house and chitchat with them. I could understand more serious conversations, but rarely collected my thoughts in Chinese fast enough to join in. I had mastered about a thousand characters, but these were not enough to make reading easy. I envied Tang Sao, our laundress. She would sit in the shade of a tree and read the Bible out loud in Chinese.

Compounding my discouragement was the fact that four of the American missionaries were China veterans: Muriel, Edie, Bill, and Chalmers. Ruth, Bill's wife, never having been abroad before, was having her own battle with culture shock and the stark living conditions. I had grown up in even rougher conditions, but had been part of the work team ever since I was nine years old. It was difficult for me to defer to the superior wisdom of my more knowledgeable colleagues and always be voted down. This was the only time in my married life that I thought about somehow going away. From Chalmers? My mind didn't explore the options. I just daydreamed about being somewhere else.

- 13 -

China Years End

Our Hunan hill country was beautiful. The air was limpid and translucent, like fragile glass that might shatter at a shrill birdcall. The venerable singing pines, the terraced rice paddies, the ancient pagodas and mountain temple had survived many troublous times. Chenhsien with its narrow streets and daily bustle, huddling close into the curve of the river, was mending itself after years of disaster. The people partook of the landscape. One felt that beneath the cheery simplicity of their daily lives were hidden deep springs more ancient than the pines and pagodas. Our household fit into this setting because of Chalmers. He was "Chinese." He loved the place and the people, admiring their integrity, enjoying their humor and empathizing with their sorrows. The small widows who hobbled about on their bound feet, the engineer bridge builder for the railroad and his cultured wife, the Chinese pastors and their families, all were close to Chalmers and a part of the church family in Chenhsien. The parish was far flung. It took in the hill villages and farmlands surrounding the city.

But we had our own concerns also. Before we were married Chalmers and I had dreamed of a family of five children. Now in the thick of things in Chenhsien I remarked to Chalmers, "Maybe three children are enough for us." Chalmers became upset at the suggestion. As we talked he showed evident desire for another son or daughter. We agreed that we were lucky to have our friend Edie, an obstetrician and gynecologist, as our doctor. I became pregnant in September. The days grew cool, then cold as Christmas rolled arouned.

Winter came with the temperatures hovering around freezing. Christmas in a non-Christian society was very strange to me. It was celebrated in the church with carols and a pageant, but there were no colorful lights in the town, no flurry of shopping and no general celebration—the other extreme to the commercialization prevalent in the West. We all enjoyed our family Christmas around the tree Chalmers brought and we decorated.

Chalmers was doing a lot of traveling, taking his turn at visiting outlying congregations. He was away on one of these trips when I began to bleed, alarming Edie. She put me to bed and asked that Chalmers be summoned.

Chalmers was at the farthest village on his itinerary when our telegram reached him. He had just finished his lunch. Either the excitement over the telegram or the fish he had just eaten caused him to feel faint, see spots before his eyes and to feel too weak to walk. He looked in his medicine kit: aspirin, milk of magnesia, an antihistamine, and atabrine (antimalarial medicine). He asked for boiled water and swallowed one pill of each kind, hoping that one of them would work. In a short time he felt able to start out. He had to walk for several hours to the town where he could catch a bus for home.

In the meantime, since I had not improved, Edie said to me, "I'm going to take strenuous measures. I'm going to give you morphine. If you don't stop bleeding, I am going to take the baby or you will bleed to death. I am telling you this now because I need your consent." I put myself in Edie's care and God's, and she gave me the morphine. I don't understand how anybody can like morphine. I was very uncomfortable in the never-never land. I did, however, like the results. The bleeding stopped. By the time Chalmers reached home, Edie felt things were under control and we could rejoice and be thankful.

Chalmers' trips to the villages, while physically hard, were stimulating and gratifying. In many places he was the first pastor to visit since the disruption of war. In one town he met a man, an elder in the Church, who sold glasses from place to place. He was also a troubadour. When a crowd gathered around to see his glasses, he would sing to them psalms and other portions of scripture set to Chinese tunes. Thus he carried the gospel message to many. He would explain to any who asked the meaning of his songs.

Chalmers visited another family, the Lis, and was warmed by their faith and happiness. Chalmers wrote this story about them:

"In the hills of south China I heard Mrs. Li tell how the gospel reached her. When they were young, her husband once took vegetables to Linhsien to sell and returned with a Gospel. The schoolteacher read it with him until someone warned against the foreign religion. Mrs. Li became afraid.

"Then one afternoon, she was washing clothes when a Chinese man stopped by the stream and politely asked the way to Mr. Li's home. This man knew her husband! She pretended not to understand his inquiry.

"But when she got home there was the man talking with her husband about Jesus. Tired and frightened, she prepared supper. After supper her husband went out to tend the animals.

"The man turned to her and said, 'I want to thank you for your hospitality. You worked hard all day and then offered this good meal to a stranger. Now I want to help finish the work in the kitchen.'

"Mrs. Li's mind was awhirl. What made this man thoughtful of a mere woman? What made him offer to do menial kitchen work? 'That night,' said Mrs. Li, "my heart opened. I wanted to hear more of the story of Jesus.'"

Chalmers' trips continued. Then springtime came with the glory of azaleas in bloom on every hillside. The small white flowers of the myrtle trees exuded their heady perfume. The creamy blossoms of the tea-oil plants drooped and swayed in the wind. Then came summer. Edie was to leave on furlough early in June and our baby was long overdue. I was busy following all of Edie's procedures to speed up the delivery. During the long days at the hospital I watched a pale white bird of paradise, with its long, flowing tail, flitting about the hospital trees like some mystic spirit bringing me solace. At this time George became ill with the flu, which developed into viral pneumonia. Chalmers was designated as his nurse so that I would not be exposed.

On June 7 the hospital staff prepared a good-bye banquet for Edie, but she could not go to her own banquet because she was delivering our daughter. Natalie Landes was born shortly before 8 p.m. Chalmers had stayed with me until about five o'clock, then gone home to see that the children were fed and put to bed. When he returned, he found his new daughter waiting for him. Edie left on her homeward way the next day.

Our beautiful new daughter also went home the next morning. We were carried on a stretcher. Natalie was a good baby and very hungry. I had the satisfaction of caring for her right from the first.

George continued to run a temperature. Chalmers was giving George an injection of penicillin, then a very new drug, every four hours. George was also taking cod liver oil and provac, a food supplement rich in protein. Even so he kept getting thinner and thinner. The Chinese doctors were afraid he might have tuberculosis, so they kept him in bed.

One morning I heard George screaming and flew to his room. Chalmers dashed past me saying, "I gave him a spoonful of alcohol instead of cod liver oil." I quickly gave George a glass of water. Drinking the water calmed him down. I looked at the bottles on the shelf. The cod liver oil and rubbing alcohol were in similar liter bottles. The alcohol was wood alcohol. Chalmers came back from the hospital with the reassurance that one tablespoonful of wood alcohol wasn't enough to poison George.

George continued to run a low-grade fever. In consultation with the doctors at our hospital, we postponed a trip to the hospital in Canton for more accurate tests because the weather was very hot. Rather, we would go to the resort in the mountains at Nan Yo until cooler weather.

Chenhsien station had a weapons carrier left to us by the U.S. military, so we packed up our household in it and clambered aboard. Yang Shir Fu, the cook, and Mei Ling, the *amah*, went with us. Chalmers drove, astonishing me by avoiding potholes, inching through crowds of people and animals in market towns, and maneuvering the heavy weapons carrier around the hairpin turns on the mountain.

We settled in a Chinese house next to a monastery. The gentle sound of the gongs that regulated monastery life was soothing. George continued his bed rest, a very patient little boy. Chalmers stayed each day with him and Natalie while I took Paul and Margie to the swimming pool. We were able to visit with other missionaries who were taking their vacation on the mountain.

Chalmers and I had a remarkable day hiking to the very top of the mountain. There were several temples on the mountain. We stopped at one to rest partway up. While I listened Chalmers had a conversation with the monks about their religion, which was half Buddhist and half beliefs already there before the Buddhist teachers came. Some of these monks were spiritual and could talk of their insights, so that Chalmers was able to share with them some of the Christian view of God and the way he reaches out to us.

We paused frequently to gaze out over a world of wooded hills and mountains in varying shades of green and blue and purple under a soft azure sky. At the temple at the very top we stayed for a hot meal. The vegetarian fare was delicious. Before long it was time to go down the great mountain in the glow of the setting sun.

As soon as we returned to Chenhsien from our vacation, Chalmers made arrangements to take George to Canton. The two of them enjoyed that trip together, especially since the Canton hospital X-ray proved that George did not have tuberculosis, only a small scar that was not significant. Were we all glad to see him back playing with the other children!

Natalie was such a sweet, happy baby. She developed an allergy to orange juice. I would pat her back and she would pat my shoulder with her wee hand. Our luck was that the persimmons, which are rich in vitamin C, began ripening on the big tree in front of our house. They were small and round and sweet, and Natalie thought they were heavenly.

In October we celebrated Chalmers' and Paul's birthdays. In November we celebrated George's and were preparing to celebrate Margie's. Margie wanted to serve noodles with chicken Chinese style to her little friends. Chalmers took her to the market in town to buy dried and salted watermelon seed, too. The party was planned and guests invited when we received a telegram from the American Consul in Hankow. The U.S. Air Force would be sending a plane, in a week, into Changsha to evacuate all Americans. We could board that plane or make our own arrangements to leave the interior of China.

It was 1948 and the Communist forces were marching southward. We felt no danger, though Bill and Ruth had already left. We couldn't travel via Hong Kong because of a longshoremen's strike on the west coast of the United States. Chalmers went to our Chinese colleagues and asked for advice. What did they want us to do? After reflection, the unanimous opinion was that we should accept the evacuation opportunity. They remembered only too vividly the times when they had had to flee. They would feel responsible for us. Transportation would be scarce, and being refugees would be hard on a family with small children.

Reluctantly we packed. But first we had the birthday party, and it was a good party despite the anxiety the adults were feeling. We stored most of our earthly possessions in the attic, for the consulate had instructed us to limit our luggage. It was already cold and on the only other railroad trip we had made to Changsha Paul's feet had been frost bitten. So we carried blankets and warm clothing with us.

The air force plane, which picked us up on the sports field of Yenging University in Changsha, was a DC-3 cargo plane. Benches lined the sides; it was not pressurized or air-conditioned. The only heat poured down from vents in the ceiling so that our heads were warm enough but our feet were freezing. We were glad to reach Shanghai. The YWCA took us in. The children, who didn't remember electric lights or flush toilets, were fascinated by all the gadgets. In Shanghai I shopped for gifts for our families.

We sailed on the Navy's USS *Breckenridge* a few days later. On this trip we traveled in the officers' quarters. The men were given cabins on one side of the ship, the women on the other. Fortunately, the children and I had a cabin to ourselves, so Chalmers moved over with us and so was able to share in the care of the children.

Before we reached San Francisco Paul became quite ill. One of our mission doctors, Dr. Stanley Hoffman, was on board. He came to see

Paul and diagnosed his malady as tonsillitis. He gave him penicillin. We were worried because of Paul's high temperature and lassitude. As soon as we docked and had gone through immigration, Chalmers put us in a taxi and sent us off to a hotel while he took care of baggage and customs.

Paul continued to be very sick, so we decided not to travel across America until he was better. We were able to rent one of the cottages in Berkeley where we had lived when we were studying Chinese. We called Dr. Oaks, our family doctor who had delivered Paul. He was concerned because the penicillin hadn't done any good. Paul was limp, unable to eat and his lips were darkened and cracked from the fever. We followed the doctor's instructions and kept watch over our son all night. With the morning light I saw a rash on Paul's wrist. I was delighted. It was the measles! With the breaking out of the rash Paul's fever diminished and he slowly returned to his normal self.

Our plan had been to celebrate Christmas with Mother and Dad Browne. Though we didn't make it for Christmas, we were glad to be able to visit them in Cleves, Ohio, where Dad was pastor of the Presbyterian Church. On our way to Cleves we stopped for a brief visit with Chalmers' Aunt Esther and her husband, Uncle Ambrose, in St. Louis. Uncle Ambrose gave George a five-dollar bill, in those days quite a fortune. George put it away proudly.

It was quite an experience for Mother and Dad to receive our family with four children into their household when they had a busy schedule of their own. On Sunday, Dad baptized Natalie at the morning service. His congregation was agonizing over the high amount the Presbytery expected the Cleves church to raise for the fund to help rebuild war-ravaged churches in Europe. Chalmers explained to George that many churches were destroyed during the war. He asked, "Would you like to give some of your five dollars to help rebuild the churches? I can change your five dollars."

"No," said George. "I want to give it all." And so he did, placing it in the offering plate. After we left Cleves Dad shared the story of his grandson's five dollars with the congregation. The Cleves church went ahead to exceed its quota. George's gift inspired them further to raise the money needed for a new organ.

We went to Wooster, where we rented a house on Quinby across from the high school until an apartment in Princeton became available. Chalmers left on an extended speaking trip to various churches.

We put our older children in school knowing it would be for a short time only. Natalie developed a fever in March and I called Dr. Wright, our longtime family doctor. He came to see her and prescribed, then turned to me. "It seems you have a cold too." I admitted to a sore throat. He looked at my throat and prescribed sulfa dyasine. Natalie improved and I got caught up in packing for our move to Princeton. Chalmers came home in time to help get the baggage off and travel with us to Princeton.

I was feeling terrible. As we settled in Princeton I became worse. My face bloomed into a moon shape, my clothes no longer fit and I was nauseated. The doctor who came to see me said I had an allergic reaction to the sulfa drug and would just have to let it wear off. Joan and Frenchy were in Princeton, where Frenchy was in his last year at the Seminary. Joan came over to see me and brought me food. I felt so grateful for her ministrations.

Chalmers plunged into his studies for a master's at the Seminary, on "China, Communism, and the Christian Response." He was also filling speaking engagements on weekends. I finally reacted strongly. "I want a chance to study some, too," I cried. "I can't take care of four children, do all the housework and study without some help."

"I'm just doing my job!" Chalmers responded with equal passion. It was an impasse. How can two married people get caught in such a web?

After looking at the situation more calmly, Chalmers agreed to stay at home three weekends out of four and help with the children and household.

I enrolled in two classes, Philosophy of Religion with Dr. Caillet and Comparative Religions with Dr. Gergi. I would get George and Margie off to school, then take Paul and Natalie to the Seminary childcare center for a couple of hours while I attended classes.

With Frenchy's help we bought a roomy secondhand Plymouth sedan. When summer came we packed our children into our car and went to Albuquerque, New Mexico, for the wedding of Phil and Mary Louise Norris. They had met as choir members at their church. The trip was fun. During the day we watched for a playground or swimming pool where the children could get out and play. In the evening after a picnic supper, we tucked the children in bed, each in his own place in the car. While they slept we put in our best driving time until at about eleven or twelve we stopped at a motel.

In Albuquerque we stayed at Menaul School. The wedding was scintillating. Margie was flower girl. She wore a sheer white dress over pink. Mary Louise's sisters, the bridesmaids, wore blue. The bride herself was very beautiful and stately in her long white dress and veil. Phil, of course, was very handsome.

The day after these festivities our family set off for a young people's conference in the mountains near Grand Junction. We drove until it was almost dark, then we settled the children all snug in their beds. Before long Chalmers said to me, "I'm just too sleepy to drive any more." I took over the wheel, but before long I was nodding. In the gloaming we could see the mountains ranging up ahead. We decided to sleep a bit in the car, curled up in the front seat, and the next we knew dawn was creeping ever so faintly to etch the contours of the mountains. We shook ourselves and drove on, up to seven thousand feet and down into a mountain valley where we found a very pleasant restaurant. We were all ready for some breakfast.

Near Grand Junction the cherry trees stood laden with dark red fruit. Up and up the mountain past the orchards and into the pine forests we drove. Columbine bloomed along the road. The camp was among glacier lakes, blue as sapphires and quite bottom-less, they told us. Snow still lingered on the north side of huge firs and pines. The beautiful setting and the great young people, zestful and with eager minds, made up for the swarms of mosquitos that descended upon us as soon as dusk approached. One afternoon George disappeared from camp. We thought with horror of the bottomless lakes. Chalmers said, "He'll soon turn up." But as the shadows began to lengthen, Chalmers went in search of George. He found him several bends down the road climbing slowly back up the mountain. "I went for a walk," our newly independent seven-year-old explained,

On our way back to Princeton, as we drove through Indianapolis in the evening, Margie's voice trilled, "Can't we sit up and watch?" We were going down a brilliantly lighted street with signs that flickered and danced in neon greens, reds, yellows, and purples. Permission given, the children enjoyed the show all the way through town. The next day I heard Margie say to her brothers, "Wasn't it beautiful?"

In July two nephews were born. Will arrived to Joan and Frenchy in Princeton. Bea and Sam brought their daughters, Rene Beth and Mary, from New York to stay with us while baby John was born. At our house the cousins had a wonderful time. They got in the big bathtub together and splashed water all over the place. Each of our children had a distinct personality. I was washing dishes. I heard Paul doing something he shouldn't in the living room, and called, "Paul, don't do that." In a bit Paul came quietly around to the kitchen. "Mother, can you see around corners?" Before I had time to respond he added, "I guess you see with your heart".

Jeanie Havlick, one of my Wilson gang, came to visit. She brought us a box of chocolates. The next day as we were getting ready to go to church, I helped the older children dress, dressed myself, then I scrubbed Natalie's face and hands and put on her dainty dress. While I turned for my hat and coat Natalie found the open box of chocolates. She came to me bearing this treasure clasped to her tummy with a smile a mile wide on her face and chocolate all over herself. I had to wash and dress her over again.

In April our lease in Princeton ran out and, before Chalmers could really finish his dissertation, we had to pick up and move to Wooster. Chalmers' dissertation was very good, except for the hasty ending.

We had been hoping to return to our friends in China, but prospects were not good. Missionaries still in China were in prison or under house arrest. Two new opportunities opened to us. One was an assignment to Thailand. The other, a request that we go to Brazil. "Chalmers, dear," I said, "I really don't feel I can learn another strange language and care for the family. If we go to Brazil, I can look after the children and household and you will be free to study Portuguese." Chalmers smiled his winsome, wistful smile and said, "You have a point." It wasn't easy for him since there are Chinese communities in Thailand. The Spirit guided us to new opportunities in Brazil. Wherever we went, the task was the same: to try to speak and live the love of God in Christ Jesus, our Lord.

- 14 -

Assigned to Brazil

Our tears as I left for China, Mother's and mine, were dried: we were going to live for a year in the same city, Campinas. The Presbyterian Theological Seminary where my father taught and the Language School Chalmers would attend were both in Campinas.

In preparation, I thought I could teach the family a bit of Portuguese as we traveled by train and then by ship. But all the interesting things to see and do along the way put Portuguese on hold. They did learn one sentence: *Quero um copo de leite, por favor* (Please give me a glass of milk).

We were traveling on a family passport. In Rio the immigration officer looked at the passport and turning to me, said, "You were born in Brazil. Where is your Brazilian passport?" I admitted that I didn't have one. I was traveling with my American husband and children. This explanation did not satisfy. He said, "This country is yours since you are a Brazilian. Walk right in. But be sure to get a Brazilian passport before you travel again." We reported this to the American consul in Rio. He said, "Try to get a foreigner's ID card." I tried and was laughed at. A person born in Brazil is Brazilian *jus soli* (right of the soil), and that's that. My dual citizenship and my marriage abroad continued to give us trouble for a long time.

The day after we arrived in Rio was Brazil's independence day, the 7th of September. We were up early to see the parade, bugles sounding and flags flying, green and gold. What a reception for us in my country! Later, we rode the cable car to the top of Sugar Loaf, first to dome-shaped Urca against Sugar Loaf and then, swinging in the wind, to the pinnacle. The view was fantastic. We had supper in the restaurant on the mountain.

When we reached Santos, one of my cousins by marriage, Geoffrey Sewell, came to the docks to help us through customs. We had a new refrigerator, which Mother and Dad had given us, and we had a hard time persuading the customs people that it was our household refrigerator. Geoffrey's long acquaintance with these officials got us through without heavy duty charges, but while we were haggling, someone stole two precious scrolls painted for us by an artist of the hill country of Hunan. We went up the mountain to São Paulo on the old roller-coaster road, replaced since the old days by a double highway.

At the Landes home in Campinas we were greeted with sky rockets. Father had them ready and set them off whirring through the air and bursting with a flash and a boom! Mother had her inimitable southern-fried chicken on the table.

Campinas can get miserably cold and windy for a few weeks in June and July. Otherwise it is a pleasant, sunny city. We stayed with my parents while we looked for a house. Mother had put all her knickknacks out of reach of little hands, but after a few days she said, "I needn't have bothered. Your children don't meddle." There was one thing which had an appeal that threatened to break down this good behavior, the strawberries in Mother's garden. Natlie found the red berries irresistible.

We found a house just a block away from Mother and Father. Chalmers was unpacking some of our things when a tricycle emerged from a barrel. Paul came running. "My tricycle!"

"Wait a minute." Chalmers started to put it together and found a cotter pin missing.

"Where can I get one of these?" he asked Mother.

"You might try the filling station at the foot of the hill." Instructed on how to ask for the pin, Chalmers went to the filling station. To his question, the garage man answered, "*Nâo tenho. O senhor tem pressa?*"

Chalmers understood the negative *Nâo*. But the next phrase was a puzzle. *Tem* is part of the verb *to have*. He didn't know what he should have, so he went back up the hill to find out. Mother laughed. "*Pressa* means *haste*. 'Do you have haste?' The man was asking you if you were in a hurry." Chalmers learned to understand Portuguese quickly, reading the newspaper daily in Portuguese. He soon had a good vocabulary, but the complicated grammar remained a difficulty for a long time. Mother helped Chalmers with pronunciation.

In the United States during the Depression and post-Depression years the U.S. churches sent out few missionaries. Now that there were again funds, several couples came to join us in Campinas. Among them were the Buyers. They rented a house just around the corner from us. Norah and Jim had two sons, Larry and Bobby. Since both the parents were studying Portuguese, I took care of the boys for part of the day along with my children.

I found going to the downtown Presbyterian Church an outlet for my spirit. Reverend Julio Ferreira, a professor at the Seminary, and his wife Dona Alzira, had an interesting Sunday School class which I joined as an assistant. Mothers with their preschool children gathered in a large room of the educational building. After an opening period of singing, prayer, and acknowledgment of birthdays, we divided into two separate circles at opposite ends of the room. Dr. Julio taught the adult class of mothers and Dona Alzira kept the children busy with Bible stories and handwork. If a child was having a hard time that day, he or she could run over to mother.

This happy year was coming to an end when we went to the meeting of the Central Brazil Mission. All missionaries of the United Presbyterian Church USA (Northern Presbyterian), to which we belonged, gathered for business and fellowship. We met this year at Bennet, a Methodist School for girls, in Rio de Janeiro. One morning Chalmers and Father were working on a committee when the lunch bell rang. As everyone filed out of the room, the person who was responsible for locking the door gave the key to Chalmers, who was still working. When he finished, Chalmers locked the door and hurried to the dining room. The only catch was that, while he assumed that he was the last straggler, my father was still in a nook of the room. We were all enjoying our meal when Father arrived. He had pushed a table to the door, hoisted himself and squeezed through the transom. Chalmers was not allowed soon to forget how he had locked up his father-in-law.

The decision which most affected each missionary family at Mission Meeting was our field assignment. The Brownes were assigned to Jatai, a town in western Goiás which was the hub of a field that extended over an area half the size of Ohio.

After Mission Meeting, with a certain amount of trepidation, we packed and set out. We stopped first in Rio Verde, where Dr. and Mrs. Gordon welcomed us into their home as if we were close kin. Our children succumbed to the intestinal flu endemic to the region. Dr. Gordon assured us, "People who haven't lived here are sure to catch this bug. But their systems soon become immune."

Dr. and Mrs. Gordon had started their medical clinic in a small rented house. Now their work had grown into a compound with hospital, school of nursing, and an organized church. This hospital became the model for health care in the whole region. The spirit of the place was one of prayer, trust in God, and the sharing of the knowledge of God's love and grace. Doctors and nurses were trained and seasoned here to go into other towns and open similar centers. Dr. Suahil Rahal, after his years with Dr. Gordon, went on to found three hospitals. He said, "I learned theory in medical school, but I learned to be a doctor with Dr. Gordon."

Mrs. Gordon had the qualities of a pastor. The church in Rio Verde eventually grew to the point that it could call and support a Brazilian pastor, largely through the work of Helen Gordon. When Chalmers came as missionary pastor, the Rio Verde congregation was still part of his parish.

From Rio Verde we traveled on to Jatai and took up residence in the Mission house. The front door opened right onto the sidewalk of a large square which suffered from the malady of many squares in small towns: it was always about to be made into something. Each mayor scrapped the plans of the previous mayor for a better, more ambitious project. So this square billowed in red dust in the dry season and ran in rivulets of red mud in the rainy season.

High-ceilinged, the house had a small anteroom which Chalmers used for a study, a large living room, a dining area, three bedrooms, a huge kitchen and a bathroom clear at the back of the kitchen. Our property ran steeply downhill with a long staircase from the kitchen to a landing by the laundry facilities and water tank and backyard. Scorpions were living in the garage under the house, but we routed them before anyone was hurt.

Jatai was an old-fashioned town, built on the side of a hill. Main Street ran into our square at the lower end of town. The building the Jatai congregation was using as a church was on a street running up the hill from Main Street. The airport was at the very top of the hill. The Presbyterian School was at the upper level, too. Our colleagues, Ruth and Samuel Irvine Graham, were the directors of the school. Dr. Graham shocked the community by donning jeans and boots and helping move materials, as he oversaw the construction of the school buildings. His hands-on style became a model and inspiration for the young people. Both he and Ruth were cheery and won a place of respect and affection.

Chalmers began to ride circuit in his vast parish. He used to say, "In the U.S.A. the early Presbyterians were the founders of institutions of learning and the Methodists were circuit riders. Here in Brazil the Methodists have been founding more schools and the Presbyterians have more circuit riders." Chalmers usually took along an elder on these trips. Senhor Pedro was one of the men who liked to go with him.

Sr. Pedro had been a lone farmer in the southwest of the state of Goiás. He had bought a Bible on a trip to Uberlandia, Minas, where he went to buy salt, yard goods, and nails. He had been reading the Bible for years when, one day, Robert Lodwick, the pastor who preceded Chalmers, paid the family a visit. Sr. Pedro and his wife asked to be baptized. After joining the church, Sr. Pedro moved to Jataí where his younger children could go to school. His adult children, who remained in the west, were illiterate.

Sometimes caught by the approach of night as they traveled, Chalmers and Sr. Pedro asked for lodging at a farmhouse by the way. They were received with courtesy, for it is the rule of those distant places to offer hospitality to the stranger. The wife would serve them a good meal, and after supper Chalmers would suggest vespers. Sometimes the householders would be distinctly embarrassed, having been taught that Protestants were heretics. More often they would be at least curious, then would warm up to the hymns Chalmers and Sr. Pedro sang. They listened to the scripture read and the explanation made. After ending with prayer, Chalmers would ask to be excused and go to bed. Sr. Pedro would remain answering questions. He carried two Bibles with him, the one he used daily and a Roman Catholic version. He would explain that the Roman Catholic Bible had more books, the Apocrypha. Otherwise the Bibles were essentially the same. He would help them compare verses from both.

In January Chalmers added to his responsibilities the pastoral oversight of Ray Pittman's field to our north while the Pittmans went on furlough. He wrote in a letter to his parents dated January 1952, "The pressures and requests are so many and varied from this vast field, and especially in this early period. I miss the team way we were able to handle things in Chenhsien. We need divine guidance to choose what should be done and trust to leave some things undone." He did have the help of the mission pilot, George Glass, and was able to circuit-ride by plane in the extensive Caiapônia area.

There were always the scattered congregations of our own parish to visit. I went with Chalmers when circumstances permitted. Mother was visiting us and I could leave our children and household in her care when we went to visit Sr. Santo. We stopped two nights for services in congregations along the way, then had only a short distance to go. We came to a stream that had no bridge. A farmhouse stood at the top of the hill and we had greeted the men sitting on the porch as we went by. There were two places where cars had forded the river. Chalmers looked them over—neither looked good, but one had some logs laid down in the stream and we chose this one. When the jeep got its wheels on the logs they slithered apart and the jeep sank down into the bed of the stream. A boy ran down from the house. He declaimed in a high-pitched voice, "You should have gone this way," pointing to the other fording place. "You wouldn't have stuck if you had gone over here." He exasperatingly repeated these words over and over.

A young woman from our last stop was traveling with us. The three of us got out in the water and tried to push the jeep, but it didn't budge. Chalmers found a long pole and placed one end under the front axle. "You two," he said to us, "sit on the other end." We sat on the pole and the front wheels lifted out of the mire enough for Chalmers to push some chocks under them. "I'm going to drive for the bank," he said. "When the jeep clears the pole, jump!" The motor roared, the jeep moved unstuck, the pole flew into the air and we fell into the stream, but the jeep was across. We were wet but unhurt. After the first consternation, we began to laugh. A bit drippy, we climbed aboard the jeep and dried out as the jeep moved through the air.

Sr. Santo and his family, living near a fast-moving river in a mud-and-wattle house with a thatched roof, welcomed us with great joy. Sr. Santo was thin and wiry and brown, as was his wife. He was something of a patriarch in his area and the influence of their lives was great upon the farm families. He was intensely aware of God's presence and bubbled over with enthusiasm for the kingdom of God.

We talked that evening by the light of a kerosene lamp, then curled up in our hammocks. About 4 a.m. we woke, feeling cold. A wind blowing across the river came through the chinks in the walls. Everyone got up and they built a fire in the kitchen, where we all gathered about. We were glad to drink the hot coffee and eat the boiled manioc roots that were passed around.

I was the first missionary wife to have come to this far place. We had brought our little suitcase organ and everyone admired it as we took it out of the jeep. I played hymns and we all sang. About ten o'clock some people from nearby farms arrived and we held a worship service. We had barely finished when a new contingent of neighbors appeared, so we had a second service with them. After lunch we started packing to go home. We had put the organ snugly in the jeep when some more people arrived. Sr. Santo urged us to take the organ back out, and we held a third service to everyone's satisfaction.

By the time we got away, it was too late to drive all the way home. We checked into a hostel in a town along our way. It was campaign time and the town was expecting the visit of a candidate. He was late and, as we mingled with the crowd, the people were restless. Chalmers drove the jeep to the middle of the square and, using the jeep's battery, showed slides of the life of Christ. He had a huge audience. We had some pamphlets and gospel portions and distributed all of them to eagerly reaching hands.

One of the families that came near was that of the house on the hill above the stream where our jeep got stuck. They proudly told everybody that they knew us, that we had gone right by their house. We returned the warmth they showed, but wished they had shown their friendliness when we needed help with our mired jeep.

That same year Seventh-Day Adventists came into that region. Sr. Santo's sister and her family moved into the Adventist church. One of their young preachers challenged Chalmers to a debate. Chalmers agreed and they met one afternoon and debated the question of the right day for the Sabbath day of rest, Saturday or Sunday. Many people attended. After the debate one man said to Chalmers, "You didn't win, you tied."

Chalmers answered, "I wasn't trying to win. I wanted only to show that we have Biblical backing for Sunday as our day of rest." The Church in that area gained strength as the people had to consider the basis of their faith. Since some Presbyterian leaders went to the Adventist Church, other members who had been lukewarm now took on leadership roles.

Back in Jatai our children were growing apace. I taught them at home so that they would learn to read and write English first. It is easier to move from reading English to reading Portuguese because Portuguese is a more phonetic language. We used the Calvert School correspondence courses, though we found that it took too long for lessons to go to Baltimore and back for appraisal. While studying English, the children had friends from our church family and the neighborhood. On Sunday mornings after Sunday School a flock of children came to play in our backyard until lunchtime. Chalmers and I had a disagreement about whether to allow the children to play with a soccer ball on Sunday in our backyard. The Protestant churches in Brazil were very strong for Sabbath observance and frowned on Sunday soccer. I felt that playing ball was better than having the children make up some possibly less savory games. We finally allowed the soccer ball on Sunday, limited to the backyard.

One Sunday an outcry from out back brought us running to the rescue. George had fallen from a board propped against a mango tree. His right arm was dangling in an odd way, broken just above the wrist. We took him to our local doctor who set his arm in a cast, but as there was no X-ray machine to verify the set, George and I went to Rio Verde. He did have to have his wrist reset. On a Sunday just a year later George fell out of the mango tree and broke his other arm. This time Chalmers took him to Rio Verde.

On Sunday afternoons the children came back to our house. We found places for all comers in the living room. I taught them hymns and choruses and told Bible stories. Then I sent them all home so that our family could gather on our bed and read stories in English or talk. A man from our congregation, who was a little strange, used to come in after the children left and look at National Geographic magazines. He would call to me to explain some picture. One afternoon he said to me, "I can't understand this English you speak with your children but I do understand Mr. Browne's evangelical English that he speaks in his sermons." This was the way he perceived the English rhythms Chalmers still had in his speech when he spoke Portuguese.

We acquired a one-year-old pet deer, Beet. We fenced an area for Beet, which doubled as a chicken yard. After we had been away for several weeks at Mission Meeting, the children dashed out to see Beet with George in the lead. Beet felt his territory was being invaded and butted George in the stomach. He was quickly driven away and George's scratches were minimal.

Several months later Chalmers had gone to a meeting in São Paulo. George Glass, mission pilot, was bringing a calf from the Heifer Project to Jataí. The heifer, in the back seat of the little Cessna, amused herself, but not George, by licking George's ears during the flight. What missionaries don't suffer for the cause! Chalmers sent me a note with George inviting me to come to São Paulo with the returning plane. We could go to a movie and then travel back to Jataí together. Regretfully I wrote my husband a note saying I felt I couldn't leave the children.

That afternoon, after the plane had left, I heard agonized screams from the backyard. I flew down the stairs and around the storage room. In the chicken yard Margie, with might and main, was holding Beet by the horns. Paul lay prone. With a stick I was able to drive Beet away, but he had already gored Paul twice, once in the groin and once in the calf of his leg.

I was able to get hold of Dr. Boris, a Russian doctor who had moved to town with his wife, Irene. Dr. Boris asked if Paul had had tetanus shots. I replied in the affirmative. Dr. Boris decided to boost Paul's tetanus vaccine, but fearful that too much in Paul's system might be harmful, he sat in our dining room talking with me in his cramped English and giving Paul small doses of tetanus vaccine every half hour. I was sincerely grateful to Dr. Boris and thankful to God that I hadn't been away at this crisis time. We soon parted with Beet after this episode of male ferocity. Unlike Bella, the little female deer of my youth, males evidently don't make very good pets.

Irene and Boris were a very odd couple. They were kind and service-oriented, but also introverted. Irene came often to confide in me. She and Boris fought to the point of throwing plates at each other. I tried to persuade her to go to church with me. She refused many times. Finally she said to me, "I am Russian Orthodox. I must worship in an Orthodox church." I looked into her eyes and realized the terrible alienation she felt from God in Jataí, the God she had left behind in Russia.

One of our eccentric friends was Grandpa, a winsome old American prospector with fading blue eyes, who would come in from the hills for a few days of civilization. He wouldn't sleep in the house, so we made up a cot for him in the shed. He always had just heard of some fabulous mine where he was going to make his fortune. Finally Grandpa didn't come again.

At Christmas time a family came to us with a newborn baby. The father was a gaunt American and the mother a Bororo Indian, and they had no place to go. They stayed with us for a week. Bororos have very different habits from ours, but we were blessed by them and the tiny child.

Each one of our children was so precious. Paul was only eight when he went off up the hill a mile to Portuguese school with Margie and George. Shortly thereafter he came home using some bad language. "Paul! Don't you know not to say those words?"

"I won't anymore, Mother," he promised. A few days later he again used strong language.

"Why, Paul!" I remonstrated.

He began to cry. "I don't mean to, but I hear the other boys saying those things." I had to comfort him.

One day Paul was helping me in the shed.

"Mother," he said, "George is the oldest boy and Margie is the oldest girl. Natalie is the baby and I'm nothing."

"You are the one named especially for us," I told him, "Paul for your mother and Chalmers for your father. You are a very special child to us!"

Natalie was five and ready for kindergarten. We had lovely material from Calvert, crayons and construction paper in all colors. I said to Chalmers, "Wouldn't it be a good idea to have kindergarten over at the church each morning and share the lessons with other five- and six-year-olds?"

Chalmers agreed and the Jatai kindergarten was born. I followed the orientation I had received in Berkeley and involved the mothers as much as possible. During the year there were between six and ten children in attendance. One day a little girl said, "I don't want to sit near her. She's black."

True, the little girl referred to was very dark. I asked, "Are all flowers white? Aren't you glad that there are blue flowers and pink flowers and red ones? God likes the flowers all colors and he decided he liked people all colors too. That's why we aren't all the same color." That was the end of racism in our kindergarten.

After this successful year of kindergarten I was ready to move on and teach Natalie her first-grade course. However, Chalmers caught me up short. "You can't start something for the community and then leave it at your convenience. You need to continue the kindergarten. Take it as an opportunity to train someone."

So I girded up my loins and asked one of Sr. Pedro's daughters, Noemia, to come in as my assistant and understudy. Somewhere we found funds to pay her. Natalie was happy to go to kindergarten in the morning and study an hour of first grade in the afternoon. After a happy second year Noemina took over. Today the kindergarten is part of the Evangelical School on the hill.

- 15 -

Brazil's Wild West

The yearly zone meeting of leaders of our region was to be held in Formosa, Goiás, one of the most distant fields. It was a real challenge to get our family of five and all the suitcases and bundles necessary for a two-week sojourn into a small jeep. George and Paul were helping in the jeep when Chalmers decided to move the vehicle a few feet. Paul lost his balance and was about to fall headlong out of the back when George grabbed him by the ankle and held on until the jeep stopped. Such episodes fill parents with thankfulness to God for his angels around about their children.

On our way we spent the night at a hostel in Goiânia the state capital. In the morning the gas in our jeep's tank was low.

"I'm afraid someone has helped themselves to a few gallons of gasoline," Chalmers said. "I filled the tank last night."

He bought a new cap with a lock for the tank, and we were soon on the road again. Our road from Goiânia northward took us over Brazil's rolling uplands. About 130 miles from Goiânia, we went past the wide, sparse plain where Brasília was to mushroom to become the new capital of the country.

John and Jean Miller welcomed us warmly into their home in Formosa. They had arranged lodging for all the evangelists, doctors, and other leaders, both Brazilian and American, in homes in the community. We spent several days in worship together, hearing one another and discussing requests for the work of the coming year. The Millers, a young couple doing a tremendous job over a vast geographical area of farms and small villages, had one dear little boy, Larry. Not long after this meeting, John was away on a trip when Larry became ill and died before his father could return. We all mourned. Despite the travails the Millers have continued working in Goiás.

On our way back from Formosa, we stopped at noon by a stream that ran sparkling over stones in the sunlight and then slipped into the dappled shadow of trees. We ate our picnic lunch, waded in the stream and played in the grassy space where our jeep was parked. An hour slipped by unnoticed. When we returned to the jeep, we couldn't find the key. We searched in the grass, along the stream bank, everywhere we had been. No key. Our situation was critical—nothing but grass and trees for miles and miles and miles. The road was seldom traveled; night might come with no one to know of our predicament. Chalmers called us together and we formed a circle with our arms about each other.

"Our Lord," Chalmers prayed. "Thank you for this beautiful place. You know our need. Help us to find the key."

We scattered to search again. Chalmers put his hand in his shirt pocket for the third or fourth time and felt the key to the new gas tank top. He marched over to the jeep, inserted the key in the ignition and turned it. The motor came to life. We all came running.

"You found it," I cried.

"It's the gas tank key! It's the same as the ignition."

We thanked God that he had foreseen our need and answered our prayer days before when Chalmers bought the tank cap. Two days later we reached home, weary but satisfied.

That was not the last episode wiith the jeep keys. George Glass arrived to take Chalmers on a trip through his parish and we all went to the airport with Chalmers to bid them good-bye. The children loved to run and play at the airport. Chalmers kissed us and clambered up into his seat, the door shut. The plane turned to taxi down the field. I put my hand into my pocket. The jeep keys! Chalmers had driven to the airport. The plane in its cloud of dust was halfway down the field. I started to run. When George turned the plane around for takeoff, they saw me panting down the field and waited. Chalmers realized why the preacher's wife was making a spectacle of herself and had the keys dangling from his finger when I reached the plane.

The next time we went to the airport, we saw Irvine Graham and his cousin, who had been visiting in Jataí, off to Goiânia. We were standing beside Ruth, who was staying on duty, as the plane curved away, catching the rays of the late morning sun. Some two hours later we received the terrible news. The plane had exploded in midair before it reached Goiânia. Trembling we went to tell Ruth. Her response was "No! There is some mistake!" But it was no mistake. There were important political figures on the plane, causing conjectures and rumors, but no answers about the cause of the crash.

When we told the children they began to cry. They dearly loved Mr. Graham. I reminded them, "You know how good it is to hear Mr. Graham's cheery 'Hello!' when he walks into the house. Just think of him calling 'Hello!' as he walks into heaven."

This idea pleased the children, but with Ruth it was impossible for mere human beings to comfort her. She went to Goiânia for the memorial service, then returned to her tasks at the school. We went up to see her and took her for rides out into the country. We let her talk about Irvine. Fortunately, she had many good Brazilian friends, very warm and sensitive. Their faith mingled with hers to give her strength. George and Helena Glass came to take her place so that she could go on furlough and visit her sons in the United States.

Chalmers and I found ourselves facing a pastoral problem. The position of the Roman Catholic Church on birth control dominated the lives of our people. Parents with five or more children legitimately wanted to be free of further pregnancies. Their own health and that of the children already born to them as well as reasonable living conditions for all were at stake. On the farms and in the small villages people had no recourse to anything but old wives' tales. The only means of birth control endorsed by the Roman Catholic Church, other than abstinence, was the rhythm method. Chalmers and I explained what we knew of the rhythm method to those who asked. We decided to try it out ourselves.

In 1954 the zone meeting, the get-together of church leaders, was in Jataí with our house used as the hospitality center. We were serving meals each day to about thirty people. On the third day of the meetings I became very ill with a high fever. I lay in bed with my face to the wall, unable to participate in anything. Meals had been planned and supplies bought, so colleagues stepped in and saw the final days through.

I got well enough to go to Belo Horizonte with Chalmers for Mission Meeting. Mother was staying at home in Campinas and we saw our foursome off to visit her before we left for Belo Horizonte.

The season was dry and our trip in the jeep was through red dust so dense that at times it was hard to see the road. We arrived at the entrance to the Methodist School where we were being housed and our best friends shied away from us, we were so grimy.

It was fun to see all our missionary friends and the new babies, some just beginning to toddle about. Still, I wasn't feeling well. The doctors suggested that I rest. In a few days I miscarried without ever realizing I was pregnant.

We drove to Campinas to pick up our kids and during the few days we spent with Mother and Father, Chalmers worked some long hours on the jeep. Father was concerned and asked me, "Isn't Chalmers spending too much time on that jeep?"

"The time he spends now will save us from being marooned for who knows how long in some desolate place. And remember, horses and mules took constant care when we traveled with them."

Chalmers found it increasingly difficult to keep up with the Jatai church and the other growing churches and congregations in his field. He was encouraging the Jatai young people to help with family groups which met for worship in outlying areas. One Sunday he took some of them to a farm. When they arrived, about sixty people had gathered under the trees beside the farmhouse. Our Jatai young folk started offering some hymn books to the people. Each person, with the exception of two or three men, refused. "I don't know how to read," was the response.

Chalmers came home troubled about illiteracy in the country. People couldn't read the Bible in their homes. We talked about it and decided that something must be done. I started by teaching the church janitor. "I know all the letters," he said, "but I don't know how to put them together." He read *banana* "b-a, ba, n-a, na, n-a, na." After spelling each syllable out, he had no idea what the word was. We made some progress in changing his habits and getting across the idea that reading is for meaning.

Chalmers and I decided to make a quick overnight trip to the farm of Jerónimo and Elvira. They were dear to us and we hadn't seen them for a long time. George and Margie were responsible enough to see themselves and their brother and sister off to school in the morning, and we would be home by lunch time. We left in the late afternoon. It was getting dark fast. The rainy season had cut deep ruts in the road. Our wheels slipped into two such ruts and the floor of the jeep caught in the middle. We got out with flashlights. Chalmers had crawled under the jeep to put the jack in place when he suddenly erupted and started feverishly tearing off his trousers. He had lain down on a red ant nest, the kind that really sting. I helped brush the ants off his legs and applied lotion from our kit.

We managed to heave the jeep back on the road and arrived at the farm. Everything was dark. We knocked; no answer. We were very weary, so we opened the door, which was made of staves that easily lifted. We spread our bedding on the pole bed in the master bedroom and went to sleep with the moonlight drifting through the slits between the upright poles of the wall.

Early the next morning we went for a shower in the cold water falling from the dug-out conduit. Water was channeled from a spring to the house in hollowed logs that ran right past the kitchen before emptying in a little waterfall for bathing. Not long after, Jerónimo arrived on horseback. He had been over at a neighbors' house for the night as Elvira and the children had gone into town. She had taken a different path and we had missed each other.

I couldn't go with Chalmers on all his trips and share his adventures. But even in town there were hazards. Chalmers had gone calling up the hill. On the way home in the dark he fell in a huge hole that reached up to his neck. The rains had gouged it into the road. Fortunately it wasn't too wet and caused only bruises and sprains.

In late September I discovered that I was pregnant. Chalmers and I had not been thinking of our early dream of five children, but the rhythm method returned us to it. Now, seven years after Natalie had arrived in the family, we were going to receive our dream, a fifth child.

Life went on and the children of our Jatai congregation practiced for the Christmas pageant and caroling. The church women made small bags of bright crepe paper and filled them with hard candy to give to all the children who came to the Christmas program. During the Christmas season we followed the custom of the town and visited our friends and neighbors to see their creches wreathed in *pitomba* branches with their dark green leaves and clusters of cherry-size, golden fruit.

In the newyear, Jim and Norah Buyers joined our Jatai family to work with the school, now named for Samuel Irvine Graham. The school was growing and becoming a real model for education in the area. Bible was part of the curriculum. Ethical and moral standards brought vitality and worth to the students and the community.

Chalmers was spending many hours helping the Jatai congregation find an architect and plan a church building. They began construction and the foundation was growing quickly. The ceremony of the laying of the cornerstone was set for the end of May. Everything seemed to be happening at once. Our baby was due in mid-May, then the zone meeting would be held in Caiaponia .

Mother came to stay with the children. Chalmers took me to Rio Verde. The baby seemed to be in no hurry. Chalmers spent May 21, our wedding anniversary, with me. He brought me a gift of a demitasse coffee service decorated with dainty little flowers. It didn't matter that the set was not of the finest china for it spoke of our sharing of life.

Chalmers went back to Jatai and I went into the hospital. On Sunday, May 28, 1955, Chalmers presided at the cornerstone laying in Jatai, jumped into the jeep and reached Rio Verde in time to hold my hand while Elizabeth Jane was born. That was an evening of thanksgiving for our perfect new daughter.

George Glass had come with the plane to move personnel to the zone meeting. I pleaded with Dr. Gordon to let us go home, where Mother would take care of us while everyone else, including Chalmers and the Gordons, would go to zone meeting. Tuesday morning Mrs. Gordon with newborn Libby in her arms went with me in the plane to Jatai. Libby had her first plane ride when she was not yet two days old.

She had been such an active baby in the womb that I thought she was a boy. Margie and Natalie were enchanted. George and Paul had wanted a brother, but forgot their preferences and delighted in their new little sister. She was a beautiful baby from her blond fuzzy head to her delicate pink toes. Mother, who had considered us a bit exaggerated to want a fifth baby, was charmed.

We were now preparing to go on furlough. Chalmers went to São Paulo to see to our passage and other arrangements. While he was away we received a request from Jerónimo and Elvira who were on a farm of friends helping to pick coffee. The note to Chalmers read:

"Please come and hold a service. It is the birthday of the owner of this farm. He isn't a *crente* (Protestant believer), but he would like to have you come."

I thought of the disappointment if I should answer, "Sorry, Chalmers is away," so I decided to go myself. I talked to Acasio, the mechanic who took care of our jeep. He was willing to drive for me the next afternoon. Libby was three months old and should be all right jouncing over the rough roads. We would be back by ten or eleven that night. Margie, Paul, and Natalie wanted to go along, but George elected to stay at home.

It was a three-hour trip by jeep. Halfway along the journey we crossed a high wooden bridge that swayed with the weight of the jeep. Then we climbed a steep hill and went along a road almost invisible in the high grass of the savanna. We were received with joy, and after a birthday party repast, we had a service of songs and prayer for the farm and the owner on his birthday. I read the story of the Prodigal Son and spoke about God's waiting love. We were ready to go home and Acasio started the motor, but the lights were so dim we couldn't see where we were going. We bumbled along for a mile through the grass, but it was hopeless. I remembered the narrow, rickety bridge and decided we would turn back.

Jerónimo and Elvira were surprised to see us return. They were all hospitality, however. Margie and Natalie shared beds with Jerónimo and Elvira's daughters of the same age. Paul and I were given a cot to share. Where would Libby sleep? The big basin for bathing hung on the kitchen wall. I took it down, put a sheepskin into it, spread a baby blanket and laid Libby in this improvised crib. I had brought an extra bottle of milk for her and she slept through the night. Jerónimo was all for sending one of the big boys to Jatai on a bicycle to let George know that we were all right. I laughed. "George will be sound asleep," I said. "He won't know if we got home or not."

We started out as soon as it was light. George was calmly making pancakes for our breakfast when we arrived. "I knew you would come or send word what I should do," he said. When Chalmers returned from São Paulo he was contrite. "I should have warned you that the battery was low."

We packed and stored our furniture and other possessions in one room so that the rest of the house could be used in our absence. Before putting things in the room, Chalmers built a platform of beams and boards painted with pitch to prevent termites from getting to them. When most of the packing was done, Chalmers sent me and the girls off to São Paulo. He and the boys stayed to finish up and clean the house. Many friends gathered at the airport to see us off.

When we reached São Paulo, we found that I was being denied permission to travel abroad because our marriage certificate had not been properly documented. Our passage on a steamship had to be canceled. Our Mission office engaged a lawyer and finally the matter was resolved and we had clearance to travel.

We were out at the Congonhas Airport with family and friends and watched the plane we were to board come in. It missed the beginning of the runway and came down midway. The pilot put on the brakes and spun the plane around to stop. Bob McIntire, a friend from Friar Club days, came up to us. "You'll not be going today," he said. "Stop kidding," I countered. But it was true. The landing gear had been damaged and would take time to be repaired.

Since we had an afternoon ahead of us, Bob and Esther McIntire invited Chalmers and me to go to the movies with them. Mother and my sister Bibetteoffered to take care of the children. So we had a night on the town.

We left for Lima the next day. There, we missed our connection with the plane coming from Santiago and were put up by PanAm in a swanky hotel. We went down to dinner and our family looked at the extensive menu with great interest and many questions. Our plane the next day did not leave until evening, and Chalmers took the children to see the ocean while I stayed with Libby. They took off their shoes and waded along the beach. The water was cold! Chalmers stopped at a flowershop and bought me an orchid. I was touched and delighted and put the cellophane box tied with ribbon on the window sill to keep cool. When we boarded the plane I asked the stewardess to put it in the refrigerator. As we approached Cleveland I took the orchid from its box. We were very much surprised to find it was artificial—it had looked so real through the cellophane.

We lived in one of the missionary houses in Wooster for the year. Mother was with us part of the time while Father underwent surgery at the Presbyterian Hospital in New York. All of the children but Libby were in school. Chalmers and I were doing a lot of mission interpretation in the churches. Then we were confronted with a decision as to our work when we returned to Brazil.

Dr. Borges, the moderator of the Presbyterian Church of Brazil, came to Wooster with Dick Waddell, our Mission executive secretary, to ask us to take on literacy work full-time with the Confederation of Evangelical (Protestant) Churches of Brazil. The opportunity seemed exciting and we agreed to the assignment.

In the summer of 1956 we went to Chautauqua for an extension course from Syracuse University taught by Bob Laubach and his father, Dr. Frank Laubach, famous for his literacy work in many parts of the world.

Edie Powers, Chalmers' cousin, was able to accompany us and take care of Libby while we attended classes. Natalie, who had never had measles, was quarantined during a measles scare. She never came down with the measles and we were glad when she was able to join George, Margie, and Paul in the many activities available to the children. Chalmers and I had a lot of homework, but we still found time to learn to play canasta with our friends.

When we returned to Wooster we started preparing to return to live in São Paulo with adult basic education as our full-time work. Then we received an urgent call from Brazil. Would we consider going to Chapecó in Santa Catarina? The whole Presbyterian field was soon to be completely without Mission work as Mr. Wright was about to retire. What could we say? Here were churches and congregations scattered like sheep without a shepherd. We thought and prayed about it and answered that if this was where the Mission wanted us, we would go.

We had been perturbed by a report that came to us in a roundabout way that the church in Jatai had been asked if they wanted us to return. Their answer had been in the negative. We knew that Chalmers' load had been so great that at times he had lost patience. We were glad that the Jatai congregation had been given a chance to make their wishes known. We discovered later that it wasn't so much our personalities as the nature of the field that had prompted their response. Jatai and Rio Verde wanted pastors of their own who didn't have to cover a large geographical area. Both churches were assigned Brazilian pastors, still supported in part by the Mission.

- 16 -

The Wild South

Neither Chalmers nor I had been in the south of Brazil. What would be the needs in our new home? Santa Catarina could be uncomfortably cold in June and July. So we set out to find some appropriate clothing for our children. But summer clothing was in full swing in the stores in America in May and June. We couldn't find corduroy slacks or winter nightwear. We settled for jeans and sweaters. Packing and moving in whichever direction was always the bane of my life. When all decisions were irreversible and all the drums and trunks and suitcases were aboard the ship, I could start to enjoy the trip.

We spent hours keeping Libby afloat in the ship's pool. The older children were on their own, since they swam like fish. We read books together and played shuffleboard on deck. In the evenings Chalmers and I walked the decks together marveling at the multitude of stars we cannot see near our brightly electrified cities. As our ship rolled over the swells and down into the troughs of dark water, the shimmering heaven high above wrapped itself about us. At the equator Neptune was welcomed aboard to hold court for a day with ketchup blood running and people thrown into the pool.

On this return to Brazil we spent six months in Campinas for a refresher course in Portuguese. We lived in a mission-rented house furnished with the basics. It was a pleasant time living less than a mile from my parents. We didn't have a car but enjoyed riding the Campinas trolleys, to school and to church as well as to the Castelo, a tower at the top of the nearest big hill, and out to the Taquaral lake for picnics.

George started going to boarding school while we were in Campinas. JMC (Curso José Manuel da Conceição) was an hour away from São Paulo on the Sorocabana railway. This secondary school served young people from interior churches who lacked opportunity for good education in a Christian environment. George could come home for a weekend now and then. Margie spent some time with my cousins Joyce and Geoffrey Sewell in São Paulo preparing for entrance exams into Brazil's secondary school.

In early 1957 we went to Jataí to get our household belongings and the older children wanted to go along. Margie, especially, was distressed at the thought of leaving all her friends in Jataí. Libby stayed with my sister, Mary Elizabeth (Bibette). Eunice Veloso Rezende had been part of our household in Jataí and the young members of our family begged to have Eunice go with us to our new home in Chapecó, Santa Catarina. Eunice's family was large and poor. Her father was ill with "fogo selvagem," a painful dermatological ailment, and her mother was a querulous woman with a heavy load on her inadequate shoulders. They were willing to let Eunice go with us. Eunice herself, a brunette with very white skin, knew a life that had its seamy side. She had a lusty romanticism that didn't want to obey rules. But as long as she was under our roof, she was tractable in her actions if not in her outlook on life. It was good for our girls to share their room and life with someone who needed support. On the other hand, Eunice's attitudes did have an influence on them.

We were now driving a large van, so we were able to take our family and hand baggage on the long move of over one thousand miles. The furniture arrived by truck soon after we did.

We rented a house on the hillside. Unlike the brick or adobe houses in the central and northern parts of Brazil, most of the houses in the south were built of wood. Pines, especially the Paraná pine, grow abundantly in south Brazil. Across the street from us was a sawmill and lumberyard and we had encountered trucks laden with logs or pine boards as we had driven south.

In some ways Chapecó was a wilder town than Jataí. There had been a lynching in the town shortly before we came and the first time we went to São Paulo in our van with a Chapecó license plate, people moved away from us as though we were dangerous.

The original immigrants to the state of Santa Catarina were soldiers who fought in the war with Paraguay and then stayed after the war and married native women. The second group to immigrate to the state were Germans, the third Italians. Chapecó still had distinct groupings of these three strains.

The huge Roman Catholic Church of Chapecó, built of masonry with its twin towers, dominated the big square at the top of the hill. Wide, unpaved avenues ran down the hill only to climb up the far slope. Our small church was a frame, one-room building on a side street. Some of the families in our church had been Lutherans, and a Lutheran pastor still paid visits to Chapecó once or twice a year to conduct services in the German language. There was also a small but lively Assembly of God church across town.

In the wet winter months the mud was ankle deep in the streets and we needed boots to walk the four blocks from our house to our church. During the three and a half years we lived in Chapecó it snowed once, but we were away at the time and didn't share in the excitement. Snow was rare, though often we woke to see everything covered with frost and a shell of ice over puddles. In our home, two wood-burning, iron stoves, one the cooking stove in the kitchen, and the other a potbellied one in the study in the middle of the house, provided heat. The living room and the children's bedrooms opened onto this warming space

Our parish stretched along the road that ran from the Uruguay River to the south of Chapecó and Xanxeré, and on to Abelardo Luz to the north. The churches in Chapecó and Xanxeré were more firmly established, and other congregations and preaching points were widely scattered along the road or up in the hills.

George had gone back to boarding school at JMC. Margie, Paul, Natalie, and Eunice attended the Catholic schools. A complaint came to us from the Protestant community that the teachers in the Catholic schools discriminated against the non-Catholic students. So when a request came from the nuns that I teach English in the secondary school, Chalmers and I agreed that it would be good to have a Protestant presence on the faculty. I liked teaching English and I enjoyed getting to know some of the nuns.

Another wonderful thing about this period of our life was the work with the youth of the church. Our own children were a rallying point and we soon had lively meetings, projects, and parties. The kingpins in the church were a couple who were of German descent. Sr. Oscar was a respected merchant in town. Dona Vale was a very self-possessed lady with strong opinions. Sometimes they differed with us on the discipline of young people, their ideas being of a more Prussian cast than ours, but we managed to iron out the discrepancies.

One project that I particularly enjoyed was the after-school tutoring that some of us, including young people, organized to help children with their homework. One girl I tutored was lively and yet was not learning to read. In just a few weeks of one-on-one work she got hold of the idea and was able to read with her class.

Xanxeré was very eager to have Chalmers' attention. We would sometimes go over and stay for several days at Xanxeré. Our family camped in the rooms at the back of the church. We held special events. People from the country round about found lodging with relatives or friends in town. The morning might begin with a worship service followed by Bible study. Then it would be time for dinner. I was usually much involved in seeing that there was enough food. The women of the congregation cooked. Rice and beans and meat and *mate* would come steaming from the large pots and kettles. In the afternoon there would be volleyball for the teenagers and favorite circle games and races for the younger set. The day ended with another service to which neighbors and friends were invited.

After we returned to Chapecó, Chalmers started out again, this time to go to Abelardo Luz at the northwestern edge of our parish, a trip of four or five hours. He returned a day later than expected and explained: "I put up in Sr. José's hotel, then went across the river to visit. As I got back I heard shots and saw a man standing on the steps of the inn next door and firing into the air. Smoke was rolling out of the building! People began rushing about with buckets of water. Sparks were threatening our inn. I climbed on top of our hotel and doused the roof as buckets of water were handed up. Our hotel was saved, but the other pretty well burned down.

"Then last night I started for Xanxeré, after a late service. I was about halfway there when, as I came around a bend, six men with guns poited at me surrounded the van. I thought they were going to rob me, but they were a posse out to find a robber. They asked to look in my car. They searched it thoroughly, then let me go on. I was somewhat shaken."

In his travels, Chalmers had discovered a farm far up in the hills where there were believers who hadn't been visited for many years. He took me to see this old couple, their children and grandchildren. To reach this place we had to go over unbelievably steep roads. At one spot we found a truck that hadn't made the grade and was sitting on its tailgate with all four wheels helpless in the air. The driver had walked for help.

We reached the ancient house constructed from logs and set in the midst of trees. Inside the rafters were black with the smoke of years of cooking fires, and the floors were of tamped earth. The people were amazingly gentle and soft-spoken, communicating their welcome with smiles and little gestures of delight.

"Yes, we remember Sr. Jorge. He used to come once a year, from Ponta Grossa." Sr. Jorge was my grandfather, George Landes, who had traveled over this field by horseback at the turn of the century. As we gathered for worship, the old couple, the sons and daughters and neighbors asked for hymn after hymn to be sung. They had read the words in the hymnbook, but did not know the tunes. We sang all the ones we knew as they chose them. After Chalmers spoke, I told them about "the fellowship of the least coin," a practice of many churches around the world. Each woman gives the coin of least value in her country. I supplied each woman present a centavo, and passed around a basket so that they could contribute their "least coin" with women all over the world. They understood and were moved. Their kind, friendly feeling could extend past the green walls of their forest to reach out to other women like themselves.

When we returned home we found Natalie, then nine years old, all packed and sitting out on the front steps. She was about to set out for her grandmother's. She planned to walk to Xanxeré, and there get the mission horse and ride all the way to Campinas. Her brother and sisters had been teasing her and she was not about to take it anymore. Chalmers persuaded her rather easily that we would be very sad if she left us and we would talk to her siblings.

Our children were all in school, so we hired Lydia, a tall, gangly, blond and freckled, eighteen-year-old German girl, to do housework and be with Libby. She came from a farm family at some distance from Chapecó. The first time Chalmers and I left the house after she came, we forgot something, and returned to get it. We found Lydia, Eunice, Margie, Paul, Natalie, and Libby all in the living room with the gramophone on and Lydia pretending to play the guitar. All of them were dancing wildly and singing at the top of their lungs. Our appearance stunned them into silence.

"What's this all about?" I asked.

Lydia admitted that at her home, they took the opportunity when their parents were away to do all the things they weren't allowed to do.

"If you want to do this kind of thing," Chalmers reasoned with them, "it is better to do so when we are at home. We can then vouch for you. When you are here without us, you have to be very careful of your reputation." They all knew that Chapecó was a place where people liked to gossip, and they saw the point.

Chalmers and I had not forgotten our calling to help people learn to read. Chalmers visited a man who was in jail for murder. His common-law wife and four children had been coming to church. While the prisoner was very fair with freckles, his wife was a beautiful chocolate. It was hard to think of this man as a criminal. He was a humble, illiterate farmer and a gentle soul. It was generally understood that he had been made a scapegoat. With a Laubach primer adapted from Spanish, Chalmers started teaching Sr. Antonio.

Before we left Chapecó, Sr. Antonio was moved to a prison in Florianopolis, the capital of the state. We helped Dona Sebastiana and the children move to the farm attached to the prison. There they could see Sr. Antonio. A lawyer who devoted his time to helping people who were dubiously condemned was going to take Sr. Antonio's case.

My pupil, Lourdes, came to me in a different way. Lourdes and her family were members of our church. Since there was no women's organization in the Chapecó church, I invited the women to get together to discuss creating a women's group. A good number of women, including Lourdes, came at the appointed hour. We took chairs outdoors and sat in the pleasant afternoon in the area beside the church. All the women were enthusiastic and wanted to get started immediately. They elected officers on the spot. Lourdes was elected vice-president.

I returned home to tell Chalmers happily about our meeting. "Dona Vale was elected president and Lourdes was elected vice president," I told him. Before I had time to go on with my recitation, there was a clapping at our front door. It was Lourdes.

"Dona Paulina," she said, "I'm ashamed. I've been pretending that I know how to read. Now that I have been elected vice president I will be found out."

She was miserable, so we immediately started lessons. She would get her husband off to work, fly through her housework, get a neighbor to look after the children and come over for her lesson. One day we were baking cookies. She had a cookie and wanted to know how to make them, so the recipe was added to the day's reading lesson.

After about three months Lourdes burst into our house in great excitement. "It works!" she cried.

"What works?" I asked

"My reading! My new neighbor came over in tears," recounted Lourdes. "She's been married only a few months. Her husband got angry and put her out of the house, so I sat her down and got her a cup of coffee. Then I read to her from the Bible and I prayed for her. Then I went with her to her house and her husband acted as if nothing had happened and everything was all right."

I'm not sure just what Lourdes read and how she made out with her reading. But, as she said, it did work.

Oceano and Leda, a young couple, and their two little girls started coming to Sunday services. Oceano came to a Wednesday evening meeting to ask for prayer. He was an alcoholic and he couldn't keep a job. Yet he was very talented. Our church people reached out to him and his family and he became one of the persons we counted on for clerical help. He had beautiful handwriting and could draw and draft, but continued to lapse back into alcoholism. Chalmers kept working with him.

George came home from JMC in the beginning of December, the end of the school year. Christmas was approaching with practices for the pageant. I was called to a committee meeting in São Paulo. Since I was a Brazilian citizen, the Mission asked me to serve on the committee to make plans for the creation of the Presbyterian Institute of Christian Education in Brasília. I wanted to be back from the meeting in time for Christmas, so as soon as I got off the plane in São Paulo I tried to get a reservation for the trip back. All planes were booked and my name went on a long list of standbys.

In session in São Paulo our committee deliberated for a couple of days on architects' plans and curriculum. Most of us went on to Brasília, still a big tract of rolling grassland, and had a service on the approximate spot where the new institute was to be. Back in São Paulo I went to the airport early the next morning. There was still no space on the planes to Chapecó, but I got a place on a plane as far as Curitiba. The flight ran late, and as we circled Curitiba, I saw the road south out of town and the bus that I had intended to catch for Joaçaba already making its way along the road. I spent the night in a hotel and left on the first bus in the morning for Joaçaba, where Chalmers met me. We drove home to Chapecó and were all together for Christmas.

We had long wanted to see Iguaçu Falls and we needed a vacation. We could make the trip in two days by car. Lydia went home to her family and the others of us set out across the gentle Santa Catarina farmland. We reached the border of Argentina to find it closed because of an uprising in Buenos Aires. The only real road ran through a corner of Argentina. There was a "road of exploration" through Brazil's Iguaçu National Park. We decided to try the Park road. Before going far we came to a house where several men were sitting out on the veranda, and we stopped to ask about the road.

"You'll never make it," was the general opinion.

Chalmers was not easily daunted. He took it as a challenge to see if we could make it. Rains had drenched the roads. Before long we came to a slippery hill. We got out and braced the car on either side while Chalmers drove very slowly down the long decline.

After a couple of hours we came to a stream without a bridge. Chalmers took off his shoes, rolled up his trousers and waded out into the stream. The bottom seemed solid enough. We all had our shoes off and crossed the stream. Chalmers tried to rush our lumbering van across, but it stuck in the middle. We all pushed energetically to no avail. Chalmers talked to the owner of the farm nearby. He brought his oxen to pull us to the bank. With a tip and many thanks to the kind people by the side of the road we were on our way again.

The sun was casting lengthy shadows and we were not too far from Iguaçu when we found ourselves in a muddy morass, stuck again. Up ahead against the sunset sky we saw a man turn into the road with a team of oxen. Chalmers took off at a run and caught up with him. The man was on his way home and reluctant to come down the hill, but finally acceded to Chalmers' pleas. The four oxen soon had us on the other side of the mud hole.

We arrived in the town of Foz do Iguaçu, which means *mouth of the Iguaçu River*. The Iguaçu empties into the Paraná River. We spent the night at an inn and the next day we drove out to the falls, about twenty miles from town.

Nature had carved out of the rock a horseshoe canyon over two miles wide and two hundred feet deep where the mighty river spilled over along the curved sides. Smooth as glass the water bows over the rim and shatters into spray as it is catapulted into the air and down to the maelstrom below. The mist from the many cataracts catches the sunlight and the voices of the falls fill the canyon with thunder. We took the walkway with railings which circles along the stony lip of the whirlpool. The path allows views of several different cascades and brings one to the edge of one of the largest falls so that we felt the fine, cool spray on our faces. All morning we basked in the magnificence of the most awesome falls in the world. We also stood on a spot where we could see three countries at once: Brazil, Argentina and Paraguay.

We became hungry. We had considered bringing a lunch along, but we were tired of eating out of our picnic basket. Certainly, we thought, there would be a stand or small store near the falls where we could buy lunch. But there wasn't—only the huge new hotel spaciously and airily gleaming amidst the trees. We looked down at our clothes, clean, but meant for back road travel. At least I had worn a skirt that morning. So we braved the hotel. They received us with joy and seated us in the big, empty dining room. We were served a seven-course dinner with four waiters hovering over us to unfold our white dinner napkins and fill our water glasses between sips. Our children were awed, and I guess Chalmers and I were too. When we paid for our stay at the hostel in Foz do Iguaçu, the bill was less than the cost of the one meal at the Grande Hotel. We went home by the road through the state of Paraná, farther but less hazardous.

After all that glory we returned to our everyday lives and new problems in Chapecó. For months, two children, Geni and her little brother José, had been coming to the house to beg. Besides giving them food, I was teaching them to read. They had never gone to school though Geni was fourteen and José nine or ten. Late one evening Geni came breathless to our door.

"My brother tried to kill me," she whispered.

Geni and José lived with an older, married brother. Even with such desperate news Geni's voice was soft. She showed me the red mark across her throat where the droplets of blood were beginning to dry. Chalmers and I conferred.

"We can't just send her away at night."

"No, we can't."

We fixed a pallet for her on the dining room floor, expecting that her brother would come for her the next day, but he didn't. Several days went by and Geni didn't want to go home.

"What are we going to do?" I asked.

"We'd better go to the judge," Chalmers answered. "We might be accused of . . ."

"Kidnapping?"

"No, just harboring a minor."

So Chalmers and I went to see the judge. He listened to our story. Before we knew it he had a writ composed in his own hand in which he placed Geni under our tutelage. For all intents and purposes we had another daughter. Where were we going to house her?

We used our garage for storage. Chalmers cleared a space in it and made a platform of boards. We put up a cot on the platform and a footlocker for her clothes. Geni was a very docile child. When I found that she was putting all her dirty clothes in the footlocker and explained to her that it was for clean clothes, she learned to wash and iron her things and keep herself neat. She may have rarely had a change of clothing before.

On a Sunday afternoon Chalmers went down to the Uruguay River, to a small village where he ministered to a group of Protestant Christians. Some of the Chapecó youths went along, including our children. Libby always loved to go with her daddy. I stayed at home even though I also liked zigzagging down the steep descent of several miles to the river and going out on the huge barges of pine boards lashed together eight deep. In constructing the barge the men left holes at intervals for keeping track of their cargo. When the river was flowing at the optimum height, the owner would take his barge down to Buenos Aires or Montevideo.

When Chalmers returned at dusk he came into the kitchen where I was preparing supper.

"Libby fell through one of the holes in the barge . . ."

My breath left me. I turned to Chalmers speechless. He saw the terror, grabbed me to him and added hastily, "Leri was right behind her, grabbed her dress and pulled her back."

I went limp in Chalmers' arms. Bless Leri! I remember him with gratitude. He was Margie's boyfriend, a good-looking young man of Italian background.

During the last year we were in Chapecó, our older children went off to JMC. Natalie, Libby, and Geni made up our family at home. There was no zone meeting in our area, or rather, Chalmers and I were the zone, since at this time there were no other mission workers in this southern field.

The Mission appointed Chalmers as a representative on the committee for the celebration of the centennial of the Presbyterian Church of Brazil in 1959. Chalmers was off to São Paulo for several meetings before the celebration and for the big event. I heard about the comings and goings of delegates and the enthusiasm of not only the people of the church in Brazil but of the many who came from abroad. The growth of the church had been phenomenal from the days when missionaries came and started house churches, translated hymns, and started the education of Brazilian pastors to the present far-flung Presbyterian Church of the centennial year with its own General Assembly, Synods and Presbyteries. It claimed over one hundred thousand members in 526 churches and a thousand other congregations, served by 415 ordained pastors.

George had graduated from JMC. He asked to travel by ocean liner and we saw him off to the United States aboard a steamship. He entered the College of Wooster in the fall of 1959. The biggest sacrifice that Chalmers and I made was the separation for years at a time from our children just as they were growing into maturity.

The Mission gave us a new assignment. The Mosers, who had been directors at Buriti for all the years since I was a child growing up in Cuiabá, were retiring. A couple with experience was needed to take their place. A newly arrived couple, the Rev. Bob Evans and his wife Gail, would take our place in Chapecó.

We started around to say good-bye to all our parish. Chalmers took us with him to Abelardo Luz at the farthest edge of the parish. After a few visits in homes the children grew restless and I took them to the river for a swim. The river was a merry sort, running shallow over flat stones and sandy bottoms. We played in the water and then walked through the shallows. The broad sheen of water gleaming and whispering softly flowed to a ledge and smoothly tumbled over the rocks, dropping some thirty feet to a pool below. We braced ourselves on the rocks beside the falls and looked over into the churning water. Libby, tight in my arms, peeked over and was fascinated. The water in the bowl below seemed to be trying to jump back up the rocks. It sprayed out in glittering droplets and fell back in dark beads among the stones. We waded back up the river and Chalmers joined us. We were filled with the joy of the sunlight on water, the peace of the softly murmuring river, and the romance of the falls.

At home that night Libby prayed one of her explanatory prayers. She told God all about the river and the falls. "The water spilled down in the hole and the ants ate it up." This was a new explanation of the ebony droplets jumping up and then disappearing in the stream below.

- 17 -

Farm School in Eden

The dream of a place of Christian nurture for the children of families from isolated farms and small hamlets where there were no schools, or very rudimentary ones, became a reality at Buriti as early as the 1920s. We moved to Buriti in 1960 as directors of the school. About eighty students from very diverse backgrounds were in our care. Being directors meant also being just about everything else. We were teachers, the only medical officers, buyers for the dining room, bookstore, and canteen, counselors, and dorm parents. We could count only on the grace of God to fit us for all these tasks. Chalmers was the pastor of the congregation of students, teachers, and farm workers.

Erasmo and Liz da Silva were in charge of the farm. With their two little girls they lived in a new residence near the chapel. We lived in an apartment at one end of the girls' dormitory. My siblings and I when we were children had played on the foundations as this building was rising.

Buriti sits on the edge of the central plains, above the valley of the Pantanal. Cuiabá is about forty miles away. Two Buriti palms rose tall by the stream that ran through our small valley.

Not only did Eunice and Geni move with us to Buriti, but Oceano and Leda with their three children followed us. Oceano's problem of alcoholism never went away. We hoped that a move and new experiences and duties along with our continued love and support would, in God's grace, overcome his addiction.

The city of Cuiabá sent us two students whose mother was of uncertain character. As school dropouts they were street children of that time. At ages twelve and fifteen, their physical growth was stunted so that they seemed younger until one looked into their faces. The first thing they did was to run away. Erasmo agreed to chase after them in his jeep. At nightfall he overtook them ten or twelve miles on their way to Cuiabá. They were tired and hungry, so they consented to come back to Buriti. They soon became acclimated.

Both boys liked the outdoor life. Ubirajara, the older brother, would take Libby fishing for minnows down in the stream using bent straight pins for hooks. He would clean the little fish, and Libby would bring them home to be fried crisp and delicious.

The boys' dorm was very small and cramped. One day when there was a misty rain falling, Lorival, the younger brother, appeared at our door. He asked to live with us; he didn't want to sleep in the dorm anymore. I explained that in a school we couldn't take him in without taking in all the other boys who might want to join us. Lorival was stubborn. An hour later I found him still sitting in the rain at our door. "Lorival!; you'll catch cold. Go back to your dorm."

After supper, when he announced his intention to spend the night at our door, I called Ireno, the teacher in charge of the boys' dorm. Ireno took Lorival under the arms and I grasped his ankles. We carried him to the boys' dorm and put him in his hammock. I couldn't let him spend the night in the rain.

Margie, Paul, and Eunice were at JMC. Natalie entered the second year of secondary school at Buriti. Libby supplemented my kindergarten lessons by sitting under the tables of teachers she liked, quietly absorbing the lessons.

Chalmers taught as much as he could. He was buyer for the school and went to Cuiabá at least once a week. It took all day to get errands done. The farm produced corn, pumpkins, manioc, fruit, and vegetables as well as milk and eggs. From town we needed flour, salt, sugar, cooking oil, soap, and school supplies. Chalmers took mail down and brought mail back.

On one of these trips he received a message that our son George wanted to speak to us from the United States. He would call the telephone center in Cuiabá again the next day at ten o'clock. Chalmers and I were in a flurry, wondering what might be the matter. When we did get on the line with George we could barely make out what he was saying. The gist of it was that someone in Colorado Springs, where he was spending the summer with my brother Phil and family, was offering him a job as a salesman. He could transfer to the university in Colorado Springs. What did we think? Chalmers answered that we would think about it and send him a letter immediately.

We went back to Buriti and Chalmers wrote pointing out the advantages of both options. Did George feel ready to give up his scholarships at Wooster, which made it possible for him to devote most of his time to study? George returned to Wooster in the fall. He had spent his vacation washing dishes in a restaurant to earn spending money.

I began to have a lot of complaints from students about stomachaches. A student would appear at my doorway, which was the unofficial clinic. I kept some paregoric on hand and gave the youngster a light dose in water. If the complaint was a bid for attention, or a passing pain, the sufferer would go away satisfied. If the student returned with the same complaint, we sent him or her to the doctor in Cuiabá. The complaints were increasing. We went to the Department of Endemic Diseases in Cuiabá and asked if they could come up to Buriti and do some lab work. No, they couldn't do that. If we rushed specimens to Cuiabá, could they process them? No, they had no lab.

"What then do you suggest we do?" we asked.

"You can take some worm medicine and give it to the students. We dispense it. It won't hurt anybody. Just keep the patient from eating anything for four hours after they have taken the medicine. Then give them iron pills, which we can also give you."

"How are we going to watch all these boys and girls to see they don't eat anything for four hours?" Chalmers asked me on the way home.

"We could give it to them at four o'clock in the morning and let them sleep until their breakfast time at eight," I said.

"But we have to weigh each kid to know how much medicine to give."

"We can get everyone who wants to take the medicine to sign up and get weighed the night before."

That's how we did it. When the alarm clock awoke us a little before four, I crept over to the girls' dorm and Chalmers went down to the boys'. We popped the right number of capsules into the mouth of each sleepy kid, then went back to bed.

At six, I was awakened by Geni whispering to me, "Dona Paulina, Dona Paulina! The girls are hallucinating!"

I grabbed my robe and ran. Sure enough one girl was leaning out of the high dorm window saying, "I have to spit." We pulled her back into the room. Another was imitating a radio sports commentator at a soccer game: "The ball is going down the field, Z, kicks it past the goalie. Go- o- o- allll!" Another was sniveling, "My mother is going to be mad at me because I'm drunk."

Two other girls were at it. "I got the best grade!"

"No, I did!"

The girls who had not taken the medicine were standing around wide-eyed. I could see panic coming.

"This is nothing," I said firmly, though I wasn't so sure. "They'll be all right as soon as they can have something to eat when the four hours are up."

About half of the girls had taken the capsules. I assigned each of the girls who had not partaken to one of the girls in distress.

"Now you are to keep her from doing anything rash. Rub her back and talk to her. Get her to lie down."

The girls willingly did as instructed and I went down to the kitchen to be sure there would be some steaming cornmeal mush with milk and sugar for breakfast. My words were vindicated. By recess time the girls were out jumping rope as if nothing had happened. The boys reported feeling light-headed, but for some reason were not as strongly affected as the girls. And there were fewer stomach aches after that.

Natalie's best friend was Sylvia, a sweet, well-mannered young woman. One day Sylvia came over to our apartment with a bad pain in her back. I took her temperature and it was about 103 degrees Fahrenheit. I was worried. The symptoms could have bespoken something serious.

I placed her on the couch and bathed her arms, face, and legs with tepid water, then gave her an aspirin. As the day progressed her temperature went up rather than down. We decided that we didn't want to take the responsibility for her overnight. To our relief, Bob, the pilot of the Wings of Mercy plane based at Buriti was at home and willing to take Sylvia to Cuiabá. We were glad when the report came back that Sylvia wasn't seriously ill. She had the flu complicated by amebic dysentery. With proper medication she was soon fit. Her parents, who were the owners of a ranch named Poço Azul (Blue Pond) were grateful for our quick action and gladly paid for the airplane trip.

Our problems were not all health related. Josu, one of our brightest students, told us that he didn't want to study anymore. We talked to him and helped him decide to continue. Jobert, a teenage terror from Curumbá, where he had been expelled from a number of schools, had us tearing our hair. He was in my Portuguese class, the one where I was almost defeated by the passive voice.

"Please put this sentence into the passive: 'The lion caught the goat'."

The answer: "The goat caught the lion."

On one particular day Jobert was feeling cranky. The benches in my classroom had no backrests. Jobert swung his sturdy legs over the bench and sat with his back to me throughout the class. I paid him no attention as if it were perfectly normal for a student to sit with his back to the teacher. After the class I watched my opportunity and fell into step beside him as he started to the boys' dorm.

"Jobert," I said confidentially, "I wanted to tell you that sitting with your back to a teacher isn't considered proper. Be careful not to do that with the other teachers."

Chalmers had to do something with him. His lack of respect and breaking of rules had gone beyond reason. Chalmers ordered Jobert's beautiful black hair shaved.

"This is to remind you and the other students to obey the rules and respect your teachers."

The school year was coming to a close. As the students went home, most of them would go through Cuiabá. Chalmers talked at morning convocation about the students' behavior in Cuiabá as an opportunity to give a good impression of their school. He said he expected good things from all of them. On our part we were going to send them off with a party on the night before the trip to Cuiabá. We would have a barbecue out under the big trees beside the dorm. There would be games and contests. They could stay up until eleven o'clock! Then we would all go to bed so as to be in good shape for the departure the next day.

The party was a big success. The meat roasted over the outdoor fire was delicious. We took the hand-cranked record player out under the trees. When we tried to wind down the festivities, the young people still had bounce, but were persuaded to go to bed when Erasmo started patrolling with his revolver in his belt. In our wild west the revolver was respected.

For the holidays Margie, Paul, and Eunice came home from JMC. We had arranged for Paul to work as an apprentice to Mr. Johnson, an American who had turned up at Buriti and taken up residence in a shack back in the woods. He was an eccentric and an excellent mechanic, but as slow as a sloth.

The girls helped about the place. We all went on picnics and long walks together. About three miles from the school there was a cave, cathedral-like with a large, arched entrance and a window opening at the back. A stream of pure water ran through the cave over sand and pebbles. It was an enchanting place in which to spend a few hours. About a mile from home another stream cascaded over a ledge and dropped forty feet or more into a wide pool, a favorite for swimming.

Christmas was coming. We announced that there would be a pageant. The children of the farm and some students who had nowhere to go during holidays became the players. There were Mary, with dark curly hair dressed in white with a blue shawl, and Joseph, tall and straight, in a bathrobe with a towel banded to his head; the three kings with gold paper crowns. There were the angels ready to sing. But especially there were the shepherds. Ubirajara and Lorival, their faces lighting up at the reading of the story from Luke, felt an immense pride and responsibility as they walked solemnly up and knelt before the manger. We practiced and then, to a packed chapel, the children of Buriti told the story of the coming of the Christ Child, bright and new-minted, for us.

The next January, the Confederation of Evangelical Churches of Brazil was convening a workshop in São Paulo for the purpose of writing a primer for adults. Sarah Gudginsky of Wycliffe Translators, a world-renowned educator, was to be the leader. We wrote to my mother and asked if she would stay at Buriti for a couple of weeks while we went to the workshop. She was reluctant, but agreed to help us out as she had done so many times before. The students who stayed at Buriti during the vacation were not easy people to deal with. Mother was wonderful with them.

The workshop was a success. Chalmers and I learned a great deal. Delegates came from various parts of Brazil, so we could thus check vocabulary and know that the sentences would be understood across the country. After we returned to Buriti, Sarah joined us there to finish work on the primer.

Mission Meeting convened at this time and overlapped with the workshop for primer building. Chalmers was chair of the literature committee of our Mission. He had established a rapport with the director of the literature program of the Presbyterian Church of Brazil, Boanerges Ribeiro. The two men had worked out a plan for funding the printing of books that were of mutual interest. While we were busy at the primer workshop, a new chairperson was elected for the literature committee and, without consultation, the Mission literature committee rescinded the plan, causing ill feelings in the literature committee of the Church.

In the new school year at Buriti, one of our students, a tall young man from an Indian reservation, was coming home with a group of boys detailed to work in the corn field. Without warning, he was struck in the shin by a *jararaca*, a large, very poisonous snake. By the time he was brought to Erasmo's house, his leg had swelled up to above his knee. His pulse was one hundred and twenty and his temperature was rising. Chalmers and Erasmo brought out their stores of antivenom. They found that between them they had the dosage this particular snakebite required. We were lucky and thanked God for the life of Altair. We consulted Brother John in Chapada, a little town about eight miles from Buriti. In his small clinic beside the Catholic Church, Brother John had been treating people for years. He came to see Altair and prescribed bathing the wound, which had grown to the size of a silver dollar, with warm infusions of marcella, a plant that grew in the fields around. The flesh began to grow back slowly. Altair stayed at Erasmo and Liz's house until he could walk easily again, and we all breathed a sigh of relief when after three months Altair was back on the soccer field.

Margie had gone to the American Graded School in São Paulo for a semester, living at the Mission Home. In August we saw her off to college. She chose to go to Wilson, my alma mater. Our strong-willed princess had flown and we returned to Buriti for the rest of the school year.

The seventh of September is Brazil's Fourth of July, and the school celebrated with a picnic to the Véu de Noiva (bridal veil) falls. A steep, slippery path down through the rain forest was a challenge. We reached the floor of the chasm and looked up in astonishment at the white swath of water falling two hundred feet from the cliff overhead. We swam in the cold water, ate our lunch and sang one of our favorite hymns. The hymn started with the words, "The birds and the great rocks . . ." The great rocks reverberated with the praise of young voices.

I had a summons to a committee meeting in São Paulo and I was packing to go when Natalie came over to our room. "Mother, it worries me so when you travel. I'm afraid the airplane might go down or something."

"Natalie, you don't have to worry. I am about the business God has given me to do. As long as he wants me to do it, he will keep me safe. He has given me you children, too, and he means me to take care of you. So I have two reasons to expect God to keep me safe. My life is in his hands whatever I am doing." I embraced my daughter.

When I did get back from that trip I found that Natalie had faced dangers she hadn't imagined. On his way back from Cuiabá very late one evening Chalmers came to a bridge on which the boards had slipped, leaving a gaping hole. He and Aristeu, our oldest and largest student, got out of the truck and tried to get the planks back in place. Chalmers was working bent over the bridge floor when Aristeu loosened a board. It flew up and hit Chalmers on the forehead, cutting a nasty gash. Chalmers saw stars and lay down on the bridge for a bit. He wiped the blood out of his eyes, tied his handkerchief around his head and succeeded in driving home. When he arrived a little after eleven o'clock, he found the girls' dorm waiting up for him. Two girls had had a cuffing and scratching fight. The teacher in charge had not been able to return order in the dorm. It took Chalmers only one minute to get everybody to go to bed when they saw his bloodied head. Then Natalie was left to help Chalmers wash and medicate his wound. The next day Chalmers went to Chapada where Father John put in some stitches. The cut healed well.

Chalmers and I did not have the time or the savvy to cope with the developing jealousies among the families at Buriti. Sr. Marcílio and Dona Anita, because of their long years of service, naturally thought they knew how Buriti should be run. Sr. Sergio and Dona Chiquita had come to Buriti from the educational center of São Paulo. DonaChiquita had gone to a Bible School. They were also, beneath their pride, an insecure couple. Sr. Delmar and Dona Madalena had graduated from the school of hard knocks in the vast regions of Brazil. They were more humble and Chalmers and I turned instinctively to them because of their knowledge of the hearts of young people.

We should have seen the trouble brewing. We had a showdown when some of the girls complained about Sr. Sergio. He, they reported, was making indecent remarks in class. Chalmers talked to Sergio alone. Everything would have straightened itself out had not Sergio told Chiquita. Chiquita went into a towering rage. She had students ready to mutiny. The tempest blew over, but not the underlying current of distrust.

We were having our last staff meeting at the end of the school year. We began with a round of prayer. Tasks were assigned for the next few days. As we were breaking up Chiquita said to me, "You know, Aristeu is at Sr. Marcílio's house. He is writhing with pain."

Two weeks before, Aristeu had come to our door with the common complaint of a stomachache and I had given him a palliative. The next day he still had a stomachache. Erasmo was going to town, so we asked him to take Aristeu to the doctor.

I talked to Aristeu when he got back. "Did you see the doctor?" I asked.

"Yes, he gave me medicine for my liver." In that part of the world *liver* is what is the matter with you if you feel unwell. So I put Aristeu's malady out of my mind. But, with Chiquita's words, all sorts of bells went off in my mind and I knew he had appendicitis.

Chalmers boiled a syringe and needle and got an ampoule of penicillin while I got ice cubes and filled a compress bag. We went through the starry night to Marcílio and Anita's house. A flickering kerosene lamp was burning in the front room where Aristeu was lying. His pain had diminished—a bad sign. Chalmers gave him the injection and we showed him how to keep the ice bag against his side. Erasmo took him to the hospital in Cuiabá the next morning.

Again God mercifully saved one of our students. Aristeu was lucky to have a good constitution, for the doctor found that he had a burst appendix. He did pull through.

Oceano and family were a real concern to us. In the two years at Buriti he had not been able to stay sober for any length of time. One Friday evening he was taking part in a talent show organized by the students and teachers. Oceano ended up making a fool of himself. Someone came to call Chalmers. Chalmers took Oceano by the arm and led him off the stage. When they got outside, Oceano gave Chalmers a hard blow to the head. The two men fell and wrestled. In a while Oceano changed from physical aggressiveness to words. One of his accusations was, "You want to make me a sober citizen because you want to write to your supporting churches and tell them about your good deeds." When Oceano calmed down Chalmers brought him to our apartment and we put up a cot for him in our living room. He wouldn't accept a cup of coffee, but was soon asleep. A few weeks later Oceano took a student with him to Chapada without permission, drank, and used bawdy language. When we heard, we told him he would have to return to Chapecó. We arranged transportation and saw the family off. We couldn't leave him for anyone else to cope with at Buriti.

Paul was graduating from JMC. Since Chalmers had been to Margie's graduation the year before, I went to Paul's while Chalmers prepared storage space for our belongings in the garage. It was good to see a large class of young people preparing now to go on with their studies or out into the work world.

I went to see Charles Harken, mission treasurer in São Paulo, to talk about our trip to the United States. Charles said, "Your marriage certificate is not registered." I sat down abruptly in the nearest chair. Chalmers had been to São Paulo only a few weeks earlier and begged Charles to get our traveling papers in order. Charles had said, "There will be no problem." I conferred with a lawyer who promised to pull all strings and ratify my Brazilian passport.

I had delayed in São Paulo two days longer than I had expected. I found Chalmers desperately trying to settle all loose ends at the school and get on with the packing. Both of us went down to Cuiabá with Raimundo Passos who, in spite of his total lack of experience, had been named director in the absence of anyone else to take that place. We introduced him at the bank and got his signature registered. The school account had only about 100 cruzeiros in it, a pitiful sum to turn over to a new director. But there were student bills outstanding which we hoped would be paid.

We did catch our plane to the States. We settled into our favorite mission house on Spink Street in Wooster and gathered our children about us. After the Christmas holidays Margie went back to Wilson, but George, now a junior at the College of Wooster, moved in with us. Libby skipped off to the second half of first grade at the Beall Avenue School. Paul was a junior in high school and Natalie in eighth grade.

Our summer was very special. We went to Green Lake, Wisconsin, a Baptist summer grounds. Chalmers and I were enrolled in the International Writers' Conference of an ecumenical organization we called Lit-Lit (Literature and Literacy). Margie and Paul had summer jobs on the grounds. Natalie was our housekeeper in a cabin on a hillock amongst locust trees and large lilac bushes. Libby attended a recreational program for children. We missed George, who was in Cleveland, where he worked in an inner city church project. This was the summer he came to the conclusion that he wasn't going to be a minister. He really had the mind of a historian.

The writers' seminar was hard work. It was also very stimulating. We had authors, journalists, and specialists in other fields to instruct us. I remember Elizabeth Yates especially, quiet, intense, and helpful.

Chalmers had a proclivity for getting into the middle of things. In the journalism class he was held up as a horrible example because he misspelled the name of the person he was writing about. He spelled it in Portuguese instead of in Spanish. We also had an Indian teacher as our mentor in cross-cultural understanding. In a paper for him Chalmers defined or explained the color saffron as golden. Our teacher objected vehemently. Others joined the search for a way to describe saffron; it never was resolved except in the negative: not orange, not yellow, not gold, not ochre. Saffron is saffron, an elusive color.

The summer and the year rolled quickly to an end. We were finally assigned to work in literature and literacy with the Confederation of Evangelical Churches of Brazil. There was one catch—this was not our only assignment. We were also to be house parents at the Mission Home in São Paulo.

Margie had gone back to Wilson by the time we set off by train for New York. Paul moved to Livingstone Lodge on campus with George. George and Paul accompanied us to the station. It was a heartbreaking moment when we had to say good-bye.

- 18 -

Double Duty: São Paulo

The city of São Paulo, nestled among hills some 2,670 feet (almost a mile) above sea level, bristled with skyscrapers. The spectacular ascent from the port of Santos to São Paulo wound through the grandeur of forested mountains over a highway of daring engineering.

We settled in the Mission Home near the center of the city, where a wide avenue ran along a ridge or spine. The avenue, Avenida Paulista, only a block away, had been lined with mansions built by coffee barons at the turn of the century. The great houses built from a hodgepodge of European marble, iron fetted balconies, and colorful tile had been an amazing sight. Now the high rises

The Home, which our Mission had bought to house missionaries on business in the city and the children of missionaries studying in São Paulo schools, was a big three-story structure. We had an apartment on the second floor, and for a time the office of the Literacy Department of the Confederation was also housed on the third floor.

Natalie went off to JMC and came home on weekends. Libby boarded the bus each morning with the other students at the Home on their way to the American Graded School.

Our double assignment was strenuous. We were responsible for the housing and feeding of a group of between seventeen and twenty-five persons each day. Missionaries who came in from interior stations sometimes had health problems. For the most part our young people were good students. Discipline was infrequently a problem. A board of directors oversaw the Home and made the rules, but we were to see that they were obeyed.

The hard part was juggling both the running of the household and the literature and literacy program. The literacy work was two pronged. Chalmers was the principal organizer and trainer of literacy teachers. I was involved more in the production of reading materials for literacy and for new readers. Some of our workshops were in São Paulo, but many were in other cities. Fortunately the Home had a good cook and three women who kept the house clean and did the laundry. We could usually arrange for another missionary who was temporarily at the Home to substitute for us if we were to be away for an extended period.

Amazingly, the Government of Brazil adopted the primer created under the leadership of Sarah Gudginsky. The Ministry of Education of the country had a million copies printed by one of the most prestigious publishing houses in Brazil. They had the guide or manual for the teacher printed in gigantic size so that the teachers could use the pages as teaching posters. However, no provision was made for training teachers to use the primer and no plan set up for organizing classes. The distribution of the primer and manual was haphazard. Though it had been designed to motivate adults, a large number of primers ended up in classes for children. Our Committee of the Confederation requested and received a block of copies of primers and manuals and was putting them into use as quickly as possible.

The printing had several severe drawbacks. One that was especially hard for adults was colored backgrounds, blue or purple pages with black lettering, or green with the printed words in red. The effect was stunning, almost grandiose, but it made reading very difficult. So after a few months the Confederation embarked on its own printing program. Chalmers was in charge. The first difficulty was to find the right type. Then the matter of the posters that the teacher would use at the front of the class proved costly. The president of one of the São Paulo banks, Bradesco, came to our rescue with financial backing for the posters.

We were driving a Mission Volkswagon minibus. Chalmers had gone to a training meeting at a home in our area. He parked the car on the steep street. When he came out, the minibus was gone. Chalmers was aghast and came home by taxi. He reported to the police. At about 2 a.m. the next morning, we received a call from the police. They had found our car parked on a street behind the Ypiranga Museum.

Chalmers started dressing. I wasn't going to let Chalmers go off to the isolated streets behind the museum by himself at that hour of the morning, so we both went and retrieved the car. Playboys had stolen the Kombi minibus and driven it around until the gas gave out.

Margie had come for a junior year abroad at the University of São Paulo. She was with a group of students in a program arranged by the University of New York. She lived at the Home with us, so we had our three daughters with us.

We attended the Bela Vista Presbyterian Church, which was not far from the Home. It was a good church home for our family. Chalmers and I both taught Sunday School and Margie, Natalie, and Libby were active in the young people's groups. Margie wrote a play for Mother's Day and helped produce it.

I began to have health problems. As mission personnel we were patients of the Lane Clinic in Campinas. Edward and John Lane were sons of Presbyterian missionaries. After studying medicine they established their clinic. I began a two-year stretch of treatments with Dr. Edward Lane, who was an obstetrician and gynecologist.

Central, south, west, and east Brazil had claimed our attention and Chalmers and I were now preparing to go to Recife in the northeast of Brazil for workshops. The first workshop was for instruction in literacy methods and community projects. The second was for teaching the techniques of writing for the newly literate. Illiterate adults who had studied through a primer now needed something meaningful to read within their skill limitations. We had some good, imaginative people write short manuscripts. Recife already had a Christian writers club led by Ann Pipkin, a Presbyterian missionary, and Juraci Viana, a talented Brazilian writer. We gladly allied ourselves with them.

I traveled back to São Paulo ahead of Chalmers, to Rio by plane, and on to São Paulo by bus. On the way I became very sick. I was desperate by the time I got home and ended up in the hospital in Campinas again.

When I recuperated and returned home, Chalmers and I talked over Mother and Dad's approaching fiftieth wedding anniversary. We couldn't all go to the States, but I urged Chalmers to go. Besides the anniversary celebration, there were a couple of other reasons for the trip. Frenchy and Joan were on furlough. Chalmers would see his brother, whom he had not seen for sixteen years. Margie had returned to Wilson, and Chalmers would see her and George and Paul. Chalmers flew to Wooster, where Mother and Dad were living. The celebration was a wonderful family reunion.

In the meantime I was feeling in need of some rest and decided that a week at the shore might get me back to normal. The Mission had a small cottage on Praia Grande (Long Beach) to which we could go. Libby and I started for the shore in the late afternoon, after I had set things to function at the Home in our absence. We arrived after dark at the beach house.

The time at the shore was very relaxing. Libby and I went swimming and shell gathering along the beach. We picked little orange and yellow orchids that grew in the sand dunes to make a bouquet for our table. We made our own meals and read together. Natalie came down by train from JMC for a weekend. The sea and sky and feeling of remoteness were healing.

Lillian and Joe Hahn and their two boys, Jody and Willie, mission colleagues who had been working in Curumbá, came to live at the Home. Joe was on a special study assignment, and he and Lillian were ready to take over the running of the Mission Home. We found an apartment a block away from the Home and moved. We had to buy some furniture as we had been living in furnished quarters at the Home. We lived in this apartment for one year, and continued working with the Confederation literacy projects.

My parents had retired and were living in their own home at Jandira where JMC was located. For their golden wedding anniversary Mary Elizabeth and I arranged a dinner in their honor. Phil and Mary Louise with their four children, Alan, Dinah, Perry, and Nancy came to Brazil to help Father and Mother celebrate. Mother's sister Julia and her brother Edward and their families were there.. The only family members missing were George and Mary Lou and their children, Toby and Katie.

My mother's faith was simple and serene, like a hymn. My father trusted God's constant care and God's "working his purpose out" in families and in all of creation and history. He spoke of these things to his gathered family.

The following period was of great stress in our professional life. Brazilians in the churches were feeling that they wanted the reins in their hands, so we were urged as Americans to follow rather than initiate. On the other hand, we were supposed to produce the results that the sending agencies wanted to see come about. Dr. Rex of Lit-Lit was the principal proponent of this double-directional blueprint for our work. We attended a Lit-Lit-sponsored weeklong conference where Rex was on hand and where we were thoroughly marginalized. We gave a report, but we were not invited into any steering committee or executive group.

On the other hand, Rex went over the heads of our Brazilian colleagues to start a literacy center in Amazonia, the northernmost part of Brazil. Rex had confided to us that he needed something dramatic like literacy in the Amazon to stir up interest in the giving churches and agencies in the United States. The Confederation literacy committee didn't feel we had the strength yet to venture so far afield. Because we had no trained personnel in that area the attempt failed.

The Confederation's literacy work needed publicity, too. Chalmers was the main mover in the creation of a filmstrip that showed the plight, sometimes comical, of a person who cannot read. We worked with a group on a story line. Then the Campinas churches provided actors. CAVE, the audio-visual center for the churches, also located in Campinas, provided the photography and other technical services in producing the filmstrip. In this project some of the future literacy workers were first introduced and trained. Rex always talked about the wonderful work these people did in creating the filmstrip. Indeed it was a very good piece of cooperative work amd we had enjoyed our ignored part in it.

In São Paulo we were involved in a tragedy in the Bela Vista church. The lovely young wife of our minister lost her tortured battle with cancer. She left a family of six young children. We were all devastated. Chalmers agreed to chauffeur a car to the cemetery while I drove our minibus with more of the congregation.

Natalie had come in from JMC to attend the funeral. After the funeral, I had parked the minibus in front of our apartment building and locked it. When we came down to the street to take Natalie to her train back to school, the car was gone, stolen for the third time. We put Natalie in a taxi and called the police. This time it was a ring that provided parts to repair garages. The thieves were caught while stealing another car and ours was found still intact.

Again we were to move. A group of Presbyterian missionaries in Recife, the capital of the state of Pernambuco, started a literacy movement called Cruzada ABC. ABC stood for *Ação Básica Cristã* (Basic Christian Action). USAID, which had a development program in the northeast, one of the most needy regions of Brazil, joined forces with Cruzada ABC and provided much of the funding. SUDENE, a commission set up by the Brazilian government to oversee development in the northeast, also had a finger in the pie.

The Confederation of Evangelical Churches of Brazil assigned us, with the blessing of our Mission, to Cruzada ABC. Natalie graduated from JMC and started off for Wooster. She and Margie both found it hard to leave their friends in Brazil, especially their boyfriends. Libby, Chalmers and I packed and, once we were on the road, had a marvelous trip until the very last evening.

We had crossed the mighty São Francisco River, and shortly after five o'clock we stopped by the side of the road for a bite of supper from our picnic basket. As we were getting back into the car Libby said to us, "I'm afraid."

"Afraid of what?" we asked.

"I don't know, but I'm just afraid."

"We've been traveling since four in the morning. You're probably tired. Why don't you lie down on your seat and go to sleep?" I suggested.

Libby was the kind of child who didn't want to miss anything. However, she lay down and fell asleep. Night was gathering its shadows as we rounded a curve. Two trucks with lights on were coming toward us, one a small tanker and behind it a cattle truck. Suddenly I screamed to Chalmers, "He's not going back!" The second truck had come around the first and was headed directly at us in our lane.

Chalmers swerved the car onto the berm just as the cattle truck, without slowing down, crushed into us. The box of the truck smashed the door of the minibus and ripped the rest of the siding off like opening a sardine can. Our car lights went off. Pellets of glass showered us. The cattle truck roared on. Libby woke to a dark silence after the crash. She began to scream. She imagined we had been crushed in the front seat. We turned to her and reassured her.

The tanker stopped and the driver ran over to us. Other cars pulled over. People were gathering around us. They expected to find us all dead, for the minibus was a gaping hole with crushed metal strewn out along the road. Some of our belongings had flown out of the car and scattered across the road. A man stepped out of a shiny black car and asked Chalmers out of the blue, "Are you a preacher?" When Chalmers had identified himself, the man said, "Come with me. I have a prophet's room built at the top of my house; you can stay with us in Caruaru. There we will notify the police."

Another man with a pickup truck offered to take our luggage into town. People helped us transfer our belongings to the pickup truck. A young man who lived in the neighborhood offered to guard our car until morning. We then got into the luxurious car of our host and went with him into Caruaru and to the hospitality of his home.

The next morning the police took pictures of our minibus with the ripped metalwork streaming from it. Though our car had been completely off the road the wide wooden grating of the truck had wrenched a slat from its side which was now lying inside the minibus right across the seat on which Libby had been lying.

After dealing with the police and making arrangements to keep in touch we tied the third seat of the minibus across the gaping hole in the side. We repacked our possessions, thanked our good friends for their generous hospitality and help, gave a thank-you gift to the man who had watched our car, and made our way over the last few miles into Recife.

-19-

Cruzada ABC

As soon as we reached Recife my malady flared up. I wrote to the Misssion office asking whether I should find a doctor in Recife or go back to Campinas. The immediate reply was a plane ticket to return to Campinas for surgery.

Before I left two important things happened to us. Paul came for a short visit. Paul was studying at Princeton University and had received a fellowship to do some studying in Brazil. It was comforting to have him with us.

The other event: Libby acquired a dog. We had rented a comfortable house with a veranda along one side. Two tall jambo trees shaded the porch. There Ginger, Libby's Dachshund puppy, took up his abode with us. He was a prince, but also very headstrong and unruly at times.

I went to Campinas by myself. Mary Elizabeth undertook to stay with me through the time I was in the hospital.

When I was well enough to leave the hospital, I went to stay with Esther and Bob McIntire, who were now living in the house Mother and Father had occupied in Campinas. Bob was teaching at the Seminary. No one could have been more caring than these friends.

I recuperated quickly and was able soon to go to my parents' house in Jandira. I spent a lovely week with them. By this time we knew that Father had cancer. Radiation and chemotherapy were not yet in common use. So there was no hope extended. It was a bittersweet time.

Margie arrived in Brazil while I was in Jandira. She had started her senior year at Wilson, but the ferment of the sixties and a series of circumstances were too much for her, so she left college, taught Portuguese for a while in the Peace Corps, then came to Brazil. How good to have her accompany me on the return trip to Recife.

When our taxi reached the front door, Ginger came sliding across the waxed porch floor to greet us, then turned and rushed back into the house and back to me, back and forth. I understood that he wanted me to go with him. I did, and he took me to see the new member of the family, a little lost kitten that Libby and Chalmers had taken in. Ginger was firmly convinced that the little cat was his.

Recife is an old city. It spreads out on the flats where three rivers flow into the sea. It is called the Venice of Brazil because of the rivers and bridges, but there are no gondolas. Like all Brazilian cities Recife has, along its edges, the ramshackle abodes of those who come in from the country hoping to find their fortune. The backlands of the northeast are desertlike, where severe droughts are frequent, but the coastal plain is sugarcane and cotton land. The shoreline extends endlessly with its beautiful white beaches and marches of coconut palms. Cashew trees grow wild in the coastal area as well as other fruit.

The percentage of illiterate adults in this part of Brazil was staggering. It was this situation that had brought us to Recife. The Cruzada ABC was just starting its work. The Protestant Churches were joining the battle. The Roman Catholic Church had tried a literacy program by radio. This program had attained some success. But with the change in governments it had come to an untimely end. The Roman Catholic Church did not want to join the Cruzada ABC officially. But at the local level the priests and other clerics gave their approval and the Catholic community participated wholeheartedly in the work.

The Cruzada ABC was being funded in large part by USAID. There was a group of USAID Americans living in Recife and working in agriculture, water management, and advising labor unions. Recife was considered a hardship post by USAID, which seemed like a joke to Chalmers and me.

The federal government of Brazil had set up a commission, SUDENE, to promote and regulate development in the northeast.

The Cruzada ABC was responsible to SUDENE, which oversaw our materials and methods to make sure they fit a certain philosophy of education. The Confederation of Evangelical Churches of Brazil, as a cooperating member of the Cruzada ABC, offered to furnish material, especially the primer, manual, and charts. The primer was not acceptable to SUDENE because it did not have what they called "content". The Confederation primer which we had constructed with Sarah Gudginsky was tailored to teach reading and writing as quickly as possible. SUDENE wanted to teach all sorts of things like hygiene and social science.

The primer was the pivotal piece of our program. If we were to write a new primer it should be done at once, so we arranged for Wycliffe Translators to send us some primer specialists. Several Cruzada writers and a couple of the SUDENE people strove to coordinate divergent ways of thinking.

We finally wrote a primer that taught both reading and other subject matter. Chalmers was not part of the daily work group, but often, when I returned home at night exhausted and despairing, he would work at the problem and come up with a possible solution. We began to call Chalmers, between ourselves, "the grey eminence."

The political climate in Brazil had run the gamut from conservative, through a socialist phase, and on to a military takeover. During the socialist regime Paulo Freire had been the bright force in literacy. He had worked with teams in the northeast. There were many young people who had been deeply influenced by Mr. Freire and had kept his writings and manuals. We were able to study these papers clandestinely and use the principles he espoused in community. While educators now studied and talked about community development, they were so entrenched in the older methods of education that many were not able to promote initiative in the community or even recognize it when it occurred.

Libby was a day student at Agnes Erskine, the girls' school founded by Presbyterian missionaries and situated about half a mile from our house. Since both Chalmers and I were away from home all day, we asked for a girl from the boarding department of Agnes to live with us and be a companion to Libby. Inalva, several years older than Libby, joined our household. She benefited by having board and room and was a cheerful, studious friend for Libby.

Chalmers and I both loved our work. I was head of the curriculum department. Chalmers was out with the people. He thrived on being in the midst of the action. A cadre of bright and enthusiastic young men and women, some of them students from the Presbyterian and Baptist Seminaries of Recife, became supervisors working on community development. They went into the suburbs and towns and sought out the leaders of the community: the civil authorities, the church leaders, and the natural leaders. To these leaders they explained the aims and strategy of the Cruzada ABC and they acquired their support.

The Cruzada offered a course in adult basic education to people in each community who could read and write and were inspired to teach. There were plenty of unemployed young people as well as housewives and men with part-time work who had some schooling and signed on. Working for the Cruzada as teachers gave them status, even though they were volunteers. They recruited their students and organized classes of fifteen to eighteen persons, who met in the evenings three times a week. The Cruzada furnished all materials, a chalkboard and chalk, primers, paper and pencils and for the teacher, a manual and charts. Besides training and the materials, each teacher and each pupil received weekly foodstuff that USAID provided: corn meal, milk powder, bulgur, oil, and soap. These people, including the teachers, really needed the supplies. The distribution was also a part of the motivation for the classes and part of the effort to teach nutrition. One of the community health workers asked a woman what she did with the bulgur, or cracked wheat, a product not common to the region.

"I feed it to my pig," she said. When she saw the horrified look on the face of the worker she said shamefacedly, "I know, but the chickens wouldn't eat it." The woman was given recipes and a demonstration of how to cook bulgur for her family.

Chalmers was under very great physical stress. He had an arthritic hip, which was causing him much pain. He decided on the surgery which orthopedists in São Paulo had advised. We went to São Paulo, leaving Libby and Inalva with missionary friends. Chalmers had what was called a "hanging hip" operation. Thigh muscles were cut and rearranged so that the pressure point of the head of the femur was changed. It was drastic surgery and Chalmers was very uncomfortable. When he was feeling better and could get about on crutches, I left him at the mission home and returned to my job in Recife.

Delmar and Madalena had been fired at Buriti as the feuding among the families continued. We heard that they were out of a job and recommended them to the Cruzada ABC. They came to the northeast and worked in the program for four years. They started out in Aracaju, the capital of the state of Sergipe and trained and oversaw the work in the states of Alagoas and Sergipe. They were then transferred to Recife and worked in the city and in the states to the north.

As the Cruzada ABC grew the Curriculum Department had a hard time keeping up with the demand for material. We were at work on five units that would carry an adult through four years of grammar school in two years. Simple readers that taught hygiene, math, history, and some basic science followed the primer. Eleven writers were working on these readers and the manuals that accompanied them. Ted Torsch was the only other missionary involved. He was in charge of graphics and preparing the booklets for the press.

To keep all the material and fill orders from the different parts of the region, the Cruzada had a big storage and handling barn. Chalmers worked there whenever he could spare time, helping to keep records and fill orders. The job was tremendous because the Cruzada ABC expanded north to Fortaleza, southwest as far as Belo Horizonte and south to the state of Rio de Janeiro. In the five years of its life, the Cruzada ABC reached seven hundred thousand people with at least the primer unit of its program. God gave us a dream and its fulfilling.

George was in a doctoral program at Catholic University in Washington, D.C. He came to do some research in Brazil. In December of 1967 he took time out to marry Mary Behling. George had met her at an event when she was Assistant Dean of Women at the College of Wooster. After that he made it his business to visit his sister Natalie, a freshman at Wooster, and see Mary discreetly. Mary and George were married in the Methodist Church that the Behlings attended in Washington, D.C.

George and Mary came to Recife in January and we had a couple of lovely days driving out to beaches and showing the newlyweds our city. Mary immediately joined the family in her loyal, outgoing way. We were charmed.

George and Mary visited Margie, then the family in São Paulo, including my parents at Jandira. They settled in a small apartment in Rio while George worked on his doctoral dissertation in the historical archives in Rio.

In late July of 1967 Mother sent me a telegram asking that I go immediately to São Paulo. My father was in the Samaritano hospital. It was late morning when the telegram reached us. I requested a leave of absence and bought tickets for me and for Libby. The next morning we were awaiting our plane in the Recife airport when I was paged. Another cable had come telling of my father's death. In Brazil it is the custom to have the burial within twenty-four hours of death, so we were concerned because our plane was running behind schedule. We reached the Congonhas airport in São Paulo around five o'clock. By the time we got a taxi and went to Mary Elizabeth's house, there was no one there. Libby and I missed the funeral at five. We stayed for a week with Mother, Mary Elizabeth, Francis, and Debbie.

My father had suffered a great deal, so we couldn't mourn his going. He had spent his life as an apostle of the gospel all over Brazil. In his last years, in retirement, he had worked tirelessly to build up the Presbyterian Church of Jandira, raising money for the church building, preaching and walking in the hilly countryside to visit in the homes. He enjoyed his family, especially his two youngest grandchildren, Libby and Debbie, taking them on walks and sharing his interests with them. Libby and I said good-bye to Mother and returned to Recife.

Chalmers was off each day to train or supervise teachers, many times in the rural areas around Recife. Sometimes I went with him out into the pleasant sunshine along the sandy roads between the cane fields. Unions from the United States were helping the cutters in the canebrakes to organize. The workers had rights, according to Brazilian law, of which they were ignorant.

The Cruzada, with its literacy program, was welcomed into the scheme of education that was going on. The U.S. unions had built study centers, pleasant places with classrooms built around a quadrangle. One time we visited two Cruzada workers who were training literate men and women from the communities so that they could teach their people. It was fun to sit down to a meal of rice and beans with the budding teachers, to feel their enthusiasm and hope and share their camaraderie. They had many stories to tell, some about the callous treatment of the workers by the owners of the cane plantations. One family had watched a bulldozer plow up their vegetable garden to plant corn.

At Cruzada headquarters we had held retreats to discuss our witness as Christians as we worked in literacy. Many of our trainers and teachers were eager to share the gospel message. We were led to believe, however, that our witness was in the joy and dedication of our service. We would not use the literacy classes as a chance to preach. As we were out that day in the center, one of the trainers came to Chalmers. "Could you bring a couple of bibles the next time you come?" she asked. Chalmers was surprised. The trainer went on, "Two of the women asked me after class how I could be so patient and cheerful. I seemed to be happy. I told them I found my inspiration in Jesus Christ as he is shown to us in the Bible. They asked me if I could get them a bible." So the next time Chalmers went to that center he took the bibles. It happened over and over that pupils came to the teachers for counsel because they yearned for the faith and joy they saw.

While in Recife we became involved in the English-speaking community church made up mostly of expatriates, many of them Americans with USAID, or business people, and missionaries. We gathered for worship on Sunday mornings at the American Graded School. Preaching was shared around since there were a number of ministers in the group. Chalmers was glad of the opportunity when his turn came. Though Libby didn't go to the American School, she had friends of her own age in the congregation. She made two sets of good friends, at Agnes and at church.

Our family enjoyed the wonderful beaches. One thing that pleased us about the beaches was that they belonged to everybody. We were there with friends from the Cruzada and with the berry-brown boys and girls of the fishermen's villages.

One morning just as it was beginning to get light, we heard a sound of many voices and then bumping noises outside. We rose to find our neighbors bringing their possessions up from a dip in the street. One couple was lugging their refrigerator onto our porch. The rains that had been falling heavily had brought floods of river water rushing towards the sea. An especially high tide caused the waters to back up and Recife was inundated. Our house was on a little higher ground. More neighbors brought other precious household possessions onto our porch. People in the town climbed up on tables and into the rafters that day and waited the turn of the tide. When the waters started pouring back out to sea, they saw their pots and pans and other loose articles swirl off on the swift current. One family lost two children. The rivers carried cattle lowing out to sea. Because of the higher ground, water only lapped an inch over our tile floors, leaving debris and muck to clean up. Chalmers put on shorts and waded thigh-deep to Agnes Erskine School where the Cruzada cars were parked. Only their roofs were visible above the water. People down the street from us pulled their completely submerged VW bug out of the water like a small whale coming to the surface for air.

A pleasant interlude was a visit from my mother. Also at Christmas time Margie brought Donald Hart to Recife. She had met him when she was teaching Portuguese for the Peace Corps. He was a very pleasant young man, charming and bright, with a voracious appetite. We were glad to have them visit for a week.

We had had little contact with the Confederation since coming to Recife, but now they wanted us to attend a workshop they were going to hold in the city of Salvador in Bahia where Margie was living. At the same time Margie asked if I would accompany her on a visit to Donald at Pilâo Arcado, a small town on the São Francisco River, where he was serving as a Peace Corps volunteer. She was his *noiva* and it would not do in a small community for her to appear there unchaperoned. I agreed to take a week just prior to the workshop to go with her.

We took off by bus from Salvador, traveling back roads to the town of Chiquechique where we put up in a *pensâo*. We visited the agent of the riverboat, which was scheduled to travel downriver the next day. This boat, which had served on the Mississippi River, made the trip from the Tres Marias Dam to Joazeiro above the Paulo Afonso Falls. The agent promised to call for us at the inn and take us to the boat when it came by about 11 a.m. the next day. He forgot us. We heard the whistle of the boat, rushed to the riverside, hired a motorboat and went out to the main stream from the inner bank, but were too late. Crestfallen, we went back to the small port behind the island and looked for a boat, any boat, which would take us downriver. After two days we arranged passage to Pilâo Arcado on a boat carrying castor beans to Joazeiro. Our motorboat owner stopped often along the riverbank to trade, a process that took time. The wide, sunlit São Francisco River became a new friend as we moved with it and listened to its lapping against the launch. We spent a night in a shack on the bank, where the family served us a good meal, and late in the afternoon of the next day we came to Pilao Arcado. We were warmly welcomed by Don and by the friends that had taken him in as part of the family. Two days was all we had left to be with Don and see the work he was doing. He was thoroughly enjoying getting to know the people and learning their ways. When we got back to Salvador the Cruzada workshop had been canceled, so Chalmers and I returned to Recife.

We knew that Mother Browne was in poor health; she had had a severe stroke, had broken her hip and had been confined to a wheelchair. Even so, it was a great shock to receive the news of her death. We grieved that we were too far away to go to Dad at this time of her going. We would miss our sweet mother whose quiet faith had been a strong stay in our lives. George and Mary had returned to the States and Margie and Don had just arrived back, too. Our children represented the family at the funeral in Wooster and burial in Cincinnati. Margie was able to stay with Dad, help with his household and do some work in the French Department at the College of Wooster.

In our literacy project we discovered the complexity of the social problems in the northeast. Delmar and other trainers found that some of the people in remote areas got the notion that if they could sign their names they were ready to tackle the big city. They sold the cow and bought tickets for the whole family and went to get a job in São Paulo. The end result was the shantytowns of hopeless people mushrooming about the big cities. In the Recife area the tension between the plantation owners and the cane cutters was growing. The tenant cutters said: "We just want the rights that the law already allows us."

The response of the owners was: "That is not what you are going to get."

It took courage and compassion to work with the people in the classes.

As our furlough time approached a new director took over the Curriculum Department. I continued working on a booklet which would afford a review of the primer. One day I received a note from the director saying that they were discontinuing the work on the review book. I realized that I had received my walking papers. I cleared my desk with a sense of shock. On the other hand, I was glad for the freedom from responsibility and the time to pack.

I now had time to accept Madalena and Delmar's invitation to visit a community development project up in the hills. Delmar drove the jeep over boulders and around hairpin curves to the place where the agricultural arm of USAID was developing this project. A schoolhouse had been built and a well dug. But people were sick because the well water was contaminated. It was necessary to boil the drinking water. There were few trees in this area, so fuel for cooking was scarce. How were they to boil the water? Madalena had discussed the problem with the women's group. As we met in the schoolhouse, one woman got to her feet and said, "I have found a way to boil water for my family. As soon as the men come in from work I quickly serve the rice and beans. Then I scrub the pots, fill them with water and put them on the hot stove. It takes only a stick or two more to boil the water. I pour it into the *pote* (large earthenware jar). The next morning the water is cool and fresh for the family, enough for all day." Thus, people in their own community tackled problems in their own way.

As we were preparing to go on furlough, Libby wanted to experience a trip on a ship. Freight ships stopped at Recife and we were able to get passage on a freighter in early December. The ship was a week late, but finally arrived.

We were told to be at the dock at three o'clock. Friends came to the apartment to say good-bye, making us fifteen or twenty minutes late. We thought that three o'clock was the time when people would begin to board. We found that the customs officer deemed otherwise. He had left. The ship company's agent who should have facilitated our embarkation was out of town. We sat on our luggage in the customs barn until about six-thirty when, after many telephone calls and urgent messages, the officer came, took a cursory look at our suitcases and waved us aboard. The ship's captain was mad. We were his only passengers and he had prepared quite a reception for us with high tea and an open bar so that we could entertain our friends. Those who came to the ship to see us off were perplexed since no one knew we were down in the customs barn.

The captain got over his peeve and we had our meals at his table. He entertained us with yarns from his long years at sea. We had a wonderful trip. Our two cabins were large and comfortable. We read aloud to each other, played games, swam in the small canvas pool and enjoyed the deck, the sea and the ever changing drama of the wide sky.

We spent a week in Fortaleza unloading wheat and loading great containers of frozen lobster. We went out each day to explore the city and spent the night in our seagoing hotel.

We had bad weather between Fortaleza and Newport News. The captain slowed the ship to protect the cargo. We wired ahead to cancel our flight to Cleveland. We had expected to be in Wooster well before Christmas to welcome our family. Instead they met us at the Cleveland Airport on Christmas Eve, and we arrived in Wooster an hour before Christmas.

- 20 -

Goiânia: Empty Nest

We had a wonderful Christmas, George and Mary, Margie, Paul, Natalie, and Libby, and Mary's older brother Jim, all around our table. It didn't seem like our table, but theirs. They had cleaned the house and prepared the Christmas dinner: squab and all the Christmas goodies. Gifts lay under the decorated Christmas tree.

Everything moved very fast. George and Mary returned to Washington, where George was still working on his doctorate.

Margie followed George and Mary to Washington and got a job and her own apartment. Margie left her marmoset, Marquis, with us. Marquis was short for Marquis de Sade because he had so abused his mate that she died. We knew that there was a rule against pets in the housing for missionaries, but, as the residence was in a very run-down state, Marquis could hardly do anything to make it shabbier.

Paul was embarked on a master's program at the Woodrow Wilson School of International Studies at Princeton. Natalie was in her second year at the College of Wooster. She moved in with us. Libby was in seventh grade at Edgewood Junior High and was enjoying school. She liked her studies and had several close friends. She was given the lead as Dorothy in a production of *The Wizard of Oz* put on by her school. Practices kept her very busy.

Chalmers undertook a master's program in developmental education at the University of Pittsburgh. It was a big challenge to get a master's degree in one year. He found it breathtaking to go back into the classroom, take exams, work on projects in groups, and write papers. Once he got over the initial shock, he had a wonderful time. He admired his teachers and found rubbing elbows with people from many countries fascinating.

To qualify for a room at Pittsburgh Theological Seminary, Chalmers enrolled for a couple of courses there. The interest in the theological classes and in becoming acquainted with another Presbyterian Seminary made up for the tight schedule. Chalmers left Wooster very early Monday morning. Since I needed the car, he went to Pittsburgh by bus or train. I usually took him out to the highway bus stop on Route 30 at dawn. He would return home on Friday, after midnight, taking a taxi from the station. Weekends were special when he didn't have a speaking engagement and the family could be together.

Dad Browne was very lonely, but he kept busy. He was serving as chaplain at the Wooster Community Hospital. He went once or twice a day to the hospital. People really loved his cheery, outgoing concern, his wit, and the comfort and buoyancy of his spirit. Dad often bemoaned his small stature, but it was part of what made him so approachable. Each day I prepared the noon meal, jumped in the car, and went to fetch Dad for dinner.

A couple of times I went to Pittsburgh to visit Chalmers' classes, and I attended a seminar on reading with him. We even went one day to the zoo, which isn't far from the Seminary.

I took a beginners' drawing course at the College of Wooster. It was fun getting outdoors and drawing trees, sheds, and other simple forms. We studied shadow and light essentially and I found it fascinating. I would have liked to study illustrating, a skill which would have helped in our making of books for illiterates.

In early May we made a trip to visit Mary's parents, Miriam and Burton Behling, and to see Washington, D.C., a truly beautiful city. The cherry trees were in bloom.

Chalmers flew from Washington to St. Louis to a sensitivity workshop. Libby, Natalie, and I rented a car and drove to Princeton to attend the impressive, open-air ceremony where Paul received his master's degree. We then loaded Paul's possessions into the car and drove the Turnpike back to Wooster.

These were Vietnam War days and Paul went to the draft board in Wooster and asked permission to enter the Peace Corps. His request was granted. We helped him get his things sorted and the gear he would need packed. Before long he was off to Ethiopia.

It was during this Wooster year that our astronauts first walked on the moon. We didn't own a TV. Chalmers rented a set so that, as the images flitted back to earth, we could see the astounding event in our own living room.

As exciting as the moon landing was, the most momentous happening of the year was the birth of our grandson, James Chalmers, to Mary and George on December 4, 1979. As soon as the news came I went to Newark to be with the family. Is there anything more wondrous than one's first grandchild, except the next one and the next? Chal was a beautiful baby, born into a loving family. His shell-pink cheeks curved winsomely; he was good to touch and hold. Mary was having some pain, so it was good that I was there for a week.

My mother had been visiting my brothers. George accompanied her to Wooster. We were glad to have his visit. Our furlough was over and Mother was returning with us to Brazil. Dad Browne advised that we travel by train to Newark.

"It would mean getting someone to take us to Canton," Chalmers pointed out. Trains were no longer stopping in Wooster. "Then we would have to change trains in Pittsburgh in the middle of the night. Better to get a plane in Cleveland."

Little did we know. At the airport in Cleveland we had checked our baggage and were ready to go to the gate when "Flights to Newark canceled" was flashed. We were transferred to a flight to La Guardia, but that flight was also canceled. Bad weather descended upon the whole New York area and we were stranded. We tried phoning the railway, but the lines were all busy. We ended up on a Greyhound bus, sloshing through wind and rain to New York.

Because of the weather we were detained in New York for a week. On Sunday we went to Newark to spend the day. Chalmers baptized

Chal, who was developing charmingly. Tears were in his parents' eyes. We had dinner, by which time the snow was falling in blizzard proportions. We spent the night all over George's small apartment. The next day we were able to return to our apartment in New York.

A number of our supporting churches in the United States had pledged program money for a five-year development project for the Department of Adult Basic Education (DEBA) of the Confederação Evangélica do Brasil to which we were still assigned by our Presbyterian Mission. This fund was to make possible a program that we would develop for the churches. During our year in the States, the Cruzada ABC had fallen apart. There had been hanky-panky in high places. In the five years of its life, however, the Cruzada ABC had produced far-reaching changes. It stimulated the desire for learning. People who had been illiterate, today have professional training.

Goiânia, capital of the State of Goiás, was chosen for our work center. Goiânia is about 200 kilometers south of the Federal District and Brasília. We did not yet have a car. Chalmers and I traveled to Goiânia by bus. We stayed with our friends, Dr. Suahil Rahal and Dona Zaida. Dr. Suahil was building an evangelical hospital in Goiânia. We roamed the hot streets on foot looking for a house to rent and finally settled on one right across from the big general hospital. The house had a small front garden and a big backyard with two coconut palms, guava, and banana trees. Three unattached rooms ran along one side of the yard. We used two of these for offices of the "Research and Development Project."

We sent for Ginger. He traveled by air; we removed him from his slatted crate at the Brasília airport. He was glad enough to get out and see us again.

A priority was a school for Libby. The school year was about to begin and all of the better schools had full enrollment. We were able to place Libby in a small private school. Libby adapted well. She soon made friends and took things more or less as they came. She read voraciously in English and Portuguese.

Chalmers' doctors advised him to swim regularly to strengthen his hip. Goiânia had a very beautiful club with two swimming pools. Friends arranged a membership for our family at a reasonable rate. The trips to the pool were a healthful source of renewal and a great boon in hosting guests.

With the demise of the Cruzada ABC, Madalena and Delmar had been helping to bring things to a close, but soon they were without a job. We invited them to join our team in Goiânia. Their coming doubled the possibilities for our work. Canvassing churches and other community organizations soon had us working with enthusiastic leaders. Goiânia had all sorts of resources. It was then a very big town of about 400,000 inhabitants where everybody knew about everybody. The church's many denominations set up a board of directors for the adult basic education project.

The first phase was that of literacy: training teachers and setting up classes for adults in churches, homes, and other centers in different parts of the town and surrounding areas. Delmar and Madalena began their community development work with the promotion of family vegetable gardens and the teaching of nutrition and hygiene. We began a new venture in the nurture of the Christian family. We developed lessons on parenting, health, family finances, and spiritual growth using slides, posters, and simple reading materials, trying out this series of lessons in our neighborhood church. Our barrio was called Setor Universitario because the University of Goiás was located there. But the houses in the area were modest to poor, the homes of blue-collar workers and unskilled laborers. Our congregation was a mission branch of the Central Presbyterian Church.

We attended this church and became involved in the ministry of its people on a volunteer basis. Chalmers preached. There was a small pump organ that no one knew how to play. We found someone to repair it and I served as organist and taught some of the young people in the congregation to play hymns.

While working with the Peace Corps in Ethiopia, Paul met Rhea Carol Dingus in Addis Ababa. She had joined the Peace Corps a year earlier. A medical technologist, she was helping to set up a blood bank in the city. Paul wrote to us, "I have found someone to whom I can entrust my life."

Carol, on completing her two years with the Peace Corps, signed up for a third. She took time out to visit her parents in Kentucky. She and Paul were married with the support of all their Peace Corps friends at the top of the mountain overlooking Addis Ababa. On completion of their Peace Corps years they returned via Brazil, having traveled first through a part of Africa.

We were delighted to see them. We loved Carol immediately. She was a slender, soft-spoken brunette with rosy complexion and a fay quality about her. Carol was awed by my mother, who was visiting us, and Mother couldn't understand Carol's soft Kentucky drawl.

Paul and Carol were having trouble with us as missionaries. Many in the Peace Corps thought missionaries arrogant and insensitive, contributing to colonial power over people in Africa and other places. Paul and Carol were also disenchanted with the narrowness they found in the church. It was hard for them to participate in our activities. This attitude rubbed off on Libby. After they left, Libby wanted to know why she had to participate in daily prayers.

"This is Chalmers' and my home," I told her. "When you have a home of your own you will order it your way." Our dear Libby accepted this verdict with no resentment.

Natalie graduated from college and, after a summer with the Peace Corps in their preparation of volunteers, set out for Brazil. How good it was to welcome her home! She stayed with us for several weeks, then went to Salvador. She taught English privately for a while, before returning to the United States and going to Tufts University in Boston for a master's in education.

Our second grandchild, Sebhat Alexander, was born to Carol and Paul in Lexington, Kentucky, near Carol's home, on September 7, 1970. Sibby, as he was called, was named for their best friend in Ethiopia. When he was eight months old, Sibby came with his mother to visit us in Goiânia He was a sturdy, sunny child with gold ringlets and a great zest for life. He liked his food, going for walks, games, learning words, everything, and Carol found it a joy, full of surprises, to see a young personality emerging from a fretful little baby. Happiness bounced back and forth between Carol and Sibby. For us, the days flew by too fast and soon we were taking Sibby and Carol back to their plane in Brasília.

Libby was fifteen, and all three of us felt she needed to prepare to go to college. We visited the boarding school of the southern

Presbyterian Church (U.S.) at Ceres, not far from Brasília. Because of her lack of academic credits, the principal wanted to place her in the second half of the sophomore year of high school. Libby was determined to go into the junior year.

We went next to Brasília, where an American Graded School was being established. The primary school and two years of high school were functioning and the junior and senior years would be added for the next school year. The principal and teachers agreed to teach Libby as a correspondence student for one semester at the level of a junior in high school. Thus when the new school year started in September of 1972 she would enter her senior year. Libby passed her tests and went to live during the week with our colleagues, the Journeys, and went to school each day with the Journey boys.

Libby had a boyfriend in Goiânia . Joviano was a very attractive young man; he had grace and flair. He and Libby made a vivacious pair. He was studying engineering at the University of Brasília. He and Libby didn't see each other in Brasília, but when Libby's bus arrived in Goiânia of a Friday evening, Joviano was there to escort her home.

Libby had a good year. She graduated first in her class of three seniors. Though the class was small the school put on a real graduation for them, with all the formalities. Then Libby was home for vacation.

The federal government launched a new literacy project which went by the name of MOBRAL. Chalmers was asked to be the temporary president of MOBRAL in Goiânia. Chalmers agreed to serve until a Brazilian president could be found. He worked at this job for almost a year and was proud to hand out diplomas to the first class to master the government primer. A woman educator who had been working through this initial period with MOBRAL, of Goiás, was now willing to take over the reins. The new appointment had not been announced when Chalmers went on a trip to Patrocinio, Minas, to hold a literacy workshop in the Bible School. While he was away, a young state legislator, newly appointed, made a speech on TV. Among other rash statements he implied that there was something sinister about Chalmers, an American, being president of MOBRAL. Then he said that Chalmers had left town suddenly and no one knew of his whereabouts. The press carried these spicy comments, not only in Goiânia, but in a Rio de Janeiro newspaper. We were blissfully unaware of this publicity.

Chalmers had barely returned home, when Jim Wright, our Brazil Mission executive secretary, knocked on our door. He came to see where Chalmers was, what he was doing, and get him out of hot water. It was bizarre and we had a laugh over it. The legislator in question didn't last many days at his post, and Chalmers was very glad to turn the directorship of MOBRAL over to his successor.

Missionaries work pretty much on their own. Our sending body, The Program Agency of the Presbyterian Church, felt a responsibility to keep some tabs on us. A kindly gentleman from headquarters visited us. For two days we answered questions on every aspect of our work. One question which pegged us as "reactionary" was, "Would you side with and take part with the university students if they went on a strike?" Our answer was, "No."

We had two reasons for this stand. First, we were being paid by an American agency. We felt it could only do harm to the student cause if we were to openly take a stand with them. The students knew that our door was open to them and that we were always glad to listen as friends on political as well as other matters. We also knew too much about the absurdities that the students committed and that many of the students themselves deplored the foolish doings of their peers. Second, our work was not with university students but with the underprivileged. We did not want to jeopardize the task we had been sent to do.

The work was spreading by leaps and bounds. With MOBRAL taking over the main organization of classes and teacher training, we were free to do special work in churches, hospitals, jails, and other places MOBRAL did not reach. The community development work was burgeoning under the direction of Delmar and Madalena. Our program taught nutrition, hygiene, and family life. The gardening project was very popular as entire families worked to produce vegetables for the table and some to sell.

In the midst of everything we saw Libby off to the College of Wooster. She and Joviano decided that, with a four-year separation, their relationship should be one of friendship. We took Libby to the airport in Brasília. Five minutes before boarding time Joviano turned up for a last good-bye, and the slight, jaunty figure of our daughter strode to the plane and turned for a last wave of her hand.

A few weeks later we received a letter from Margie saying that she and Don were going to make a trip together through Europe. We were stunned. Our whole concept of the role of the family was being challenged. We requested they come home first and get married. They didn't accede. These were the sixties, the early days of the "new morality" and Chalmers and I felt shattered.

A group that had trained with us was forging ahead with their literacy program in Anapolis, a burgeoning city between Goiânia and Brasília. Teresinha, their leader, set up a workshop and asked us to spend a week with them training teachers, demonstrating the use of new materials, running a new readers' library and helping to assess resources and opportunities in Anapolis.

The only problem with the workshop was its timing. We had planned a seminar in Goiânia to take place two weeks later and the Anapolis workshop drained off many of those whom we had hoped to host in Goiânia We had to reduce the program to a weekend retreat. We had invited Emília, the secretary of DEBA (Department of Adult Basic Education), who planned to come to the seminar as a leader. We wrote to her that the seminar was off because we didn't have enough registrations. Emília was highly intelligent and very hard-working, but she was also morbidly jealous. Our relations were often strained. She was angered by this canceling of her participation and took her complaints of us to Jim Wright. We received a blistering letter from Jim. Fortunately, we had her letters to us and copies of our letters to her and to other persons involved so as to show our good faith and that Emília had twisted matters. So ended that skirmish.

I was invited by Lit-Lit to go to a workshop in Mexico. Again Emília, who had expected to receive this invitation, was hurt. She arranged funds privately and went to the Mexico workshop. On the way she stopped in New York to visit the Program Agency and carried her complaints of us to headquarters.

I got off to Mexico. A great thunderhead illuminated by the setting sun towered over Mexico City as our plane came in to land. It didn't look so much ominous as beautiful and powerful. From Mexico City

I took a bus to Pachuca. I walked through Pachuca streets looking for the church where the workshop was already under way. One man of whom I asked directions in what I thought was Spanish answered, "I don't understand English." I felt deflated but went on to find the church and participated in a very good workshop with classes in methodology and in health training. Alphalit, which for many years has helped people to read and write in Spanish, was in charge.

Pachuca is up in the hills where silver is mined. I was billeted in the home of a Mexican family. They were dear people. I enjoyed their hospitality and the bright red geraniums on their patio with sunny marigolds and blue delphinium against the whitewashed walls. But my most lasting impression of my hosts is of their laughter. They thought me immensely funny with my foreign accent and my ignorance of how to make tortillas.

From Pachuca we returned to Mexico City via the pyramids to the Sun and Moon. Looking down the central avenue between the pyramids the extraordinary symmetry, the purity of line and the fall of light and shadow amidst the gently eroding stone was like walking with angels, with the spirits of the long-gone builders of this place.

We were in Mexico City for a week at a conference on strategy. This was Lit-Lit's conference and Rex was in charge. One morning as we were at breakfast Rex and I sat at the same table. He began to tell me all of Chalmers' shortcomings. He had no good word to say. "Dr. Rex," I said, "no wife likes to hear anyone say such things about her husband." I wasn't going to argue with him, and he begged my pardon.

We took a two-day trip to Pascuaro to visit a literacy research center with lovely grounds, buildings, and equipment. But I was puzzled by how little actual field work was being done. No illiterates mingled with the intellectuals. Maybe it was just the time we were there. Gladly I returned to Goiânia

Hard times were hitting church budgets in the United States. Ten couples of our mission were asked to cut their terms short by a year. Perhaps because of the assessment of the interviewer who reported us as unwilling to support a student strike and the grievances of Emília, we were among the ten couples. John Sinclair, Latin America coordinator of the Program Agency, came to bring us the news. We pointed out that our supporting churches had provided special funds, not for our salary, but for our program, for five years. A compromise was reached. We would stay for four and a half years, six more months. Delmar and Madalena would carry on the project for the remaining six months. We moved the DEBA office from the rooms behind our house to a downtown, second-floor suite of two rooms. As we transferred the work to Delmar and Madalena, they took over with fervor. They had about a thousand households enrolled already in the vegetable-garden-nutrition project.

We packed up rather sorrowfully and stored our furniture with the new minister at the downtown Presbyterian church. He and his family were friends from Recife days. We had attended their wedding. Delmar bought the little red VW we had been driving. We took Ginger with us to my sister Mary Elizabeth and Francis and Debbie, where he spent the remainder of his days.

We were off again to the United States, this time to look for a job. We were not anxious, for God had always opened doors for us. We trusted that the Spirit would guide us to the right door.

- 21 -

Choosing Mozambique

The Presbyterian Church of Lambertville, N.J. had a lovely apartment, which it rented to missionaries at a very modest price. We were fortunate to live in it for a year. George and Mary lived but an hour away by car in West Orange with Chal and Russell David, born on December 29, 1971. Russ was now a debonair young gentleman of one year, curious and lively and into everything. Paul, Carol and Sibby were living in Washington, about three hours away. Natalie was at Tufts University in Boston.

Margie had written us that she and Don would soon be leaving for Israel to live in a kibbutz. When George met us at the airport he informed us that Margie and Don had been refused the opportunity in Israel because Margie was pregnant. Libby was at the College of Wooster, enjoying her first year. We talked to her by phone. She wanted to come East immediately for a visit, but we put it off as we were planning to go to Wooster shortly.

We went for a short visit to Dad and Libby in Wooster. We found Libby in the infirmary with chickenpox. She was soon well enough to be about and show us her dorm and have us meet her roommates.

As we settled into our new apartment in Lambertville we thought we might be able to do without a car, but we discovered that there were only two buses each day through the town and no other form of public transportation. Trenton, the nearest railroad or commuter plane point, was some thirty miles away. Mary and George had a friend who was offering to sell a car for seventy-five dollars. It was a Pontiac Le Mans, about ten years old. We bought the car and it served us for twenty thousand miles of driving before we turned it over to George and Mary, who used it for another two years.

All our children and their families came to visit in March. They helped me celebrate my birthday. We were a noisy bunch with our three little grandsons. We were beginning to learn to be grandparents.

Though Sibby was older, he and Russ were about the same size. Sibby had a big beach ball and the two little boys held it in a tug of war. Each had hold of one side of the ball. Sibby was yelling: "No way, Russ, no way!"

The next morning Chalmers and I were having breakfast when Sibby walked into the kitchen. "Have some breakfast, Sibby?" we invited.

Sibby sat at the table and accepted some of the toast we were eating and some orange juice.

Then Libby appeared with a hug for Sibby. "I'm going to have an egg. Do you want one, Sibby?"

Sibby readily agreed. He was consuming the egg when Natalie arrived with a cheery greeting. "Want some cereal with me?" she asked.

Sibby had some cereal and when he was finishing, Paul and Carol came in. Sibby continued having breakfast with them to our astonishment at a small boy's capacity..

I offered Chal some banana. Always the meticulous one, he dissolved into tears when I cut the big banana irrevocably in two: he had wanted it whole.

At Easter time we went to Boston to visit Natalie. She was working towards her master's in education, and was rooming in a house with several other young people. She showed us around Tufts University. We went to the chapel at Harvard for the Easter service: the music and worship were moving.

Back in Lambertville, Mary and George came visiting for a few days. Mary was writing a paper. "Go upstairs, Mary, and write. I'll take care of the boys. We'll call you for lunch," I said. It was a beautiful day and I invited Chal and Russ to go to the park. Russ got into his stroller and Chal stood on the back bar. I pushed them both along. At the park we played for over an hour on the swings, jungle gym, slides, and seesaws.

I looked at my watch. "Time to go home and make lunch," I said. Chal immediately ran over to the stroller and took his place; Russ ran away. I chased him and carried him to the stroller. As I turned the stroller around he climbed out and ran away again. After several repetitions of this game, I was out of breath and time was passing. "I guess I'll have to spank you," I said. Magic words. Russ climbed into the stroller and we were on our way.

Over another weekend Carol and Paul left Sibby with us while they went on an excursion of their own. Sibby was interested in everything as we went for a walk and he counted dandelions along the way. I realized that though he was counting only to three, he was really counting, not just saying the words. Not bad for a two-year-old. All went well until lunchtime the next day, when he suddenly turned an anxious face to me and started out of his chair. "Where's my Mummy! Where's my Daddy!" His voice was full of panic.

"Sibby, your mummy and daddy are driving," I said. I turned an imaginary driver's wheel and made the noise of a car engine. "They're coming right now to see Sibby. They'll be here soon." Sibby calmed right down and continued to enjoy everything until, blessedly, his parents arrived in time for supper and bedtime.

When they were not able to go to Israel, Don and Margie moved to Rochester, N.Y., where Don continued his doctoral studies at the University of Rochester. Chalmers and I were having a difficult time accepting their lack of marriage, considering they had a baby on the way, but they were children of the sixties. They did not need the government or the church to "marry" them; the decision was theirs alone. We persuaded Don and Margie to allow us to send out a formal announcement of their decision to form a family so our relatives and friends would know about them.

Libby got a summer job at a camp in New Jersey, so we picked her up every other weekend to spend Saturday and Sunday with us.

Natalie was with Mary and George when she had an urgent call from the camp where she had worked the previous summer. They were short of counselors. She was able to spend a few weeks in her beloved camp where we visited her and saw a group of counselors building one of the distinctive tents which this camp had developed.

I had a commitment to speak to a church group when it was one of Natalie's days off duty. Chalmers went to the camp for her and they wandered in the countryside in green and shadowy places by brooks and waterfalls. It was a day they cherished. After the time at camp Natalie made a trip to Europe with a friend. They enjoyed Paris, London, and the beaches in Portugal.

We were busy and happy but perplexed. We were reaching the end of our six-month furlough and would soon be off salary, so we were glad when a church in southern Pennsylvania contacted Chalmers. A delegation from that church came to a service in Narberth, Pennsylvania, where Chalmers preached. After the service we met with the delegation. They explained about the manse and living conditions as well as the challenges of the church work. One of the men turned to me and asked, "What do you think of it?"

"It sounds like heaven," I answered.

The following week Jim Wright visited us on behalf of the Program Agency of our church. The United Methodist Church had approached the Presbyterians with a request that we be seconded to them to work in the Portuguese colonies in Africa. The Methodist Church was especially concerned about Mozambique, where missionaries involved in education were not being issued permanent visas. The McKnights, who for years had spearheaded the literacy and literature program of the Mozambican Methodist Church, were living in South Africa and obtaining tourist visas to spend three months of each year in Mozambique, a most unsatisfactory arrangement.

Our supporting churches were willing to underwrite us to return to Brazil for a year to facilitate our entry into Mozambique. The Central Presbyterian Church of Goiânia had requested of the Program Agency that we return to do full-time urban mission work with the congregation in the University Sector where we had been volunteering earlier. The Methodists believed that we would more easily obtain a permanent visa to work in Mozambique if we requested it from a work base in

Brazil. We accepted the challenge and reluctantly said good-bye to the very appealing Presbyterian church in southern Pennsylvania.

On July 3, 1973, Ezequiel Olinto Hart was born in Rochester. We immediately went to visit Margie and Don and our new grandson. I was impressed with Zeke's eyes. They were very keen and seemed observant of everything. Greta was very happy with her little son. We had to get used to this new name for Margie. All her friends called her Greta, as did Don.

Marcel Wallbridge Browne was born to Carol and Paul in Washington, D.C. on July 16. Carol's mother, Janice Dingus, came to help in the home. We made a trip to meet our new grandson who, unlike Sibby, was a large, placid little boy, very fair. Now we had five of them! This was truly the year of the grandsons.

We were still without salary until the next calendar year when we would return to Brazil, so we responded eagerly when we received a call from the First Presbyterian Church in Evansville, Indiana. They were looking for a missionary in residence for a couple of months. We drove to Evansville for an interview, then returned to Lambertville and packed up our belongings.

On our way to Evansville we took time to visit Bea and Sam in Menominee, Michigan. Sam was now Episcopal bishop for the Upper Peninsula. We made the trip in one day, over 700 miles. We were being frugal with our dwindling bank account, but it turned out to be devastating for me, since I was ill during our visit in Menominee.

In a few days we drove on to Evansville. The Evansville Presbyterian Church had rented for us a small cottage that belonged to a member who was in a nursing home. We visited her and told her how much we appreciated her place with its rose garden and comfortable living.

Chalmers became part of the church staff. Our days there were a continual round of meetings and speaking engagements. First Church was unique in that it had two sanctuaries and two programs. The old central church was no longer where most of the congregation lived. A new modern complex was built in a growing suburb. But members who cherished the beautiful downtown building continued with their services each Sunday and a program of outreach to the neighborhood. We were impressed with the youth program of the church and the outreach to hurting people. First Presbyterian of Evansville was willing to share us and we spoke in other churches in the Presbytery.

We received an invitation from the First Presbyterian Church of Colorado Springs, where my brother Phil and Mary Louise were members, to spend a weekend with them as they focused on mission. On our way west we had a couple of hours between planes in the airport at St. Louis. We were trapped with no one to visit, all to ourselves. We went out on the deck and watched the planes coming in and going out, a plane every few seconds. The evening was dying in a haze of cloud and light. It was beautiful and we felt at peace and glad just to be with each other.

First Church of Colorado Springs had five thousand members. The weekend was very full of events and promotion of worldwide involvement of the church. We were caught up in the enthusiasm. It was also special to visit my brother and family.

From the Evansville assignment we moved to Southminster Presbyterian Church in Mt. Lebanon, Pittsburgh for two months. Southminster was one of our longtime supporting churches. Here Chalmers functioned as a calling pastor among the members of the church. He liked this work and the months passed quickly. We lived in a beautiful home of a member of the church who had just lost her husband and was staying with her daughter.

Chalmers had sprained his ankle in our move to Pittsburgh. I went with Chalmers to see a doctor. He was told to keep off his foot for a couple of days, a very hard task under the circumstances. After the doctor had finished with Chalmers I told him of my cold that had lasted all summer. The doctor prescribed an antibiotic and I was soon so much better that I wondered why I had not sought help before.

Christmastime at our temporary home was very special. Margie and Don arrived by bus with their six-month-old son. As they alighted I took Zeke in my arms. As he looked into my face he began to laugh. We both laughed and laughed. It was an extraordinary moment.

Friends in the congregation invited us to their Christmas party. They had a lovely home with antiques and old paintings and etchings of Pittsburgh. We were assured that Don and Margie would be welcome. Zeke went along too and spent his time in a bedroom upstairs. It was not altogether a successful evening for Margie and Don were definitely of the hippie generation and dress. The party was Pittsburgh bluestocking. It was really too great a contrast and our friends were embarrassed.

Natalie and Libby arrived also. Natalie and Libby employed themselves in decorating the house for Christmas. They made a wreath for the front door. During the holidays Paul and Carol also visited us. We took our cue from Zeke and laughed a lot and sang carols in English and Portuguese.

With the new year it was time to return to Goiânia. As soon as we reached Brazil we got in touch with the Portuguese embassy about visas to Mozambique. It was good we started early for it took us all of a year to get the visas.

The next item on the list was to find a house. We wanted to live in the area of our congregation, and after much searching we rented a house that had no bathroom—with the understanding that we could install one. The creation of the "throne room" turned out to be a major project. The house was at the back of the lot and the street was about eight or ten feet above the house. We were not allowed to run the pipes down to the lower street behind our house as we had hoped. In order that there would be a great enough fall into the sewage system at the upper street level we had to raise our bathroom floor several feet. Three steps led up from the hall to the bathroom.

Our house was small, but it was mighty. We had a lovely front bedroom and a guest room. We extended our living room space into the front yard under two trees entwined by a passion fruit vine, which bloomed with large purple flowers and rained down pulpy yellow fruit. We had fresh passion fruit-ade on our lunch table every day. Under the trees we affixed a picnic table and benches where, in the good weather that is plentiful on the Goiás plateau, we entertained visitors. We ate our family meals on the back porch just outside the kitchen. Teresinha, who became a very loyal friend, reigned in the kitchen. She cooked Brazilian food well and learned to make American and Chinese dishes.

The church was about five short blocks away. Madalena and Delmar lived one block from the church with their family, including a new adopted baby daughter, Cristiane. It was a real boon to have them helping in the church as well as continuing their adult education project.

Chalmers was the minister of word and sacrament under the official sponsorship of the Central Church and we worked at counseling, teaching, and reaching out to those in need of physical and spiritual healing. Our people were the salt of the earth, many of them struggling under the handicap of poverty. One member sold popcorn and spun candy for a living and his wife was a seamstress. They were relatively well off.

Greta and Don moved to Brazil after Don received his Ph.D. in English literature from the University of Rochester. Their idea was to acquire some land and live close to the earth, and they stayed with us while they looked for a place. We made several trips of exploration with them in our red Volkswagon bug. Zeke was walking and enjoyed these adventures.

The land they bought was near the small town of Cocalzinho with its lime processing plant and farms all around. Don and Greta's farm was about five miles into the wilderness. There was no house. Greta and Don put up a tent in which they lived while their house was being built. Their household water supply came from a spring in the wooded hills.

Our congregation was growing and expanding its activities. Dr. Suahil was the elder from the Central Church who took special interest in the University Sector Congregation. He and Dona Zaida came to Sunday School and services and Dr. Suahil taught a men's Bible class. We also had a weekday adult education program.

The youth group enjoyed their meetings and activities. The thing they liked best was a trip to the hot springs south of Goiânia. We would get up before it was light on a Saturday and travel three hours in a rented bus to the hot springs. A hotel with special pools at the hot springs was expensive, but the waters of the stream that flowed from the springs were deliciously warm and free. We would picnic and play in the shallows for carefree hours until the setting sun warned us to climb aboard the bus for the return home.

Madalena and Delmar wanted their oldest daughter, Angela, to go to the University on her graduation from high school. Angela and her boyfriend Melquinho were too deeply in love. They came to us for support and we listened to them but could not take sides. They did what many a couple has done before them—they forced their parents' hand. Angela became pregnant. So the wedding was set and Chalmers and I went searching for flowers and decorated the church. Chalmers married the young couple in a beautiful formal wedding.

Frenchy and Joan were working in a parish in the United States after returning from their service in India. They took a vacation trip to Brazil to visit us. The youth group of our church threw a party for them, a St. John's Day party with a bonfire, firecrackers, skits, and special food. The language barrier did not dampen the enjoyment. We then took our vacation and traveled with Joan and Frenchy in our little red car to São Paulo, sightseeing along the way. We visited Mary Elizabeth and Francis, Debbie and Mother, and missionary friends. We were glad they could be with us to see a little of Brazil.

The Brazilian Presbyterian Church with whom we served, had severed its ties with our sending denomination, the United Presbyterian Church U.S.A. We were therefore becoming somewhat of an embarrassment to the Central Church in Goiânia. One of the elders in the Central Church was a good friend of ours, but also the treasurer of the General Assembly of the Brazilian Presbyterian Church. When the time came for us to leave at the end of the year we were thanked and given a farewell party, and we all breathed a sigh of relief.

We packed and gave most of our furniture to Greta. She was teaching English in Cocalzinho and had rented a small house in town. She would ride horseback or walk into town with Zeke and spend several days. She was glad of the furniture for the farm and the house in town. We set out in our little red car, which was now of ancient vintage, hoping that it would get us all the way to my sister's where we had a buyer for it.

We were tired and decided to go as far as the hot springs to spend the night. We arrived at the hotel at about dusk. We spent a delicious evening in the lighted hot pools. It was a blissful hour suspended between the job we had left behind and the unknown, uneasy adventure ahead.

The little car behaved beautifully and we were able to tell the new owner about its good performance. We visited Mary Elizabeth and Francis and Mother. They had added a large room and bath onto their house especially for Mother. It was good to be with the family.

We had worked on our visa through the Portuguese embassy in Brasília. When we went to pick up our passports and visas a few days before we left, we were told that we would find them waiting for us in São Paulo, and we did. A week later we left Brazil for Angola and Mozambique.

- 22 -

Independence for Mozambique

*I*n preparation for bilingual adult education, Chalmers and I, before we left Brazil, spent several days with Gloria Kindal at the Wycliffe Translators' headquarters in Brasília The Wycliffe teams were specialists in working with new languages and in helping people move from their native tongue to other languages. It was a quick course, but invaluable to us. We left with a better understanding of what we could do.

Somewhere between Brazil and Africa we metamorphosed: we became Methodists. Doris Hess of the Methodist Board of Global Ministries, who had worked with us in Brazil, had asked that we go to the Portuguese-speaking countries of Africa where the Methodist Church had work, Angola and Mozambique. There was a need for people acquainted with Portuguese and the field of adult basic education.

In Angola Bishop Emílio de Carvalho met us. He had set up a ten-day workshop to create a primer for adults. We were put up in a very nice hotel and walked each sunny morning to the Methodist compound. We met some fascinating church people and worked out an adult literacy book in a short time.

We were able to take strolls around the city in the daytime, but at night there was a curfew. The war with the Portuguese was over, but tribal differences had flared. We could hear the barking of guns throughout the night. Each morning there were new tales of deaths and destruction.

On Sunday we went to a church in a suburb where the service was in the native tongue. Though we couldn't understand the words, the fervor, joy, and dedication of the Christian community were clear.

After the service we went to the pastor's home for dinner. As we were at table the door opened and a gaunt-looking man entered. He stood just within the door with all eyes upon him for an instant. Then the pastor jumped to his feet and rushed to embrace the newcomer. There was a time of great jubilation with all present hugging the man, exclaiming and laughing. He was a relative who had fled for his life during the time of conflict with the Portuguese and was back from a long exile.

While we were in Luanda, fighting in the city became worse. Fear and a sense of helplessness pervaded the atmosphere. Meetings at night were canceled. We were sorry to leave the people of Angola in this rather desperate situation.

Our journey to Lorenzo Marques, the name of the capital of Mozambique at that time, was through Johannesburg. We spent the night in the Johannesburg airport hotel. We arrived in Lorenzo Marques in the bright morning. Barbara Kurt, evangelist and educator missionary, took us under her wing. We stayed in her apartment while we bought furniture for ours. Both apartments were on a court that could be reached by pedestrians through an archway from Eduardo Mondlane Avenue or by a long alley for vehicles.

Our second-floor apartment was lovely. The living room had French windows opening onto a small balcony overlooking the court. We bought some cotton goods patterned in big medallions with stylized starfish in the centers, inky blue on a beige background. We found office furniture made of metal, cushioned in the same rich blue as the curtains. We were pleased with the effect.

We were quickly into the tasks of learning a new culture and tribal language, Xithswa, and understanding the literacy and literature program of the church. The Methodist Church, true to its name, tends to be more structured than the Presbyterian so that it is easy to know what one's job is. We belonged to the Committee for Literature and Literacy. Our predecessors had worked out a very good program to teach reading and writing in Xitshwa. The hope was that, working with our Mozambican colleagues, we would be able to expand the program. The Bible had been translated into Xitshwa by early missionaries and was a source of life-giving hope and satisfaction. The word of God reaches us best in the language of the heart, the language of our home and people.

But Portuguese was necessary, too, because it is the national language of Mozambique. Also, contact with the outside world is dependent on a European language. Instructions accompanying any machine or appliance would be in Portuguese, English, French, German, or Spanish.

The head of the Literature and Literacy Committee was Bento Navˆs, a man small in physical stature, but very big in his abilities and capacity to give of himself. His knowledge of Xitshwa was phenomenal. He had been deeply marked by the years of discrimination and humiliation at the hands of the white people in South Africa as well as in Mozambique. Bento's wife, Ana Navˆs, was a large woman with irrepressible energy and good will. Her work was largely with the women of the church.

The Mujongues were another dedicated couple. Chadreque was not only the treasurer of the United Methodist Church of Mozambique, but a sort of pivot in the workings of the programs. Margaret Mujongue was the head of the Subcommittee on Literacy and our immediate work partner.

When we reached Mozambique, the Bishop was away. One Sunday morning we saw a tall handsome gentleman at the church service and learned that he was Bishop Zunguze. He was a warmhearted man who enjoyed the jacaranda trees in bloom with their profusion of glowing lavender flowers. His wife, Thelma, was a lovely lady who didn't speak much Portuguese, but was a mother to the women and young people.

Another early friend was Penicela. He had studied in Brazil and in Portugal and now taught at the University of Mozambique. He and his wife, Angelina, helped us get acclimated. The Mozambican people are rich in their capacity for friendship and pure joy, even in the midst of tribulation.

Lourenço Marques, now Maputo, is a port on the Indian Ocean. It is not far from the southern tip of the country at its border with South Africa. The country extends along the Indian Ocean almost as long as the Atlantic coastline of America from Florida to Maine, and is fringed with lovely beaches, reefs, islets, and lagoons.

The Methodist Church, and most of the other Protestant churches, had been restricted by the Portuguese to the southern third of the country. The Methodist Church had work as far as the Vilanculos River, four or five hundred kilometers north of Maputo.

The main centers of the work were Maputo, and three hundred kilometers to the north, Cambine and Xicuque. The main hospital of the Church was in Xicuque, a coastal area of fishing villages. Cambine is inland, a beautiful place with sunny fields and glens of wide-spreading trees. The first missionaries who came to Mozambique from Sweden more than one hundred years prior found favor with the chief of this region. The chief gave them land where springs of clear, fresh water fed the valley stream. A Bible School, a gracious church, a clinic building, and residences were now scattered about the parklike mission station, which follows the good Mozambican fashion of villages hidden among fruit trees, cashew and avocado, and coconut palms. Cambine was a place of serenity, and Chalmers and I were privileged to be in the home of the Persons on our first visit to the Bible School to teach methods of literacy.

Since we were in Mozambique on a temporary visa, we were advised to get our permanent visa before the end of the year of transition. Portugal was going to turn over the government of Mozambique definitively to Mozambicans on June 25, 1975. To get our permanent visa we were required to leave the country and apply at a Mozambican embassy abroad. The nearest embassy was in Swaziland, so in May we boarded a bus headed for Mbabane, capital of Swaziland. It isn't very far from Maputo to the border, where we changed from our Mozambican bus to a Swazi one. We had passes to cross the border. From the bus station we went to a Holiday Inn to spend the night. The next morning we went into town to the embassy. In no time at all we had our permanent visas to live in Mozambique. We had time to walk about the town and drop in on the pastor of a church we came upon and do some shopping.

We missed our bus back to Maputo the next morning because the taxi we had engaged was late. The taxi driver said he could overtake the bus, but the taxi cab broke down and left us stranded. We hoped for another bus, but none came. It was windy and very chill. Finally a car stopped suddenly just beyond us. The driver stuck his head out and asked where we wanted to go.

"To the Mozambican border."

"I'm going that far," he said. "Hop in."

Our rescuer was a salesman and a warm Christian. We had a good chat until we were set down at the border. We thanked our new friend, and crossed the border on foot. A bus stood ready to go to Maputo. "I'm just going to stop a minute down the road, then we will be off," said the driver. We waited hungry and cold for an hour while we imagined the driver having a good hot meal. We finally pushed off and were never so glad to reach home.

The great festivities of June 25 included a parade with floats and marching groups of many descriptions: military, school children, and citizens clubs. We watched from the sidelines. The biggest event was the massing of the populace in the large stadium at the edge of the city. Friends drove us out to the meeting, but the crowds made an impenetrable wall around the stadium, which was full to capacity. Speeches and singing went on until midnight when the Portuguese flag came down and the new Mozambican flag fluttered, red, black and yellow with its star, book, hoe, and gun on the night breeze.

The churches put on a daylong pageant recounting the deliverance of the chosen people of Israel from their bondage in Egypt. We sat for two hours in the morning in the principal gymnasium in Maputo, then went home for lunch. We congregated again at two for the continuation of the spectacle.

The churches in Mozambique, including the Methodist, had great expectations for the new independence that would come to all. Surveys and plans had been made to extend the network of schools and first-aid clinics into areas that had been off limits during the Portuguese regime.

Samora Machel, the president of Mozambique, in his long, inaugural speech on Independence Day, said "We are going to move far to the left: you will be surprised how far left." Mozambique became a communist state overnight.

On the Fourth of July the American embassy invited all U.S. citizens to a picnic on the beach. There was a sober note to this get-together, for a missionary of the Nazarene Church had been jailed. Several days later another American missionary and his companions, one Brazilian and the other from a French colony, were also put in prison. These missionaries were victims of odd circumstances. One had made enemies among the revolutionists by unwittingly helping someone who was fleeing from them. Three others had been running a halfway house for drug addicts. Some of the men in the house were unsavory characters from South Africa; thus the missionaries were harboring enemies of the people. Many missionaries who had worked for years in Mozambique now felt threatened or no longer useful and, in time, left.

It was a difficult process to urge the Mozambican government to release these prisoners, who languished for years in jail. The embassies kept up their pressuring until finally all five of them were allowed to leave the country. In the meantime, week after week, families attached to the American embassy and missionaries like us took meals to the men in prison.

The Mozambican Church was faring ill. Land and buildings belonging to the churches were confiscated. Church schools, hostels and hospitals were nationalized. Some churches were closed because they were too close to the schools and would be a "distracting influence."

For us this moment was one of truth. Here were people who had lived under restrictions and had endured humiliations. They had expected at last redemption, political freedom, and widening opportunities. Instead they suffered severe curtailment, despoilment of their properties, and relegation to second- or third-class-citizen status. They absorbed the blows without complaint. Their faith and hope were not in buildings or in recognition, not even in the services taken from them, but in their Lord.

The government set up rules about places of worship. No new churches could be built. People could not congregate in the open air for worship services. In many subtle ways religious people were circumscribed while the government proclaimed freedom of religion. Religion was not prohibited, but it was considered a superstition, a benighted vestige that would just fade away.

A government official was haranguing a large crowd gathered under some trees about the matter of superstition. He pointed out, with arguments, that there is no God. Convinced of the force of his eloquence, he threw out the question, "Now, do any of you believe in God?"

An ocean of hands went up and a roar of "We do."

One place that was left to the church was the Interdenominational Theological Seminary at Ricatla. Once a week we went out to Ricatla, which is about thirty kilometers from Maputo, to teach methods of literacy. We also taught reading and writing and Portuguese to the wives of the ministerial students. Most of the students were married and had their families with them. They lived in round houses and tried to grow vegetables in the meager, sandy soil with very modest results. Large trees shaded the expanses of thin grass between the few buildings. Simâo and Adelaide Chamango were the directors. There was a sense of calling, almost of passion, out at Ricatla.

Now Libby was coming to visit us. She had completed the necessary number of courses early at Wooster. She had studied in Italy one summer and for a term at the University in Nantes, France. Her major was in Romance languages. She decided to visit us in what would have been her last trimester. Libby sent us detailed information about her travel plans. We made joyful arrangements to receive her on Wednesday. It was our Ricatla day, so Chalmers went to Ricatla, but I stayed in Maputo to be at the airport early. Chalmers kissed me good-bye and left.

Not long after, someone knocked, a messenger from the office of the Mozambique Council of Churches. A phone call from the airport reported that Libby had come in on a plane that had arrived at 6 a.m. She was not being allowed to leave the airport until someone came to claim her. The Secretary of the Council himself drove me to the airport. Because we had no phone in our apartment Libby had no phone number for us. It was lucky that someone thought of the Council of Churches. How wonderful it was to see her coming from beyond the barrier and into my arms. We collected her luggage and were soon home, where Chalmers joined us.

Libby stayed with us for two months. We took her to Ricatla. Barbara drove us in her car because our Volvo, assigned to us by the Church, had suffered an accident when a Mozambican pastor borrowed it. We went to Cambine, traveling as far as Maxixe by bus. Methodist missionary Mary Jean Tennent met us and took us over the narrow, winding road to Cambine. Mary Jean shared her large airy residence with us.

On this visit we enjoyed the colony of yellow chattering birds that made their hanging nests in the palm trees near the house. They tore strips from the palm leaves to weave into their nests. Mary Jean's African violet plants were amazingly large and bright. Walking along the many paths, visiting the families in their round houses and picking passion fruit for juice made the days fly.

Libby was somewhat disconcerted with me because I complained and made a big deal of the difficulties of getting food on the table. We had to wait in queues for hours to get a kilogram of sugar or a few onions. One morning I got up at 4 a.m. to get in line to buy meat. Finally, at about eight o'clock, we were told there would be no meat that day. Libby was a blithe spirit. She loved the people of Mozambique as we did. They loved her back. They invited her to go along to a conference of the Methodist Church in Zambia where delegates from various countries of southern Africa would be speaking English, French, and Portuguese. Libby was fluent in all three. Our Mozambican delegation asked her to go as their documents translator, so we had to let our Libby go.

Libby, of course, had her passport, but the Mozambican delegates had not yet been given visas. On the day of departure we took Libby to the airport and found our delegates all sitting on the curb in front of the building waiting for their passports and visas. These documents came just in time for them to make the plane, and Libby was off with them.

At the Conference Libby was called on to do instantaneous translating as well as written translations and nearly had a nervous breakdown.

From Zambia Libby went to Brazil to join Greta and Don and Zeke at the farm. She lived there for two years teaching in the equivalent of a one-room schoolhouse. Libby rode horseback from the farm to her school each day. Her pupils came from homes where books were an unknown entity.

While we were in Africa Natalie married Al Kondo, a young man of Japanese descent. The couple moved to Texas so that Al could pursue his doctoral studies in public health at the University of Texas.

We finished our two years in Mozambique and were invited to return for two more after a three-month vacation. We visited George in West Orange, New Jersey. George was teaching Latin-American History at Seton Hall University and he and Mary had bought a house less than a block from St. Cloud's Presbyterian Church. We went on to Wooster and stayed with Dad and spoke in churches.

Then finally we were free to visit Natalie and our new son-in-law. Al's quiet, assured ways and warm welcome endeared him to us.

We continued on our way to Brazil via Quito, Ecuador, where Paul, Carol, Sibby, Marcel, and our first little granddaughter were to be found. Kathryn Illiniza was born on February 15, 1976, and was an adorable little lady. Her mother was especially delighted with a girl. "She is really different from a boy," she exclaimed. Paul and Carol took us sightseeing before we flew on to Brazil.

We touched down in Brasília and went out to the farm to meet our next new granddaughter, our first Brazil-born grandchild, Sofia Cristina, born on March 1, 1976. She was petite, blue-eyed and blonde, a little sweetheart.

We found Libby ill, and unable to go with us for a weekend in Goiânia. We took the bus to Goiânia. Sitting beside Greta and Zeke I was holding my little granddaughter on my lap. Greta told me that Don was being unfaithful to her with many other partners. Besides her anguish for herself and her children, Greta was concerned for the women who thought Don was in love with them. I know Greta would have liked me to say something. I found nothing to say. How was she to decide between her own wholeness and the family that counted on Don as a parent, a father? I couldn't choose for Greta and she continued for yet a time living on the farm with Don.

We had an exciting weekend with our friends in Goiânia. On Sunday Chalmers preached and we rejoiced that the congregation of the Setor Universitário was growing and had a spirit of enthusiasm.

When we got back to the farm, it had become obvious that Libby had hepatitis. I longed to stay with her, but she was with Greta, who would watch over her and see that she rested and had a proper diet.

We went on to Sâo José to visit Mother and Mary Elizabeth and family. Aunt Charlotte, Father's sister, when she was no longer able to care for herself in her Rio apartment, came to live with Mary Elizabeth and Francis and Debbie who gave generously of their love to both Mother and Aunt Charlotte. Debbie found it very hard to have her young life overshadowed by the pressing needs of the elderly, so different from her own. Aunt Charlotte died later that year.

Mother was frail and subject to sudden drops in blood pressure and she didn't want to let me go. How very hard to say good-bye. But Mozambique was calling and we must go.

23

On the Shore of the Indian Ocean

When we returned to Mozambique, a new group of students had come to Ricatla, six families and a single man from northern Mozambique. In the north a church had been growing as native Christians from the south carried the gospel to them. These congregations in the north had challenged their young men to study for the ministry.

They spoke Lomu, a language very different from Xitshwa. The men and one of the women were literate in Lomu and Portuguese. With their help we created a Lomu primer. We used the same Bible verses as in the Xitshwa primer, and so we could use the same book in Portuguese as the transition reader. The New Testament had been translated into Lomu, and was a great help.

But the women who spoke Lomu could not communicate with the women who spoke only Xitshwa. Classes in literacy became boring to the women who had studied with me the previous year. Chalmers was teaching a class in theology in Portuguese to the men, and Mr. Chamango, the director of the Seminary, allowed the women who were in their third year to join the theology class.

We also did some very interesting work in literature for the new reader in Xitshwa. The women wrote a bilingual book about a family who had suffered under the Portuguese colonial government. I learned of the deep feelings people still had about the grinding poverty which they had endured under colonial rule. To teach the women to speak Portuguese, I was using skits. They performed one of these skits at the graduation program. Their husbands were amazed when they heard their wives speaking in Portuguese.

Our literature committee's writing workshops were producing some Bible study booklets. We asked the participants to write some meaningful experiences of their lives. One young man wrote about his father and mother's custom of family prayers each evening before dark. They would sing a hymn, read from the Bible, and pray. A neighbor passed their house often and heard them singing. One evening he stopped and asked to stay and listen. The family welcomed him and he came several times, then brought his family. A house church started in this way. This story was written in Xitshwa and translated into Portuguese. We added a printout of Psalm 150, in Xitshwa and Portuguese, then a series of questions about the story and the Psalm, also in both languages.

We did not have access to printing because the government ruled that our material was not "high priority" and could not take up the presses. So we laboriously mimeographed and stapled our books. We bound several of these stories together to form booklets.

We could not keep up with the demand for one of our books. The Reverend Felisberto Manganhele wrote a story in Xitshwa entitled "The Slipshod Family." The Slipshods just couldn't get their act together. The children could never find their shoes or lunchpails so they couldn't get off to school on time. Meals were late because no one brought firewood for the stove. One day, the Slipshod house burned down. Some kind neighbors who took the family in ran a well-organized household. On Sunday everything was taken care of so that the whole family could go to church. When the Slipshod house was rebuilt and they had moved back, they fell into their old ways. Mrs. Slipshod went to talk to her neighbor.

"While we were here with you," she began, "you managed everything so easily. At our house everything is disorganized. I think it's my husband's fault. What can I do?"

The neighbor was sympathetic and gave Mrs. Slipshod tips as to how to change her own behavior. "Your family will like the new things you do and will change too," she said. Mrs. Slipshod took heart, spruced up herself and the house and made better meals. The family responded to her requests to cooperate. The ending of the story is daring. Mr. and Mrs. Slipshod step out together à deux. In Mozambican society some of the younger couples were going places in each other's company, but the older people still went out of the home only in the company of those of their own sex. In church men sat on one side of the aisle, women on the other.

Felisberto and I translated the story into Portuguese and trimmed it to a stapled booklet size even though Felisberto didn't want to see his creation diminished. "The Slipshod Family" became a great success. People from north to south in Mozambique were asking for copies. No matter how many we ran off, there were further demands for this bilingual booklet.

The most painful experience we went through in Mozambique was the accident of our very dear friend, Penicela. He would come to our apartment taking the steps two at a time to bring us a piece of good news. At the retirement of Bishop Zunguze, Penicela was elected bishop. A man of intelligence, probity, and kindness, he was the best-educated of the clergy of the Methodist Church in Mozambique.

The ordination was to take place at Xicuque, a central location for the gathering of the whole church. Everyone was in a flurry of preparation. Penicela planned to drive from Maputo to Xicuque with his family a couple of days before the great event. Mulamula, our pastor, had experience as a driver for the Portuguese navy in the days before he studied for the ministry. He offered to drive for Penicela, but the car would be full and Penicela felt he could do the driving. Penicela, Angelina, their four children and a sister were in their car when a tire burst and the car ran over the bank. Penicela clambered out and extricated everybody from the car. A passerby took them to a clinic in a town some distance away. The next day Penicela could not move his legs.

The family went back to Maputo, where Penicela was placed in the hospital. It was an interminably long time before arrangements were made to get him to a hospital in Switzerland. He and Angelina were in Switzerland for months, but irreparable damage had been done to his spinal cord and he became a paraplegic. He returned to Mozambique in a wheelchair. The male nurse who accompanied him taught Chalmers and others how to move Penicela and care for his needs. Penicela was consecrated bishop and served for many years despite his handicap. For the remainder of our stay in Mozambique Chalmers was Penicela's chief chauffeur and aide.

Chalmers stayed in Maputo to work with the literature committee while I spent a month in Cambine at a program for the women of the church. This event was very special because it represented a new understanding by the church that the women should have chances to learn and grow. The husbands of the eighty women who came proved, by allowing their wives to be away from home for a month, that they were indeed enlightened.

The program at Cambine was dynamic. The women reveled in study, fellowship, and worship. I taught reading and writing in Portuguese; Mary Jean taught Bible, and Ana Navˆs taught singing. Mozambicans harmonize by instinct and the rafters rang with the beautiful voices.

I enjoyed being at Cambine. At Mary Jean's house the outdoors came right in through windows and doors. The sandy paths between buildings wandered under the trees amidst purple and coral bougainvilia, flaming poinsettia, and hedges of delicately blue plumbago. There was time in which to read and reflect.

Soon after, Chalmers and I held a weeklong workshop near Xicuque. Church leaders from various regions were intent on learning to teach and run literacy programs and use the various readers our committee was producing. As we packed up at the end of this week, one of the pastors was helping put boxes in the car.

"Put that one here!" I said to Chalmers.

The pastor turned to me and said, "You should say 'please' to your husband." I felt duly reprimanded.

We had a marvelous trip into elephant country, only we didn't see any elephants. We drove for what seemed a long time through high grass such as we had seen before only in movies. The narrow road wound on and on with glimpses of round houses now and again until we reached a place of trees. As we neared the end of our trip, fruit trees became more plentiful. The pastor and his family had introduced new fruit and garden plants into the parish and given the people incentive to cultivate a greater diversity.

Margaret Mujongue and Bento were along on this trip and we were all received with great joy. It was not often that visitors came to this distant place. Chalmers and I were lodged in a round house with a double bed in it—pure luxury! As I was sitting on a stool at the door of the house a young girl came shyly to my side. She knelt on one knee beside me and looked into my face. "Your bath is ready," she said. She handed me a towel and showed me to the bathhouse made of rush in the shape of a caracole. It was open to the sky, but its walls supplied privacy. On a rustic table with its legs set in the sand was a basin of steaming water and a gourd with which to ladle the water over oneself. Again, what luxury!

At eventide we went to the outdoor church, a venerable place under six huge tamarind trees. Benches and a worship center had been constructed in the same fashion as the table in the bathhouse. In the dim light filtering through the feathery leaves, we sang and prayed to the maker of all things good and beautiful.

The men had built a shelter for our classroom. The people who came to the workshop were all men and had walked for hours and days. Most of them knew little or no Portuguese, but as they began to use the bilingual books they were amazed. "We would have attempted to learn sooner if we had known it would be this easy!" one exclaimed.

The women of the community spent their time making our meals. They walked some distance to get water and firewood. They ground corn and husked rice in their mortars. Their fires glowed under the trees as they boiled water and prepared rice and stew. We really wanted them to join us for some study. So Margaret arranged a class for them in the afternoons. We all gathered in a big circle in the open, men and women, and studied "The Slipshod Family." It was a great success here too. There was a good deal of discussion and merriment.

On the last day the women danced and sang for us. As part of the dance they brought us gifts of chickens, pumpkins, and fruit. They were charming in their manners and graciousness.

After this workshop Chalmers and I went to Chonguene for time to ourselves. Chonguene is a beach of awesome beauty at the end of an almost impassable road over the dune hills. *Chonguene* means *little river*, for a strong current runs along the beach inside the reef when the tide is high. When the tide is out the reef holds pools, some as large as a swimming pool, where we swam in quiet water. In the shallow pools we could observe the beautiful small fish—red, orange, green, blue, striped in black, of many shapes and sizes. These exotic fish swam about in their natural display tanks until the water swept over the reef with the next tide. At one end of the beach an old tugboat lay rusting, half buried in the sand. High sand dunes rose beyond the beach where shrubs and scraggly trees and vines took over. Climbing the dunes we could look up and down the coastline along the vast extent of uninhabited beach and out to sea. The warmth of the sun and the song of the sea was balm for our spirits.

The Chonguene hotel, built in the lush colonial days strictly for white visitors, many of them tourists from South Africa, stood practically empty. It had a skeleton staff to accommodate the few people who arrived on weekends. We became good friends with the staff and shared the Bible with them.

Later, in Maputo, we received the joyous news that Natalie and Al, who had moved to Baytown, Texas, had welcomed their first child, Andrew Takaki Browne Kondo on March 3, 1978. Baytown, Texas, seemed very far away but so did Areias, Brazil where Greta and Don welcomed their son, Victor Hart, on October 19, 1978. We wished we could go meet our new grandsons who were reported to be both healthy and beautiful, but our reality right then was Maputo.

Despite such good family news, I was feeling a bit restless and decided to take the camera and get some pictures of the area around our dwelling. Chalmers was the photographer in the family, so I felt rather daring as I went out on the avenue. There was a queue of brightly dressed women waiting to buy something at the grocery store just down the street from our archway. I stood back, took a couple of pictures of them and was returning through the arch when suddenly I was mobbed. A young man grabbed for the camera. I had the strap over my head and across my shoulder and I hung on tightly. People surrounded me and started pinching and poking. The din was terrific. I couldn't hear anything that was said and it was useless to try to say anything. The crowd started dragging me back to the street. Something I did not recognize in myself rose up in me like a tiger. I wanted to scratch and bite. At that moment two soldiers came by and, at their intervention, the mob fell back. I told the soldiers what had happened and I let them take the camera. They asked me to accompany them to the nearest military post. At the *quartel* (army headquarters), the soldiers on guard did not know exactly what to do. They took me to an office where a young man questioned me.

"Where do you live?"

"In an apartment right where I was when the soldiers came by."

"Why were you taking pictures?"

"I keep pictures in my album as remembrances."

"Do you know that the people of Mozambique are our special care?"

"Oh, yes," I said. "I was taking pictures of them because I think they are beautiful."

The young man was somewhat mollified. He went on to explain that the people were asked to keep watch for spies and exploiters. They were doing their duty. He said I could take the camera, but he wanted to develop the film. I tried to open the camera, but didn't know the trick. I agreed to leave the camera and bring Chalmers to open it. The soldiers who had escorted me to the barracks now escorted me home in case any of the mob were lurking about. No doubt they also wanted to check out my story of the place of my residence. We returned by the side street and the alley.

Chalmers was reluctant to go over to the quartel. The missionaries who had been imprisoned were all men, but we went. Chalmers removed the film and received his camera.

"We will develop the film and return it to you in three days if we find nothing subversive." We never recovered the film.

As two more intensive years of workshops, writers' seminars, and pastoral work were coming to an end, in May, 1979, we received word that Mother had died. Mary Elizabeth wrote that we should be glad for Mother. She had been getting very feeble and life was no longer a pleasure. She was now her young and beautiful self again with God. But we missed her.

The furniture in our apartment belonged to the Methodist Church and we sold other household items to friends eager to get scarce goods needed for ordinary living, such as dishes and kitchenware.

We packed a trunk and a steel barrel with personal items and books in English. We were required to list each object and each book title for the authorities. The paperwork and hanging around offices waiting for permits took days. We had arranged for the trunk and barrel to go on a cargo ship that was due in Maputo from Tanzania. It never came. "But what about the cargo that was to be shipped on it?" we asked in distress.

"It will go on a freighter which is already in port and will be leaving in three days, but there won't be time to finish your paperwork. The deadline is tomorrow."

With some pleading and much legwork by Chalmers, we got the barrel and trunk and the papers to the docks in time for inspection before the fatal hour. The alternative would have been to postpone our trip, since the owners of the baggage must dispatch it themselves.

We had been approached by Afro-Lit, a pan-African church organization for literacy and basic adult education. Could we go to Guinea-Bissau and report on the state of literacy work in that Portuguese-speaking country? Guinea-Bissau was formerly Portuguese West Africa. We agreed to go.

It was wrenching to leave our Mozambican friends. We flew from Maputo to Nairobi, where we met with Afro-Lit personnel. They treated us royally. We talked over our assignment as they drove us to St. Paul's Theological Seminary to visit some of our Mozambican friends who were studying there. St. Paul's is high in the hills and was cool and misty that day. Our friends prepared a Mozambican lunch for all of us.

There wasn't time in one day to go to the large animal preserve, but our Nairobi friends took us to a park where animals at risk in the larger reserve could be tended and still live in their own habitat. We saw at close range rhinoceros, pigmy hippos, and a most beautiful cheetah lying along the branch of a tree, its marvelous coat glowing like coals.

On the trip to Bissau, the capital, our plane touched down at various airports, hopscotching across the continent until we reached Dakar, Senegal, on the western edge of Africa. We checked our baggage at the Dakar airport and took a DC-3 south to Bissau.

In Bissau, Mário, secretary for Adult Education of the Ministry of Education of Guinea-Bissau received us. For four days we heard reports of the Paulo Freire literacy project initiated in Guinea-Bissau three years earlier. The primer was in Portuguese. Freire's chief contribution to the literacy process was his *concientização* or consciousness raising. His reasoning was that men and women in underdeveloped countries needed more than all else to discover their own worth and participate in the political process. Therefore primers should be built around words that had motivational meaning in the lives of the people in their political reality. In Brazil and Chile the people were at a cultural and economic crossroads that warranted this approach, but the tribal culture of the Guinea-Bissauans lacked much of the patterns that made concepts like "unity" and even "work" meaningful in a political sense. Their culture was not in touch with communication as we know it. Reading and writing were not desired and motivation was needed at a more basic level in their tradition.

The country has at least twelve basic languages. Portuguese is spoken by a minority, mostly by those who have had some schooling. The army and businesses, such as hotels, had some success with the Paulo Freire method by requiring class attendance on company time. The students soon saw that opportunity came with literacy. Mário asked us if we would return and help the ministry with its adult education project. We left him with a "possibly" answer.

After a very hot trip back to Dakar on the little DC-3 plane with no air-conditioning, we boarded our plane to Brazil at midnight and reached Viracopos Airport near Campinas the next morning. We were going through immigration and my Brazilian passport had been stamped when Chalmers presented his American passport.

"You don't have a visa," said the officer. "You will have to return to the plane."

Stunned, I broke in, "I am a Brazilian and he is my husband."

All our arguing and pleading went unheard. Americans and Brazilians had not needed visas before, but the laws about visas had changed while we were abroad and no one had informed us. Chalmers returned to the plane, which was flying on to Assunción, Paraguay, then to Buenos Aires, Argentina.

I went on through customs in a very agitated state of mind. When I was asked to open suitcases I realized that Chalmers had the keys. The officer saw my tears welling and, noting no inspector nearby, marked my luggage with the necessary chalk marks and waved me on. I wheeled the luggage out to the walk to await the bus into São Paulo, but shortly Libby arrived. How glad I was to see her and go home with her!

When we had last been in Brazil we had left Libby with Greta at the farm. Shortly thereafter she had moved to São Paulo and joined Guara and Smitty, friends of earlier days, in their new venture of a language center. She now lived in an apartment on Avenida Pamplona. At this new home we waited for some word from Chalmers. It finally came through Julian, one of my Hodgkiss cousins. Chalmers had found his number in a São Paulo telephone book when he reentered Brazil at Foz do Iguaçu. Two days after being extradited he got a visa in the Brazilian embassy in Asunción, Paraguay. He had had little cash in his pocket and just managed to survive the weekend. We were reunited at the Congonhas airport.

George had been pursuing his studies on immigration into Brazil on a research fellowship. The first time, he and Mary and the boys had taken up residence in Blumenau, Santa Catarina. This time they were living in Florianópolis, the capital of Santa Catarina. They came to visit Libby and see us. We went out to Sâo José dos Campos together. Mary Elizabeth, Francis, and Debby had taken care of Mother and Aunt Charlotte with quiet kindness and love until their deaths. I noticed that now Mary Elizabeth was having trouble with coordination, the beginning symptoms of a long, progressive illness.

In São Paulo Guara and Smitty invited us to dinner at a Chinese restaurant to tell us of their plan to make Libby their business partner. Libby would own a third of UNIQUE Language Center. We were astonished and pleased for our youngest child. We came to the end of our sojourn in Brazil and returned to Wooster.

While we were away Dad Browne had spent a year with Frenchy and Joan in Renoldsville, Pennsylvania, where Frenchy was pastor of the Presbyterian Church. Now that we were back in the United States, Dad returned to his apartment on College Avenue in Wooster and we took up our abode with him.

That fall we were known as the Van Brownes since we drove the Synod van on a mission interpretation tour of our Presbytery. We spoke in most of the one hundred churches, some of them out in the Ohio wilderness much like the land of frontier days.

As we projected our last year before retirement, several entities entered into an arrangement whereby we would go to Guinea-Bissau for a year. We would receive our salary from the Program Agency of the Presbyterian Church. Afro-Lit would pay transportation and the Ministry of Education of Guinea-Bissau would provide hospitality, including housing.

Our new tour of duty was put off for nine months while Chalmers underwent a hip replacement at the University Medical Center in Cleveland. Chalmers did very well and was soon able to move back to Wooster. However, Dr. Goldberg would not release him to go overseas, away from high-tech medical care until June of 1980 when we left for Bissau.

- 24 -

Down by the Geba River

In early June of 1980 we flew again from Dakar into Bissau on the little DC3. I had high expectations for the housing because in Maputo the guests of the government occupied beautiful homes in the lovely residential area on the bluff overlooking the harbor. But we were assigned a two-room apartment in what had been junior naval officers quarters down near the river. One room was furnished with a double bed and dresser and the other with a few chairs and a table. There was a bathroom with shower between the two rooms.

This apartment was on a compound of about twenty apartments around a rectangular court of cement and wild grasses. Most of the occupants were teachers. All were expatriates from many countries, such as Russia, East Germany, Palestine, and Portugal. Our closest friends in the complex were a young couple from Angola, who were both teaching in the high school.

This couple had employed a young African girl named Sábado to wash clothes and help with household tasks. They were willing to share her with us so that we had someone a few hours each week to help with washing clothes, which had to be done by hand.

We managed to acquire a one-burner kerosene stove so that we could heat soup, and water for tea and coffee. Our hosts, the Ministry of Education, arranged for us to have one meal a day at a hotel less than a mile away. Mango trees along the streets furnished some welcome shade as we walked to and from the hotel each noon. The hotel was a stolid, dark building with a pleasant dining room and good cuisine. We especially enjoyed the seafood: shellfish, shrimp, and squid as well as various kinds of fish.

On the first Sunday we were in Bissau we found a Protestant congregation that met in an old warehouse around the corner from the hotel. This congregation was of the Evangelical Church of Guinea-Bissau, which came into being through the mission of the World Evangelism Crusade. World Evangelism Crusade had its main headquarters in London, but also had headquarters in Philadelphia. Its missionaries were drawn from many denominations and many countries. Even though the government changed from a colonial to an independent socialist form, the Mission was allowed to continue its work unimpeded. The Roman Catholic Church continued to be the dominant Christian presence in the country. A small group of Seventh-Day Adventists also worked in the city. Beside the animistic religions of the different tribes, the Moslem faith strongly influenced the culture, especially in northeast Guinea-Bissau. These religious entities had all been in place when the government change occurred, but no new missions or religious organizations were allowed into the country.

The literacy program in Guinea-Bissau was practically at a standstill. People found the literacy classes a complete puzzle because they couldn't understand Portuguese. We were asked to take some material of the Party—there was but one—and create a bilingual reader based on the civics of these lessons. The Department of Adult Education furnished us with informants who were to help us learn Creolo. Creolo, a centuries-old language, is understood across tribal groups. It is made up of basic African grammar and thought patterns and incorporates a great deal of Portuguese vocabulary.

When European nations carved up Africa into the countries that have continued to exist, they did so with little regard to the peoples inhabiting the areas. Thus, different tribes with their own languages were found spilling over into different countries. Creolo emerged in Guinea-Bissau as an African substitute for Portuguese. It is mostly used in speech, whereas Portuguese is used as a written language. It was not at all easy to capture the spirit and culture of our new situation.

The Swedish government was funding the adult literacy project in Guinea-Bissau. Marcela Ballara came as their envoy to investigate the state of the program and to assist in its expansion. Marcela was originally from Chile, but she had to leave with the change in regimes after the death of President Allende. She had a sociology degree from the University of Santiago and validated her diploma in Sweden. We found her a very good fellow worker and friend.

We were taken on field trips to classes in progress, mostly in the city. One weekend we flew to one of the Bijagós, Islands where literacy work had been started. The teacher was away and there were no classes, so we were disappointed. A hotel with cabins made our stay on the island very comfortable. We could have gone by bus to the beach on the far side of the island if we had known in time that there was no literacy work to attend. We did see the fishery plant, including a refrigeration system set up by the Swedish to train local fishermen.

The Bijagós tribes have a matriarchal system. The women plant the grain and the gardens and the men fish. If a woman decides to divorce her husband, she puts all his possessions outside the door of the house, and that is that. We were learning much about the diverse tribal cultures in this small country.

A new American ambassador came to Bissau. Chalmers wrote him a letter of welcome. The couple became very good friends to us. We were also welcomed warmly at the Brazilian embassy. One of our pastimes was to go for walks along the river road, a good form of exercise. On these walks we met people from the Chinese embassy and had some rather hedged conversations with them.

Sunday by Sunday we became better acquainted with the church people and the missionaries in Bissau. When we had time we visited at the mission compound. It was good to be with Christian friends and feel the fervor of God's love in their lives.

At Christmastime missionaries from Biombo on the coast invited us to their station. We enjoyed the Christmas pageant the church people of Biombo put on. We were much impressed by the clinic the two nurses ran. The women of the Papel tribe in that area give birth to their children right on the earthen floor of their kitchens. Animals are all about, and so many of the babies and mothers die of tetanus and other infections. The nurses had to be very patient to overcome suspicion and a long tradition of superstition, but healthy babies, born at the clinic, were persuading the families. The nurses taught hygiene and nutrition and also dispensed large doses of love and joy in the Lord.

On Boxing Day, the day after Christmas, we all went out to the beach with a wonderful picnic basket and had a marvelous time enjoying the water, the sun, and the sand. The next day we visited a Papel family and saw their compound built of wattles, mud, and thick hedges, an African-style fortress. At another the cattle were kept in a central court because stealing someone's cow was considered a valiant deed.

Soon after, Mario, the head of the Department of Adult Education, received a scholarship to study in Switzerland. When he left Bissau his wife, Miguel, who worked in the department, moved with her baby daughter into an apartment in our complex. Augusta was assigned to take Mario's place as director of our department. Things were still moving very slowly if at all.

One day when we returned to the compound we found a group of about seven persons sitting on the curb with their hand luggage waiting for someone to show them their lodgings. They were a delegation from the Ministry of Education of Brazil. Their task was to help the Guinea-Bissau government work on a curriculum for its high school. All were high-ranking Brazilian educators. Guinea-Bissau had no idea what to do with them. These highly trained professionals sat around, homesick and disillusioned. After the shock wore off, they made the best of what was to them appalling housing and food and took the time on their hands to read and write and joke, especially about Creolo, which they found hilarious. We were pleased to have the company of compatriots.

Without warning Chalmers developed a very grave illness. The first symptom was several black and painful toes. There followed fever and generalized pain throughout the body. The ganglia or lymph system in his legs went into panic—he looked like he had small bunches of grapes under the skin on his inner thighs. When the pain became unbearable I would put cool compresses on his legs until he could sleep again. We were blessed to have a very good friend at hand, a Brazilian doctor assigned to the embassy in Guinea-Bissau in his last year before leaving the diplomatic service. He came to see Chalmers almost every day. The doctor and I were worried. With nursing and the limited medication we had, the fever, swelling and pain subsided and Chalmers slowly improved. We took a deep breath of relief.

Our walks by the river mornings and evenings provided us with a glimpse of rice farming during the course of a year. For several months the bottom land lay fallow under brackish water from the Geba River. Bissau is not far upriver from the sea. When the rains came, the farmers let the fresh water wash out their paddies. Then at low tide they closed the dike openings to prevent the return of the river's salty water. The men turned over the muddy earth with long paddle-like tools. Their seedlings had been growing in special nurseries with much ritual and blessing. The women and men planted them in the newly turned field. The green of the field as the rice plants grew glowed with life. The heads of grain appeared and in a few more weeks boys and girls were out in the field driving away the birds that came in graceful flight but with pilfering intent. Finally the grain was cut and bound and carried away by the whole family. The fields were again empty and the dikes open to the brackish water from the river and sea.

From Libby we heard interesting news. Joviano, her old Goiânia flame, had visited her in São Paulo and they were again going together. "This is it," I said to Chalmers. We were glad for them.

Sábado, the young girl who helped us with our housework, wanted to learn to read. I took a story from a book of Creolo folk tales and constructed a primer for Sábado. She found learning written symbols very hard, but it was fun to work with her.

Up to this time Creolo had been written with Portuguese orthography. For example, all the symbols for the sound "k" were in use: *c, qu,* and *k.* African alphabets use only *k* to denote this sound, and it was adopted for Creolo by the Ministry of Education. *Creolo* is spelled *Kiriol* in that language. There were many such changes and we had long discussions about the sounds and the symbols for the emerging written language.

We felt close ties to the Mission and to the church people of Guinea-Bissau. Their need for literature and for literacy materials was great, so we held a couple of evening training courses for them, in writing simply, and in bilingual literature. Missionaries were at work on a translation of the Bible into Creolo. It was in its early stages so we passed on the thought and planning of the Ministry of Education to the missionaries. The churches and their work were accepted on the scene, but they were not taken as partners in national development.

One Friday evening we were teaching at the Church's city meetinghouse when the lights went out. There was a terrible rumbling in the streets. Tanks were rolling by. All of us stayed inside and it was several hours before we were told that a quickie revolution had occurred. The epicenter was down at the naval yard and we were not allowed to return to our compound. We were invited by our missionary friends to go with them to the Mission compound on the edge of town where we spent Saturday and most of Sunday. On Sunday afternoon Gene McBride drove us back to our compound. Everything was as usual. There had been only one death in the revolution, a high military officer who remained loyal to the ousted President Luis Cabral.

President Cabral disappeared quietly. Luis was a brother of Amilcar Cabral, who worked for the liberation of Guinea-Bissau and was assassinated before he saw the new nation come into being. These men were known as *assimilados*. They had acquired European education and culture. The tribal peoples felt antagonism to assimilados, who were felt to be tainted with colonialism. This revolt put a large tribal chieftain in the presidency.

A devastating telegram arrived. Joviano, who had started his own construction engineering company, had gone to inspect a bridge. He and the pilot of a small plane flew into the side of a mountain and both perished. We wished we could rush to Libby's side, but there was no possibility until our year in Guinea-Bissau came to an end. We sent Libby a cable and wrote to her.

Chalmers wanted to take me to Europe. I had never traveled in Europe and Chalmers had not been back since his trip home from China for college. We thought Libby might join us for a couple of weeks. Then Augusta saw the primer I had made for Sábado. "Stay and make a primer with us. I didn't know you could do this!"

We were upset. We had been in Guinea-Bissau for a year with very little to show for it. Reluctantly we gave up a vacation at this time to stay through May to make a primer. The primer I had made for Sábado was not acceptable because the story on which it was based, though a Guinea-Bissau folk tale, was considered to lack the social teachings desired. We explained that we had commitments that would make one month all we could spare for the primer project, and we also told

Augusta that it would take serious concentration to finish a primer satisfactorily in a month. But we were willing to try.

No sooner had we agreed to do this work than Augusta announced that she had invited a linguistics expert from the University of Senegal to spend a couple of weeks that month with our department and lead a workshop to review the phonics and alphabet of Creolo. It hit us like a bombshell. We had given up our trip to Europe to spend our vacation month in Guinea-Bissau and it looked like our work would be again frittered to nothing. We went to talk to Augusta. She managed somehow to turn the matter around so that we were at fault—she said we did not trust her. I was in tears, but the session did get results. She put a team to work on the primer with us. She wanted us to be at some of the meetings of the workshop also so as to give our input.

A couple of the more imaginative members of the staff took on the creation of a story that would mirror the lives of the people. *Kebur*, which means harvest, began to emerge. The first page began, *Arus kusido* (The rice is ripe). The story continued through the preparations for feeding all the people who gathered to help with the harvest, an accident when one man cut himself with his machete, and the festival when all the grain was in. Chalmers and I worked to cull from the words of the developing story all the phonetic symbols of Creolo. Then we constructed drills to fix the letter sounds and to use them in new words.

The workshop was fascinating. The linguist from Senegal lectured and worked in French though he was conversant with Creolo. We were glad we had enough French to follow and learn. The fine points of just what the sounds of the language were and how the alphabet should mirror them was long debated. An alphabet for Creolo emerged, and we finished the primer.

The American Ambassador and his wife, the DuBois, threw a party for us. What a special honor! They asked us to choose our guests and they invited all of them.

We returned directly to the United States this time. We were retiring and we planned for a family reunion in Wooster. We first went to Houston, Texas, where the 1981 meeting of the General Assembly of the Presbyterian Church was taking place and to which Chalmers was a delegate. Since Natalie and Al, Taki, and our new granddaughter,

Natasha Mimiko Browne Kondo, were living in Baytown, near Houston, we hurried to see them. Tasha was a roly-poly seven-month-old, with dark hair and eyes and winning graces. I spent most of the week with them and attended General Assembly for one day with Chalmers. It is always exciting to be in the whirl of activity and find old friends. Greta on her way to the United States from Brazil joined us in Baytown with her three children.

Dad Browne was in Rices Landing, Pennsylvania, with Frenchy and Joan. He was desperate to get back to his apartment and we had committed ourselves to caring for him. We stopped to visit in Rices Landing and asked Dad if we could borrow his apartment for our reunion before he returned to Wooster. He was a bit dubious about all the children, but gave his consent.

- 25 -

Dad Browne

Chalmers and I were on the doorstep of Dad's apartment to greet him when Frenchy and Joan brought him home. Dad was glad to be installed in his own living quarters again, but his health was a grave concern. He had Parkinson's disease. The doctors agreed that he should not have medication then available for the relief of Parkinson's because his nervous state would become intolerable, so we cared for him with nourishing food. Chalmers helped him bathe and dress, and we read to him.

Moving from Africa to the United States can have its culture shock. I found it difficult to throw away grocery bags and plastic milk jugs. So many people in Guinea-Bissau would have been most grateful to receive what we so easily discarded. I found it difficult to adjust to the expectations of neighbors. Americans have a fiercer sense of their personal freedom and privacy than do those who must live in closer quarters and more rugged conditions. It takes time to learn sensitivity to the comparatively rich.

Chalmers and I needed a car. We decided on a four-door Chevrolet Citation. We found a new one unsold because it had a small scratch—we would have had to wait six weeks or more for an ordered car. So we happily rode off in our camel colored Citation.

Along with Dad's business affairs, Chalmers took on those of Grace Miller, Aunt Natalie's stepdaughter. After Uncle Clarence and Aunt Natalie died, Grace remained in the big brick house. When we returned from Africa, we found that Grace had broken her hip and was in a nursing home. She was a bit confused, believing she was still in her own house, but she was glad when we visited her. She gave Chalmers power of attorney to care for her needs.

Her assets were low. It was important that the house be sold to assure her care. Bea had come to stay with us. Chalmers, Bea, and I spent as much time as possible going over the contents of the house from the third floor to the basement. We had the able help of Grace's cousin, Bea Ebert. We sold furniture and other valuables and eventually the house.

The house we lived in on College Avenue was divided into three apartments. Dad's apartment was on the first floor, and when Bea came to live with us, Chalmers and I were able to rent the apartment above him. It was a relief to have somewhere to put our things and to have study space.

Chalmers and I programmed our lives so that he would take speaking engagements as they came up and I would write. In Guinea-Bissau I had started to write a story about people in Africa. As part of my writing project I went to a seminar at Pittsburgh Theological Seminary. Dr. Roland Tapp, who led the seminar, pointed out that my story was too long for a short story and too short to be published as a book, and he suggested I write more. The story to this point was about a Muslim village in the interior of Africa that I knew from what I learned from our informants. I moved my characters to the city of Bissau, which I knew personally. Dr. Tapp continued to guide me even after the workshop.

Our home was across the street from the First Presbyterian Church. Each Sunday morning we helped Dad across the street and to a place in one of the first pews. Bea went to the first service at St. James Episcopal Church then joined us for the ten-thirty service at First Church. I think it was a source of great satisfaction to Dad to have two of his children beside him at worship.

We kept in touch with the work in Guinea-Bissau. Augusta wanted our continued help in creating follow-up books to the primer. Marcela had finished her report on the Portuguese literacy program—the results were very meager. She and the Swedish government were now committed to developing the Creolo-Portuguese project. We were retired and could do volunteer work, and the Program Agency of the Presbyterian Church agreed to pay our travel expenses.

Chalmers and I could not both leave Dad at the same time, so we decided that I would go for six weeks to Guinea-Bissau. Chalmers drove me east in October and he and George took me into New York City to pick up some traveler's checks and documents at the Program Agency offices. George parked the car and joined us. When we returned to the car the trunk had been jimmied open and all my things were gone: tape recorder, two cameras, my carry-on bag and almost everything out of my suitcase. Only the case itself remained. I had my passport, ticket, money and traveler's checks in my purse with me and decided to go ahead. My menfolk were devastated, of course. George gave me, as consolation, a calculator which he had in his pocket. Chalmers gave me his trust that I would be able to manage.

I reached Lisbon in the early hours of the next morning. A whole day lay before me until my plane left for Bissau. The air company placed me in a resort hotel near the shore. Instead of going to the beach, I spent the day in a shopping area near the hotel. I bought underwear, a nightgown and a blouse. Then I went to a shoe store. While I was trying on the shoes someone stole the shopping bag with the articles I had just bought. The shop people were concerned at my distress and gave me a special on the shoes. I then went to an open-air market nearby and bought clothing, and collected paper, pens, shampoo, toilet soap and toothpaste in a specialty shop. I made my plane to Dakar, then on to Bissau.

Augusta was not in Guinea-Bissau when I arrived. She was pregnant and had gone to Portugal for care in hopes that she could carry her baby this time. The Department of Adult Basic Education now had a good work group. Miguel, who had been with the Department from the beginning of the literacy work, was in charge. She was pessimistic, feeling that nothing done under her leadership would find acceptance with Augusta. I persuaded her that there were things we could do and that

Marcela and I would tackle Augusta. We worked together on a unit for teaching oral Portuguese and on a bilingual reader to follow the primer.

I was housed again in the compound. Electricity was rationed and evenings were dark. There were no candles or kerosene on the market, so I would sit and talk with friends, especially Ana and Jorge, the family who had shared Sábado with us. They had one little daughter about six years old, and were expecting a second child. I went to bed about nine o'clock and left the light switch turned on to wake me when the electricity arrived at about two. Then I typed material for the next day.

I was in Bissau at the time of crickets. Once a year crickets invade the city by the droves. They get into shoes, share one's bed and shower, chew up clothing, pinch one's skin and fly in one's face. But they do not bite.

Time flew and I left with work still to be done. I had a day in Lisbon between planes and went to visit Augusta at her sister's apartment. We had a long talk and she agreed to OK what we had done.

Greta had settled in Bethlehem, Pennsylvania. She began a correspondence course with the Goddard program on the campus of Vermont University. To qualify for a B.A. in psychology she would require three semesters of work, including three two-week residencies. I went to Bethlehem to stay with Zeke, Sofia, and Victor while Greta did her first two-week stint. Greta returned very happy with her program. The people were caring and encouraged a sense of group camaraderie amongst the students.

Don accepted a job as the director of the Peace Corps in Niger, Africa. He wanted his family with him and Greta agreed to go to Niamey with the children as soon as school was over for that year. Don agreed to provide for trips to America so that Greta could return to Vermont for the residency requirements of her course.

When summertime came, Chalmers and I went to Bethlehem to help Greta pack. She was in a flurry of enthusiasm. Chalmers helped her buy the tools Don had requested, then on a very rainy day we left Bethlehem with our car loaded to capacity on our way to Kennedy Airport. We saw Greta set off for Africa with brave new hopes.

On arrival in Niger she found that Don had slipped back into his old ways despite promises of a new lifestyle for the family. Getting used to the new climate and environment and the emotional blow caused Greta to become very ill. The Peace Corps doctor and the friendship of his family brought her through. She stayed on in Niger for the two years, continued her studies, and Chalmers and I attended her graduation from the Goddard program.

In January of 1983 Chalmers took his turn going to Bissau. I drove with him to Columbus to get a plane for New York, and again we were parted. The drive home was harrowing. It was snowing and I missed my way. It was dark before I reached home.

Chalmers worked on didactic material, manuals for teachers. He had a room at the hotel, accommodations that left much to be desired. One day he fell in the shower and wrenched his shoulder—the sprain took many months to heal.

That summer we had a family reunion in Ventnor on the New Jersey coast. We made sandcastles on the beach with Victor, Taki, and Tasha. The waves rolled exuberant swimmers about. Moms sunned themselves and dads joined ball games. We played parlor games together in the evenings.

Libby was young enough and our bigger grandsons old enough to have great fun together. They walked into Atlantic City along the boardwalk, exploring the many kinds of entertainment offered, and they fought water battles. Sibby played some water trick on Libby, so she asked Paul to take Sibby's picture against the front of the house. As Sibby stood while his father focused, Libby and her coconspirators dumped a bucket of water upon him from the porch on the second floor. We gave thanks for the graciousness of the blue sky, the sunshine, and the wind and waves which we shared as a family.

The next January I went again to Bissau. Our main project this time was a math book. Augusta and the other members of the team were not sure of mathematical terms in Creolo. Since math has a language of its own, we proposed to write the first booklet without Portuguese or Creolo and use only math symbols. We also took into consideration that some tribes do not use the decimal system. They may count by fives instead of by tens. The second math booklet would be written for students who were beginning to use Portuguese and we could offer problems in that language. Page after page of exercises that helped show relationships and the value of numbers were hammered out as the team discussed, accepted, rejected, and revised.

Marcela invited me to live with her this time. I was grateful. She had a nice house and gave me her second bedroom. Food was scarce. We had a meager diet, one small serving of chicken or fish at our noon meal, with rice and maybe a vegetable. For supper tea and crackers, and cheese if one of Marcela's friends, who was a pilot, had managed to bring her a few things from Senegal. One day I stepped into a building that had been an air-conditioned supermarket. It was like an oven. There was nothing on the rows of shelves except some white beans and some small cans of exhausted Royal Baking Powder. Some fish had come in and there was a long line of people all trying to get some of the meager catch. I lost six pounds in the five weeks in Bissau.

In the evenings Marcela and I went for walks along the streets to get some air. Again there was little electricity. An oil tanker arrived with crude oil and gasoline. The ship remained in dock for about three days while the government tried frantically to find collateral to be able to acquire the needed fuel. Finally the tanker moved off, without delivering its cargo, to try its luck in the Cape Verde Islands.

While the tanker had been in dock a ship from Portugal had arrived with potatoes and onions in its hold. Since there was only one dock in the port of Bissau, the freighter sat in the middle of the river under a broiling sun. When it was able to unload, the onions and potatoes were half spoiled and smelled horrible.

We finished a couple of math workbooks. When I left, Augusta, Marcela, and the team were tackling the instructions for teachers. Augusta was much better at creating study materials than in the field work of classes and community support.

Back in the United States, when Frenchy and Joan were able to substitute for us, we took a short vacation and drove to Baytown for a week with Natalie and family unaware that we were going to meet Alicia too. We arrived at Natalie's home at about five in the afternoon and that night at about two o'clock hurricane Alicia struck the area. It was an awesome spectacle. We marveled as we watched the trees bending before the one-hundred-mile-per-hour gale that sent the rain pounding out of the leaden skies.

Natalie and Al were living in a beautiful brick house on parklike grounds. They were caretakers of the property for the county. The house was solid and didn't much mind the high winds and downpour, but many of the pecan trees on the property were uprooted and the power line pole beside the garage toppled over, leaving us without electricity. It was very hot with no air-conditioning or fans. Neighbors shared ice as one, then another, made a trip to a distant town. We camped out in the house for the week. We played games, shared toys, and went for walks, Tasha in her stroller and Taki with his tricycle. The children were less stressed than the adults. At the end of the week when we left, Natalie and Al still had no electricity. And they had a big job on their hands to clean up the grounds.

Dad Browne was failing. He wanted very much to reach his one hundredth birthday, but his ailment made eating and absorbing of nutrients problematic. We blended food for him and tried to coax him to eat. One day he told me about salt-rising bread. "When I was a boy I would go each Tuesday, the day the bakery made it, to buy a loaf." I called the Wayne County extension agency and they supplied me with a recipe for salt-rising bread. I made a loaf for Dad, but it was heavy, chewy bread and he was not really able to eat it.

During the day Bea and I were beside Dad to read to him and move him about, but through the night he felt very much alone. Chalmers rigged up a buzzer system between Dad's room and our bedroom on the second floor. Chalmers was the one he wanted at night because Dad was a very private person. When the buzzer sounded, Chalmers would make his way downstairs and attend to Dad's needs. No sooner would he crawl in bed again than the buzzer sounded once more. Fran Curtis, a nurse who was a close friend, became available and substituted for Chalmers two or three times a week.

In December Dad ran a temperature, so his doctor sent him to the hospital for tests. His two days in the hospital were an agony as the nurses made him follow hospital routine. We were relieved to get Dad back where we had the control of his comfort. We were all up with him in the night to ease his restlessness.

Then on the 13th of January Dad did not respond to us anymore. Our friend Mayla Roots, who was a nurse, came to see Dad and was shocked that we were not feeding him. We had tried, but he didn't swallow what we put in his mouth. Chalmers and I bathed Dad, who was unconscious, and I saw how terribly thin he was, like a famine victim in a refugee camp.

After lunch on January 15, Chalmers said, "I'm going to the bank to check out Dad's box." Bea was wrapping a package at the dining room table. I went to Dad's side and stood for a minute. His breathing was even and strong. He was lying quietly, all the restlessness gone. I murmured something to him and went upstairs.

Bea stayed where she could hear Dad's steady breathing. When she needed something from her room she walked past Dad's bed. A moment later as she returned she heard complete silence. She realized that Dad had quietly stopped breathing. She called me and together we noted that it was four o'clock, teatime.

I phoned the doctor and asked him to come, then I called the bank and told Chalmers that I had called the doctor. I avoided making a statement, but Chalmers understood. Dr. Cebul Jr. certified Dad's death.

The open casket was placed in the chapel of First Presbyterian Church and friends were invited. In early evening the casket was closed and placed at the front of the sanctuary. The service was simple but meaningful as the faith that Dad had exemplified and preached was expressed in song, in Scripture readings and in the testimony of those who had known the dedication of this man who, though small in stature, was great in heart.

The coldest trip I ever made was that to the Spring Grove Cemetery in Cincinnati. It was not only very cold but it was icy and snowy. Libby was with us and George drove for us. It seemed to take forever. After the service on the Browne family plot, we drove immediately back to Wooster because of the continuing bad weather.

Months earlier Chalmers and I had talked over our future. We had thought that when we retired we might spend some years in volunteer work in Brazil, but now Chalmers was feeling he wanted to stay in Wooster. "I know you don't want to live in Wooster," he said in a rather bitter tone. He was tired and downcast.

"Of course I will stay in Wooster if that is what you want," I said. "Let's make a deal. We'll live in Wooster and we will buy our own home."

Chalmers knew that this was a longtime dream of mine. I was tired of living by the rules of the owners of rented property and I wanted to be able to have our children and grandchildren around us without any stipulations. I wanted to plant my own garden.

We started looking for a house. Our realtor friend Bob drove us about to see houses, but just from the outside.

"This one is attractive," he would say stopping in front of a house. "But you see that the driveway is steep, so I don't recommend it for you." At the next stop he might say, "This is a nice house, all on one floor, but the owners are asking too much." After many of these viewings from outside, we stopped on Kieffer Street. "This is your house," stated Bob. "The wide driveway is flat. The brick house is solid."

The house sat back from the street. A sunburst locust tree dominated the front lawn. In the back a maple tree cast its wide shade on the far lawn. Daffodils bloomed profusely in the spring sunshine. We went inside. It was our house.

We had hoped to move slowly over a couple of months while we worked out our mortgage arrangements and sorted the accumulation of stuff in Dad's basement. But the Lukes, owners of the College Avenue house, were in a hurry to reclaim it. The Lukes had been very caring and generous to Dad and we were grateful. We moved a bit helter-skelter, but it was wonderful to be in our very own place for the first time.

- 26 -

Promised Land

These were the carefree years. Our garden was full of delightful surprises—yellow and white daffodils, grape hyacinths, and merry blue windflowers. We planted our first rosebush. In the late fall we boldly set forth to visit our children.

We flew to Brazil. Libby had bought an apartment near the Congonhas Airport where we could hear the planes going and coming into São Paulo. Lissa, my cousin Joyce's daughter, invited us to a Christmas party where we had the fun of being with all the Hodgkiss clan. For the week after Christmas Libby rented a cottage at a secluded beach. It was wonderful to be out in the sunshine and sea breezes and to bounce about in the waves. On New Year's Eve people came to the shore to celebrate Iamanjá. Candles glowed in the sand all along the beach and offerings to the goddess were tossed into the sea.

Next we visited Delmar and Madalena Machado in Ibiraci, Minas Gerais. After the ending of the adult basic education program in Goiânia, the Machados had served for a time as the directors of three different homes for needy children. They were very good at this work.

When Delmar's father divided the gains from a sale of property amongst his three children, Delmar bought a farm with his share. His new property was just outside the town of Ibiraci in the southeastern corner of the state of Minas.

Delmar enlarged the small farmhouse so that Delmar's mother and father could live with them. All about were meadows and copses with a wide variety of trees. An orchard of orange, tangerine, banana, guava, and avocado trees stretched down to the pond behind the house. Up the hill before the house rose a stand of coffee trees. Delmar and Madalena were still hurting from injustices done to them. They needed time to mend. They considered Chalmers their pastor and talked to him of their defeats and fears, but also of their hope that the farm would make them self-sufficient and they could again do work in the community and with young people. We talked about a church for Ibiraci where no Protestant church existed. The Machados had attended a strict charismatic congregation, but found they could not follow all the rules. The Catholic Church dominated the social life of the town. Most people were baptized, married, and buried by the Catholic Church, but many of them also went to spiritualist séances.

We returned to São Paulo and Libby. On Sunday her building was without electricity. Libby's apartment was on the twelfth floor, so we had to walk down the eleven flights of steps to reach the street. Chalmers thought it was on this descent that he first felt his replaced hip begin to give way.

Our tickets back to Cleveland were from the Newark airport, so when we arrived at JFK we looked for a way to get to Newark. "Why don't you take the helicopter?" suggested the agent whom we consulted. We found that the helicopter shuttle cost only twenty dollars per passenger. So we had our first and only helicopter ride. The day was lovely with clear, open skies. We could see a wide landscape from our bubble enclosure: cemeteries, houses, factories, and waterways. We stopped at La Guardia Airport for passengers and crossed Manhattan north of the wondrous skyscrapers. The helicopter landed again at the Trade Center in the Battery. Each time we took off the helicopter reminded me of a camel rising to its knees as it tilted forward before rising into the air. We looked down on the Statue of Liberty and Ellis

Island as we crossed the Bay before reaching the New Jersey coast. We caught our plane in Newark and arrived in Ohio without incident.

Driving East from Wooster to Paul's house, we stopped at Greta's. She and Don were separated and we met Rod, her new friend. We had a good visit with our Hart grandchildren, Zeke, Sofia, and Victor. The morning we left, Greta and Chalmers discussed religious subjects and found themselves diverging strongly. The emotional tension was great. After we had driven for an hour we turned off a country road and sat under the shade of the overhanging trees to talk. Chalmers always found that speaking his thoughts cleared his mind. We also needed to simmer down. We drove on to George and Mary's house and then to Paul and Carol's. We had a lovely time with Sibby, Marcel, and Kathryn, very grown-up teenagers, while their parents took a short vacation.

We returned with real pleasure to our home in Wooster. Chalmers began serving as chaplain for Hospice of Wayne County. He was pastoral counselor to the staff, nurses and those who visited the patients. He was the link with the pastors in the area, letting them know when one of their parishioners came under the care of Hospice. If persons did not belong to any church, Chalmers became their pastor. He visited, comforted, and helped as he could. Sometimes I visited patients with him, and we attended Hospice workshops together.

I was writing a mystery story for my grandchildren *entitled Summer Days at Robinson House*. I created a character to represent each of my children and grandchildren. It was fun.

During the time we lived with Dad on Ciollege Avenue, I beame a member of First Presbyterian Church. Chalmers, as a minister, was a member of Presbytery, made up of an equal number of ministers and elders, representatives from the churches in the area. The Session of First Presbyterian Church asked me to represent it on the Hunger Subcommittee of the Social Concerns Committee of the Presbytery.

Reports came from missionaries in Mozambique that the students at the Ricatla Theological Seminary were going hungry. The prolonged civil strife in Mozambique was having disastrous effects on the country as a whole. The Hunger Subcommittee of Presbytery on which I served decided on a special drive to raise funds for the Ricatla students and their families. I was asked to present information on the project at a Presbytery meeting.

The following month the Presbytery convened at First Presbyterian Church in Wooster. A bombshell of condemnation fell on our Hunger Subcommittee. One member of the Presbytery thought we were overstepping our bounds. He told a horrible joke to make his point. The ExecutivePresbyter made an impassioned speech defending his staff. But the speech gave no comfort to the Hunger Subcommittee. Things were in an uproar. The storm blew over. A vote was taken, and the Presbytery was able to send about four thousand dollars for the relief of hunger at Ricatla Seminary.

Our friends and coworkers from Brazil, Jim and Alma Wright, were with us at that meeting. Jim spoke to Presbytery about the work he had been doing with Cardinal Arns of the Roman Catholic Church in São Paulo to unmask the political imprisonments and torture in Brazil during the days of the military regime. Paul, Jim's brother and our companion of Santa Catarina days, was one of the persons who disappeared and was killed.

In June we went to the PY (P'yongyang Foreign School) reunion at Montreat, North Carolina. Chalmers, Bea, and Frenchy had all graduated from the PY high school in Korea. PY opened its doors at the turn of the century and its last class graduated in 1941. The joyous reuniting of old schoolmates was splendid to behold. Reminiscing went on in formal and informal settings, including an outing into the hills for a picnic. The reunion culminated in a service at the Presbyterian Church in Black Mountain followed by picture taking.

Chalmers came away with a job to do. At PY Chalmers had been editor of the school paper, the *Kum and Go*. There was also a literary magazine, the *Kulsi*. An update of the news about PYers seemed appropriate after the reunion. Chalmers accepted the formidable task.

We were blessed by the fact that during the summer Frenchy and Joan finished their ministry at Rice's Landing and retired to Wooster. Their children gathered at Rice's Landing to honor their years of devoted pastoring and teaching and we went over for the service and festivities. We were glad for the opportunity to see our nieces and nephews and their children.

Frenchy and Joan bought a house on Spring Street, a mile away from our house. Thus Frenchy was able to work closely with Chalmers to put together the *Kulsi Kum and Go Update, 1987*. Our basement was turned into an editing workshop. Letters went out to as many of the PY alumni as it was possible to locate, soliciting information about their lives since PY days.

Then other matters intervened. My brothers out West invited us to join them for a week on a houseboat at Lake Mohave, Arizona. Chalmers had some initial difficulty adjusting to the Landes family way of doing things, but soon we were thoroughly enjoying the trip to the lake and the beautiful days on the water. The boat was a bit crowded for six adults, but on the whole was very comfortable. The expanse of blue lake and blue sky was both exciting and relaxing. We went for walks along the shore and saw friendly roadrunners and glimpsed an occasional coyote. On the lake mallards and many other waterfowl swam and dived. We tied up at a sandbank every evening while we played card games and slept.

On Sunday we went looking for a church in nearby Bullhead City. We found a Methodist Church sitting on a hillside. I had a strange experience in that little church. Suddenly I heard the words: It won't be long now. For an instant Jesus stood beside me. He had on a white robe striped in pale green and pink, and he held a small, dark boy by the hand. His presence was electric and from him emanated the sense of deep desire for me. I had experienced desire for him, but did not know that his wanting of me was even more intense. The charged moment vanished as quickly as it came and we were there in the church on the hillside. We went to a Chinese restaurant for our dinner and then back to our boat for a few more days of blue water and sunlight on the surrounding white cliffs.

Returning to Wooster we were occupied for six weeks in the Miami Presbytery mission study emphasis. Frenchy, Joan, Chalmers and I drove on weekends to speak, each in a different church. We savored the trips to southwestern Ohio, the hospitality of warm Christian people, the encounter with groups making an effort to minister in their corner of the world, and we welcomed the opportunity to share our commitment to global spreading of the good news of God's grace by word and by deed.

At Christmas time we had a reunion of the Chalmers-Browne family. There were twenty-one of us. Chalmers and I put up all the grandchildren, ten of them, in our house. We found a lovely bed-and-breakfast on Bever Street where our children were royally entertained. Though separated from Greta, Donald wanted to be with his children for Christmas. We welcomed him at our house with all the grandchildren.

In the midst of the excitement some of our number had sad feelings. Tasha didn't like being the youngest and Libby saw her brothers and sisters with their growing families and wept that she was unmarried and childless. (Libby has since had the blessing of righting both conditions. She was married in 1988 to Maurício Dias, an electrical engineer, and has two beautiful little boys considerably younger than Tasha.)

For several years we had been having tension in our midst because some in our family were reacting against the ethos of church attendance, an ingrained tradition of the Browne and Landes families. I'm not sure that anyone was too clear as to the dynamics at work but the whole matter became an issue between generations. Both Chalmers and I were moved by the attendance of all members of the family at the Christmas Eve candlelight service at our church.

How fast those gracious days flew by and the New Year was upon us! Chalmers had been getting around painfully with a cane, so there was no more putting it off. Dr. Greenburg scheduled the surgery for the second replacement of Chalmers' hip for late January.

Frenchy and Joan took us to the University Medical Center in Cleveland. They and Pastor David Ross, then interim minister at First Church, stayed with me during the four-and-a-half-hour operation. Chalmers' bone had splintered and grafting was necessary in addition to the replacement of the whole prosthesis. Chalmers worked hard at curbing his propensity to lash out at the nurses and technicians when he was in pain. I stayed in the nurses' house so that I could be with him most of the time.

At home again he recovered day by day and learned to use the gadgets introduced to him by the therapist so that he was able to do much for himself.

Our oldest grandson, Chal, was looking about for a college. He borrowed our car to go to nearby Oberlin and then Kenyon College. He was on his way from Oberlin to an interview at Kenyon when the Citation motor burnt out. Fortunately he was close to an AAA station. He was towed back to Wooster and Frenchy drove him then to Kenyon. He eventually chose Kenyon as his college.

The question now was what to do about our car. Chalmers was still not in shape to search for a new car, though we had been considering buying one. We were offered a very good deal on a Citation motor from a totaled car and decided to take it. Chalmers would be able to look for a new car at his leisure when he was well again.

Chalmers was soon about on crutches, then graduated to a cane. He was doing very well except that now and then his new hip would rotate out of the socket. I learned to help him get it back into place. We had many good outings and Chalmers continued his work for Hospice and took on some preaching engagements.

In July we were getting ready to go to the wedding of Chalmers' cousin, Lois Cowen Donheiser's daughter, in Maryland. We were ready to get on the road when Chalmers sat down on the edge of the car seat to read a map. Suddenly, his hip went out. No matter how hard I tried, the hip would not go back, so we sadly drove to the emergency entrance of the hospital. As Chalmers was getting gingerly out of the car the hip went back in place. We rejoiced, climbed back in the car and were on our way.

We attended the wedding in a quaint old Episcopal Church at St Mary's on Saturday morning. We rejoiced in the family reunion and in the fresh young couple plighting their troth. We stayed for the wedding luncheon.

Chalmers had a preaching engagement back in Ohio on Sunday morning. We left the wedding festivities a little after two and drove through the evening and into the night. Part of the time Chalmers slept and I drove. At the wheel I was feeling scared. How lethal is a car racing through the dark, even though on a four-lane highway! We were home sometime after midnight and got a few hours' sleep before taking off for Chalmers' preaching point.

Those were days of visitors: Takashi Simizu from Brazil and Julia and Jim Crothers, old friends. Frenchy and Chalmers were finishing up the PY update. The manuscript went to the printers, orders came in and Chalmers and Frenchy were busy mailing off the booklet.

One afternoon Chalmers was mowing the lawn and I was watering my flower beds. Chalmers called to me. When I did not respond immediately he called more sharply. I jumped and went to him. He had nothing to say to account for his summons. He called to me again with no apparent reason. The third time he called me out on the back lawn. I imagined that he wanted me to take over the mowing, so I took the mower in my hands. Evidently that was not what he wanted. He got his cane and went for a walk. I was puzzled. That night before we went to sleep he asked me, "Are you still upset?"

"I'm still frustrated," I answered. He did not offer any explanation. Maybe we should have taken the matter more seriously.

Chalmers was feeling pretty good because the arduous work on the PY project was completed. There is a sense of accomplishment in getting a job well done. That Friday afternoon we sat at our dining room table and looked at the contract which Vantage Press had sent us. Vantage Press publishes books subsidized by the authors. We had a fund which we had been holding for something special.

"We could use our fund to publish your book," Chalmers suggested.

"What about the trip to Europe?" I asked. That was one of our dream projects.

Chalmers smiled and shook his head. "That isn't important."

We decided to take the contract to our lawyer. On Friday afternoons she closed at four, so we missed her. We went shopping. "Let's go to Odd Lots and get the teakettle," said Chalmers. Odd Lots had advertised a teakettle and we'd burned ours. We bought the kettle and Chalmers picked up a tool. On the way home we stopped at the grocery store.

"What kind of meat do you want?" I asked.

"Lamb," was the predictable answer.

On Saturday Chalmers and Frenchy mailed late orders of the *Kulsi, Kum and Go* directories. The job was finished. Chalmers was ready to turn to other things that had long been waiting for his attention. I roasted the lamb, made mashed potatoes and gravy and served Sunday dinner on Saturday since we would not be home on Sunday. Chalmers was to preach at Malvern.

We were up early on Sunday and reached Malvern well ahead of time. We went for a walk in their park where we circled a picnic area and playing fields and walked under the trees.

Malvern is a small town and the Presbyterian Church is traditional with a loving spirit. Chalmers preached a good sermon. After the service we stood at the back of the church and talked with the people, then started home. At about one o'clock we stopped for lunch at a small roadside restaurant. The food was good home cooking.

Sunday evening we went to the College to the dinner for overseas students. We were one of the host families. Chalmers drove and I took the dishes I had prepared into Westminster House. Chalmers parked the car and joined us.

The next day I went with Joan and Margaret Pittman to a Presbyterian meeting in Youngstown. We were away most of the day.

Margaret was driving when we arrived home. Chalmers was out mowing the front lawn. He cut the motor and came over to greet us. As the car drew away he kissed me and said "Wuyani." I answered "Wuyili." This Mozambican form of greeting means "You have come." "I have arrived." I think Chalmers was inspired by the fact that I had on my green Mozambican dress. I ran upstairs and changed into jeans. Chalmers was back mowing the lawn. "Do you want me to finish up the mowing?" I asked.

His answer was, "I'm doing fine."

"Then I'm going to the grocery store," I said.

"Don't forget the milk," Chalmers called.

We were to host the Missionary Circle the next day at our house. I bought two baskets of Concord grapes with which to make grape pie for the dessert. As I drove up Kieffer Street to our house there were two police cars parked in front. One of the officers came over to me.

"There has been an accident," he said. "Your husband has gone to the hospital."

My first thought was that Chalmers' hip had gone out. "I'll drive over to the hospital," I said.

"No, I'll take you," the officer answered.

I noticed as he led me to his patrol car that the other officer was putting the mower in the garage and closing up the house. At the hospital emergency I found Frenchy and Joan in the waiting area. Frenchy told me that he had stopped by to give Chalmers some papers. He found Chalmers finishing the lawn. "Our gals are home," Chalmers said. He asked Frenchy to put the papers on his desk. As Frenchy laid the papers on the table he heard the motor of the lawn mower stop. He returned outside and found Chalmers fallen on the driveway. Frenchy immediately started mouth to mouth resuscitation. A neighbor saw them and stopped. Frenchy asked her to call an ambulance. She rushed into the house and phoned. The ambulance came in less than ten minutes while Frenchy continued CPR. Chalmers was transported to the hospital only a block away where Dr. Campbell, our personal physician, was on duty.

A nurse came to tell me that all efforts were being made to revive Chalmers. Not much later John Campbell came to tell us that Chalmers was dead. The nurse led us into the room where his body lay under a sheet. There were leaves from the sunburst locust tree caught in Chalmers' hair. I pushed back his hair from his dear face.

"May I touch his hand?" I asked.

I ran my hand down Chalmers' arm to his hand. His arm was warm but his hand was cold. That was all. Chalmers was not there. I turned and we left.

Telephone calls to our children, the wounding words humming along the wires. A call to Dr. Greenburg to cancel an appointment. Shock. The undertaker, a friend. I asked that Chalmers' body be cremated.

Duane and Susan, our pastors, came. I knew exactly what the memorial service should be as if it were scrolled before me: "Be Thou My Vision, O Lord of my Heart," sung at Chalmers' ordination, and "For All the Saints," the hymn he taught the congregation we visited on our honeymoon. All the dear, favorite, comforting passages in the Psalms and Gospels.

All our children came to the memorial service, all our grandchildren and brothers and sisters, except Mary Elizabeth, too distant and unwell to come. We sat together and lifted our voices together in praise and thanksgiving.

Libby came all the way from Brazil. She went with us a few days later to Spring Grove Cemetery in Cincinnati where we laid the urn with Chalmers' ashes in the Browne plot. Frenchy and Joan drove. Frenchy read the committal service.

The venerable elm tree stands guard over the graves of two centuries of Brownes waiting until my urn rests with these gravestones.

We turned and I took the first steps that will continue my mortal and earthly journey. The strong arms of God have reached out for Chalmers and will reach out for me. His steadfast love and graciousness can pierce through rebellion, grief and weariness until that day. For now faith, hope, and love remain, and abounding grace.

CPSIA information can be obtained at www.ICGtesting.com
Printed in the USA
LVOW042154251111
256524LV00001B/101/A